Valhalla

with a

Twist of Lethe

&

Other Strange Tales

By

Satyros Phil Brucato

Quiet Thunder Productions • Seattle, Washington

Valhalla with a Twist of Lethe, and Other Strange Tales

A Quiet Thunder Productions Book

ISBN 978-1-953203-00-7

Cover photo by Sandra Damiana Swan

Author photo by Cedar Blake

Cover and interior design by Sherry Lynne Baker

Typeset by Quiet Thunder Productions, Inc.

Printed and bound in the USA

Quiet Thunder Productions, Seattle, WA, 98133, USA

Dedication

For Sandra Damiana Swan

My Belovedest partner, lover, spouse, collaborator, and friend.

Love is a verb. Family is a verb. Life is a verb.

Beloved, you are magic.

Thank you for sharing your magic with me.

Table of Contents

Valhalla

with a
Twist of Lethe

&

Other Strange Tales

TASTING THROUGH
THE ROOTS

For Ann Lenore Taylor

You're gonna think I'm crazy. But the trees talk to me.

Not in voices. I'm not psychotic or anything. But I can feel something inside them that says "Hey, I'm alive." It's not as simple as words. It's a feeling. I've always had it. Back when I was a kid, there was a magnolia tree in our front yard. Whenever Mom went looking for me, I was usually roof-high up that tree, with a book in my hands. No wonder Mom went gray early! I was a quiet kid but was never good at doing what I was told.

So anyway, I never worried about climbing that tree. She said it was okay. The tree did, that is. She would take care of me, and if I fell it was only because I was being dumb and not trusting her. So, I never doubted, and I never fell. There are plenty of trees I've climbed before and since, but never – not once – have I fallen out of one.

See, I listen to them. The ones who talk to me, I trust. The ones who stay quiet, or who warn me away, I don't climb those trees.

We have an understanding, the trees and I. I don't carve in 'em, break off branches, throw trash in the woods or chop 'em down, and they don't dump me when I climb up in them.

There's a language in the trees, y'know. They watch everything nearby. They taste it through their roots and brush it with their branches. Birds bring them gossip, ants eat little notes in the bark. Everything that stops or dies or pisses near a tree leaves a little bit of itself in that tree's body. Everything that munches on some leaves or climbs up branches is remembered somehow. So, every tree is a living museum, a little bit of history that can speak to you if you know how to listen.

When I climb a tree, I can feel its stories. They sing beneath my hands and feet, vibrate through my soles and fingers. Here, gimme your hand.

Feel it? Deeper.

Now?

Yep.

Believe me now?

Heh.

Scared yet?

No? Good.

Let's go running in the woods. Tell me what you hear…

SWALLOWED

That stupid fly.

As Henry Rollins said, once you're up on stage in front of a crowd, absolutely nothing can go wrong. Whatever happens – falling light rig, sudden cramps, out-of-tune guitars – you roll with it. Gotta piss? Hold it in. Feel like your lungs just collapsed? Suck it up, cupcake – you're living the dream, and these folks paid good money to see you enjoy it. Now, unlike Hank, I never knocked myself out onstage. Still, some things are worse than public unconsciousness.

So, there we are, opening for Triplesixxx at the Psychlotron in Riverhaven, late summer a few years back. Great crowd, fucking huge, mad as hell and wild for a good time. It's hot and loud and we're laying down thunder like you wouldn't believe. Blake Chisholm himself had given us our intro, so we had the crowd from word go. Chipper was making sawdust of her drumsticks, wearing through them like a psycho lumberjack. Brian, as usual, was beating his head against the bass amps, and Dervish made her Fender sing in that strange pitch halfway between a growl and scream.

I had one green Doc planted rock-god style on the monitor, and a million hands reaching up and out like some stygian sea. In short, it was fucking *awesome*, and nothing could go wrong.

About that thought…

We all want badass nicknames, right? Especially those of us riding this rock 'n' roll beastie, we want to be legends. Not the people our parents made us, but the gods we christen through our own awesomeness. We're not Heimie Fucking Witz but Gene Fucking Simmons, Henry Goddamn Rollins, not Henry Lawrence Garfield. And so, I'm not Gregory Phillip Oliver – I'm Ravenwolf Grigori.

Or at least, I used to be.

So again – there we are, wrecking that crowd like titans on crack. There's a cyclone mosh going at the foot of the stage and a few brave souls have already started surfing. Stage lights shining across bodies soaked with sweat, open mouths, security dudes rising like idols from a pagan surf. Fucking epic. I'm loving life.

Funny thing about the Psychlotron: It's an outdoor stage. And with an outdoor stage, the lights draw every bug in the goddamn state. After dark, the bugs swirl like clouds in the spotlights. Bats dart back and forth, filling their little bat bellies with the feast of a lifetime. Everyone's having a party, y'know?

So, like every other band on earth these days, we do the video-screen thingie. Cameras zoomed in on our faces from the world's most epic angles, casting our images huge behind us so that we're holding mass to deify ourselves. We've got two videographers – Argo and Bliss – catching the action from the foot of the stage. Argo swings his lens from Dervish's riffing fingers to my face. I'm screaming my head off, bigger than life.

You see where this is heading, don't you?

It took three years and half-a-dozen bands before people called me Ravenwolf with a straight face. In a world where guys go by names like Mortiss and King Diamond, you wouldn't think it'd be that difficult to score your nickname. But it kinda was. Chipper got this little sneer when she used my name… but then, y'know, I expect that much from *her*.

Anyway, I think it's a matter of letting yourself *believe* you're so-and-so – not just calling yourself a name, but getting swallowed up by your persona. I'm willing to bet no one's called Gene Simmons "Chaim" for decades, except maybe his rabbi… if he has one, anyway. That dude's been eating his persona for breakfast, lunch and dinner for 50 years or so, and now the whole world calls him Gene Simmons, God of Fucking Thunder.

(Okay, yes, I know – Gene didn't write his signature song. Paul Stanley did. I'm trying to make a point here.)

So here, I worked out and grew my hair all shaggy and shit, and kept it dyed the right kind of black and *finally* I had people calling me "Ravenwolf." Well… all of them except Chipper, who had somehow found my birth name out and called me "Oliver" just to piss me off. Right. All good. So, no shit – there I am, my Doc up on the amp, full-face screaming right in Argo's lens. Behind me, that scream's filling the video screens on either side of us.

Like I said, epic.

Until that stupid fly flew in my mouth.

Remember how I said, "nothing can go wrong?" Try eating a goddamned fly in mid-sentence, with a sea of flailing limbs and hot punky chicks and sweaty dudes stripped to the waist in August southern heat.

7

Try imagining six hairy legs and a pair of wings buzzing at the back of your throat, crusted with whatever shit the fly had been dining on just prior to making a swan-dive down my trachea front of hundreds of fans and a goddamn video camera.

Things went *wrong*.

First I choke. Then I cough. Then I swallow that goddamn fly and feel the little bastard do a death-dance all the way down. All around me, I hear this loud "*AHHHHHHHHH!!!*" as people watch me gulp down the world's biggest goddamn fly right on video. I pull back and start trying to spit the fucker out of my mouth. Then I throw up, right on Dervish's combat boots.

Brian starts laughing. Chipper goes off-beat. Dervish looks up at me with this smear of compassion, disgust and fury running across her face. We trainwreck the song, and fucking Argo tapes the whole goddamn spectacle.

Dude.

In the back of my head, I hear Rollins lecture me. "Nothing can go wrong," he says. So I swipe my hand across the back of my mouth, shake my hair out, and roar like a furious god.

That scream rolled up out of someplace primal, some inner pit of molten lava that remembered every insult, laugh or fumbled word I'd ever suffered through. Every night I'd coughed up lungs after singing my throat raw. Every hot-chick date that slid through my fingers after the wrong words jumped off my tongue and ran across the table screaming "*LOSER!*" Every ounce of sweat I'd baked off under bright stage lights. I roared for every person in that crowd, channeling *their* pain, *their* hate, *their* defiance at a world determined to make them small.

And I got them back.

And I turned it around.

And Dervish ripped a perfect matching chord out of that guitar, echoing the sound that explored from my throat. Chipper slammed a four-beat, four-limbed tag and Brian took it up, busting out a bass chord that sounded like Tyrannosaurs farting out his last meal.

All four of us cracked back into synch right where we'd left off. Bliss and Argo filmed it all.

We were back, and the audience rolled with us.

The set blurred by in a storm of flying bodies, sweat, and screaming mouths. We got the requisite ovation, and we happily obliged. As we stumbled offstage in the afterglow, Blake slapped me on the back. "Good save, Raven," he told me. "You pulled that back together like a pro."

Bliss handed me a beer to wash away the fly and raw-puke taste. As I raised it to my lips, Chipper knocked her plastic cup of beer against my own. She flashed that mean grin of hers: "All hail," she said, "to the Frog Prince!"

What a bitch.

Oh, well. Some things, you swallow, and some things swallow you.

I guess every legend needs a healthy sense of humor.

THE KING OF SLEEP

Tell me a story."

Charlotta's dark face is flushed and fevered. Her eyes have the blear of someone who wants to sleep but can't. Marlene Watkins tests her daughter's head for the third time in minutes, wishing the sickness away. Her wishes do little good.

"Mom-*mee*..."

Marlene's nerves pull a bit at the whinging sound in that little voice, but who can blame the child? Nobody likes being sick, and a girl like Charlotta... well, she's not exactly the patient type to start with.

So, Marlene casts about in her head, fishing for an idea to comfort both her daughter's misery and her own. Something to soothe a path for the King of Sleep.

The image comes to her, then, of the King all in his robes: A large dark-skinned man with kindly eyes. Too skinny for his height, all angles and planes outside the sweeping yellow of his garments. A smile like a handful of cool sand, soundless feet, comfort. He's standing in a garden all entwined with creeper, washed in sundown and drowsy flowers. From nowhere, then, the words come flowing:

"In a kingdom long ago…"

Marlene tells Charlotta of the King, of the twelve sons of Ndoki and the feast they made of the King's slumber gardens. How the people of the kingdom could not rest until the King had changed into a breeze and swept over the Vembo Woods, seeking out the lair of the sorcerer who had ruined his harvest. How the King had dropped a cloak of sleep upon the thirteen feeders, then tickled them until they breathed out the fragrance of the gardens. That fragrance drifted back across the plains and lulled the people of the kingdom until they too fell into deep and restful dreams. Then the King of Sleep drifted off and returned to reap a full and wealthy harvest.

She tells this tale even though she's never heard anything like it before, even though she's a New York City girl born and raised, even though, until now, she's never told a story in her life.

And when Marlene looks down Charlotta is asleep, fever cooling and a smile upon her face.

Marlene kisses her daughter's forehead for luck and tiptoes from the bedroom, thanking the King of Sleep and wishing him good harvest.

ELYNNE DRAGONCHILD

The dark man in the metal dragonskin seized Elynne's arm. She cried out and pulled away. He grabbed her again roughly and shook her, barking words she could not understand. Another armored man laid his hand on the first man's shoulder, speaking to him in soft tones. The first man quieted but kept hold of Elynne, the leather of his gloves warm and sticky with fresh sweat and spilled blood.

Across the vaulted rock chamber, two other men gazed at three charred corpses in smoking armor. They fanned their faces to chase the burnt smells that choked the cavern. Elynne's own gaze blurred and swam. Spilling tears mingled with sweat as she sobbed. Her pained wails echoed through the twisting cavern complex.

The dark man rattled her again. The second man, pity in his gaze, pulled a cloak from his pack and draped it about her bare shoulders. It itched. She shrugged it off. He wrapped it around her again, murmuring a soothing chant. The cloak and the closeness of the two men pressed in, crushing her. A ringing sound rose in her ears.

Not two dozen paces away, a gore-spattered man struggled to rip the heart from the massive dead beast sprawled in its last-stand corner. Elynne's stomach lurched, her legs gave way. The two men caught her as she fell into darkness.

They hadn't even let her say goodbye.

ELYNNE. Her christened name was one of the few things she remembered from the days before the riders came, sheathed in iron and leather. Barely six summers old, Elynne had slipped away into the forested hills while her village burned. She'd wandered for days, going ever higher in the hills her people had shunned, and had been near death when the dragon found her.

She had frozen like a rabbit in the dragon's shadow, dropping to her knees in both awe and supplication as it swooped from the sky. The dragon seemed to stretch across the clouds as it landed, blotting out the sun, buffeting Elynne with the blast of its massive wings. Knocked down, stunned on her back, the starving child had felt terror give way to admiration at the majesty of the beast. Its scales shimmered in the autumn sun as the dragon's muscles shifted and slid beneath the armor. Elynne lay transfixed as the dragon's supple neck lowered a massive head down to sniff her, its hot breath snorting like a blacksmith's bellows. Then it withdrew and regarded her with washtub eyes. Despite herself, Elynne giggled as the monster sat back on its haunches like some titanic puppy dog. The creature cocked its head at the unfamiliar sound. After a moment, the dragon reached for her with a monumental claw.

Screaming terror shot through the girl. But days of exposure and starvation had robbed her of the ability to do anything but howl as the dragon wrapped her in its paw and flapped its ponderous wings, rising away from the ground, the trees, the hills where she had wandered. It felt like both dream and nightmare, this flight, and after a while Elynne stopped screaming and simply watched the land spill away beneath the dragon's wings.

The girl had been near-breathless when the dragon alighted at last. It set her gently on the ground before a great cave, and then withdrew its claw.

Fear returned. Would the dragon eat her now? Elynne stood trembling, unwilling to meet the monster's gaze but unable to avoid it. The dragon stared back, waiting, then flicked its head impatiently at the cavern mouth. Elynne started forward, hesitant, waiting for the slash of teeth of a blast of flame. None came. The dragon simply waited.

When she'd reached the stone arch doorway, Elynne stopped cold, unwilling to trespass. The musty air was sweet with the dragon's strangely pleasant scent – a smooth leathery musk, not an animal smell. To the girl's surprise, the creature seemed to nod and grant her access to its lair. She stepped across the threshold, and the dragon unfurled its vast wings again and rose impossibly to the sky. She watched in wonder as it left, and then entered the cave alone.

Inside felt surprisingly warm – a marked contrast to the windy chill outside. A towering hallway narrowed and snaked up a short distance to an anteroom where the smell of smoke and dragon hung like incense in the air. The cavern floor had been worn smooth, and the great walls – sloping upward like the battlements of some fabled city – glowed with a similar polish in the light of a huge fire burning near the center of the room. Smoke from the firepit floated into dark chimneys far above, and smaller passageways twisted off in several channels from the main room. The stonework, though clearly natural, had been just as clearly carved and smoothed by giant claws and tempered with fiery breath. To Elynne, the cavern seemed like a storyteller's dream world, a faerie kingdom or a playground for elves. But then, wasn't this a dragon's cavern? All the fireside tales the older children had mocked suddenly seemed real, and Elynne's fear and hunger drained away, replaced by a drowsy sense of peace. Whatever the dragon intended, she seemed *safe* for the first time in days. A small stream bubbled from a cleft near the floor, and thirsty Elynne drank her fill. Exhausted, the little girl lay down beside the firepit and slept.

She bolted awake to the clack and scrape of claws on stone. The dragon had returned… and with it, her fear. As the monster approached the firepit, Elynne realized that it carried a limp and mangled stag in its nightmare jaws. She screamed. The dragon stopped beside the pit and cocked its head again, paused, and then dropped the stag and quickly rent it to pieces with deft passes of its claws. Being a village girl, Elynne was not so much shocked by the swift dismemberment of the animal as she was by its method. When the dragon plopped chunks of meat to sizzle on the rocks beside the fire, Elynne's stomach roared with hunger.

That night, Elynne and the dragon shared the first of many meals together.

"Tell them to look *harder!* After losing three good men, I don't intend to go away empty-handed."

"Don't let your thirst for gold get the better of you, Fredrick. If nothing else today, we've saved a young girl from the jaws of Satan's hosts. And come through it all *alive*, by the grace of God. Surely that's enough to be grateful for?"

"It isn't that I'm ungrateful, Father, but gratitude won't pay the men or feed the widows. Blast it, the gold must be *somewhere*."

Elynne heard the voices from far away. She could not understand the words, but the tone was clear enough. Hollow pain sang behind her forehead. Sickness tugged at her throat and stomach. She forced her eyes to squint open to the blinding sunlight outside the cave. Wheels creaked. Bridles jingled. Horses snorted. Elynne lay wrapped in soft leather and a fine-spun cloak in the back of a wooden wagon, nestled between sacks that smelled of bread and oil. Groaning, she forced herself to sit up.

Outside the dragon's cave, armored men ran to and fro like ants. Another wagon sat waiting off to her left. A few paces away, the dark-haired man sat high in a saddle while a bald man – the one with the soothing voice – sought to calm the dark one's temper. Hearing Elynne moan, the two men turned to look at her. Elynne shivered. Though she'd held no shame of her body, she felt exposed before these two men's gaze, and so she clasped the cloak in front of herself.

The standing man smiled and spoke gently to her as he moved to her side and drew a sloshing sack from the stock beside her. She stiffened as he clambered aboard the wagon and offered her the waterskin. The dark man dismounted as the bald man coaxed Elynne to drink. She wanted to scream, to spit the stale water in their faces and fling herself at them with a sword in hand and hack them all to pieces. She felt weak and dizzy, though. *Later*, she consoled herself. Later, when her strength returned.

The dark-haired man's voice rang out across the clearing. The man beside her scowled while the first man strutted between the wagons. Elynne's eyes burned as she glared at him. The dark man built to the crescendo of his speech, leaped aboard the second

19

wagon, and whipped the leather tarp from the grotesque trophy underneath.

When Elynne saw the dark man's trophy, she screamed out and was sick.

SHE HAD GROWN UP wild and strong after the dragon took her in. As she matured, Elynne had thrown off the clothing, tools and language of mankind. She hunted, fished and foraged with her bare hands, growing accustomed to the weather regardless of the season. As there was no one who could listen, Elynne ceased to speak. She and the dragon did not need words to converse, and in time Elynne forgot what words she had known.

Near winter that first year, and for every year thereafter, the dragon and the girl would build themselves a winter store of food within the caverns, piling up extra wood to keep the fire going. Her guardian would then hibernate through the cold season, leaving Elynne to her own devices. The caverns trapped the heat of the fire and the living earth, and they remained warm all year 'round. During these months alone, Elynne grew bored. Sometimes she would drape herself with fur and wander barefoot in the snow, delighting in the winter's clear, cleaning bite until the cold became too bitter. Other times, she would heft a brand or two from the fire and explore the endless warrens of their home beneath the hills.

In the warmer seasons, all the world was hers to explore. She swam in the lakes and streams, hiked the vast wilderness and scaled the granite hills. She grew strong and brave and self-assured, her hair a wild dark mane. Nothing was beyond her. Each year, she ranged further, dived deeper, climbed higher... and the dragon seemed pleased as she grew to womanhood.

On the day she finally reached the summit of the highest of the hills, she stretched out her bruised and aching limbs and basked in triumph, winds, and sun. For leagues in all directions lay unspoiled land, as gorgeous as the dragon or as Elynne herself. As the sun began to color the horizon, the dragon rose and soared above the hills. Laughing, Elynne called to it. The beast circled the mountain she had climbed, eyeing her with concern. Elynne, though, laughed and danced upon the hilltop... and the dragon understood. Fading sunlight glittered rainbows on scales and leathery wings as the dragon capered in the air. Elynne motioned it toward home. With a nod, the dragon flew off across the sunset. Alone, Elynne drank in the sun-washed sights as nightfall came, then picked her way down the hill again in darkness.

SHE BOLTED when the wagon struck a rut. The draft horses yelped as the harnesses snapped them to a stop. The wagon pitched forward, and Elynne leapt to the ground. Behind her, men shouted, and horses whinnied. She rolled to her feet on the stony turf, flung off the cloak, and ran.

If they'd hit the rut in the forest, she'd have gotten clean away. Even many leagues from home, she knew the woodpaths from long familiarity. But the track the riders had chosen was open, bordered by trees but clear for passage. As she pounded across the naked ground, she heard thudding hooves behind her. She threw herself down and rolled as the dark man rode past her, grabbing at empty air. Another man pulled up short before his horse could trample her. She scrabbled rocks from the earth and hurled them at the riders… but to no avail. They surrounded her, bore her down, and carried her – lashing and spitting – back to the wagons. Against the protests of the bald man, she was bound.

WHEN SHE WAS A CHILD, Elynne and the dragon would sometimes play. She found her guardian a willing and gentle, if formidable, playmate with a keen sense of fun and an endless imagination. Yet despite the dragon's power and gargantuan size, Elynne was never hurt beyond the usual childhood scuffs and bruises.

The girl often watched and longed as her adopted parent flew away on some errand or another, remembering her first ride in the dragon's grip. Until she grew older and stronger, however, the dragon refused to take Elynne into the sky again.

As the years passed, Elynne realized that the dragon, though far larger than a cottage in the village where she'd been born, was far smaller than it had seemed when she was young. Back then, it had seemed enormous; as she grew older, though, the dragon appeared to lose some of that forbidding size. Ten summers, more or less, after her adoption, Elynne had grown large enough to straddle the dragon's back. One day, as they played, she grabbed one wing and slipped across her playmate's shoulders. Its cool scales, familiar to her touch, seemed to slide beneath her thighs. The beast rose on its haunches and raised its head to question her. Elynne's heart thundered and her skin tingled as she hugged the dragon tighter, willing it to spread its wings and hoist them both into the sky. Tendons tightened and huge bones shifted beneath the dragon's armored hide. Her fingers clenched at scales. She met the dragon's gaze and nodded. *Now.*

Huge wings, furled to the sides, unfolded, lifted, spread, flapped. Elynne's pulse sped beneath her skin. She feared that her hammering heart would explode as her breathing deepened, quickened, then held itself with awe. Clouds of dust and leaves swirled, rose, blew away as both girl and dragon lifted and the ground fell away.

Wind caressed Elynne, whipping hair and rippling skin. She felt her stomach lurch as the trees danced far below. She strained to clutch pounding wing muscles and cobbled dragonhide. Startled birds squawked and wheeled from distant skybourne paths. The air chilled. The clouds approached. A league or so above the ground, the dragon leveled out into a glide. Elynne raised her head, shook the hair from her eyes. Her heart skipped as wide eyes peered down upon the world spread out forever. Not even the highest hill had been anything like *this.* All below was green and brown. The sun seemed closer, the clouds whisping near enough to touch. Freedom sang within her – the freedom of gods. Vertigo and exultation whirled and warred and stole her breath. Gripping tightly with her legs, Elynne pulled back, sat up, and spread her arms in joy. She sucked breath from the wind that roared in her ears and then bellowed her soul's song. The dragon peered over its shoulder to confirm her safety, but Elynne's eyes were closed and her mouth was wide, and her throat sang wordless praise for a long, long time.

Though they rode the skies many times together, Elynne never forgot the first time that she had dared to ride.

The somber hall flickered torchlight. Courtly ladies tittered as Elynne's long fingers fumbled with her eating dagger. The stench of animals and unwashed bodies seared through cooked food and rank perfume. The dragon would *never* have tolerated such a stink. Elynne's long gown itched as she fought against tight corsets for each breath of foul air.

They'd brought her to a castle larger than even the dragon's cave. Instead of wild nature or solitude, though, the place was packed with reckless pets and ill-mannered people. They'd forced her body into graceless, scratchy clothes, and her feet into graceless, clumsy shoes. They tried to twist her tongue around their words and her deeds around their manners. When she refused, they cuffed her, shouted, or brought strong men in to hold her down. The dark-haired man, Lord, wooed her with gentle words and gifted her with finery. What use, though, was flattery or finery to a girl who'd ridden naked on a dragon's back? Elynne loathed him. His new-found honeyed manner felt insulting to her honesty. The other people clearly thought her mad, and they treated her accordingly… though with caution and restraint. From daggered looks and appraising glances, she guessed that they found her beautiful. Dressed, though, in their clothes and weighed down by their stone castle walls, she felt ugly and alone. Only the bald one – the one they called Father – could soothe or cheer her… and just a little even then.

Now she sat at Lord's table, blushing at the chuckle of fancy ladies and their servants. Two hands' worth of days and nights following their arrival at the castle, a crowd of strangers packed the banquet hall. Elynne had been wrapped in stifling gowns and led to the table. As she'd entered the room, Lord had bellowed some speech or other and the assembly had cheered. "Smile," said Father – one of the words he had taught her. Stiffly, she obliged. Then came the food, and the fumbling, and the mockery. Father tried to scold the snickerers, but Elynne didn't care.

The banquet was torture.

After too much eating, drinking and suffocating shame, Lord leapt upon the table and addressed the crowd again. Elynne couldn't understand his words, but knew that he was bragging again. She sighed. Lord bragged a *lot*. At length, he clapped his hands and hollered. Two servants came in, dragging a small but sturdy cart. Elynne stopped chewing as Lord strode, jaunty, to the cart. Her throat clenched around the food.

She shuddered.

Lord reached for the drape.

She tried to tear her eyes away, and could not.

Lord gripped the drape and pulled.

The crowd gasped.

Elynne choked on her food, and screamed.

The dragon's head had been mounted on a huge wooden shield covered in the dragon's own skin.

Elynne spat food, grabbed her eating dagger, and flung herself, shrieking, at Lord and his trophy.

The table tumbled as she jumped upon it. Food flew in all directions. Guests screamed and guards scrambled.

She thrashed to her feet and dashed toward Lord, holding the dagger high. Father grabbed for her and missed. Lord stumbled back in surprise as guards rose in Elynne's path.

One blocked her with his halberd. The other clouted her with a heavy mailed fist. Elynne, though, had wrestled with a dragon's claws and tail. Their blows, to her, meant little.

She swung the blade. Felt it bite into mail. One guard cried out. The other dashed her across the wrist with the butt of his weapon, knocking the dagger from her grasp.

Other guards grabbed at her arms and shoulders. From behind her, she heard Father crying out. Now he stood before her, shaking her, pleading while the guards pinned her arms behind her back. Elynne's vision reddened and swam. Strong as she was, she was helpless now. Lord's voice bellowed as he pointed to the corridor.

The guards bore Elynne away while Father followed, begging at her with his soft, soothing voice.

ONLY ONCE had Elynne roused the dragon's anger. Being long-lived and wise, such creatures had near-infinite patience. A growing, willful child, though, could tax even a dragon's calm… as Elynne had quickly learned.

Once, and *only* that once, she had refused to bathe. The dragon's finicky nose could not tolerate uncleanliness, and her guardian had insisted from the first that she bathe as regularly as the dragon did itself. That day, though, Elynne chose to test her limits as children will. She threw a tantrum, yelling and kicking and refusing to budge.

The dragon remained unmoved.

When Elynne started to run away howling, the dragon merely stepped into her path. She spun around, but again the dragon blocked her.

She stood and shouted. The dragon paid no attention.

She kicked its foot and hurt her own.

She burst into tears and slammed herself to the ground.

The dragon waited.

She rose and stalked away.

It blocked her again.

She stood firm.

The dragon scooted its paw across the ground, pushing her gently toward the pond.

Snarling, the child picked up a rock and pitched it at the paw.

It bounced off.

She heaved a larger one.

No effect.

The dragon lowered its head to glare at her.

She threw another rock at the dragon's eye.

It connected.

The dragon whipped back its head in pain. The sudden shock tossed Elynne to the ground. Horrified, she watched the dragon thrash its head in tearful agony.

Then it stopped.

Blinked.

And turned again to her.

She blanched with terror.

The dragon growled.

The sound would have sent an entire village trembling.

Fire burst from its flaring nostrils. Tears welled in the dragon's eye. Its huge jaw dropped open, baring teeth half as large as the child herself.

Slowly, deliberately, the dragon raised its talon and lowered it over the whimpering child. Just as slowly, it tightened its grasp. To the dragon, its grip was tender. To Elynne, the dragon seemed to crush her.

Child in hand, the dragon hobbled to the pond's edge and then lowered both claw and child into the pool. Then it shook her, pulled her out, put her back under, and then shook her again. Several shakes and submersions later, the dragon released the clean and chastened child on the pool's rock edge, glared at her again, and stalked away.

Elynne never again dared the dragon's anger. Strong and stubborn though she might be, her guardian was unstoppable. Or so she had believed.

THE COURTYARD OUTSIDE the tower window was quiet now. The revels had ended, and everyone seemed to be asleep, save the night watch. And Elynne.

Inside the room, the finery was dashed. The guards had locked the door, and Elynne had let fly her rage on every object in the room. Even Father had wisely stayed away. She had shredded her gown and the strangling underthings, and hurled the clattering shoes out the window. Hours later, all was quiet.

Elynne sized up the climb from the window to the cobblestones. It was far steeper than the rocks she had climbed at home... but better death now than continued misery. She waited until the watch passed by, then lowered herself out the window, trying a fur wrap about her waist for later use. Hugging bare flesh to cold, rough stone, she recalled her mountain climbs in darkness as she sought toe-and-finger holds. Every floor or so, she would rest and flex in a window crevasse. She reached the courtyard without incident and crept stealthily toward the castle walls.

Once, twice, she ducked the approach of passing guards, moving and freezing like a forest hunter. At length, not long before dawn, she reached the battlements.

She padded to the top of the stairs, then froze.

Father stood not far off, gazing from the wall to the distant hills. He glanced over his shoulder at her and then quickly averted his eyes.

Elynne stood, wary, and then approached the wall – if need be, ready to strike. Father whispered to her, but she understood almost nothing of what he said. Then he sighed and turned to face her, ignoring her nakedness as if she had been clothed. She spread her hands and tried to explain herself but could not find the words. In Father's eyes, however, she saw that she didn't need to.

"Go with God," he said, and that much she understood.

She nodded, gauged the distance between herself and the moat, and leapt.

DURING THE ENDLESS winter months, Elynne had laid claim to many passages and rooms within the caverns – many of them too small for the dragon to enter. There, she often entertained herself by drawing on the walls with burnt wood, sharpened sticks and home-made dyes. Chipping impossibly gorgeous designs from the raw stone, she shaped nooks into the caves that only she could fit into or find. Those rooms became her refuge, task, and treasure.

The men who'd killed the dragon – her protector, playmate, and friend – had scoured those passageways but left them disappointed. According to the childhood tales she had remembered, dragons were supposed to hoard gold, jewels, and other riches. Her dragon had kept none of those things. And so, the men took its head, hide, and foster daughter as their prize.

But the dragon *had* left a treasure, one all the men had missed. And now Elynne set off for home to claim it from a painted room set deep within the hills.

She traced their path from memory, skirting villages and towns as she went, living off the land as she had since childhood.

Nearly three seasons later, she returned.

A strong scent of old decay greeted Elynn's homecoming. She tossed aside her walking stick and what was left of the tattered wrap, and then descended, trembling, into the cavern. Fading dark stains marked the way.

Tears spilled, but she kept on walking.

Grief hit her as she entered the largest room, burning worse than dragon's fire. The tattered carcass lay ravaged by killers and scavengers alike. She dashed across the smooth stone floor and fell sobbing at the dragon's side.

She wept for a very long time.

Rising at last, she swept the tears away and turned her back on the remains. The firepit, too, was cold and dead. She returned to the surface and retrieved a stolen tinderbox from a makeshift pocket in the discarded wrap. Gathering deadwood, she built a small fire, lit a torch, and carried both wood and torch inside. She re-lit the firepit and built it up with winter-stock wood. Then, carrying a large brand, she went off in search of the painted rooms.

A handful of seasons past, the dragon had taken Elynne aside and led her to its treasure. In the silent way they had shared, the dragon asked her to hide the treasure. Elynne, shaken by both the honor of the request and the nature of the treasure, agreed, and soon buried it beneath the dirt floor of her favorite painted room.

As she reached the room, she found the floor disturbed, the treasure missing.

Brittle fragments littered the floor.

Had she been too late?

Desperate, Elynne searched the room, then followed the tracks upon the floor.

She traced them through the corridors to a refuse heap in a crevasse where she'd tossed winter food remains. Falling to her knees, she dug through sharp-edged bones until she found what she had sought.

The hatchlings grumped and whined as she uncovered them from their hiding place. She figured they were hungry. Even now, each one proved to be a heavy armful. Still, Elynne hauled them both out to the largest chamber and set them by the fire.

It was cold outside.

But as darkness fell, Elynne set off to hunt.

As the dragon had done for her, so she would do for the dragon's children. And perhaps, if she lived long enough, she might even ride the winds again.

LOOPHOLES

For Damiana Swan and
Clary Lucretia Pollack

Tap.

Tap.

Tap.

Jack's there at the bedside. I can't see him, but I hear him. Feel him, too, a dense presence with barrel-thick arms. The club in his hand falls without striking a blow. He doesn't need to. The sound is enough. Jack Dunning's clever enough to hurt you inside.

Tap.

Tap.

Tap.

Oak shouldn't fall so lightly. Calloused palms shouldn't sound so thick. There shouldn't be an ogre in a three-piece suit standing at the foot of my bed. And I shouldn't owe him something I just can't pay.

"You 'wake?" Jack says. His voice rumbles through the framework of my bed.

"Keep it down," I hiss. "You'll wake my roommate."

The dark-on-dark shape shrugs. I shouldn't be able to see that, but I can. My eyes must be accustomed now to the lightless room we share. The club keeps falling steadily, soft as rain, hard as thunder.

Tap.

Tap.

Tap.

Sigh, deep, finally.

"Okay, Jack," I say. "Let's talk…"

IT'S THE AMERICAN WAY. Make money, spend money, borrow more money for both. I'd spent the better part of a decade as a hotshot law-shark, acquiring all the toys such status brings. New cars, new house, new clothes, new stuff. My wife Mari and I lived well. If we seemed extravagant, there was always more coming on.

Until there wasn't.

Boom. Bust. Pretty words. Harsh feelings. Economic onomatopoeia doesn't capture the crushed-chest pain of bills you could have paid a year earlier. My credit was still high, though, so the plastic got a workout. It was only a matter of time, we figured, until the good times rolled back up again.

Something stalled, though. So did my career. Soon, my marriage did the same. The bills, though, kept arriving. The good times, then, seemed over and done with.

But you don't get where I had been without accumulating a few favors along the way. So about three years after the boom had busted, I walked down a flight of stairs I promised myself I'd never descend again.

He was still there, waiting.

The door to his office swung open, silent as a Mob witness on testimony day. Inside, the office was much as I recalled. Floor-to-ceiling bookshelves. Clutter everywhere. Burnt tobacco and paper rot. Endless ticking from countless clocks. Gargoyles perched on precarious shelves. Occasionally, they moved. It'd been that way since I was a kid, when Dad first brought me down to visit…

"Gino," he said in a cigarette voice. His parchment features crinkled with something like joy.

"Hello, Sal," I replied, raising my hand to wave. My fingers, I noted, were trembling.

Salantazi DiVoraccio was from what you might call the Old Country. The *very* old country. Not my ancestral lands of Sicily, but someplace far more ancient than human civilization. His name was a convenience, not even truly Italian. Like most names, though, it conveyed certain hints about his identity.

"It's been too long," he scolded, unfolding from his overstuffed chair. On the table he'd been sitting at, a watch spilled its guts across black velvet. A jeweler's glass overlooked a glittering dissection of bright lights and miniature tools. Sal liked things that ticked. The walls of his shop clustered with cuckoos and other novelty clocks. He couldn't care less about passing hours, but precision fascinated him. If something stopped ticking, Sal would want to know why.

I arced a shoulder to shrug. "Time gets away from me."

Sal chuckled like wax paper. The watchmaker's spotlight cast his dry features into sharp relief. He stilted toward me, trailing smoke like a grasshopper with a nicotine fixation. "Such a busy boy," he said. "So many things to do." He reached out to hug me. I hugged him back, of course. He felt like old twigs wrapped in steel. "It is good to see you, *bambino*."

"Good to see you, too."

His wagged a thin finger at me, smiling. "Ah, ah, ah… lying again. Haven't you learned better than that?"

I half-smiled. "Sal, I'm a professional liar."

"Small wonder, then, that you are doing so poorly with it."

"You know?'

"I always could read you, *ragazzo*," he said, motioning to another chair. "Sit."

"Then you know why I'm here." I sat. The trembling in my hands went bone-deep.

He shrugged, sitting back and turning his chair to face me. "Tell me anyway, yes? Confession is good for the soul…"

I HADN'T PLANNED on the law degree. I liked solving problems, though, and Dad always claimed I was great at arguing. "You can debate circles around me," he'd said once. "That doesn't make you right." I didn't need to be right, though. Just paid. As long as I was getting paid, everything seemed fine.

Sure, I made compromises. Who doesn't? Law school teaches that your client is never guilty, even when he *is*. I had plenty of "never guilty" clients, and lots of favors I didn't cash in. One of 'em sat at the bottom of a flight of stairs that sometimes was there and sometimes was not. "Stay away from him," said Dad after I asked about his old "friend" Sal. "Some people, you don't deal with unless you're ready to meet their price. And trust me, son, you never are."

Dad wouldn't discuss the prices he'd paid. I only knew about my own. Late nights bleared with arcane facts. Precedent and argument. Missed meals and brokered deals. Mari spent many 4:00 a.m's with my nightmares and compromised positions. Shakespeare said, "First, kill all the lawyers." You don't have to. Our livers do it for you.

It was my friend Steven, though, who helped me soldier through. Over more beers than I'd like to count, he claimed we lawyers kept the American clockworks greased. "This is why it all works, Gino," he'd say, his lanky frame hunched over the bar stool. "It's us. In a nation of 'laws, not men,' we're the men who work the laws that work the men." He didn't understand that some laws are stronger than men. I didn't understand it either. I sure as hell get it now.

Our firm seemed to be rolling right along. Then the track ran out, fast. When Steve hopped off, I saw the end coming. A few months later, the pink slip hit my desk. I thought my client base would take care of me. I thought wrong.

Folks say you're only as good as your last paycheck. Soon, I wasn't feeling too good. Pride made things worse. I couldn't admit how desperate things had become. "Never let 'em see you sweat," and all that. Or bleed, in my case. Lawyers deal in the red stuff, real and otherwise. Sharks smell blood, and I know the scent well. I smelled it all around me, even as I slept. Stepping out of the shower, I stank like a slaughterhouse. The smell drove me insane. It clung to me in each interview and got stronger with each apology. Three years out, I was breathing failure.

That's when Steven called again.

By that time, Mari and I were history. Most my cash and credit had gone with her. I was fighting wolves back from the door, and I had the bites to prove it. Sure, I scored the occasional client. Getting ahead, though, took money I didn't have. So, when Steven called, I jumped. You need me, Steve? You got me.

JACK LOOMS across my bed. His breath smells of garlic and alfredo sauce. Faint light through the curtains glints on the tusks jutting from his lower jaw. Jack rumbles in his chest. Is that interest I hear from him, or hunger?

Tap.

Tap.

Tap.

I choose my next words carefully.

"Thanks, Sal," I'd said to the papery old troll. His eyes held a sympathetic light. His dry hands, however, held something far more valuable: a contract with my name on it. No blood – nothing that melodramatic. Just ink, the blackest kind. The kind that won't come off your hands no matter how much you wash.

"You're good for it, *mio piccolo bambino*." He offered a single nod and a vaguely barbed smile. On a nearby bookshelf, one gargoyle flapped lazily and settled back onto its perch. I tried to act like that wasn't unusual. Instead, I nodded back. "I am, Sal. You've got my word on that. Literally."

I tried not to notice the scent of blood there, either. Was it something in the room, or was my wounded pride bleeding again? Underneath the paper-rot smell and subtle glide of watch-oil hovered a rich carnal aroma. Maybe I just knew, then, what my bargain with Sal would cost.

Like Dad said, some folks cost more than you want to pay. Sal was one of 'em. He didn't ask me for anything right then, but I knew that when he smiled and said, "Just you remember me when I come calling," I had better damned remember. There are worse things than broken knees and concrete shoes, and Sal dealt with those "worse things."

My trembling had nestled south of my heart, and my ticker was doing its best to stomp its way out through my ribcage. My wallet, however, held a check for a quarter of a million dollars – the buy-in price for partnership in Steven's practice, plus a bit extra for me to live on.

Who'd have thought that something worth so much could weigh so little?

That thought shook me. I glanced at the clock guts scattered across black velvet on the table. "You realize," I reiterated for the third time that afternoon, "that I *cannot* pay back this kind of money yet. Not now. Not soon. Not for a while."

Sal waved his parchment hand. "Money? It means nothing. Nonsense and trickery. Five thousand years and it still amazes me that you *ragazzi* take it so seriously."

"So why do you have this shop at all?"

He waved his hand at the clockwork corpse. "To see why things tick, *un giovanoto*, even when they are taken apart."

"Is that what happens, Sal, if I can't pay you back?" My voice stuck. "You'll take me apart?"

DiVoraccio shook his head. "I won't have to." He replied, lighting another cigarette. "You will."

"I'M WAITING," Jack says. The words remind me of Mari's tone just before a fight. Drop the voice three octaves and you'd have a perfect match... but then, I know why it sounds familiar. It's part of Jack's nature to embody your guilt.

They train you, in law school, to keep your voice steady. Some things, though, can't be trained away. Facing down a jury is easy. When you've faced down a seven-foot leg breaker with Boschian dental work and a tone like your ex-wife, then come talk to me about training.

Deep sigh. "I know I can't pay you right now," I say as steadily as I can manage. "You know it as well as I do."

"And…?"

"And you know why I can't."

I feel the shadow shrug again. The pressure in my chest grows. Pain swells. The ogre hasn't moved an inch.

Maybe it's the dawn light through my curtains, but I can see him now. He fits in my room with appalling ease. Given his height, Jack should be stooping. Instead, he stands like a butler of the damned. Folks say that Jack was once a man, a warden in an English debtor's jail. Stories of him, though, are as old as debt itself. In Hebrew writings, he's called Yacob the Mountain. Sumerians referred to him as Gud-alim, "the Bull." Germans named him Jakob der Golem, while Chinese debtors regarded him as Fang Yu, enforcer for the God of Justice. I've had plenty of time to study him, see. Jack's been assigned, you might say, to my case. This isn't the first time he's dropped by, and mere bankruptcy won't make him leave.

It had been going so well for a while. Once again, I was nailing my game. Castrovinci & Hall, Attorneys at Law, had a small but busy practice. In a year, we'd broken the two-mill mark. Not bad for a couple of has-been hot shots. The beer tasted sweet then, and though my bed lacked Mari, it didn't lack company.

Sal's first client showed up around then, long after I should have gone home. The doors were locked but he found his way in.

There were spiders between his teeth. "Sal sent me," he hissed before I could protest. "I have a special case…"

Some laws are stronger than men. Stronger than other things, too. There are laws carved in the pillars of heaven. And they have loopholes, too. That was Sal's payback from me: he wanted a lawyer to find loopholes for his friends. God help me, I did.

They weren't *demons*. I knew that much. Sal didn't handle Hell's trade. Some things are worse than demons, though. Things with baby-skin belts and razor-blade eyes. I began putting aside funds to pay Sal back. A quarter-mil didn't seem like much of a price for a good night's sleep.

And then? Well…

I noticed it first when my card was declined. I checked my balance and almost died. Sixty grand and change had vanished overnight. The shock took me like a hammer to the chest. Shaking, I hustled out my laptop. Logged in. Checked my savings.

Gone. All of it, gone.

I flew to the office without stopping for lights. Our doors were open. Our furniture, gone too. Five staffers wandered, dazed, appalled. Regina, Mark, Valerie, stunned. He'd even taken their private things. In Steve's office, one word – "Sorry" – stared back at us from a single index card propped up in the center of the room.

I counted five holes in the wall before my fist started hurting.

He took our money. Took our books. Took our client lists, notes, computers. Worst of all, he took my files, the ones I kept for my "special" clients. He took the library of loopholes I'd started to amass. And my copy of the contract with Sal.

What could I do now?

I never saw the knife coming. I hadn't wanted to. Steve had always felt above the law. For a while, I had, too.

Soon afterward, I learned better. I was poison in town, untouchable. The blackball went rolling through, squashing every job in sight. My contacts dried up. My references disowned me. Each compromise I'd made came down on me like a thick oak club.

And that's when Jack showed up, to make me pay my debt.

The thunder in my heart deepens.

"You signed a contract," Jack murmurs. "How are you gonna make good?"

Deep sigh. "I have no idea."

Tap.

Tap.

Tap.

"That's not good news," Jack rumbles.

"It's been a while since I've had some myself."

"I can make it worse," he says. His eyes narrow, dangerous.

I don't have words for what he does to me then.

But by the time I can think straight again, my throat is raw from screaming.

My roommate Ben never so much as knocked.

"It's just you and me," Jack says when I can think clearly enough to understand his words. "No one else will know."

There's not a mark on my body. They're all on the inside.

I can't speak, just moan.

Jack shakes his head as he fades into gloom. "Don't make me come back again…"

SAL HAD SPREAD his nicotined hands when I told him about Steven's theft. "Bad business," he kept saying. "Bad business."

"So, what can we do?" I asked. My left eardrum pulsed in time with my heartbeat. My right hand featured a cast for the five bones I'd broken against the wall.

"Do?" repeated Sal. In the background, a gargoyle gnawed on something that could have been a mouse skull.

"About my contract. My work. My debt."

DiVoraccio grimaced, stretching the corners of his wide mouth down. His eyebrows bristled like silver thickets. "Our old arrangement has not changed."

I'd been afraid of that.

He brought his hands together, rubbed them vigorously. "*Un poveraccio*, this changes nothing. You asked for a favor. I granted it. You got what you needed. Now *I* need things. Your partner is no concern of mine, *capisci?*"

"But my books. He took them, too."

DiVoraccio tapped his bald temple with a steel-twig finger. "You're a smart boy, Gino. You go to school, you learn many useful things. These things are not so easily forgotten. Debts still need to be paid."

I felt as though I was drowning in that over-cluttered office. "But… I *can't!*" I insisted. "I can't do the things you want without my books…"

He dismissed me with a wave. "So buy more books."

"With *WHAT?*"

DiVoraccio glared. "Make *do.*" For a moment, I glimpsed the thing he truly was. A face that made centurions crap their togas 2000 years ago.

I didn't crap my toga. But as I stumbled up the stairs a minute later, I threw up on the landing.

I refused, then, to take on more clients from Sal.

Jack dropped by for our first session a month later. He's come once or twice a week in the two months since. And each time, I feel a bit more dead.

I HATE THE HOURS before dawn. The twisted-sheet sickness of a mind against itself. A bed peopled with too many ghosts. Small apartment. Memories. A roommate I hardly even see. Boxes of junk. A knotted gut. A Rolodex of phantoms that never call back…

Pain chases my mind in circles. I can't get away from myself.

Jack will be back soon enough. I have no more to give him than I had before, and no way I can think of to come up with what I need.

A handful of favors and a few scraps of paper are all that remain of my professional life. Bastard even took my diplomas and the contract with Sal. If I had even *that* much, I might be able to figure a way out of this mess.

Contracts have loopholes. Even Sal's. If I could only *see* it again, I could find my way out of it. Figure out what makes it tick…

Problems. I solve problems. Puzzles. Rubick's Cubes. Debates. Rhetoric. Creation itself. Everything has laws. Laws have loopholes. I *find* loopholes. There's got to be one here.

GOD'S A LOUSY LAWYER. His contracts are full of holes. Maybe He didn't want to get stuck with the details. Point is, there's lots of room in reality for interpretation. If you can find the loopholes, you can bend or even break the deal.

Folks like Sal, Jack, and their kind… they're not bound by many of our laws, but they're utterly bound by their own. Mortals often use that to their advantage. In the case of Rumplestiltskin v The Miller's Daughter, for instance, the little guy could no more break his sworn oath than the girl could spin straw into gold. We know how that case went, and I can't say poor Rumpie got a fair shake in it. Arguing by that precedent alone, you can see why Sal's friends wanted to change the deal. They don't like mortals "pulling a Rumpie" on them. My job, then, was to find ways around those laws so that folks with blood-red caps and razor-blade eyes could cheat like humans do.

Yeah, God's a crummy lawyer. He just keeps paralegals busy with the paperwork. Me, I became part of the opposing counsel. The price of my quarter-mil from Sal was to take on clients *pro bono*. Clients like the faceless woman, or the sea-stallion with a thing for kids. They weren't *all* horrors, but I parceled off enough of my soul for that partnership that by the time Steven made off with the office, I halfway thought I deserved a knife in the back. Funny thing about loopholes: just because you can use 'em doesn't mean you'll feel good about it afterward.

And that's Jack's loophole: guilt. That's why I can't get away from him.

I can't tell you what my contract says, but it's as binding as any physical law. That contract was 26 pages long, with more clauses than a Christmas mall. It's the contract that binds Jack and me together. The legalese would make your head spin, but the gist of it is this:

Jack Dunning is Sal's insurance policy on me. He can't be bribed, bought, distracted or defeated. I fly to Tahiti, he'll be there when I arrive. Why? Because he's part of me. I signed on that dotted line myself.

Jack is guilt incarnate. Everything you owe, every mess you ever made, that's him. That club in his hands only *looks* like wood. It's actually something far heavier: regret. He doesn't even need to hit you with it. You do that for him. And compared to what I feel like after *that* kind of beating, I'll take the oak club any day.

Like I said, Sal's people don't work by human laws. Jack's immortal, but he's part of me as well. The money ogre lives inside of me, the part of me that feels obligation and guilt. Jack manifests the shitty way I feel about myself. And as long as I'm bound by my contract to Sal, Jack will come around to make sure I fulfill my end of it.

Ironic, really: my inner leg-breaker works off the feelings that made me quit Sal's service. No wonder he hurts me so bad.

WHEN STEVEN cleaned out the office, I lost everything that helped me handle Sal's clients. Not that I wanted to, anyway. Guilt is something every lawyer learns to live with. I mean, no matter how ethical you try to be, you'll help some lowlifes to get things they don't deserve.

In my case, the lowlife that had broken my nerve had nine tails, a big mouth, and a taste for little girls. When I'd read his profile (courtesy of some really nasty Japanese folk tales), I tried to turn the case down. Sal waved me away like a handful of smoke. "Gino," he wheezed, "you're a good boy but you think too much."

"This isn't a matter of letting some brownie skip K.P.," I protested. "This guy eats…" My mouth didn't finish the sentence. My imagination did.

Sal had turned back to his black velvet playground. That day, he'd been eviscerating a Mickey Mouse watch. Mickey smiled despite his missing arms. I thought of my nine-tailed client's dietary preferences. "I don't think I can do this, Sal. Not even for you."

His parchment hands stopped. His thin shoulders stiffened.

"Let me buy you out," I offered. "I know I owe you, Sal. I never forgot that, and I'm grateful to you. But this... this is something I cannot do. *Capisci?*"

A drift of smoke rose from the face turned away from me. I'm not sure it came from his mouth.

Tick.

Tick.

Tick.

"I understand, *bambino*" he said at last. His voice sounded drier than usual. "Half a million of your dollars and your debt to me is paid."

"Half?" The word caught on its way out of my gut. "I borrowed a quarter..."

He turned back to me. Seeing his face, I understood why Dad drank so much. God needed better lawyers when He made things like Sal.

It took me almost a full minute to find my voice. "Half a million, then. I'm good for it."

A voice like paper burning. "You'd better be."

From that point on, I swore never to help Sal or his clients again. I'd clear my debt the same way I'd incurred it: with cash.

I'd been six grand short when Steve took it all. And if he hadn't taken Nine-Tails' file, too, I might have sicced my would-be client on that bastard just for fun.

51

THE COPS had searched for Steve, of course. Nothing. Wherever he'd gone, it wasn't Stateside. South America, probably, maybe Eastern Europe. Someplace where the law couldn't touch him.

Man's law, anyway.

I knew other kinds of law.

If only I'd had my books…

It had taken me almost a year, and some really messy favors, to acquire my *other* library. The one my daytime clients never saw. The fairy tale books weren't too bad, and the Bibles looked downright respectable. It was the rare books, the ones bound in moonlight or human skin, that I hid from everybody else.

At times like this, when there's nothing left to do but think, I wonder what Steve and his crew thought when they dug *those* books out.

I wonder if he's kept them.

If he ever reads them.

If he knows what to do with them.

I doubt it.

But what if he tries to *sell* them?

People would notice. People I know.

Of course.

I was a fool not to have thought of it before.

And just like that, I've got a plan.

It's not great, but you work with what you have.

Steve didn't leave me much to work with.

And I owe *him*, too, for that…

I WAS *RAISED* CATHOLIC, but I'm not a *good* Catholic, if you know what I mean. The things I've seen and done don't fit in anybody's book. Still, I know there's *something* out there, and before I get started I figure it's time to set things square with the Man Upstairs.

Figure I should make this a one-on-one conversation. There's this lawyer-client privilege thing to think about, and I should honor the rules of the game, especially if I want turn 'em to my advantage. So, I light up some candles and dust off my Bible and take out a rosary I haven't used in ages, kneel down in near-darkness and make the opening statement no Catholic ever forgets:

"Hail Mary, full of grace, the Lord is with thee…"

Soon, my eyes go dark and my knees go numb. I keep speaking. After a time, I feel like someone hears me.

And I let it go.

All the guilt. All the shame. All the compromises and "never-guilties" that I still feel guilty about. It takes forever, this conversation. By the time I see the room again, it's full morning out and the world feels lighter.

"Thank you," I say. And I rest.

My clock is digital but ticking haunts me.

Time is my loophole… and Steven's noose.

Her name is Dami, and she lives outside of time. Dami could go walking through Pompeii's gardens, cop a bender with Edgar Allen Poe, and show up at your door a few minutes later with Poe's booze on her skirt and 2000-year-old grass on her heels. Not long ago, I helped Dami bend a few rules so she could step through time and still retain her clothes. When I head toward her favorite oasis, I've got favors of my own ask.

Benito's opened just before the Civil War. It hasn't closed since then. A 24/7 Manhattan rat-hole, it's timeless as a broken clock. I wave at Francesca behind the bar and snort some forbidden tobacco air. The smoke's so thick Jack the Ripper would get lost, and I have to wonder whose mojo keeps the Breath Gestapo away. "Perfumes of heaven," I declare, and the bartender laughs. Faint light catches diamonds in her shark-tooth smile.

A few quick words, some flattery, and a half-serious peck on the cheek later and Fran sets me up with a bottle of green faerie at the table near the back. Sure, the stuff's illegal as hell, but so's a barroom full of smoke. Dami always had a taste for absinthe. She claims the stuff was better a century ago, but she'll knock it back like a frat boy on a binge. I can't stand the taste myself, but I get two glasses from Francesca anyway. Best to appear sociable when Dami arrives.

On the table, I lay out the charm: Six Indian head pennies, a few drops of mercury, and a pinch of burnt oak ash. Dip my finger in the ash and draw a circle on the deep-scarred tabletop. Whistle "Greensleeves" badly, and wait…

She steps up a few minutes later, a tall shadow in the nicotine gloom. Thick silver hair cascades across a black velvet jacket stitched with matching silver filigree. Dami spots the green bottle and glasses, and she smiles. "Someone," she says with an English twist, "is speaking my language tonight."

"Thought you might like it."

"That I do," she says, sitting. "So, is this a social call, then?"

"More or less," I say, breaking the seal on the absinthe bottle.

"You're a very bad liar."

A shrug from me. "If I was that bad, you'd be standing there naked."

"And you'd hate that so."

She spills some of the green stuff in her glass. No sugar, straight up. Dami swirls the liquor around. Inhales with cat-eyed pleasure. Sips a bit of green faerie and grins again. "So, what's this job, then?"

"No job," I assure her. "Just a favor…"

STEVE WAS MY MENTOR and the big brother I never had. Skinny and pepper-haired, he stood a half-head taller than me. I think he was gay, but never asked. His real lover was his work, and he taught me well. Too well for my own good.

He'd convinced me, one beer-soaked night, to sign non-triggering full partnerships with one another. That way, both of us had full access to the firm's resources without consent from the other. He claimed it would allow either one of us to tend the firm if anything went wrong. His dad, after all, had died suddenly without provisions, leaving his estate and business tangled in red tape. Steve had health problems of his own, and he didn't want to make them my problem. "It's all business, partner" he assured me as we signed. "We've got to take care of each other."

He'd taken care of me, all right. Cleaned out our bank account and forged his way into mine for good measure. Stupidest decision I ever made, that contract… but that decision cut both ways… *if* I could find the contract to prove it. That's why, I think, he'd stripped my office clean. Steve wanted to make sure I couldn't pull the same stunt in reverse.

But he didn't know about Dami. Or Sal. Or Jack Dunning.

If I'm right, that's about to change.

MAY 25ᵀᴴ. The day Steve knocked me from powerhouse to poorhouse. It's easy enough to give Dami directions to our office and tell her where to leave certain files. She can't take things back and forth through time. She *can*, though, move things around. So, I send Dami back to the night of May 23ʳᵈ, to copy and stash a few items of interest before Steve cleans the place out. Items like our partnership papers. Sal's contract. And a few select books and files.

Dami can't make major changes in history, but Steve won't miss what he doesn't know exists. I figure he was looking for the contracts we shared between us, so I ask Dami to photocopy those and put 'em back where they'd been that night. He didn't know about my gig for Sal, though, or the details of my special collection. So, over licorice-and-peppermint bites of absinthe, I give her access passwords and ask her to shift my stuff to a safe location: a box in my closet that I haven't opened since before Steve cleaned out our office.

Like I said, Dami can't change history. Here's the loophole: if I suddenly "remember" those things I forgot until now, it doesn't count as a change. Steve still cleans out the office, my life still goes to hell, Jack still shows up to collect his due… until I "remember" the box that winds up containing my things. Coincidence. Sure, there are risks: Dami might get caught in our office. She might put things in the wrong box. My past-self might even catch her rifling through things in my old apartment. She might not even be able to pick the locks on the office or my old apartment. Hey, no plan is perfect. This way, though, I had a chance to "find" the long lost files, books and contracts. With them, I'd have the tools I'd need to set things right.

One more call to make. To my favorite bookseller, the place in Soho with a back room only certain people know about. On my past-due cellphone, I call in one more favor from the guy with rainbow hair. Give him a list of books taken from my office. See if he can track down any recent sales, and then find out where they came from. If I'm lucky, Steve won't think I've got that covered. He might stick a tome or two on eBay and use an address I can trace.

It's a long shot, but that's all I have left. Long shots and loopholes and promises in the dark.

When I get home, Ben's cleaning out our dishwasher. He says nothing as I walk past, but his silence weighs heavily. *Did I miss something?* I wonder, heading toward my room. Another bill I forgot to pay? Rent due? Something I borrowed and didn't return? This is nuts. I can't live like this anymore. No matter what happens with Dami's errand, I need to sort my life out. Fast.

Jack's waiting in the shadows as I open up my door. The kitchen light shines on his three-piece suit. As I softly close my door, he begins to tap his club against his palm.

Tap.

Tap.

"Drop the drama, Jack" I whisper. "It's getting old."

"Sal wants to see you."

Oh.

"When?"

"Now."

The clocks have stopped ticking when we enter his shop. Even the gargoyles are still. Sal sits at his workbench, his back turned to me.

58

A cuckoo clock lies scattered on black velvet, its innards glaring in the worklight shine.

Jack shuts the door behind us. Click.

Sal turns around in his chair to face us, his smoke-wreathed smile more awful than a wound. "Gino! What's the good news, *mio piccolo bambino?*"

Try to smile back in that terrible stillness. "I've almost got it, Mr. DiVoraccio."

He uncrumples from his chair, the creases of his suit smoothing into devastating sharpness. "A half-a-million dollars, yes?"

"Maybe that," I allow. "Maybe better."

He picks his cigarette off an overflowing ashtray. "I like the sound of 'better.' The 'maybe,' not so much."

"The devil's in the details, Sal."

He stops smiling.

"It's an expression, Mr. DiVoraccio."

"I know what it is," Sal replies, taking a puff from the cigarette.

Beneath my jacket, my heart pounds like a heavyweight. "I was just saying that I'm working a few things out."

He takes a single step. "When you worked for me, Gino, you worked much faster, yes?"

Nod. "I did, yes."

"So, you will be working for me again. Yes?"

59

Swallow hard. It's tempting. But then I remember little arms and a promise made to God. "I don't think so, Mr. DiVoraccio."

His smile disappears.

"I'm changing my line of work."

He shakes his head. "I asked you for good news. This is not good news. Not to me. Not to my people. Not to you. Especially not to you."

Stillness.

"I may have good news."

A thick puff. "Go on."

Here goes. I breathe deep and assume my best case-voice.

"What *do* you value, Sal? I mean really *value?* It's not money, you've told me that. What is it you really want me for?"

He waves a parchment hand, impatient. "You know this, *un giovanoto.* I have problems, you sort them out for me."

"That's true." I press my case. "I *can* sort out your problems. But I have to do that my way. I must be able to say 'No.'"

He shakes his head. "This was not part of our agreement."

"You're right. It's not. But it can be part of our *new* agreement."

Behind me, Jack cracks his own neck.

Sal scowls. "Explain to me this new agreement."

And I do.

Jack looks dubious when I finish. Sal seems slightly more impressed. "If," he says, "you can do what you claim, and pay my fee, I will call our old deal done. This, I promise you."

Inside, I feel like the cuckoo clock. "Thank you, Mr. DiVoraccio."

He lights a new cigarette with a loud fingersnap. Old-school, but it works. "I promise you this, too, *ragazzo o giovane*: If you make me send Jack for you again, he will take you somewhere *else*. And then, there will be no more deals."

Now I feel like the ash on the end of his cigarette. "I understand."

Sal nods. "You have seven nights to do this thing."

Try to smile as if I'm not shaking inside. "I've done more with less."

I try not to run on my way home. Has Dami taken care of my errand yet? The empty streets seem to stretch into endless hallways of fitful light and passing shapes. My steps *clop-clop-clop* on sidewalks flecked with dog poop and spit. My guts throb softly in time with my heart. I want to check the box in my closet, but I know that it's a one-time-only deal. If I open that box before Dami's had a chance to put my stuff in there, the laws of the universe might keep her from placing it there afterward. New things in that box would create a paradox. I'm not sure what would happen if she tried that, and I don't want to find out.

These thoughts keep my brain spinning all the way home.

Almost there, I change my mind, turn around, and head back toward the subway. Benito's is open as always, its smoky depths shadowed with the desperate and damned. I fit in well. Francesca's gone to whatever passes for "home" in her world, but the new guy behind the bar has a message for me. Taped to a bottle of Horka Absinthium 1792, there's a note in elegant script:

G.

You've forgotten something in your closet. Best go check it again.

Have a drink, darling. And no sugar, either!

PS: You owe me, hugely.

Cheers,

D.

It tastes like burning mouthwash going down, but I step lighter on my way home.

MY ROOM feels cleaner as I step inside. Jack's gone to wherever phantom legbreakers go when they're off-duty. Through thin walls, I hear Ben snoring. How he slept through all my screaming, I can't imagine.

Quiet as I can, I open the closet and move the boxes within.

Hands shaking hard, I check the proper box.

It's all there.

Thank God and all His little loopholes.

Fire up my computer and get to work.

In my email, there's a note from my Soho connection. Yep, Steve's tried to sell my books. They'd even bought some from him. Yes, there's an address.

Paydirt.

For the first time in months, I can truly breathe.

By the time my eyes blur, it's past noon. I haven't slept, but that's okay. Everything I need is here. Steve even used his new Belize address as the contact point for the book sale. I'm half-surprised by that. After all, he's a wanted felon. Then it occurs to me that he might secretly *want* to get caught... at least by me. That fits what I know of Steven, and it suits my plans perfectly.

Normally, Steve's beyond guilt. He could care less about laws or ethics. He's such a hotshot because he holds most people in contempt. Law is his power trip, and working it is his compulsion. Normally, that would make him immune to the likes of Jack Dunning. You have to *feel* guilt in order to be hurt by it. Like everything, though, Steve's immunity has a loophole. And that's where I'll take the bastard down.

Like I've said, he and I shared lots of beer and conversation. He was kind of closed off about personal stuff, but every so often the beer would take over and you'd see what made Steve tick.

One night, I remember, he was especially depressed. It was near Christmas but Steve was spending it alone. No family. No longtime partner, no kids, no relatives. I think I may have been his closest friend. It gutted him that night.

Now normally, Steve was all piss and vinegar. Nothing ever seemed to bug him. That night, though, he drank lots more than usual and wound up toasting his dead brother, his mom, his dad, and everyone else in the bar. Seems he hadn't spent much time with family back when they were still alive. Once he hit law school, Steve had better things to do. One year, he didn't even go back home. That was the year his brother hit a patch of ice and slammed into a phone pole two days after New Year's. His mom went a few months later – heart attack, I think – and then his dad, slightly afterward. The following Christmas, there wasn't a home to go back to.

Now, I was never much of a family guy myself. I never had a brother. No sister, either. I was an only child – a weird thing for a Catholic household, but there it is. Talk to my folks once in a while. See 'em on holidays. That's about it. So, when I admitted that I've never felt especially close to my family, Steve leaned in and gave me hell. Breathing a brewery in my face, he told me never, *never*, to forget my family. "You might wind up like *me*," he slurred, "spending your holidays buried in other people's misery." *No wonder he works so hard*, I thought that night. *It's all the poor guy has left.* That was the only time I'd ever seen him feel guilty about anything. I used it to get nice Christmas bonuses for all our staff. That felt good.

Now I'd use it as Exhibit A in my case against him.

That was gonna feel good, too.

SEVEN DROPS OF BLOOD, dripped in a circle. Seven drops of blood on an oak leaf placed at the center of my overdue cellphone bill. It's the first time I've employed the charm to call Jack Dunning. Normally, he comes on his own. In the darkness of my room that night, I light three candles, cut my finger, arrange the charm, and wait.

Tap.

Tap.

Tap.

"I can always tell it's you, Jack."

"You got the money?"

"I needed to check certain provisions in our contract." For the first time since we met, my voice remains steady. This is my turf, now. The realm of law.

The club stops tapping. Jack scowls.

I press my advantage. "Section 1, subsection B, employs the term 'perceived mortal value.' Am I right to assume this means the human value of the money lent by Mr. DiVoraccio?"

"Um… I think so."

"Just as I thought. And Section 9, subsection C, where it refers to 'agents of collection.' I assume that's you?"

His tusks flash in the candlelight. "Yes."

"So, in Section 13, subsection E, when it refers to 'tangible and external manifestation of the Lendee's internal sense of moral obligation,' that describes you as an extension of my sense of guilt."

"Yeah."

"And in Section 14, subsection F, the reference to 'all and sundry locations on any or all planes of earthly existence,' means that you can go any place that I have gone. Correct?"

A growl. "Correct."

I'm having fun for a change. "Now, when I read Section 1, subsection E, I take it to mean that any party that benefits from the 'perceived mortal value' of Mr. DiVoraccio's loan is also bound by the provisions of this contract and its strictures, provided that they are also beholden to the legal provisions of partnership with the signee of the contract."

Tap.

Tap.

Tap.

"Please answer the question, Mr. Dunning."

"I… guess so."

"So, by my reading of Section 13, subsection E, you should also be able to manifest for collection purposes to anyone who shares a legal obligation to the holder of this contract, provided they have an associated feeling of guilt about that debt."

Jack's brow crinkles like a Park Slope sidewalk. His eyes roll back and forth, as if reading an answer from invisible cue cards. Finally, he speaks. "I think so."

"Yes or no. This is important."

"I need to check with Mr. DiVoraccio."

"Understood. But I need an answer tonight."

Confused by my sudden shift from shrimp to shark, Jack nods. "Okay," he rumbles.

"Here," I say, offering Jack a copy of my partnership contract with Steve. "This contract verifies my full and legal partnership with a Mr. Steven Robert Hall, current benefactor of my loan's 'perceived mortal value.' Please take this to Mr. DiVoraccio."

Jack frowns. "I think you'd better take it yourself. With me."

Damn. Ah, well. I didn't think it would be that easy. Fortunately, I'm ready this time out. My briefcase is already packed and I'm wearing my best courtroom suit. Blowing out the candles, I hope it's enough to win this case.

There's no clock on black velvet this time. The chronographic operating theatre is bare. The gargoyles perch, expectant, as Sal crackles his parchment hands. "So," he breathes with nicotine malice. "You plan to pull a Rumpie on me, *bambino?*"

"Not at all, Mr. DiVoraccio. I have the new agreement here for you to examine."

Sal squints at the papers I hand him. I've seen snakes with kinder eyes. As he reaches for a pair of wire-rimmed glasses, I glance around the clock-lined walls of Sal's cluttered shop.

"Ever wonder," Jack rumbles, "where Mr. DiVoraccio gets all these clocks?"

Shake my head. "Not really."

"Maybe you should."

It takes a moment for me to understand.

My bones turn to cold glass inside.

God *really* needed better lawyers when He made Sal DiVoraccio.

I truly hope this works.

"Oh, shit. It's you."

I'd had my rainbow-haired friend whip up a pretext for sending me to Steven's office in Belize. Some nonsense about verifying Steve's book collection for future business. The details aren't important. What *is* important is that two days later I'd passed gratefully from the humid streets of Orange Walk into an air-conditioned office where I now stood face-to-face with Reginald Robert Hallister, alias Steven Robert Hall.

Steve's aged. His face has lines that his new tan can't disguise. His salt-and-pepper hair has gone almost totally gray, and several patches of it are just plain *gone*. Steve still knows how to dress for success, but his tailored suit can't cover the skinny frame beneath it. He looks ten years older than when I last saw him, but it's been less than ten months since he left. "Jeeze, Steve," I say. "You look like hell."

He tenses behind his polished oak desk as I close the door. "How did you find me, Gino?"

"That's not important."

"It was the books, wasn't it?"

Nod.

"I knew I should have left those damned things behind." The look in Steve's eyes lends extra emphasis to *damned*.

Sit down, uninvited, in one of his client chairs. "So why *did* you do it, Steve?" My voice thickens. "Why did you dick me over – dick *all* of us over – that way?"

He looks down, away, anywhere but at me. "I really can't talk about it, Gino. It's… complicated…"

The sun-washed room seems to darken.

"Complicated?" My voice sounds like a stranger's. "*Complicated?* I'll bet it's complicated." My fingers tighten around the armrests with five months' worth of pain. All it once, it hits me: What I went through, what everyone in our office went through, when he disappeared. Our clerks. Our secretaries. What we *all* lost to bring him here.

"So, tell me, Steven," I continue, "how 'complicated' your life is. Tell Regina, whose kid had to drop out of that special school of his because you took Mommy's job away. Tell Valerie, whose old yearbooks wound up in a Dumpster three blocks away after you cleaned her office out. Tell Mark and Merci and the half-dozen people you put out of work because your life was 'complicated.' And while you're at it…" I lean forward in the chair. "Tell your partner, your best friend, the guy who's spent the last four months with a goddamned sledgehammer in his chest, just how *complicated* your life had to be before you *cleaned out his fucking bank account* without so much as a 'good-bye.'"

Lean back. Take a long, deep breath.

"Tell me *that*, Steven. Because I'm really dying to know."

Steve looks back to me at last. "You were getting ready to do it to me."

"*What?*"

"Tell me you weren't." He stands up tall, his old courtroom self. "Tell me you weren't conducting business behind my back. Tell me you didn't have clients coming to see you after hours – clients you never told me about, never processed through the partnership." He leans across his desk. "Tell me you didn't have books of *sorcery* and God-only-knows what else hidden in your office, Gino. I'd noticed you moving money around in our account, checked up on you, and found out that you were getting ready to screw me over." He folds his arms across his chest. "So, I decided to screw you over first."

Silence. I honestly hadn't expected this.

Steve goes on. "I had… medical problems… I wanted to talk about them with you, but… when I found out about your off-the-record business and the money shuffling and the weird things you'd been up to *in our offices*, well… I knew I couldn't trust you with that information. Or with much else."

For a few seconds, I almost feel sorry for him.

Then I spot his new Rolex. One bought with the money he stole from our firm.

Tick.

Tick.

Tick.

"Oh, bullshit."

Steve glares back at me.

"Sorry. I'm not buying it." Rise to my feet. "Maybe you *were* sick…"

"I was. I *am*."

"And you know what? I. Don't. *Care*." The word falls like a dagger on his desk. "Once, Steve, once I would have given you *anything*. Anything you needed, you would have gotten from me. All you had to do was ask. But you had to be clever. You had to assume you knew what was going on."

"I did…"

"You had *no idea*, and you didn't even try to find one. Thing is, you've *always* been like this, Steve, and you always will be. *That's* your sickness, your real sickness. You have to be three steps ahead of everyone else, even if those three steps are wrong."

He glares back. "I wasn't wrong about this…"

"You were *totally* wrong. It had nothing to do with you, nothing to do with us. Yes, I had some extra business, extra clients on the side. I *had* to, to pay off the bill for buying in with you. But I was *loyal*, Steve. Loyal in ways you can never understand."

I pause, then let the bomb drop:

"I was loyal like a *brother*, Steve. You were the brother I never had. And I was the brother you threw away."

That hits home.

"And that's where you and I differ, Steve. I still *care* about people. And you never did."

Silence.

"So," Steve finally asks. "What do you want me to say? What do you want to hear?"

"I want to hear you're *sorry*, Steve. I want to hear my old friend apologize to me."

"Is that it?" He looks hopeful.

"Of course not," I reply. "I also want back the money you stole from me. My books. My things. My client list. My trust. All the things you took from me and our staff and from everyone else who depended on us and looked to us to make things *right* for them. I want that all back."

He looks ten years older now than he did when I walked in. "I can't do that."

"No," I say heavily. "You can't. You can't undo that day and all the days since then. You can't turn back time, Steven. Neither can I." I grant myself a private smile. "But I *can* demand a half-million dollars from you. Now. Right now."

Steve sits down. "I can't do that, either."

Minor flash of panic, but I don't let it show. "Where *is* it, Steven? Where *is* all the money you stole from us?"

Now it's Steven's turn to smile. "What are you going to do, Gino? Call the police? Tell them that the respectable businessman who's been handling exports here for almost half a year is actually your ex-partner from New York?"

"Something like that."

"Get out of my office, Gino." He waves me off like a gnat. "Get out and go back home to your witches and gremlins and your other fairy tales." He leans back in his chair. "Go to the police if you want. Hell, I'll call them myself. I'm covered, Gino. I'm *legitimate*. Sure, you might get an investigation started, but no one's listening here. By the time somebody takes you seriously, I'll be long gone."

I see him now like the stranger he is. Guess I never knew him that well. But at least now, I know myself better.

Get up and take out the papers I've been carrying. Set 'em on his desk. Our contract. "Remember this?"

His eyes widen. Then his sneer returns. "Yes. And?"

"Our agreement. Our partnership. Our signatures. What I have is yours. What you have is mine."

For a second, he looks fragile. Then he sweeps the contract off his desk. "That was another life, Gino. Another man. Not me."

I pick it up again. "Believe that if you want, brother. But a contract is a contract."

He shrugs. "Only if you can enforce it."

I head for the door, then, like a shark tasting blood. "I won't have to, Steve. You will."

I GET THE E-MAIL two days later.

Swiss bank.

Credit Suisse

Reginald Robert Hallister

CH10 0023 000A 1098 2234 6

Take what you want.

Just make it stop.

Thank you, Jack Dunning. He'll make *this* deal stick.

I take out exactly half of Steve's account. After the half-million buy-off for Sal, that leaves me with just shy of two million for myself. I resolve to pay a hefty chunk of that to Dami. The rest I set aside for other creditors, our former employees, and some seed money for my new business. And that night, I thank God for a very long time.

I LEAVE Sal's office the next day with a new contract and the lingering smell of stale tobacco on my clothes. Under the terms of this agreement, Sal still sends clients to me and Dami. We have right of refusal, though, and there's no money-ogre clause to twist my arm. I take on the cases I *want* to take on, and my word – yes or no – is final. All other debts are paid. This time out, I owe Sal nothing but good work and a fair shake. The rest is at my sole discretion.

Yeah, I'm still working with God's little secrets. I get paid well, but not *too* well. Now I work a fair practice. My clients, after all, need someone to keep things ticking smoothly. A mortal who knows loopholes and how to work 'em right. Every so often, the Rumplestiltskins of the world can use an edge when some wiseass thinks she can cheat her way to a golden future.

So yeah, I'm back in business. Ginelli Castrova, that's my trade name; some folks shouldn't know your true one. I provide a necessary service, and I do it well. Hey, *someone's* got to read the fine print on Creation. And after what I've been through, no one's better suited for that than me.

GRIMBLEGROTH

For Danielle Curry

Jenna learned the hard way not to litter.

Back a few years ago, she used to go out hiking every weekend. Just take her day pack and some Powerbars and head out to the Smokies. She'd come back after nightfall, full of stories about the gorgeous things she'd seen.

Now, you'd think Jenna, with her love of the outdoors, would be one of those "pack it in, pack it out" types. Nope. If the one hike I took with her was any indication, she'd just toss the wrapper from her Powerbar wherever seemed convenient. I remember giving her a hard time about it, and she told me to stop bitching. "It's a big world," she said. "No one's gonna notice it." That was the first and last time I went hiking with Jenna.

Anyway, one night she didn't come home. By ten, I was getting worried. Jenna's in good shape, but she's still kinda tiny. Finally, after midnight, I called 911. *Where'd she go hiking?* they asked me. I admitted I didn't know. They told me to go down to the police station and fill out a missing person's report if she hadn't gotten in by morning. I tell you, I didn't sleep at all that night.

Around 5:00 a.m., Jenna came back, all muddy and wide-eyed and shaking like a scared cat. When she told me what happened, I understood *why*.

She'd been hiking down a particularly lovely winding trail when she stopped for a snack. In her usual way, she'd dropped the Powerbar wrapper under some bushes and headed off again. Not ten minutes later, she swears a bird with bright blue and deep black feathers alit near her. "I'd pick that up," it chirped. "Or Grimblegroth will be unhappy."

Jenna did a double take. "I'd pick that up," the bird repeated, "or Grimblegroth will be unhappy."

It was a long way back up the trail, and Jenna wasn't so sure she wasn't hearing things. So, she blew the warning off (hey, I didn't say my roomie was *smart*, did I?) and kept going.

A few minutes later, she says, a deer walked up to her. Just walked right *up* to her, not hesitant or anything. That deer had bright blue eyes with dark black pupils, which, if you know anything about deer, is not exactly common. Jenna says that deer cocked its head at her and said, very clearly, "I'd pick that up, or Grimblegroth will be unhappy."

Okay – now *me*, if a bird and a deer both walked up to me and said something, I think I'd listen. But you know Jenna, right? Again, she just shook her head, blew it off, and kept going. (She admitted that even if she *had* gone back, she couldn't remember where she'd left the wrapper anyway.)

So, soon after, it's getting dark. Not supposed to – it's only two or so – but it is. Jenna's scanning the sky for clouds. Nothing. Just tree cover growing thicker and thicker. Now she's starting to get a little creeped out – I mean, she's not a novice hiker or anything, and her instincts are telling her something's wrong. She turns around to head back.

And doesn't recognize a thing.

Like I said, Jenna's got experience. She knows how to follow trails, even make new ones if she has to. But when she turns 'round, she has *no idea* where she is. The trail is gone, and the forest looks all wrong.

She turns back around, and now *none* of that forest looks familiar, in front of or behind her.

And then she hears this rustling nearby. Big, like a bear might sound. Or bigger.

Now, she knows enough not to run away from animals, 'cause most big ones can catch you anyway. But she's seriously scared. That sound's coming from everywhere and she doesn't know which way to go. The breeze picks up, starts shaking the leaves, and she swears she hears them whispering *Grimblegroth. Grimblegroth. Grimblegroth.*

And then she sees eyes in the forest. All around her, glowing in the shadows. Bright blue with dark black pupils. Dozens of 'em. Maybe hundreds. And birds come fluttering down from the sky, dozens of 'em, maybe hundreds. All bright blue and dark black feathers.

Grimblegroth. Grimblegroth. Grimblegroth.

That's it. She's outta there.

They chase her all over those woods. Up hills, down slopes, through creeks, across clearings. Sometimes she can see them, most times not. All the time, though, she hears 'em coming. Hears that whisper: *Grimblegroth. Grimblegroth. Grimblegroth.* She's got no idea where the hell she is, but the light keeps growing dimmer till there's just enough to see by. Finally – and I mean *hours* later – she spots a familiar slope with a patch of trail running up it.

Bang! She's up that thing, pounding fast as tired legs can go.

You see where this is heading, don't you? Not ten yards up the trail, there's this flash of bright orange in the brush. A Powerbar wrapper. She grabs the thing out of the branches (where it wasn't before, by the way), screaming *I'm sorry! I'm sorry! I'm sorry!* Jams that wrapper into her pack and takes off up that slope.

She still hears the wings. Still sees the eyes. Still feels the crash of angry legs behind her. But now she recognizes where she is. It takes a while, but eventually she's out of the woods. By around midnight, she's at her car again. You know the rest already.

Now, I'm not sure whether to believe that story or not. But I tell you this: far as I know, Jenna hasn't gone hiking for a while. And I've never seen her so much as spit on a sidewalk since.

VALHALLA WITH A
TWIST OF LETHE

Thor built his first guitar out of lightning and oak and a few hairs plucked from Freya's head. He crafted it with passion and a touch of envy, too. Taking up the instrument, he used Mjollnir as a plectrum and shot sparks from his beard as he played. The sound drove trolls into hiding and cracked the mountain where he stood. Ships sank. Hel's whole face turned pale, and Fenris scratched some stars into oblivion.

Hmmmm… Thor thought. *Perhaps a bit too much.* He dialed things back to avert Ragnarok, and the Midgard Serpent retreated to its bed again and slept.

The thunder god took his guitar to Bifrost Bridge. As he played, the rainbows changed colors to match the notes. Nerids writhed in their watery beds; when they woke, five hundred men were drowned. Lightning laughed and thunder tolled. The shades in Helheim swooned. Yet Thor shook his head and chewed his beard. "Not yet," he muttered. "Not quite." Impressive spectacles aside, the music did not move him. His efforts paled when compared to mortal art.

And so, Thor grooved on purple haze. He went down to the crossroads and saw smoke on the water. He weighed in on chromatic scales and raised Dorian temples to the majesty of Rock. He even smashed his guitar in a fit of rage, breaking new tributaries for the Rhine. Still, all was for naught and the God of Thunder moaned. "All flash," he mourned, "no substance." Thor ground his teeth and wondered why.

As he built his next guitar (with wolf's-hair humbuckers and a dwarf-forged tremolo bar), Thor pondered his technique. He asked advice from Thought and critiques from Memory. He took lessons from Yngwie Malmsteen and sat in with Blackmore's Night. He even gouged his eyes out a few times… but, being godly, he grew them back in time for his next gig. Yet although he pulled groupies like Tommy Lee on Viagra, Thor himself remained unmoved.

Lo, he rock'd not.

T'was enough to drive a sane god *man*.

Ripping limbs off Yggdrasil, Thor heard an evil hiss. The serpent coiled in the world-tree's roots had dark insights to share with him. "Young Thorrr…" spoke the serpent, its eyes thin with secrets, "'tis *mortality* thou lacks. Thou fearessst not death, so thou underssstandest not *life*."

The frustrated god set down the broken boughs. "Go on," he said.

"Thou knowest *truth*," the serpent continued, "and ssso ponderessst not the universe." It flicked its tongue at him at him in mockery. "Sssuch things make mortal heartsss inspired."

"I don't follow you," Thor replied, hefting his hammer to smash the serpent flat.

Fearless, the serpent beneath Yggdrasil eyed the god. Moonlight glowed along its fangs. "Thou doest not know what it isss to *die*, young Thorrr," the serpent purred, "and thusss thou cannot know what it issss to *live*."

Wisdom dawned like sunlight on the Rainbow Bridge.

Life was not merely slaughter, beer, and wenches, Thor understood at last, but the daily understanding that upon some day, everything would end. True enough, the Norns had forecast the death of gods and men alike, but passing ages dulled that prophecy. In Thor's world, death was an *inconvenience*, not a curse. And without that curse to give it meaning, his music rang hollow on Asgard's hills.

This, he decided, was a puzzle worthy of a god. "To be the bolt of lightning," he pondered, "not the hand that hurls it. To grasp what the flash feels like is to know the essence of its thunder. Mad mortals wring passions from their ignorance. Gods know too *much* to understand so *little*, and thus they understand less about life than man."

"Verily" – the serpent flicked its tongue again – "thou hassst blooded the rune of Rock." And so saying, it slid off to go eat a cosmos or two.

Thor wandered the hills of Arcadia. His bootfalls shook the temple of Poseidon. Nymphs cringed and centaurs fled. "How might a god," Thor mumbled, "forget all that he has known?" Resting for a light snack, Thor ate some goats and sulked.

A sharp laugh broke Thor's revere. "So *like* a god, to eat my kin!" Pan shook his shaggy head at the carnage of the goats. "Truly, wolves endure less appetite than you." Trip-trapping to Thor's side, he helped himself to Thor's tankard of mead.

"Not now," Thor snapped, snatching back the mug. "I'm thinking."

"A rare enough event," Pan quipped, one eyebrow cocked in dubious surprise. Thor shot him a storm-dark glare. "And sullen as a titan, too," Pan replied. "Forethought doesn't bring much light these days, you know." He poked Thor's belly: "Though perhaps a bird in *your* guts would do you some good."

Thor snarled. Lightning fell.

Pan dodged aside, amazed. "Good gods," Pan cried, "you *are* in poor temper, aren't you?"

Thor bared his teeth at his old friend. "Says the goat whose music makes men run for the hills and hide. And nymphs too…" he grinned with cruelty. "Let us not forget the nymphs."

The goat-god scowled. "A low blow, even by your standards."

Thor gestured at the Pan pipes. "At least I don't craft my art from paramours."

"Ahhhhh…" purred Pan. "So *that's* what this sulk's about. The God of Thunder can't rock 'n' roll."

Thor turned away. "'Tis all sound and fury, signifying naught."

"Mortals have been deified for less."

"Mortals are not *me*."

Pan scrutinized his friend. "No indeed," he said at last, "and that *is* the core of this dilemma, is it not?"

"Perceptive," grumped Thor, "for one thought dead."

"Long live me," Pan replied. "Long live us all." He lifted the pipes and played. Uneaten goats danced a jig. The skins and bones of their dead kin skipped across the fields.

"Nice trick." Thor scowled, looked down at his hands, and sighed.

Pan set aside his pipes. Looked Thor up and down. "Bloody Vikings," he muttered, then clapped his hands. "My brother," he cried aloud, "let's go *DRINKING!*"

"Best thing you've said all day," said Thor, rising to dust the grasses from his butt. A troupe of maenads joined them then, all sharp teeth and naked flesh, howling with elemental glee.

Pan's laughter shook the hills as the two gods and their retinue set forth, with Kali, Inanna, and the Monkey King for company.

And so, their revels came to pass.

Jim Morrison groaned in envy. Keith Moon heiled a salute. G.G. Allin rose from his coffin, farted, threw a handful of shit for good measure, and then went back to sleep again. It was a night that shamed Led Zeppelin, the Stones and Mötley Crüe combined. When at last the gods and maenads staggered home from their festivities, the very pillars of heaven sagged with relief.

Perhaps it was his mood. Perhaps it was his mead. Perhaps it was because Thor partied with divinities known for drink and trickery. In any case, the night ended with Thor face-down in the River Lethe.

His companions shrugged. Thor couldn't drown. No Hendrixian swan-songs for him, then. They left a curse to guard their friend and went their separate ways.

"Ow," said the man who rose from the mud.

"Ow," he said again, for hangovers sound much the same in English and Old Norse.

"Ow," he said a third time, combing muck from his beard.

What he *didn't* do was hail a six-legged horse-ride home. Thor, you see, had forgotten who he was. The River Lethe drowns memories, and not even gods are immune.

All he knew now was pain in his head and sewage in his guts.

After puking up a toxic spill, Thor sprawled beneath a willow tree. Tired beyond reckoning, he judged himself to be a mortal man. The certainty of godhood had fled his mind.

All that remained were mortal doubts. *Why did I do that?* he pondered. *Did I have a good time? Did I break anything expensive, and can I still show my face at home?*

Oh, yes. Home. Where *was* home, exactly? *Hmmmmm...* Heading off into the sunrise, Thor began rambling with no particular place to go.

(Meanwhile, the three frat boys who'd been set to steal Thor's pants were transformed by Pan's curse into gnats. Krishna later swatted them into their next incarnation, where they were promptly eaten by a carp. Moral: Don't steal pants. Payback is a threefold bitch.)

Thor headed on down the highway. He stayed away from Copperhead Road. He shook hands with Mr. Brownstone and hopped aboard the Crazy Train. He rambled from the gallows pole to the Temples of Syrinx. The Alamo, when it saw him coming, grew legs and ran away. (God-piss burns, you know.)

Hell-hounds dogged his trail. Stairways to heaven closed their gates. Levees broke and shooting stars fell. Thor turned the page and boogied down, all thoughts of godhood gone. Amidst rivers deep and mountains high, he nursed his achy-breaky heart. There were devils and drugs and dust on the wind.

Finally, there was a guitar.

And by then, the amnesiatic god remembered how to play it.

Thor pressed his calloused fingertips to tight strings and polished wood. Nothing fancy, nothing gained. For the first time in dog-years, a smile broke across his face.

All Creation held its breath as Thor's first notes rang out from the strings.

Those first few notes were tentative. Revolutions often are. Thor scowled and squeezed his eyes shut tight. In the play of steel beneath his fingers, he chased that implacable moment when fear gives way to ecstasy. Where the cry of a new child meets the sighs of dying men, no god may truly go... until, like Thor, he forgets how to be a god and simply plays the song.

And so, he did.

Over the hills and far away, Pan smiled at the sound.

Lightning spoke from Thor's fingers, then. Thunder answered in between the notes. At his coaxing, the paradox unwound. From the soul of a god forgotten by himself came the essence of mortality and divinity in one. Let there be rock, indeed.

And there was.

Spirits joined in. Mortals, too. And ghosts. And gods. In his pastures, Pan danced and laughed and fucked. In her underworld, Inanna flayed herself with joy. Kali stomped Shiva flat in a demonic mosh pit while the Monkey King rocked heaven down… again. Christ and Lucifer dropped Stryper into a Slayer gig for laughs as Evanescence sat moping in a corner, all alone. Mötörhead kicked Nickelback's ass, and a grand time was had by all.

Thor's music, stripped of all pretensions, rocked Creation to its core. A simple man, once lifted on a song, can chase the gods and win. When Thor finished playing, even Robert Johnson smiled. "Not bad," said the bluesman, "for a white boy."

Thor laughed so hard the Himalayas broke.

All Creation, some say, is music. The trick is to forget what you know and recall what you feel. Thor did both, they say, on the day he rocked. In forgetting, he remembered… and yet, that memory helped him to forget again. We are the beasts our arts have made us, and in that regard mortals and gods become one.

Thor looked across the horizon, to a sea of lighters, skin, and faces eager with regret. *They look to ME*, he thought, *to speak for THEM*. What more precious sacrifice could be laid upon the altar of a god? Not blood or fear, but trust. Trust in the sharing of a dream.

And so, Thor raised his ax – not the blade of war but the chariot of sound. All Creation waved lighters in response.

"ARE YOU READY" Thor boomed, *"TO MAKE SOME NOISE?"* The heroes cheered. The Serpent stirred. Let Ragnarok arise!

As he cranked his amps up past 13, the God of Thunder grinned. In his stein swirled a twist of Lethe mixed with Jack Daniels and a hit of groupie tears. *"I don't know about y'all,"* he drawled, *"but I'd rather be a ROCKER than a GOD!"*

With that, he took a swig and hit the strings. And although his first chord deafened half the population of Helsinki, they later all agreed that it had been the hottest rocking they'd ever heard.

RAVENOUS

For Ann Leone Taylor, SJ Tucker,
Elizabeth Leggett, Lonesome Crow,
and Coyote Ashley Ward

I've got that just-before-the-cages-open feeling in my chest. Wipe my fingers. Check the tension in my strings. There's a pack of drunken faces just beyond the stage. Stale beer perfume. Leather and sweat. Black tees with faded band names. Showtime.

The wood feels good beneath my boots. Solid. Strong. The Fender's weight hangs tight across my shoulder, giving comfort like a gun. My corset's too tight, though, and it's shoving my boobs to my chin. I can't breathe. Stupid corset.

Glance across to Chipper behind her kit. Brian's shadow cocked behind his bass. Rice's fingers flexing just before the storm. Hunger from the crowd. Hunger inside.

Nod to our secret weapon in the wings.

Her familiar luminescence emerges from backstage. The crowd hushes, then it roars. Kelsey slips brave and barefoot through the cable mess. Bright wings unfurl, shimmering, from her back.

She smiles, and even with the lights down you can see her grin. She steps up behind the mic stand. Breathes. In the twilight, someone starts to howl. The crowd picks up the sound until it screams.

Kelsey grins wider, lifts her arms high like a priestess. The scream becomes an invocation. She brightens, feeding off the surge. Behind me, Chipper shifts her weight. Drumsticks click, cymbals hiss. The Beast is waiting.

Kelsey looks to me.

I nod, and it begins.

Our first note hits like a thunderclap. The lights blast up and everything goes white. For a second, we're suspended in a single power chord. Then we crash in toward the verse. Kelsey screams in perfect pitch. The crowd goes apeshit. They love it. They love us.

This is what I live for. Ravenous. That's me. That's us. That's Kelsey. That's the Beast.

Who'd believe this could be me?

Let's be honest: I'm a dork. Strip away the Docs and corset, peel out my contacts, snatch my Fender and cover up my ink and I'm just a sullen tubbo *World of Warcraft*-playing geek. I read too much bad fantasy and haven't had a date in months. I still sleep with my stuffed *Tigger*, for fuck's sake! Yeah, I'm so Rock Star I could die.

Kelsey, on the other hand, is magic.

Really magic.

What *was* I thinking when I made her up?

Kelsey began as a voice in an old oak tree, three broken necks above the ground. I was about ten years old then, reading more Dragonlance than homework and practically living in Old Man Ivan, this huge oak tree outside my parents' house. I'd climbed up as high as I could go to get away from everyone that day. Mom. Dad. Teachers. Even my cat. Anyway, I was up there moping and reading and singing some old Tori song and feeling all pity-me party and then this girl's voice said *What's wrong?* and I almost fell out of the tree.

She caught me, then. I told myself for years afterward that it had been my own fingers that stopped me, but the truth is that Kelsey grabbed my wrists as I fell. She wasn't any bigger than me – smaller, in fact – but the pretty little girl who just *happened* to pop up next to me thirty feet off the ground was strong enough to pull me back onto the branch I'd fallen from. I totally lost my shit at her then – started screaming that she'd pushed me and all this other stuff. The girl just smiled. "At least you're not sad anymore," she said. And that's how I met Kelsey.

She was a thin kid, about my age. Her eyes glowed green and her hair changed colors. She had wings on her back like a big butterfly, and when they flexed I saw rainbows dancing. She never wore shoes, never had to go to bed. At night, she'd appear in my room all glowy and cool. Always asking questions – *Why is this?* and *How is that?* I answered her with stuff like *Because the sky is full of fish.* Looking back, we never made much sense together but that was just part of the fun.

Soon I had Kelsey wearing my clothes, too. We cut holes in the backs so her wings could fan out. Mom wasn't amused. I didn't care. We went everywhere, Kelsey and I. The mall. Church. Mercy Creek. Even school. That part made my life hell – not just with my parents or my teachers but with the other kids as well. Not only was I Weird-Ass Nicole, but now I was Weird-Ass Nicole Who Talked to Nothing. Y'see, no one else could actually *see* Kelsey except me. No one else could hear or touch her. To me, she was as real as Mom or Dad. To everybody else, though, she was Nicole's little imaginary friend. And that made Nicole a walking freakshow. Soon, even *I* began to think I was crazy.

Maybe we were right.

TIME GOES GORGONZOLA. We're halfway through "Dead on Your Feet" before I even know what's happening. My fingers hit most of the right chords in more-or-less the right sequence without my brain having to issue marching orders. The adrenaline shake in my knees gives way to Metal God posing and I find myself with my foot up on the amp without remembering how I got it there. Kelsey blazes neon green, and all I can see in front of us are flying bodies and thrashing heads. To me, everything seems like frozen lumps of time all hopping to the beat.

Chipper's roaring into "Destiny" by the time my mind catches up with my fingers. Sweat and splinters fly behind her drumkit, and her arms are a blur. I named her "Chipper" because of how she wrecks her gear. Brian, meanwhile, beats his head against his amp like always. Rice's eyes are squeezed shut, but somehow he still sounds tight. He may be an asshole but he plays a mean guitar.

For now, we own this place.

Kelsey shines like a glowstick goddess, blazing so bright it hurts to look. No one asks why – they just accept it. Kelsey glows and sings and fucks like a tornado. She's got wings and changing hair and Wow, those special effects *rule!* That's all anyone has to know.

I wish that's all *I* knew about her. I wish I couldn't feel her voice ring through my bones. I wish I didn't feel like throwing up when she fucks someone else. I wish a lot of things.

Some of them even come true.

MOM GAVE ME MY FIRST GUITAR when I was twelve. She wanted Jewel. She got White Zombie. Turns out I was a natural – who'd have known? Soon I could shred like Dimebag Darryl on the rag. That's when people started asking me who my friend was, the barefoot kid with colorful hair. Too many questions, too much detail. We had to think fast or be destroyed.

The night I finally realized that other folks could see her, I begged Kelsey to go away. We huddled under my blanket but I couldn't stop shivering. Kelsey just put her cool, dry hands on my forehead and held me close. She kissed my forehead, then my belly, then my lips, then deeper. It wasn't the first time she had done that, but it was the first time I kissed back. She tasted like spring leaves and budding flowers.

Some lies are sweeter than others. The lies we cooked up that night for her went down like green candy. After that, I never wanted her to leave.

THE BEAST SCREAMS NOW, fists high in the air. We pause to pose a bit. Red lights and smoke backlight us like gods of hell. Rice and I lock eyes. He grins his crazy grin, and I've probably got one too. Kelsey, blazing green amidst the red, lifts her arms and flexes her wings again. This close, I see light pulse through the membranes. She catches me looking, reaches out, grabs a fistful of my hair, and pulls me to her with the biggest grin of all.

The crowd goes psycho. We melt together and I taste warm green.

Time locks up again. I feel her tongue on my soul and I don't care. Far away, my Fender's screaming feedback. It blends with the Beast. I'm lost.

Then she rips me back. I'm at arm's length suddenly, gasping like a fish held by a fistful of hair. Red light. Green light. Everything is fire and fog.

Now it's Rice's turn. I try not to watch. It's not the first time I've seen them kiss but my guts twitch anyway. I don't want to watch. I can't *not* watch.

Red light. Everything goes thick and flat and red.

WE MADE UP HER HISTORY that night. Where she went to school. Who her parents were. How and where we met. *Kelsey* may have been real, but not much *about* her was. I'm not sure how believable our stories were but no one called us out on any of it. If

Mom and Dad wondered why my new friend shared a weird name with my imaginary one, they never asked me why. To be honest, they didn't ask me much of anything by then that didn't involve slamming doors. I didn't spend much time at home around that point.

School wasn't much easier. Now that folks could actually *see* Kelsey, I couldn't take her to class with me anymore. That didn't stop us, though. Sometimes she'd meet me between classes or at lunch, colored hair streaming, eyes warm green. Tucking her wings up underneath a jacket, she'd wait out by Crown Hall or toss a Frisbee with the East Wing stoners. I didn't dare make out with her in public, but all high schools have dark and secret corners. For those four years, she was one of mine.

Chipper brings us back around with four quick, angry shots on her snare. I hit the cue with the first long chord of "Centrifuge." Brian and Rice come in wobbly, but Chipper holds it tight. Kelsey chokes on the first few words. I shouldn't smile but I do anyway.

A few wrong notes later, Rice is back in line. His smile's gone and he savages the chords. Rice locks eyes with me again but there's nothing playful about it now. Months ago, I'd made the mistake of fucking him. That sick feeling in my gut returns when I catch his glare.

Curious experience

In things that don't make any sense

Young and dangerously borrrrrrred...

Kelsey spits the words out. "Bored" sounds feral. I glance up at her. She *looks* feral, too, and not in a good way. I don't like what I hear behind her words.

It doesn't sound like love anymore.

I wish I could say it stayed good between us. But nothing teenage is forever. By the time I hit senior year, Kelsey and I fought constantly. Over boys. Girls. Time together. Time apart. The only moments when the anger fell away was in the arms of Old Man Ivan. There, we remembered the children we had been. That sounds crazy, but really – wasn't *everything* about us crazy?

Crazy is a good word for those days. We formed our first band when I was sixteen – and if you wanna know how much trouble two teenage girls can get into, give 'em a metal band to play with! We had plenty. Pyrotic Angels was the first. Then Wrecker Bitch. Jesus on the Half-Shell. The more it pissed my parents off, the better a band name was. Kelsey took center stage, I wrote the music, and everyone else in the band became our personal bitch. Mom and Dad hated it, of course. By the time I slammed my last door back home, we'd all gone too crazy to care.

We burned through eight band names and over a dozen lineups before we came to Ravenous. That name suits us both. It's hungry. Volatile. So are we all. It's like riding rockets, this beast of ours. I keep waiting for something to tear off or explode.

Rice and I go head-to-head, pressing our skulls together. Behind us, Chipper sounds like she's gone through two sets of drumsticks at least. Her beat never breaks but you can feel how mad she is.

And Kelsey looks out to the crowd, reaches out into the pit, grabs a dude, and lifts…

I still forget how strong she is. Strong enough to lift a man without straining.

What's on her mind?

The crowd screams like happy wolves. The dude grins like a lost soul.

She kisses him, soul-deep. Kelsey's green fire spreads. Takes him in. Drags him down. But he's not one of us, and that's not good. Dude doesn't know where he's going and seems too gone to care.

The crowd cheers. I feel sick.

Not here! I want to scream. *Not a stranger! Not on stage!*

Even *we* have rules. And limits. I hit mine.

I don't know if it's the lover, the friend, or the scared human being who yanks herself back from Rice and hollers *NO!!!*

Maybe I just want her all to myself.

I'M NOT A PEOPLE PERSON. Never have been. Never will be. Kelsey is, though. Totally. She's our walking nuke. I'm just trying to keep up. So back when we formed Wrecker Bitch, I stopped being Nicole. The name sounded boring. I wanted to be exciting. I tried Nikki. Raven. Even Shade – how lame is *that*? Nikita stuck. I liked that one. It sounded romantic, like that killer on TV. I wanted to *look* like her, too: tall and strong and badass blonde. My body, though, had other ideas. I stopped growing *up* at five-foot-four, and started growing *out* instead. No matter how little I ate or how much I threw up, I still looked like a tank with tits. I had my guitar and Kelsey, though, and that counted for a lot.

Kelsey was the gorgeous one: long, changing hair, greenfire eyes. She got the body I wanted and had the charisma I lacked. So yeah – Kelsey and Nikita. Two-headed beast of fuckatude. I wish I could say I was happy with that arrangement. But after you cry yourself to sleep alone or walk in on your girlfriend being an utter slut for about the millionth time, it gets old. Sometimes it's like sticking your heart in a candle flame.

One of those nights, walking home from a gig, feedback stuffing my ears with nothing, I made a weird connection: Until I'd picked up a guitar, I realized, no one could see Kelsey but me. Now when I played, she seemed to glow. When we kissed, that glow got brighter. And sex... well, we never needed candles.

She was *feeding* on me. On my music. Maybe on more.

I began to shiver then, and even now I couldn't tell you how much of that shaking came from adrenaline or cold and how much of it was fear. Where do you *go* with that? What do you do when the only person you love in the world is literally living off of you? What does their attention cost? Worse, what if that person *stops* loving you? What if you're not good enough to keep them? After that, I was less jealous about her flings with other people and more worried that someday one of them would be better at keeping her around than me.

I never told Kelsey, but that's the night I came up with the name Ravenous. Like I said, it fits us both.

I PULL BACK. Rice falls forward. Kelsey and the dude are glowing. Dude burns with green fire. Kelsey blazes with it too. Rice makes feedback thunder as he hits the floor. My Fender goes flying before I think to throw it. It's all a blur again.

Me screaming at Kelsey. Kelsey screaming back. The guy in her grip, jerking like a spaz. Brian's bass punching through his amp. A drum flying past my head. Hands on my shoulders. Rice shoving me off stage.

Falling.

I feel empty air. Three broken necks to the ground with only a mosh pit to break my fall.

But this time she isn't there to catch me.

This is gonna hurt. A lot.

"*WHAT THE FUCK WERE YOU THINKING?*" I don't know if Chipper's yelling at Kelsey, me, or all of us.

She shreds us both like paper flowers. Her words all blur together except for the kicker: "*I. FUCKING. QUIT!!!*"

The wreckage of our gear fills the alley where the bouncers have thrown it all. The door's locked. No way we can go back in. Brian holds what used to be a sweet black Fender J. He hasn't said a word. Finally, he looks up, tear-eyed. "Well," he adds in that soft voice of his, "Yeah... that was..." – a grimace – "*fun.*"

"Brian..." Is that my voice or Kelsey's? I can't tell.

"*DON'T!*" he snaps, glaring at us both. "Don't even *try* to make nice with me!" That soft tone sharpens. "You're both insane. You're sick. You use people like toilet paper, and... and... I'm tired of wiping your ass." He looks down at the broken bass in his fist, and for a second I'm afraid he'll pitch it at us. Then he shakes his head. Slumps his shoulders, sighs. "I'm with Chipper."

"Don't call me that anymore," she adds, gathering her gear. "I'm taking *nothing* from this band, not even a nickname."

"Like she said," Brian adds, quiet. "I'm with her. I'm leaving. Don't call me again. Ever."

I want to cry but can't even breathe. Stupid corset.

Beside me, Kelsey whispers: "I'm sorry." Over and over, like it'll turn back time. Her glow has faded. Her wings sag. Her eyes no longer shine, and the broken glass nearby makes her bare feet seem... no longer brave but *helpless.*

Again, I feel Rice's hand on my shoulder. This time, though, he's gentle. "You guys," he says, almost kindly, "have some stuff to work out." From far off, I feel myself nod.

Rice turns me around to face him. He looks like some Zen death god. His thick guitar fingers dig tight into my skin. His bright blue eyes size me up, but it's not rage I feel from Rice. It's compassion.

A long pause, then, for everyone to breathe.

"Nikita," he says at last, "I like you. A *lot*. More than a lot, if you can believe it. You're a great songwriter and an amazing guitarist. I want to see where you go when you get your shit together." One corner of his mouth twitches into something that could be a smile if you looked hard enough. "I might even be there when and if you do," he says finally, shrugging. Then he lets me go. "But before then, you have to get a lot of things straight inside your head. A *lot*."

I dip my head to agree.

"As for you…" Rice says, addressing Kelsey with more bitterness. "I don't know your story and I'm not sure I want to. But you need to figure that out, too, before you both destroy everything that means *anything* to you."

"Haven't we already?" she says, like a child.

"That depends." He glances at each of us in turn. "On you two. Getting your heads out of one another's ass."

I'm glad when my eyes finally blur. It's easier than looking at Rice, Kelsey or the others.

Under the roaring in my ears, I hear Not-Chipper open up the van and toss her stuff inside.

THERE'S A TORRENT OF SILENCE where love falls away. I sense it swirling as we walk. I don't really know *how* or *where* we walk after the van drives off. It's all black silence and a storm of loss.

Everything blurs to midnight pavement and the sounds of feet booted and bare. Stores lit with nothing inside. Lonesome traffic lights. Glass diamonds on the shattered street. Blocks and miles without speaking. We don't share a word as we walk, but we both know where we're going.

And finally, near dawn, there he is. Old Man Ivan. Where it all began.

My parents' house is dark. It's just us and the tree where we met. Beside me, Kelsey shimmers, hardly glowing at all. Closing her eyes, she reaches out and lays one palm against his bark. Sighs deep. Unfurls her drooping wings. I reach out too. We're home in more ways than one.

I wait for the music that never comes.

Silence.

I surprise us both by speaking first. "So…"

"Yeah?" She sounds husky. Deep and calm.

"We made a mess of it again." I wish I didn't sound like such a goddamned frog.

Her mouth twitches. Her eyes close. "Big mess."

"Again."

"Yep. Again."

"What's wrong with us?"

No answer.

Silence.

"I'm sorry," she says finally, "for what I did."

"Me, too. For what I did."

I look up again. Her eyes shine with soft green tears. "God," I say, "sometimes I really want to kill you."

"Same here."

"Couldn't you?"

"No more than you could."

"Point taken."

"Besides," she says with a faint smile, "misery loves company."

"*Are* you miserable?" I watch her face. "That's a serious question."

"Not usually, no." She looks with real concern at me. "Are you?"

"Usually, yeah."

"I can tell."

"Yeah."

"Why?" It's the same tone she used in the tree long ago.

I take my hand away from the bark. Stand on a ledge I've avoided all this time. Look out, then leap: "You."

Silence.

"Me." It's not a question.

"Yeah." I nod. "I love you, but yes, these days it's you."

Nothing.

"You take all the happiness from my life," I go on. "You're…
too beautiful, too talented, too… *everything*. All the best parts. All
that's *best* about me, I think, you… *become*."

Still no reply.

"So, what's left there," I conclude, "for me?"

Kelsey's eyes go flat and hard.

Silence.

Finally: "That is *such* a cop-out."

Cross my arms tight against my chest. "Is it? I'm not sure it is."

"You *know* it is!"

More silence. We glare at one another.

"Are we done yet," she finally asks, "with tonight's pity party?"

Glare back at her. "No. We're not close to done."

It's her turn to cross her arms. "What if I say we are?"

"Then we both go hungry."

The venom in her stare could kill half of Asia. I probably look
the same way.

She closes her eyes first. "Then say what you need to say."

"You too."

"Fair enough." Like a judge telling me to choose the blade that kills me. No matter now – I'm falling so I might as well go down brave.

"Admit it," I say at last. "You've been... *feeding* off me. For *years*."

She nods. "That's true."

"It is?"

"And you've been *letting* me. For *years*."

Small and fragile voice. "So, I was right."

She sighs. "I thought you knew."

"*Knew?*"

Half-accusing, half-surprised. "*Didn't* you know?"

"*KNOW?*" A sudden shout. "How the *FUCK* would I *know?*"

Her eyes go wide. "I thought that's why you sang to me."

"Why I *what?*"

"Why you *sang!*" She's horrified. "You sang me into this world, you stupid bitch! Didn't you even *know* that?" Green tears glitter in the corners of her eyes. "Didn't you *mean* to do it?"

The next words in my mouth crawl up and go back to where they came from. Instead, I whisper "No, I didn't know that."

"Songs were your gift to me." Her voice goes thick. "Your call. Your summoning. Wasn't that why you sang all those times?"

My voice can't say *no*. My expression says it for me.

I'm an idiot.

"I thought you did that for me." Her face is every breakup I never wanted to have. "The singing. The music. Because you loved me. Because you wanted me to be with you..."

"I *did*–"

"But you don't *now*, do you?" She pulls back. The look on my face must be everything she's ever feared. "You're *scared* of me. Look at yourself, Nicole! You never meant to have me be like I am at all."

Shake my head, quiet. Backpedal. Fast. "That's not true..." Try to breathe. Can't. Damn corset. "I *do* love you. Always have... still do... It's just..." I shake my hands in total frustration. "It was a mistake..."

Shit.

"I'm a *MISTAKE?*"

"That's not what I meant!"

"It's what you *said!*"

"*FUCK!*" It's all wrong, what I'm saying. "*You're* not the mistake! *I* made a mistake! I wasn't trying to sing you into... whatever you are... from whatever you were..."

"You keep *saying* that." Tears spill across her broken voice. "'Whatever you are, whatever you are' – Christ, I'm not some *monster*, Nicole. I'm who I've always been. I'm *Kelsey*. Your *best friend*. Your *lover*. Why do you keep acting like I'm something else?"

110

"You *are* something else!" I don't mean to shout but I do anyway. "*Look at you!* You've got *wings!* You *glow!* Nobody could see you for years and then they *could* and then you kiss like I don't know *what* and you…" If I had an oil rig, I couldn't dig myself any deeper.

"Fine," she spits. "I'm a creature. Some fucked-up thing. Fine. I get it." The sudden calm in her voice cuts like broken glass. She reaches for the tree again. "Monster's going home, then. I won't bother you any more…"

"Kelsey…"

"*No!*" A snap, then softer. "No. No." She looks away. "You're not *all* wrong. I *have* been all the best of you."

My hand, halfway to her shoulder, stops. "Huh?"

"Most of it, anyway," she continues. "All you couldn't bring yourself to be, all you didn't think you could be – I took it on. And yes, I became those things."

It's my turn to be silent.

Her hand begins to melt into the bark. She swallows. Hard. "I didn't do it to steal anything from you," she says. "I did it because I didn't want you to lose those dreams. I wanted to become them for you."

"Why?" More a breath than a word.

She looks down. Her arm begins to fade. "I told you: I *loved* you. You believed in me and you had a good heart and imagination and… and more…" Kelsey goes all ghostly, like fog at morning light. "And… and I wanted to share them with you…"

111

"…and you wanted to be more than you were without me." A lifetime's worth of puzzles click into place.

Her green eyes close. "Is that so bad?"

I don't have an answer for that. My hand stays frozen in the air between us, halfway between her shoulder and my own.

"Don't I feed you too?" She hardly more than whispers.

I have no answer she would want.

There's just silence as she fades.

"I think…" she says finally, her voice air-thin, "that I should go."

I fall 10,000 feet without moving at all.

LIFE IS HUNGRY. Ravenous. All things feed on something else and are fed upon in turn. Tool said it best: *This is necessary – life feeds on life, feeds on life, feeds on life.*

Who are we to argue?

I remember one time up in Old Man Ivan, watching the ants and spiders in his bark, all marching in their own worlds, all eating one another, all oblivious to any life except the contours of their tree. *Each tree*, I thought, *is like this. Full of lives and deaths. All separate but bound together.* I was just a kid when I understood that, and something inside me changed forever. I remember reaching out and running my fingertips over the bark, so soft I could barely feel the scrape of it, and I swear to this day that I felt that hungry pulse of life.

And I swear I felt life reach back into me.

Maybe I was even singing when I touched that tree.

Maybe that's where we began.

Life feeds on life.

Songs feed on songs.

Dreams feed on dreams.

Can I really blame this dream of mine for living out the things I'm too afraid to face?

Don't I feed you too? she asked me.

Yes. You do.

I can't let her go.

So, I reach out before she fades away. Like Kelsey did so long ago, I grab hold of her skinny wrist and pull.

And now we're both falling. Falling where there's no place left to fall except into one another.

There's a place where lovers touch. Where skin meets skin and goes *beyond.* Where you fall inside one another until it feels like flying. That's where I go when I grab Kelsey now. Where the world disappears until there's nothing left but us.

This time, I hear the music, faint like a solo lost deep in the mix. You have to listen, have to stop, have to breathe lightly so the notes don't get lost in the thunder of your heart.

It's the solo I always want to play but can't. The notes that flee when I place my fingers to the strings. The words that rise in my throat at 4:00 a.m. when love or fear grow so thick I want to scream. The sound of Together. The sound of Alone. The music that gets stuck when I try to say, *I love you.*

Damn corset. Not the one on my skin. The one inside. The fear strapped tight across my gut.

I need to breathe. I need to sing. I need to fall and catch myself. And capture her as well.

She reaches back to me. Cool dry hands. Cool green eyes. Grasps my fingers. *Sing to me*, she says without words. *Let me know I'm wanted.*

Sing to me, I say, silent. *Let me know I'm more than songs to you.*

And both of us – we sing.

Music is power. We know it. The Beast knows it. Groupies fuck it like infernos. Rock stars shoot it up like diamonds. The angel singing at the heart of a Marshall amp has a pitchfork and a tail but his kiss is the sweetest thing alive.

Music is the dream of life. And so, eyes locked, we sing together.

And there is love and fear and hunger from us both. On those wings, we fly.

Soar over heartlands. Glades. Cracked homes and bitter dives. Soar across *I Miss You* plains and alleys ravaged by *But I Forgot*. Ice wind and lava tears and the ecstasy of silence. We sweep across them all and move beyond.

There is promise in this flight. Not an end to pain, but an understanding.

There are no mistakes in life, you see. Only promises we hadn't meant to make. But promises have wings. They fly even when you're falling.

Sometimes they even bring you home.

So yes, we fly. In what world? Does it matter? There are no corsets here. No shackles or illusions. All there is, is vertigo and the love that's worth our pain.

We fly for an eternity, then fall to earth. This time, though, the descent is ours to choose.

And when we reach the ground, we're laughing ourselves to tears.

At the base of Old Man Ivan, we hold one another tight. I've still got her. She's still got me. We've even got a sunrise.

All we need is a guitar solo and a band.

Know what? *Fuck* the band.

I breathe deep. "Wow."

She's glowing. "Yeah."

"God," I say, smearing Kelsey's makeup with her tears, "you're such a *freak*."

"God," she replies, "you're such a *psycho*," smearing my face with mine.

"Well..." little-girl voice: "Maybe the sky *is* full of fish."

"And maybe... you're just full of shit!"

We laugh, and it feels like home.

"No more lies," I say finally. "Nothing else held back."

She grins, serious. "No more lying to yourself."

"You either."

"Me neither."

We're lying now and we both know it. But hey, it's a step toward truth.

"No more snacks," I add. "I'm serious."

Her stare could stop a tank. "Then stop *letting* me have the best of you."

Sigh. "Point taken."

"It better be."

"It is." I make a fist then, crook one finger: "Pinky swear."

She laughs, does it too: "Pinky swear."

We kiss deep, and it tastes like dawn.

Look out, folks. The Two-Headed Beast of Fuckatude is back.

Sure, we're crazy. But it's a crazy world.

And if love's too sane, it's just not hungry enough for us.

KEYSTROKES

For Kraig Blackwelder and
Carla Sanders

I can still hear his fingers on the keys. The soft chimes he used to ring from that piano. I was way too young to be in his league, and way too male, I thought, to win his attention anyhow. Still, I used to linger in the hallway outside the practice room and listen to Kraig play, the timbre of each keystroke echoing through the halls.

By then, I was convinced I'd been wasting my time chasing that music degree. Sure, I'd been good enough for high school band, but college was a level I'd never imagined. My fingers fumbled across the strings of my guitar, thudding where my classmates made them sing. There was Carla, whose bow slipped across her violin like water over fingertips; and JD, whose drumsticks attacked the skins like warlords on the march. *What the hell*, I wondered almost every day, *am I doing here?* I was so far out of my depth that I felt drowned. Each Friday, I resolved to quit.

And then I'd hear Kraig practicing, and I'd stick around a little longer.

He had the figure of a jungle cat, lean muscles and tanned skin. Curls of dark brown hair fell across his eyes and faintly furred his arms. I'd close my eyes sometimes and imagine that fur soft and thick across his chest as well. Then the storm would boil up under my skin and I'd want to rip my cock off and throw it across the room with shame.

Yeah, you could say I had issues back then.

Carla slipped up beside me one night as I stood outside the door, listening to the notes trickle out from Kraig's piano. "What'cha doing?" she whispered, raindrops shining in her dreads. Silver trails slid down her leather jacket as she smiled at my fumbled explanation.

Realization lit her face up from inside. "Oh my God," she said. "You're *crushing* on him!"

I probably said something articulate like *Um* or *Uh*.

"Brady's got a *man-crush*," Carla sang, and the chilly hall suddenly felt too hot to stand.

That's it, I decided, *I'm out*. No way I was gonna stick with the program after *that!*

I guess I said something stupid as I grabbed my guitar case and turned away from her, because Carla reached out to grab me. "*Wait*," she called out, but I wasn't listening. My sneakers thudded heavily on the hardwood floor.

I hadn't heard the music stop.

But I heard his voice: "Hey." Soft and musical as the notes he'd played.

Kraig.

Oh fuck.

I stopped. I'm not sure if I really had been trembling, but I remember it that way.

"Brady?" His voice carried, somehow, over the rain outside and the storm inside my head. It sounded close, but as I finally turned around, I saw him in the doorway to the practice room, leaning one hand against the edge, standing four or five yards behind me. Carla smiled at both of us, nodding me back to join them. "Hey," he said again. "You wanna practice?"

I don't remember what I said, but it must have sounded something like "Yes."

ECHO CHAMBER

For Echo, Chesh, and the
old-school White Wolf Crew

I know it's not much," Brian said, "but it's the best we can do for now."

Dennis nodded as he took the envelope from Brian; inside, three weathered $50 bills folded around a gift card. "The card's got an additional hundred-fifty on it," Brian added. "That's a food allowance for you. Anything that's left when we get back, you can keep."

"Cool. Thanks." Dennis nodded again, tucking the envelope into his pocket. "Half now…?"

"…and half when we get back," Brian affirmed. "Plus, if you do a good job, you can pick out a few goodies from the warehouse next week." His voice held a note of apology, and he reached behind his neck in the age-old gesture of silent discomfort. "Sorry we can't do more."

Dennis shook his head. "It's all good, dude. I know how things are these days." He did, too. He'd gotten this gig by way of his buddy Rig Chen, graphic designer and *de factor* art director for Storm Dragon Game Studio. The company was hurting, and Dennis knew it. He was hurting too. Even at three hundred bucks for a week's work, he needed this gig more than he wanted to admit.

Brian Beckett, Storm Dragon's co-founder and acting CEO, continued rubbing the back of his neck. The past five years had aged him at least ten. Brian still looked fitter than you'd expect the head of a gaming company to look, but the stress was starting to show. His rangy good looks had begun to grow hollow and a bald spot crested his once-boyish hair. "I think this'll be a good con for us," Brian said, his words straining toward optimism. "There's a lot of anticipation about the new line, and I think it'll go over well this year."

Dennis Kitcher nodded, grinning. "I heard. Rig says it's badass."

Brian grinned back. "It is. Wanna see?"

"Of course!"

Around them, the offices of Storm Dragon Game Studios bustled with activity… or at least did the best approximation of "bustling" a company can do when it consists of nine people and a cat. Editor Kathleen Crowley hauled a case of bottled water toward the door, while the company's sales manager Travis reset the reception office phone messages. Outside, incongruous against the background of a neighboring cemetery, an Enterprise rental van purred near the main entrance, packed to the brim with luggage, pillows, and boxes of stock. Marjorie Stoner, the warehouse manager, sat behind the wheel, battered combat boots kicked up on the dashboard and a bored look creasing her face. Her sweaty assistant Scott shoved another cardboard box into the van's crowded interior. Meanwhile, the company's CFO, A.J., checked the offices for burning candles, smoldering incense, or drugs left in conspicuous places. "Geeze, guys," he told Cheshire Martin and Echo Stern, the company's two remaining rock-star designers, "I hope y'all are getting that out of your system before the drive."

In the kitchen, the two women held court with a belching contest. True to her name, Echo seemed to be winning. "C'mon, Chesh," Rig urged, "you can beat her!" He waved to Dennis as his friend passed the kitchen with Brian. "Dude! You made it. Thanks!"

"Thanks for getting me the gig, man," Dennis replied.

"Hey, Rig," Brian added. "Wanna come help me show off your masterpiece?"

"Cool!" Rig exclaimed as Chesh ripped forth with a devastating burp. "I call this duel in favor of the pretty redhead from Atlanta!"

"Jesus, Rig." Echo sneered in mock disgust. "You're such a fucking suck-up."

"Um…" Dennis held the new book at arm's length with fascinated disbelief. "It's… wow."

Chesh prodded Rig in the belly as his friend scanned the pages. "Hey, Mikey," she said, "I think he likes it."

"God," Rig whispered back, "that shit's *archaic*, yo."

Brian stood behind them, his hand again clasping the back of his neck. "So," he asked Dennis, "thoughts?"

Dennis pored over the pages of the lush hardcover, his eyes darting across the red-and-black images within. "It's gorgeous," he allowed. "They're gonna let you sell this at *GenCon*?"

"Nope," Rig said, grinning. "They already said no."

"Then why–"

"…are we piling into the van?" Echo added, leaning one elbow on Chesh's shoulder and the other on Rig's. "Because we're going black market with this bad girl."

Brian winced and Dennis turned his head to her in confusion. "I don't follow you."

The brawny designer flashed a grin that had floored fanboys and fangirls alike for almost a decade. Her biceps flexed as she leaned her weight against Rig and Chesh. "They told us in advance that we couldn't sell *Crimson Key* on the exhibition floor," she said. Dennis felt his heart catch as Echo's mischievous brown eyes locked on his own. "So, we won't. We'll be selling it outside the hall, out of the van and our backpacks…"

"…and making sure everyone else knows about it," Chesh finished, offering the cock-eyed smile that had inspired her nickname. "Twitter is our new best friend."

"That way," Echo finished, running her fingers through Chesh's red-dyed bangs with knee-buckling effect, "we keep everything we make from the *Crimson Key* sales, generate scads of free publicity, *and* hold exclusive distribution of the hottest-ticket item at GenCon!"

Brian's expression showed what he thought of the arrangement. Still, desperate times called for desperate measures, and Storm Dragon was pretty damned desperate. If *Crimson Key* didn't pan out, everybody'd be looking for work. And then there'd be the legal battles over ownership they'd face if the company went belly-up. Gavin McRea, Storm Dragon's co-founder, wanted the Intellectual Property rights to everything the company had produced, and no one here wanted to see him get them.

Rig fished a folded flyer out of his pocket. "What'cha think, yo?" He held it out to Dennis. *Crimson Key*, read the words grouped around a scathing hot bondage babe. *Dark Erotic Roleplay – the book THEY don't want you to see!!!*

"Seriously?"

Rig frowned. "You don't like it?"

Kevin backpedaled. "It's not *that*, exactly…" He noted Echo giving him a look that might be appraising, thoughtful, hostile, or some combination of the above. "It just seems a bit… *extreme?*"

"Extremity," said Echo, "is the point. Everyone's concerned with being so fucking *polite* that everything has just gotten so…" She searched for the right expletive. "*Boring.*"

"And boring," Rig added, "does not save companies."

"Or," Echo finished, "*jobs.*"

And jobs were not anything anyone could afford to lose.

Two years out from the biggest economic crash since Black Friday, everyone who still had a job was struggling to keep it. The new guy in the White House talked a good game, so to speak, but layoffs were still the order of the day. "Hope" was a slogan for banners and election parties. Hope didn't pay the rent. *Attention* did. *Extremity* did. And yeah, sex did too. Storm Dragon had been founded on all three, and if they were lucky this year, those traits might keep the place in business.

127

Fortunately, Chesh and Echo excelled in those regards.

Seven years earlier, everyone at GenCon had declared Echo and Chesh to be the hottest booth bait in the show. They were wrong. The two young women weren't booth bait – they were Storm Dragon's newest game designers. Gavin's furious departure that year had left Storm Dragon in the lurch. Enter two college friends who'd met in their local gaming group. Echo and Chesh had started off as interns but didn't stay that way for long. In short order, the girls charmed Brian, teamed up with Marjorie, kicked ass on everybody else, and led Storm Dragon to its hottest days that decade.

Trouble was, it had still been a lousy decade. The book-based roleplaying market had crested in the mid-1990s and then steadily declined. Between collectable card games, miniature games, computer games, and those thrice-damned Massive Multiplayer Online RPGs, the demand for Storm Dragon's specialty collapsed almost as soon as the company released its first product, *Angelicus: War in Heaven*, in 1995. Computer-game license attempts hadn't panned out, and two ill-fated card games and a misconceived zombie board game soon drained the company bank account to critical levels. If it hadn't been for the wildly successful *Angelicus*, Storm Dragon would not have survived the turn of the millennium. As things were, that survival had been a near thing.

And then suddenly, there'd been *Blood, Roses & Steel*, a swashbuckling success story with a heavy live-action component. In the hands of the traditional dude-male game designer, the game might have warranted a shrug. Thankfully, *Blood, Roses & Steel* had come from two smart, attractive, badassed young women instead. When McRae quit, Echo picked up *Angelicus* and ran with it, hard. The resulting books – and some tie-in jewelry – had kept the company afloat while Chesh and Echo created *Blood, Roses & Steel*. The pirate-themed RPG reached the market just as Disney's own pirate films made pirates cool again. The timing had been just what Storm Dragon needed… and when the two designers hit the con circuit with gleaming corsets and cutlasses, the game exploded. Since then, Echo and Chesh had been golden. Still, book-based games no longer paid the rent. *Crimson Key* was a make-or-break gamble. It was all-hands-on-deck time at Storm Dragon Games, and the storm, as the saying goes, was upon them now.

Thankfully, it seemed, Chesh and Echo were ready to face it. Being female game designers, they were obviously used to storms.

"So – you like it?" Chesh asked Dennis. A full head shorter than her friend, the designer stood as curvy as Echo stood lean. Her short hair blazed red as a bull-baiting flag. She looked, Dennis realized, like the model for half the pictures in the book. He felt the spit dry out in his mouth. "Um, yeah," he mumbled, glancing between the pages, her face and the floor. "I do. A lot."

"Cool," she added, her tone suggesting that she'd known as much already. *The dudes at GenCon*, he reflected, *are doomed.*

"Check *this* out, yo," Rig added. He took the book from Dennis' hands and flipped to a section printed in graceful red ink. The sumptuous line art recalled Alphonse Mucha by way of de Sade. "We adopted the LARP system from *Blood, Roses & Steel*, then added some real kink and sex magic!"

"*Dude!*" Dennis grabbed the book back as the designers laughed. The pages swirled with arcane designs. "Are those real, like, real occult thingies?"

"Kinda," Rig confessed. "I messed with 'em a bit."

"We didn't want to put real magic in a game book," Chesh said, her cropped bangs twitching as she shook her head.

"Not cool," added Echo. "Seriously not cool."

"You never *know* what people will do with it," Chesh added, smirking. *Are they messing with me?* Dennis wondered, and decided that they were.

"Echo did some kick-ass research," Rig said. "She got all these wild books back in her office, and…"

"Guys," Brian interjected in his *Boss said so* voice, "we really need to go."

"Yeah, I guess we gotta," said Rig, disappointed. "Still, check that shit *out*, yo!" He pointed to some ominous squiggles. "My head hurt for *days* after I drew that shit!"

Dennis scanned the diagrams, which looked like tantric spaghetti on crack. "I see why, man," he said, nodding. "That's seriously complex!"

Echo squeezed Rig's shoulder affectionately. "Rig came through, big-time," she said. "The book wouldn't be nearly as good without his art."

Dennis eyed Chesh, connected the dots between her looks and his friend's illustrations, and glanced down at the floor again. *Lucky bastard*, he thought. *I wish I could draw like that!*

"So, Dennis," Echo added. "Have you been to the office before?"

"Nope."

"Lemmie show you around then," she said, taking his arm. "If you're gonna be stuck here for a week, you really should know what not to touch."

"See the books up there?" she asked, pointing to a series of battered spines crammed into the top layer of Echo's bookshelf.

"Yep," Dennis answered.

"*Don't. Touch. Those.* If and when you want something to read, you're welcome to browse through anything else in here. But not those. Seriously." She looked eye-to-eye with him. "This is so *not* a Bluebeard's keyhole thing. I mean it. Those books are old and rare and valuable, so pretty please, with sugar on top, don't fuck with 'em."

"No problem." Dennis decided he could get used to looking eye-to-eye with Echo. She was tall enough… or he was short enough… or something. *Damn*, he thought, *do I have stuff in my teeth? Did I brush before I got here? Is my breath doomish?* She didn't seem to mind his proximity, but closeness to a woman like Echo made a dude self-conscious.

Dennis himself wasn't that bad, really. Just kinda… y'know, *geeky.* He spent too much time playing *World of Warcraft* and not enough out in the sun. Dennis hadn't worked up a sweat since that warehouse job two years ago, and his hair stayed stuck in that awkward range between "delightfully scruffy" and "Dude, see a barber." As Echo leaned against the bookshelf, her six-pack abs teasing the edge between her Venture Brothers T-shirt (with the sleeves ripped off) and a low-rise set of urban camo cargo pants,

Dennis found himself poking between his teeth with his tongue. Her office smelled like coffee and girl-sweat. Its walls glared with sullen prints by Royo and Brom. She'd painted those walls a dark forest green, and the light oak of her bookshelves made them pop in the dim light. He recalled the pictures in the books she'd just written, and his mind wandered. *She just invited me into her office,* he thought, *and told me I could borrow her books.* Did that foretell further intimacy? Or was she just being polite, pitying or both?

"So, yeah," she continued, "feel free to come in here while you're here if you need something to read or anything. Just put stuff back where you found it when you're done. I have a system here, and I'll be hacked off if it's ruined."

Dennis put his hands up, open-palmed. "No problem," he said again. "I'll make sure that I keep track of anything I move."

"All good," she said, flashing that killer grin. She leaned in closer to him. "Hey, we really appreciate you coming in on short notice like this. Thanks."

"No prob–" He threw himself into verbal reverse. "I'm glad to do it." He glanced around, noting the pagan-god statues and vintage McFarlane action figures. Three swords hung by brackets on the wall – one, a wooden practice sword, the crossed ones, actual steel. "Cool office," he said at last. "I like it."

"It works."

He indicated the swords. "You really use those?"

"Ten years of kenjutsu, plus some fencing and a stint in the SCA."

"Bad*ass!*" he breathed.

Echo brushed his arm with her hand. "Thanks," she said, and he could almost spot a shy girl underneath her grin. It was easy, he thought, to see why Echo made such a hit at conventions. She had a gift for seeming aloof and intimate at the same time. The combination made him flush. "I spend way too much time in here," she went on, "so I have to make sure it's comfortable."

Against one wall, a Papa-San chair rested against the wall, its contours draped with blankets and pillows. "You sleep in here, too?" he asked before he'd thought better of doing so.

"Yep." She grimaced. "More often than I'd prefer to."

Dennis flushed at the mental image of her curled up in that chair. "Bum…" he started to say, but his voice caught. He coughed. "Bummer."

She giggled. "People still say that with a straight face?"

Face burning, he shrugged. "I guess."

She slapped him lightly on the shoulder. "Well, you can look through the books, except for the ones I told you not to touch." She grinned with just a hint of edge. "But you should probably do your sleeping elsewhere."

"Oh, no question." *I might be a perv*, he thought, *but at least I'm not a creep*.

"So, you canned the interns?" Dennis whispered when Echo and Chesh had gone to finish loading the truck. Out back, a small Ryder rental idled, its cargo bay stacked with product.

"Dude!" Rig shook his head. "They were totally skeezing hard on Kat."

"And they *lived?*"

Rig chuckled like dry leaves crunching. "More or less. Echo, Chesh and Marjorie took turns tearing strips off 'em before Brian finally gave 'em the big ass-boot."

"No doubt!"

"You do *not* fuck with those ladies, my friend," Rig said. "They've had every kind of shit this industry can throw at 'em – an' when you think about who most of the people in the gaming business are...dude, that's a *LOT* of shit!"

Dennis nodded. He knew some gamer-girls, himself. Until today, though, he'd thought all game designers were dudes. "So, you're driving the truck up with Chesh?"

"Me an' Cheshire, all the way to Indie!"

"Dude..." Dennis glanced in the direction of the departed designers. "Are you and she like...?"

Rig laughed. "Me and she are like *friends*, yo. Friends and brothers-in-arms. Yeah, sure, we spend some nekkid time, but it's not like that. That's like business. She's an artist, man. So am I. We make art and war, not love."

"Sounds all right, man," he said, jostling his buddy's arm. "Not prying, just frying."

Rig looked at him. "'Frying'?"

"Forget I said that."

"Done."

"Yeah. Well, hey – I'm glad for the caretaker gig. Thanks."

"All is good, grasshopper," Rig said, checking his desk drawer for a flash drive. He found one, nodded to himself, then stashed it in his black Tripp jacket. "All is good. 'sides," he added, "I'd rather have you here minding the shop for a week than leave *those* two geeks gone wild in charge while we're away." Rig skritched absently at his spiky black hair. "They were on my last nerve in a *week*, yo, and I was glad to see 'em gone."

"Their loss…"

"Your gain."

"No doubt."

"Hey," Rig added, dropping his voice to conspiracy level. "The intern slot's still open. You want I should drop a bug in the boss's ear while we're conning?"

Dennis nodded. "Yeah. A fucking centipede, dude."

Rig laughed. "Right to his *brain*, man. Right to Brian's brain."

"Thanks, dude."

Rig shared the infamous fist-jab with his friend. "You got it, yo. Just don't fuck shit up, you got it."

THE KEY RING RATTLED as Dennis locked the door. Up Boulder Avenue, the Ryder truck's taillights flashed red for a moment at the intersection, then disappeared around the curve. Above the tree line, dimming skies hinted at dusk. Six days until the Storm Dragon crew returned. Six days, and the office was all his.

Cool.

"Keep visitors," Brian had told him, "to an absolute minimum. We don't expect you to be a hermit, but for God's sake don't host any parties here. Honestly," he'd said, rubbing the back of his neck again, "I'd rather you didn't have anyone out here except the pizza delivery guy."

"Understood," Dennis had replied in his most professional voice.

"Good." Brian fished out – with some hesitation, Dennis noted – a bright new key. "We had to change the locks last week," he said as he handed the key to Dennis. "I think you probably heard why."

"The interns."

"Yeah." A cloud of anger drifted across Brian's face. "They probably won't come back, but they know we'll be gone, so…"

"Travis gave me the security company code," said Dennis. "And I know how to call 911."

"Good man."

"And if all else fails," Dennis added, "I can always grab a sword from Echo's room."

Brian laughed, and all was good with the world.

There was beer in the fridge (good stuff, too, he noted – Canadian microbrews and some Sapporo), a ton of books, and no end of games to play. *Of course*, he thought, *I'd need someone to play them with...* and since Brian had discouraged visitors... Oh, well. There was still online gaming, and this time out he'd be getting *paid* to sit on his ass and veg on *WoW*.

The office sat in a crappy run-down industrial space on the curve of Boulder Road. All by its lonesome self, it nestled between two empty office fronts, a bunch of trees, and that nearby cemetery. Train tracks passed by the intersection of Boulder and Stone Ridge. Not long before the van pulled off, a freight train had rumbled past, shaking the floor like thunder. "Is that a storm?" Dennis had asked, and Chesh had laughed at him. "That's what I thought, too," she said, her red bangs fringed across her eyes. "When I first got here," she continued," I kept looking for thunder clouds and wondering where they were."

"That's why," Marjorie added as they checked the warehouse one last time, "Brian and Gavin called their company 'Storm Dragon.' It used to be 'Rabid Hamster' or something like that, but when they moved into this office space, they always thought it was getting ready to rain."

"So yeah." Dennis nodded. "Storm Dragon. I get it."

"Sounds better than Rabid Hamster, anyway." Chesh stretched herself into interesting shapes. "God, I hate long drives!"

"Now these," Marjorie continued, indicating rows upon rows of stock, "have been taped shut while we're gone. If you open them," she said, her jaw tight with menace, "I *will* know, and I'll feed your spine to my iguana."

"I'll keep 'em shut," Dennis assured her.

"You'd better," she said. Watching Marjorie move with the grace of a wrestler and the single-minded focus of a Shaolin monk, Dennis wondered why anyone in right mind would even dare to risk her wrath.

Marjorie showed him how to take deliveries, pointed out the pallets that needed to go out, and handed him inventory instructions. "Everything I know about has gone out already," she'd said, "and most of our customers will be at GenCon, too. Still, I want to keep track of anything that comes in. So, if and when a truck arrives," she asked, her face mild yet significant, "what do you do?"

"Follow the instructions, keep out of the way, and open nothing."

"Right." Her grin revealed some missing teeth, and her nose lumped like it'd been broken once or twice. The shoulders beneath her hoodie stretched with muscle. Her tattooed forearms would make Popeye doubt his chances in an arm-wrestling match. *Those interns*, Dennis thought, *had been the dumbest motherfuckers on earth.*

As a fresh train rumbled past, Dennis checked the sky. It *did* look like it might rain tonight. He felt sorry for Rig and Marjorie, driving through the storm. *Yeah, right*, he reflected. *They're going to GenCon, and you're holding down the fort.*

All things considered, though, this wasn't a bad place to be.

BATSHIT THE DEMENTICAT – named for her tendency to tear through the offices at lunatic speed – arched with tortoise-shell abandon. Dennis skritched her under the chin as he wandered his temporary home. In his arms, Batshit stretched out her paws and tilted her head back for more effective spoilage. Outside, the sunlight faltered and a train rumbled past on its tracks. The pizza guy would arrive at any moment; in the meantime, Dennis paced the Storm Dragon halls, cat in hand, and contemplated his evening's activities.

His ramblings took Dennis through a dim-lit office space. Posters from previous Storm Dragon releases (*"Angelicus: Thy Name is Wrath!" "Blood, Roses & Steel – a Girl's Best Friends!"*), scatterings of art prints, and the doleful "wall of shame" where awful submissions were posted for mockery at large… Dennis scanned them all. As Batshit pawed Dennis's chest, Dennis eyed the empty offices. More than half, he noticed, were *empty* empty – or at least abandoned by regular staff. The layoffs that had bled the company dry had turned those forlorn offices into dusty storage space. Old computers, battered toys, stacks of expired promo material… *Damn, dude*, thought Dennis, *this shit's kinda depressing.* Even game companies, he reflected, could be grim places to work.

Most of the doors were closed. Some sported shiny new doorknobs, with keyholes that the other doors lacked. *I guess that was to keep the interns out*, he guessed. *Or maybe me?* The thought troubled Dennis, though he couldn't say why. Echo, however, had left her door open – had, he reminded himself, explicitly invited him to go in and borrow anything he wanted or needed. *Except those*, he recalled, glancing up with inevitable curiosity at the volumes on her top shelf. *I'm supposed to stay away from those.*

What better way is there to invite someone to do something he's *not* supposed to do?

Echo's oak bookshelves reached almost to the ceiling. Unlike the OfficeMax specials that filled the offices, these looked expensive and serious. The forbidden volumes ranged across the bookshelf nearest to her desk, an obvious reference library within easy grabbing range of both the computer seat and the Papa-San chair. A grungy pair of Reebox nestled beneath her desk, their weather-beaten look at odds with the meticulous way they were arranged. On the wall nearby, a new poster for *Crimson Key* ("*Sin & Sorcery at the Devil's Knee!*") gleamed within a glass frame. Rig's work, Dennis noted… and damned if the model didn't look like Chesh. She knelt in an alluring pose, her parted lips and half-shut eyes reflecting strength, submission and sarcasm all at once. It was the kind of image that would seduce boys and girls alike. *Those posters*, he thought, *will be* very *popular this weekend.*

And then, there were the books…

What *is* it that makes us do the things we're not supposed to do? Dennis scanned the shelf, eyeing the titles with a scuttling thrill of curiosity, arousal and distaste. *Screw the Roses, Send Me the Thorns. The Encyclopedia of Erotic Wisdom. Dark Eros. The Sadian Woman.* There were art books with titles like *Bondage Obsession* and *Cry for Pain.* There were other titles, too – ominous tomes of old leather and gold-etched spines: *Hymns of Matangi. Daughters of Joy. Codex Licentia. The Feast of Flutes.* A roleplaying supplement, *The Book of Erotic Fantasy,* perched incongruously in the midst of these disconcerting volumes. *Oh, well,* thought Dennis, *I guess Echo's system makes sense to* her, *anyway.*

As he thought so, his hand reached toward the top shelf. Batshit mewed her displeasure as those fingers ceased their tribute to her majesty. *Dude*, Dennis reflected, *don't go there. She said not to...*

So just take out one at a time, he replied to himself, *and put 'em back in the right place when you're done. She won't know.*

His tingling fingers slipped across the spines. Rested on *Cry for Pain*. Began easing it from its place on the shelf.

DEENG-DONG! Dennis jerked his hand back at the sound. Batshit spilled from his arms with loud complaint, hitting the floor and racing off before the source of that sound kicked in. *Oh yeah – the door.* The electric bell rang again as his heart hammered against the ribs that restrained it. Slipping like a sinner through Echo's open door, he hustled off to get the pizza.

Minutes later, he returned, his fingers smelling slightly of garlic and cheese. The pizza cooled on the break room table, filling the office with the welcome scent of chow. Still, the bookshelf drew him back. When he walked into the office, he saw way. The copy of *Cry for Pain* tilted out from its position on the shelf, held there by the press of other books. *Oh, crap!* Dennis thought. Not a half-hour into his week and he was already breaking the few rules they'd given him! Reaching up, he pushed the slender volume back into its proper position...

...then slipped his fingertips across the heavy-bound spine of *Feast of Flutes*. The other books shifted slightly, as if inviting him to ease the volume from its place among them. Shaking with guilt and curiosity, Dennis slid the book out... and then caught himself and stopped. *Nope*, he thought, and pushed *The Feast of Flutes* back where it belonged.

Someone's watching me.

He turned slowly toward the door, expecting either some wild-eyed demon or – worse yet – Echo.

Batshit the Dementicat *rowww*ed at him, her eyes shining in the dim light.

"Yeah," Dennis said aloud. "I need to get my ass of here and go eat some pizza before I do something really dumb." With those words of wisdom, he followed Batshit the Dememticat toward the kitchen, pulling Echo's door closed till it clicked shut behind him.

"Dude," he whispered aloud, "this fuckin' *rocks!*"

Dennis stretched out in the break room, his high-topped Keds propped on a neighboring chair, his belly plumped by half a Meat Lover's pizza. Batshit nestled on the table next to him, gnawing on a crusty peace offering he'd left on her very own paper plate. A deep purr signaled her acceptance of the new cat-slave.

His hunger sated, his fingers wiped thoroughly on a half-dozen paper napkins, Dennis now turned his attention to the copy of *Crimson Key* that Brian had given him before they left. "All yours, Dennis," Echo had said as she blew her wet-inked signature dry. "You're the first one outside the company to see it." She handed it to him with a grin. That flash of teeth alone had been worth a week of baby-sitting real estate. Every member of the staff signed the book for him – even Scott, whose contribution to *Crimson Key* consisted of hauling it around the warehouse. It was a collector's item of immeasurable value now. Better still, it was actually *good*. Really good.

"Life," it began, *"is lust. Lust for pleasure. For power. For immortality. In this lust beats the heart of our existence. And from it, those of us without fear or scruple bring lust to its grandest heights."* Written in Echo's lilting prose, the book went on to describe a world where ultimate pain and pleasure were the keystones of enlightenment. Players in this world were invited to become *Talashi*, masters of sensual bliss. The game drew bits of *Vampire*, *Witchcraft*, the Kushiel and Gor novels and God-knew-what else and then wrapped it up in the romantic dedication of two young women who clearly believed in what they were doing… or who at least did really good imitations of people who did.

He had to wonder how much they truly practiced what they wrote.

The art was every bit as good as the writing, if not better. Rig had outdone himself here. Each illustration looked like a page from the *Kama Sutra* by way of Luis Royo channeling Gustav Doré on an absinthe-cocaine bender. The book was smaller than usual, more like a novel than a game textbook. Its hard red cover gleamed with red-foil embossing. *No wonder Brian's nervous*, thought Dennis. *The printing alone must have cost a fortune.*

Years back, Chesh had won awards for her world-building work on *Blood, Roses & Steel*. If anything, she'd surpassed herself on this book. *I wonder if they run a* Crimson Key *game here*, he thought, and then wondered what he'd have to do get invited if they did.

143

A CRASH jolted Dennis from his reading reverie. Another crash dimmed the light. Something rattled the ceiling overhead – a metallic wash of sound. Dennis looked up, puzzled, as the light came back on. "Jeeze," he said after a moment, "is that… *rain?*"

Apparently, it had decided to storm after all.

Rain roared thick against the corrugated roof. Putting his signed copy of *Crimson Key* on one of the few clean countertops, he rushed out to see if everything was safe. Light flickered from outside as he headed toward the plate glass door.

Across the parking lot, sheets of rain steamed against the asphalt. Branches caught in the sudden tide surfed out from the edge of the grass. A sudden southern storm boomed down from the pink-gray sky. Dennis winced as yet another bolt of lightning knocked the power out.

This time, it stayed dark.

Great.

Candles, he thought. *I know I saw some somewhere.* Thankfully, it wasn't quite dark enough to render the office impassible. The maze of doors and corridors glowed with what was left of daylight. He grabbed his book and fumbled his way in the direction of Chesh's and Kathleen's offices. They had candles, he recalled. Lots of them. Now if only they had matches, too…

Again, he flashed sympathy for the drivers caught in the blast. *It can't be easy,* he thought, *driving a truck or van through* this *shit!* He hoped that Rig and Marjorie had cleared the path of the storm before it hit. Kathleen's doorknob rattled but refused to open. Locked.

Okay, fine – Cheshire's office, then.

It was locked, too.

Don't they trust me? he wondered as the building shook again. But then, given those asshole interns, why should they take chances? *Hmmmmm… there must be flashlights around here somewhere. Why didn't they cover that stuff in the tour?*

Batshit the Dementicat raced past Dennis, yowling distress. She darted into an office down the hall. He heard dull thumps, a meow, and a muffled crash. "Um, Batshit?" he called out, and was answered by a boom of thunder.

A dull red glow infused the front offices. Dennis glanced up to see the sky bloom into a disconcerting crimson shade. "Uhhh," he said, shaking his head. "That can't be good." Tornado? Forest fire? Incursion of demonic forces? From where he was standing, nothing seemed unreasonable.

You did this, he thought. *You were fucking with the books.*

"Oh, *please*," he snarled aloud. "I put the damn thing back – I didn't even *open* it!" Still, the idea nagged at him. What if – in breaking Echo's rule – he *had* brought on some kind of…

That was too stupid to think about.

He went back to searching the drawers. Finally, he found a small Maglite with half-dead batteries at the bottom of the reception desk. Lightning flickered through the red skies, throwing the rain into silver shards.

Dennis popped his cellphone. No signal. He blinked. No bars. The display glowed with bright blue promise, but the reception field was blank. He tried the phone anyway. Dead.

"You're kidding, right?" he said, but got no answer.

145

Outside, a green Prius – headlights glaring – sheared down Boulder Avenue, fishtailed across the rain-slicked pavement, and disappeared beyond the trees. Dennis waited for the sound of a crash, but nothing followed.

Caught between the dark labyrinth of offices behind him (populated by Batshit and God-knew-what-else) and the red-tinged storm on the other side of that fragile-seeming door, Dennis stood thoughtfully for a moment, hefted the tiny Maglite, and sighed. "This," he said, again aloud, "is gonna be a long few days."

As THE SHOCK of the storm wore off, Dennis headed toward Echo's office. There'd been candles in there, too, and the room hadn't been locked... or had it? *She left it open for me*, he recalled, *and I closed the door*... He hustled toward the room through dark hallways, lit only by the faint beam of the Maglite and a wash of distant red from the sky.

In that disconcerting twilight, the posters seemed to shift and dance, their faces following as he passed. Dark fantasy was Storm Dragon's stock-in-trade, and the hungry figures on the walls capered with sinister allure. A half-naked witch girl howled from her stake. A grim knight, bristling with spiky plate armor, hefted an axe large enough to chop Buicks in half. A blaze-eyed beast-thing hefted a young chick in artfully tattered clothes. In the red-washed shadows, these cheesy archetypes reached something dark and primal within Dennis' skull, pulled it out, and had a snack.

Around him, the walls rattled with the fury of the rain. Rolls of thunder shook the floor beneath his sneakers. Batshit yowled from her hiding place, commanding the new cat-slave to find the source of this disorder and make it stop at once. Echo's office lay at the far end of a narrow corridor, flanked on each side by closed doors on the facing walls. The first bore a picture of a scar-faced man pointing a huge pistol at the viewer. "*I'M BUSY*," the sign declared. "*GO. AWAY. OR. DIE.*" The second door held a poster of the Devil grinning with mustachioed aplomb. A short-haired brunette lashed a two-fisted dude with her riding crop. A blonde in torn lingerie cringed behind him as the poster proclaimed that "*SATAN WAS A LESBIAN!*"

Echo's door was blank. And slightly open.

I could have sworn, thought Dennis, *that I closed it when I left.*

The Meat Lover's pizza waved *Hello!* to him from within his guts. *Remember what we shared?* it cried. *Set me freeeee!* He clamped down on the churning below his belt line and gently pushed open Echo's door.

Behind him, storm-sounds rumbled down the corridor like Lucifer belching through a megaphone. *Six more days of this?* he wondered as he stepped gingerly inside. The dark green walls felt oppressive now. The bookshelves bore their burdens with stoic resolve. Dennis spotted three fat red candles clustered on the paper-strewn desk.

DEENG-DONG! Dennis shrieked, springing back from the desk. Again, the doorbell rang. His heart threw a hissie fit inside. *Someone's at the door*, he thought through a hopping maze of panic. *Someone's out there in the storm. I should let them in.*

No, his wiser self replied. *You really shouldn't do that.* Still, he set down his book, grabbed the candles and hustled toward the door.

Batshit hissed from her hidden niche. Dull thumping sounds echoed down the hall. Dennis passed the posters again, grimacing at their lurid splendor. *Dude*, he pondered, *why the creeps?* There was nothing in these hallways worse than the stuff on his walls at home. *Those* posters didn't freak him out, he puzzled, so why should these?

Red light still glowed on the reception area walls. Weird shadows danced off boxes and furniture. That annoying doorbell pitched its electronic insistence through the halls. "*Christ!*" yelled Dennis, "Knock it *off*, already. I'm *coming*. Jeeze!" The muffled thumping grew louder as he reached the doorway, entered the reception area, and stopped.

Outside the plate glass office front, clustered by the door and bumping together beneath the overhang, a crowd of people packed themselves against the glass. One leaned his shoulder against the doorbell, sending that affronted *DEENG-DONG!* bouncing through Dennis's skull. The red skies threw the crowd into silhouette, casting thick black shadows across the sullen carpet. The people outside were soaking wet. Silver drizzles spilled across their limbs. Instinctually, Dennis flicked the light switch near his hand. Nothing. He raised the Maglite. Its illumination shimmered off the glass. It caught the faces of the crowd. Or what was left of them.

"You're shitting me," said Dennis.

Back behind him, Batshit hushed. Far off, deep in the warehouse, something boomed against the loading dock door. The impact echoed through the office building, blunted but not silenced by the doors and walls.

Again, he sent the timid light brushing across the features of the crowd. Their gaunt faces. Their sunken eyes. Their bared teeth and tattered clothes. The occasional missing limb.

"Seriously?" Dennis shouted. "*Zombies?*"

Lots of zombies.

"But I didn't *DO* anything!" he wailed. "I put that stupid book back on the shelf. I didn't even *open* the damn thing." The loading dock door thundered again behind him. Batshit had nothing to add to its eloquence.

"This is *bullshit!*" He crossed his arms defiantly. "I did not do *anything* to deserve a fucking zombie horde! And zombies are. *So. Played. Out.* Fuck. *OFF!*"

In answer, the shambling things beyond the glass door moaned, their rotting mouths swelled with preternatural hunger.

"Uh-uh," Dennis insisted. "Take it elsewhere, dudes!" The zombie by the doorbell pushed the button again. "*AND CUT THAT SHIT OUT!*" Dennis banged the wall beside him, and the zombie lurched away from the buzzer. "That's better," Dennis said.

Now what?

Okay, zombie hordes. He'd seen this movie already. You beat their brains in and ran away until either the Army showed up, the zombies ate your guts out, or someone bigger and meaner than you arrived to kick some ass… yours included. The plate glass, he noticed, was reinforced with thin wires. It would hold, but probably not for long. There were zombies at the back door, too. This wasn't good. No phone, no lights, no way out. *George Romero*, he reflected, *you suck.*

Mental inventory time. The Maglite was pretty much useless. The kitchen held a microwave and some junk in the fridge. The knives and forks were probably all plastic. There'd be box cutters back in the warehouse. And yeah – Echo's swords. *Well, that's a 'duh,'* thought Dennis, turning back toward Echo's chamber. Swords it was, then. He'd never used one in real life, but it couldn't be *that* hard. Sharp, pointy, made of metal. Swing at things until they die. It's not like zombies used swords, too.

I don't want *them eating my guts out*, he thought.

And so, he went to fetch the swords.

…which would have worked better had they been sharp.

"Practice swords," he cried. "*Dammit.*"

Still, a set of aerodynamic baseball bats was better than no weapons at all. So as the zombies battered themselves pulpy against the front door (and the unseen yet ominous-sounding trespassers at the loading dock added their efforts to the overall din), Dennis tucked one dull metal blade into his belt, did the same with the wooden sword, took a practice swing with the best of the lot, and accidentally demolished a plaster bust of Cthulhu on Echo's desk. "Oops," he said, wincing as pieces bounced off the dark green wall. "Sorry, Echo."

He wondered if he'd get the chance to apologize in person, or if his intestinal spaghetti (*possibly*, he thought with a grimace, *polished off by the cat*) would be the closest thing to contrition she would see. *Talk about spilling your guts*, his inner voice added. The image of a Tom Savini special effect with his face on it reintroduced Dennis to the Meat Lover's pizza in his aforementioned guts. *Hiya*, it said. *Miss me?* A sharp, sour taste rose up the back of Dennis's throat. *With my imagination*, he reflected, *who needs zombies?*

As Dennis picked up the biggest chunks of Cthulhu's shattered skull, he noted a loud cracking sound from the vicinity of the front door. The warehouse still rang with the sound of zombie fists on corrugated steel. The cat had probably disappeared to whatever dimension cats head off to when things get bad. *Alas, poor 'Thulhu,* Dennis mused as he placed the busted head on Echo's desk. *Dude, we hardly knew ye.*

Anger surged again. He looked back up at Echo's books. "It's not *fair,*" he insisted. "I put you back without reading you! Dude, why are you fucking with me *now?*"

Dennis, said the calm inner voice, *Why are you talking to a bookshelf?*

He slammed his free hand against the bookshelf in frustration. "'Cause I don't *want* zombies to eat my guts out! 'Cause all I wanted was to score an easy gig and a few bucks for rent! 'Cause I was tempted to read those stupid books up there and I didn't and *IT'S NOT FAIR!*" The zombies out front took up the cry, moaning loud enough to be heard down the hallway. Dennis felt chills racing underneath his skin. It was one thing to play *All Flesh Must Be Eaten,* and another to be the main course for real.

I'm a gamer, he thought. *In a gaming company's office. That's got to give me some kind of advantage here.* In a way, after all, he'd been training for this his whole life. *Problem is,* he thought, *zombie survival horror games don't teach you how to fix the problem. They just stall your messy and inevitable death.*

As if to provide an express stop for that train of thought, he heard the front door shatter and bodies spill through.

The warehouse shuddered beneath the blows at the loading dock door. *There's a side door, too,* he thought. *They're probably at that one, also… or already through it.* He heard thumping in the hallways, clumsy bodies butting into walls and doors as they plodded through Storm Dragon's office space.

Dennis glanced around. At the green walls. The heavy bookshelves. The desk and Papa-San chair. Echo's computer and the seat beneath that desk. Cued by the hollow sounds from the warehouse door, he looked up at the flimsy drop-tile ceiling. And then at the door and the hallway leading to it. He swung the sword again, this time in a more careful arc. Dennis smiled. *It's a defensible position.* To get him, the zombies would need to cram themselves down the hallway, pile up against the door, and expose themselves to attack if and when they smashed it open. The ceiling wasn't worth a damn, but since when could zombies climb? Although backed into a corner, he might just survive this mess! *As long as they don't hang around until I starve*, he thought, *I may be able to wait them out.* And if they *did* come for him here, down that long and narrow hall, he could hold them off like those dudes in *300* until someone came to help him out… or at least till he died like some barbarian badass on a Frazettian heap of corpses. *That*, he decided, would be *cool*.

It sounded like a plan.

But a *cowardly* plan.

Dennis scowled. He kinda *had* been training for something like this his whole life. Even though that "training" took place in his imagination or on a computer screen, the adrenaline rush had been real… and so had the feeling of victory when he'd won, or at least gone down fighting. He glanced around Echo's office again, this time feeling ashamed. The swords he'd taken, the action figures on her desk, the games she'd designed, the posters she'd framed… this was the domain of a woman who worked out hard, practiced with swords, and collected and created fantasies of heroism.

Heroes didn't hide and wait for monsters to come kill them. Heroes went looking for adventure. And if it killed them, well at least they died with style.

Would Echo want him to make a last stand cowering in her office? Would she respect that? Dennis shook his head. *He* wouldn't respect it, either. It might have been *smart* to stay there, but it wasn't *heroic*. And if he'd learned anything from a lifetime of fantasy, it was that it was better to be a cool corpse than a live coward.

And then the crashing began.

First it seemed as though someone had overturned a table full of silverware. Then the unmistakable *BOOM* of something heavy dashed against an office wall. Another "something" – this one glass – shattered against the kitchen tiles. An object both mechanical and fragile (*the microwave? A computer?*) whoooshed through the air and slammed against carpeted concrete floor. *Holy shit*, he thought, *they're trashing the place.* This wasn't incidental damage – it took effort to make that kind of mess. Vandalism, not hunger, appeared to drive the zombie horde.

"Like *hell*," he said aloud. "I'm gonna kick some zombie ass!"

He strode forward manfully and tripped over the swords in his belt.

ONE OF THE BENEFITS of a sedentary lifestyle is a built-in cushion when you fall on your face. Dennis felt the impact mostly in his front-loaded gut and the wrists he'd put out to slow his descent. By the time he was eye level with the floor (which needed *serious* vacuuming), Dennis was more angry than stunned. With a grunt, he pushed himself upright, yanked the swords out of the way, and watched a computer monitor bounce itself to pieces at the far end of the corridor. The red light from the sky illuminated just enough office space to reveal moving shadows and shimmering ruins. From the floor, the Maglite cast a dim yellow sun against the doorway's edge. Dennis felt the vibration of some other item being smashed. Snarling with territorial offense, he hauled himself upright, rearranged the swords, and started down the hall.

Glass glittered across the carpeting as Dennis crept out and raised Echo's blade.

Not ten feet away, three zombies stomped the remains of his pizza into the rug. None appeared to sense him.

Heart pounding, Dennis tiptoed into position, drew back the sword, and swung it powerfully into the nearest wall.

Dude, he thought as his palms stung with impact and the zombies turned, as one, to face him, *how the fuck did you miss hitting a zombie from behind?*

"*RUGGGHHH?*" cried the nearest zombie, jaw slack with decayed disbelief. He pointed at Dennis, his skull bobbing like a bobble-toy as he glanced between the other walking corpses as if to say, "What a *dork*."

"Eat me," Dennis snarled, immediately regretting his choice of words.

The first zombie had been a beanpole. The second one looked grannyish, while the third had probably gone by "Bubba" in his past life. All three zombies had endured some fairly extensive rot, and they seemed to have died or been buried in formal clothes. Now, however, those clothes hung in muddy ruin. The zombies gaped at Dennis for a moment, flexing their devastated hands.

Then they attacked.

This time, Dennis was ready. He yanked the blade from the drywall and took the zombie's bobble-head off at the neck. That neck crunched like a handful of crepe paper wrapped around some Kentucky Fried chicken bones. That skull hurtled through the air and bounced off the second zombie's face, knocking the Granny corpse askew. Dennis brought the sword around in a backswing, mulching through Bubba's ribcage and spilling rank intestines across the floor. "Holy hopscotch *Christ,*" he cried at the wave of rot-formaldehyde stench. Who knew death could smell so *bad?*

Dennis recoiled as the first and third zombies collapsed in stinking heaps. *Huh,* he thought in the part of his mind that wasn't gagging, *they're pretty fragile.* The second zombie steadied herself drunkenly against the wall. Dennis let loose a barbaric yawp and brought the sword down through Granny's skull. *BWANG!* The metal blade shuddered against the bone. Both combatants staggered, knocked away from one another by raw kinetic force. Dennis swore with geeky eloquence, his palms stinging from the impact, as half the zombie's face slid down her sundered skull. Granny shuddered for a moment and then joined her fellows on the floor.

"That was easy," Dennis marveled.

Then a laptop hit him in the head.

SOMETHING RANK and squishy pinned him to the floor. Behind the dark wall of pain, he sensed a pile of soggy weights on his back. A cold, wet tile floor pressed against his cheek. Nasty fluids bathed his face. The smell made him cough. "Hey," cried a female voice, "he's *alive.*"

"Good," replied another voice. Echo? A muddy Doc Martin boot came down beside his eyes. Dennis tried to speak but the effort sent sparks of bright pain across his head. Someone started lifting the weights off his body. *Dude*, he thought. *Zombies. I'm buried underneath dead zombies.* The redundancy behind the sentiment did nothing to alleviate its Ick factor. Dennis tasted his Meat Lover's pizza heading for a swift return trip.

A crunchy burden lifted off his head. Dim light greeted his half-open eyes. Groaning, Dennis squeezed them shut again, clamping his lips shut and swallowing the pizza down. Rolling over slowly, he opened his eyes again and looked up.

Echo towered over him, the crotch of her cargo pants posed right over his face. "I thought I told you," she said as she tossed the last zombie aside, "to leave my goddamn books *alone.*"

"I *did* leave your goddamn books alone," he rasped. "I had nothing to do with this."

She wiped her hands on her pants. "You swear?"

"I swear." Despite the view, he closed his eyes again. His head felt like aliens were kegging it up in the back of his skull.

The lights had come back on. All around him, the office was trashed. Broken bits of zombie flecked the walls, floor, and

156

drop-tile ceiling. Not far off, yells and thumps and crashy sounds suggested that the battle was not yet won. Echo reached a slime-coated hand toward Dennis. Groaning, he took it. "Okay, then," she said. "Sorry if I was wrong."

Together, they shoved the other zombie corpses off of him. "They didn't eat me?" he marveled.

"No," she said. "I think they just came to fuck shit up."

"Good," he replied. "Not good that they came to fuck shit up, but…"

"…good they didn't eat you," she said with a grim smile. "Yeah, I count that as a win too, I guess."

"Man," cried Rig, rushing over with a brain-clotted baseball bat. "What the *hell*, dude?" He helped pull Dennis to his feet. Dennis clenched his jaw against the pain. Still, he held the sword he'd taken from Echo's room, its blunt and battered edge smeared with zombie gore. "Check *you* out, yo!" Rig exclaimed, slapping Dennis on the shoulder. "You went *Conan* on those muthafuckas!"

"Not bad," Echo observed. "Though you probably would have done better without two swords in your pants."

Dennis shrugged. "I wanted backup in case I lost the one in my hands." He regarded the spray of bodies, fluids, and destruction. As near as he could figure it, he must have gone berserk when the zombie clubbed him with the laptop. There was indeed a Frazettian strew of carnage from the break room to Brian's office. "Did *I* do that?" he marveled.

"Looks that way," Echo said. "I'd guess you buzzsawed your way through the bulk of 'em, then tripped over the bodies and got dogpiled in the corner."

"And that's around when we showed up," Rig added with a cocky grin, "and played pināta with their undead butts." He shook a splatter of gunk off the bat. "We figured they already ate your ass. But hey…" he added when Dennis grimaced, "I'm glad they *didn't*, yo."

"Yeah, me too." Dennis added. "So, what's up with that – you coming back so soon, I mean?"

Echo laughed, a nervous sound punctuating the smack of a crowbar against a distant zombie's head. The door toward the warehouse was open, Dennis noticed, and Marjorie was making all zombies on her turf rue the day they had returned from death. Around them, the office was a shambles. "God," Echo said as she surveyed the damage, "I really hope *Crimson Key* does well at GenCon."

"Yeah," Dennis agreed. "Like I said: What's up with that? Where are the others, and what brought you back so soon? Not that I'm not grateful and all."

"Well," Rig said, "we're about half-hour out when Echo sees the sky go all red 'n' shit." He prodded a zombie with one pointy-toed boot, but the sack of bones and bloated skin remained stubbornly deceased.

"So, I tried to call you," Echo said, heading back toward her office, "and got nothing. We called the office, called your cell…"

"Yeah," said Dennis, following her lead. "I tried calling out, too. Everything was dead… well, y'know, the phones and power and stuff. The zombies showed up later."

"I still want to know," she said, grim, "where they came from, and why they all came here."

"It didn't happen everywhere?" Dennis asked as they passed through the hallway and returned to her room.

"Nope," she said, brows creased with irritation. "Just here."

"Which means…"

"It was personal," she agreed.

"There was some *serious* arguing, when Echo told Brian we needed to stop." Rig followed them down the hallway, checking the locked office doors.

"I'll bet," said Dennis, flushing with embarrassment when Echo spotted Cthulhu's head on her desk. "Sorry," he added. "Bad practice swing."

Echo frowned. "Dammit. That was an old Sideshow Collectable, too." Her attention, though, focused on the top shelf of her reference library. Spotting something, her eyes narrowed. "You said you left these alone, right?"

Damn, thought Dennis. "Um, pretty much, yeah."

Her mouth curved dangerously. "'Pretty much,'" she mimicked. Echo reached up toward the volumes. "Then what," she snarled, "is *this*?" Dennis gaped as she slid *The Book of Erotic Fantasy* down from the shelf. "Well?"

"I had nothing to do with that," he replied. "It was there when I got here."

Rig stood in the doorway, blocking escape. Echo brandished the book as if to hit Dennis with it. "So how," she demanded, "do you *know* that?"

Dennis spread his gore-slimed hands. "Okay," he said, "I looked at them, yeah. I read the titles. I was curious. I did *not*," he insisted, looking her dead-on, "pull them down, or move them, or read anything from off that shelf… or any *other* shelf, either." He pointed to the copy of *Crimson Key* they'd given him, perched on her desk where he'd left it. "All I read tonight was *that*…" He looked at Rig. "…and it was awesome, and you did a great job with it and I hope it sells a million copies so *GET THE FUCK OFF MY BACK!*"

In the warehouse, a zombie went *squish* beneath Marjorie's bootheels.

Echo glanced at Rig. "You believe him?" she said.

Rig shrugged, looking at his friend. "Fuck yeah."

Echo nodded. "Me too."

Dennis sighed with relief. "Cool." Then he added, "But who *did?*"

"THOSE IDIOTS," Echo said, careful not to step in the bloody shreds that had once been their ex-interns. The cemetery mud was churned red with their messy and inevitable demise. She fished a tattered page of *The Black Seals of Ganzir* from the mud. "I knew," she said as they surveyed the ruined graves, clawed open from the inside out, "that I should have kept that book at home."

The red skies had faded to their rightful black by the time Echo, Rig, Marjorie and Dennis sorted out the mess. They'd decided it would be best if no member of Storm Dragon Games

– not even a hired hand like Dennis – was anywhere near the offices when the delivery truck came by the next day. "That way," said Marjorie, "we have what the politicians call 'plausible deniability' when the cops show up."

"What's that mean?" asked Dennis.

"It *means*," she said, her own voice full of meaning, "that we don't know *shit* about what happened." Dennis got the feeling she'd had experience covering up crimes.

"The place is enough of a wreck," Marjorie had continued, "that they won't be able to pin anything on anyone here." They'd already wiped the hilts of Echo's swords clean. The evidence of Dennis's presence would be explained by his new intern status.

And his alibi?

"Well," said Echo, shrugging, "wanna come to GenCon?

Naturally, he'd said yes.

Now they stood in the middle of the last loose end: A churned-up graveyard with two fresh bodies and some old pages of a book. Empty cans of cheap-ass beer littered the site for yards around. The dead boys had embarked one hell of a bender before hauling out the book and calling up the bodies.

"So, what do we do with *them*?" Dennis asked. By now, he was feeling kinda detached. *Still*, his inner voice insisted, *I think we'll have a few rides on the Nightmare Express soon, don't you think?*

"I don't think we do *anything*, yo," said Rig. "I think we let Five-O figure out what lies to tell, not us."

Echo nodded. "Stupid bastards," she said, each word crusted with sorrow and disgust.

"Dude," said Dennis, shaking his head in agreement. He felt bad and all… *But hey*, said the inner voice, *they called up what they couldn't put down*. You *didn't do this*. They *did*. And with that, his conscience could agree.

Echo ground the remaining pages under her Doc Martins, blotting out their weird designs. The rain still fell hard enough to wash away all signs that they'd been there. By morning, they'd all be in Indiana, facing a new kind of zombie horde. "Let's get outta here," she said, glancing at the sky. "We've got *Crimson Keys* to sell."

"We do?" said Dennis, liking the sound of *we*.

Echo smiled as she took his arm. "Yeah," she said, "I guess we do."

WAVES

I gave my voice for love and drowned myself in silence. For him, I walked on knives and left my weightless seas. I bargained with my fear and turned aching eyes toward the sun.

And for this, he left me and gave his heart to someone else.

The song of my sisters calls to me across the waves. I hear the thunder of my father's voice. Alone on shore, I clutch the instrument of liberation in my pale and unfamiliar hands, weighed by the gravity of this new and hostile world. Even in its dimmest light, the realm of my beloved dazzles me near-blind. The roaring of my lost surf haunts me even as I try to sleep. For this love, I have surrendered the swirling comforts of my home. There, I swam with family; here, beheld by eyes of multitudes, I feel exposed. Forsaken. Alone.

For love, I've suffered gladly. And yet, his love belongs to *HER*.

So, *rise*, waves! Churn to froth! Pour the challenge of my sacrifice upon his false and freakish kingdom! Flood their streets. Dash their falseness clean. I will *not* melt, not drift away like foam on morning tides. My voice, returned, calls tempests high. Once more, I am a *princess*. Let the people know my song.

THE LORD'S GREATEST JEST

Every lord must have his cruelties, and my Lord was no exception. The horses strained against their ropes as if in horror of their pending chore. Being but poor brutes, they had no true comprehension of the depth of our king's humor. Still, God's creatures are imbued with some measure of His grace... save, perhaps, we poor fallen specimens, made in our Lord's image and yet born, it would seem, to defile it.

The men cowered in their chains, some begging for mercy, a few soiling themselves. The men-at-arms grumbled at the turn of their task, yet none dared to offend the king's honor by questioning his commands. The stink of terror and vile waste offended my nostrils and compounded the dank atmosphere of the day. Clouds piled up in solemn sky-veils, as if to shield Almighty God's view from the pending deed.

Would that such mercies had been allowed to us.

It is our state to live in fear

Our poor knees to mercies bent

And fair to tremble at the threat

Of some well-pointed argument.

My liege lord availed himself to wine – fine red stuff purged from Tuscan vineyards and carried by main force through the hills. I am familiar with such techniques, as I myself was procured through such adventures. In the carpeted pavilion where my lord took his shade, noble men and women gossiped, distracting their attentions from the activities underway. He gestured to me, and I attended. It was by his grace alone that I was not within that queue, or else long gone to the crypts or shattered like some discarded plaything somehow flawed by its maker's hands.

"Hop-Frog," he said, his fingers twitching with excitement, "It is a marvelous jest, don't you agree?"

"It is," I avowed, nodding my capacious, if marginally overlarge, head, "the very toll of Irony's bell."

The king was fond of jests, which is why he sought my company. He regarded himself as quite the humorist, and if in truth his humours favored a brutish, scatological bent, none within his court would dare make tell of such. His ministers and courtiers roared at the king's japes like cruel boys with some rocks and a frog pond. It fell to me to instill some measure of refinement in that court, however poor my efforts may have been.

"The day is hot, my hopping prophet – *drink!*" My master pressed the wine cup to my hands. I took its measure, then downed it without protest. I fear, however, that I am not much fond of spirits. They skew my wits, and my lord knew this. My sardonic wit had amused him from the day I'd first set foot within his presence. Though I must confess I found his manner quite appalling, I could not argue with the favor of his office. I was one of many celestial pranks gathered into our king's court as entertainers for the noble kind. Yet it was *my* wit (if not my humor) that most pleased our gracious lord. And so, here I was, a partner in his latest jest.

The first team of horses found themselves hitched to the first man drawn from the line. He howled as if the pain had already begun. Like a kitten dangled over fire, he shrieked and clawed and struggled but to no purchase or relief. The men-at-arms hitched his legs to the team – one-half of the team to the right leg, one-half to the left.

Our good king gave the gesture, and the horses were loosed.

Arms pinioned to his sides, the man was drawn to the stake in awful mockery of the carnal act as was practiced in the halls of Sodom, damned yet sacred in appeal. For truly, what *else* could rouse such divine reproach but that which is, by some man's measure, sacred?

God cares not for petty things

To gain His favor, man's deeds must be

Keen of edge and iron-rich

Splendid in depravity.

And so, the deeds of my king were, for his appetites were as capacious as his humours… which is to say (like his belly), vast.

Delicacy forbids me to describe in detail the king's foul spectacle. Let us simply say it was an excessive jest.

By evening-fall, three-score men were writhing in dances of excruciation, dancing a pine-jig of dim theatricality.

"Let it be known," said our king for the third or fourth time that day, "that such is the punishment in my realm for buggery."

And this too, may I say, dear reader, was *also* the very toll of Irony's bell.

For in all the kingdom, I knew of no more prolific a buggerer than our good king himself.

GIVEN MY CLOSE (might I say pointed?) acquaintance with our king's true predilections, I remained wary as we watched that spectacle. Not a one of those so terribly speared had *not* been a member of the King's inner secret circle – those men most tenderly taken in our lord's awful favor. Given the normal instinct for self-preserving acts, you would be forgiven for thinking that such men might avoid our lord's attentions. But just as birds often dash themselves against inviting windowpanes, so we men find ourselves drawn (if I may say so) to morbid fascinations in the hopes that some catharsis might be found. We are creatures of pity and terror by inclination, and our tastes seem sharpened by the risk of some fell thing.

In this case, that fell thing was the king himself – a magnificent hallmark of God's handiwork, I must confess, yet tinged with a Saturnian glare. His opulence – grand foods, grand drinks, clothing fit Papal lords – was well-known, even if his bedchamber-pursuits were not. The finest musicians, acrobats and courtesans were summoned to his palace every fortnight, to entertain men and women elevated to grand opulence by God.

And *I?*

I had the fortune to be master of his revels (both public and discreet), my chambers as capacious as my skull. I was well-barbered by a host of concubines purchased at fine price for the purpose of gilding one of God's mistakes. For just as our good king was charming and well-formed by the Craftsman's hand, so I had been tumbled off the lathe at some imperfect juncture, my wits full-formed and my body, sadly, not.

This, too, I take and gather

As sure sign of my King's wit:

To employ a half-formed Hop-Frog

In service of his etiquette.

Nor was I alone among my countrymen in being granted such an office. One other – a sweet-faced boy named by our liege *Triptolemus* – had been taken from my distant village. We forged a kinship, he and I, in shared captivity. For be assured, dear friend, royal captives is what we were – well-favored slaves, most certainly, but beaten or worse when the king's humours darkened toward night-black.

Triptolemus and I had good reason to fear our king's attentions. For by some gracious blessing of celestial wit, this young man and I shared a common secret with the king. Had truth prevailed in that forest of lies, all three of us would have been hoist upon the buggerer's spikes. But while the king's appetites were as gentle as his cruelties, Triptolemus and I held common comfort in the touch of a secret angel's wings.

I cannot in good conscience claim he loved me. How could *any* man desire in his heart an accident of flesh such as I? It speaks of strange devotions that so beautiful an Adonis could cradle my misshapen head, stroke a perfect finger down my cheek, suffer slights and rantings from our king when tendering on my behalf. Triptolemus kneaded my bent shoulders, rubbed balm on my frequent whip-burns. He held me at night when the torments took me, whispering that he would never leave my side. What inspired such dedication, I cannot say. He never told me then, and he cannot tell me now.

Unlike the coarse blunderers who peopled our king's court, Triptolemus moved like air across a flame. So delicate that he could cross a rope across a gorge, yet strong enough to lift me without drawing a hard breath, Triptolemus shared my acrobatic skills. For though my legs force me to a perpetual half-hop along the ground (hence my name – all hail my master's wit!), my arms are strong as cables on a carpenter's high scaffold. With such ropes and scaffolds we entertained our king, swinging like apes through torch-lit halls in defiance of death and common sense. I may have been the stronger man (or *half*-man, if you will), but Triptolemus was our Orpheus, so delicate in art that he could look Hell in the face and return to the living world unscathed.

Perhaps our bond grew from that kinship to our distant home, or from the brutal method of conveyance we shared between that home and the good king's court. The trust of wrists and well-timed leaps may well have united us. But perhaps it was our *stature* that struck such affection from our souls. For like me, Triptolemus was judged half a man – well-formed as any artist's statute, but far shorter than even a common girl.

What jesting Maker shapes such men? What heavenly laughter shook the clouds on the nights when we were born?

When His wits are up

And His humours sing

The Lord of Hosts

Is cruel as a king.

As our good king laughed at Triptolemus and myself, so the King of Kings must have laughed at us all.

And yet, Triptolemus showed no defect. His small height could be judged his only deformity. Diminutive in stature, he may have been; but in form? Generosity? Intellect? Grace? He was as perfect as any man I have ever seen… and far more so than our noble lord.

I miss him. Curse me for a fool, I miss him still.

Our king, of course, shared no such sentiments. We were prize foals in fools' motley beneath his royal gaze. And as we sat together, my king and I and his seven man-sized crows, drinking ourselves toward happy oblivion, the stench from our lord's jest filled the air.

I confess I was not in good humour then, myself.

Drink is my Golgotha. If my cup could have been taken from me, I would gladly have wished it so. But my lord bid me drink, and so I did, my head growing heavier than usual with the mixture of thick wine and thicker smells. The men on stakes (still living, and what cruel jest was *that?*) writhed and spilled their entrails most pitifully. I stared down at my boots, uneasily aware that they had not escaped the legacy of humours spread out around us. I wished for Triptolemus' arms about me then, his soft words soothing my pulsating skull, but was glad to see him spared this spectacle. Back at the palace, our king had decreed a feast to be held in honor of his wit. Triptolemus had remained behind to oversee the preparations, while I followed the king's train to witness his glorious jest first-hand.

"Dance for us," my king commanded. "Raise that heavy head of yours and amuse our company."

My stomach roiled with revulsion and wine. "I fear, my lord, that I've had far too much to drink."

"Nonsense," replied Bartholomew, the most demanding of my lord's advisors. His sour moustache twitched with disapproval. "Our *king* bids you dance, Hop-Frog. Do so."

I glared at him with all the venom a slave dares display. Behind him, a man I'd known as Antony shrieked for mercy. I could not look up without seeing the forest of violated limbs and trees. Squinting, I could render them into shadows, but nothing stopped that *smell*, that *sound*. "What sort of dance," I asked our king, "would you see me do, my lord?"

"A jig of spring, my toad. As graceful as you can be."

Grace was never, I fear, an attribute of mine.

Bowing, I rose to my feet. My head swirled and throbbed. I tilted as if the world itself had tugged the carpet from beneath me. The king and his advisors laughed. I spread my arms out in pale imitation of a swan.

"*No*, my fool," the king said.

My heavy skull bobbed at the end of my neck. "My lord?"

"Not here," he said, gesturing to the carpet rolled out across the mud by his servants. "You'll soil the carpets."

"Where, then, do you wish me to dance, my king?"

He pointed, not to my surprise, to the forest of budding corpses. "Out there."

The courtiers barked flatteries at my king's command. Bartholomew cackled as he took a sliver of lamb from an ill-looking servant's tray. Caught between two pointed logics – the wall of courtiers and men-at-arms before me, the wall of staked men and men-with-stakes behind me – I bowed again and took my leave of the carpet, stumbled into the reddening mud with as much dignity as I could muster. Once there, I raised my gaze to the skies. A trio of musicians began to play beneath the pavilion, and I danced.

I wish I could say that my eyes remained closed, but that would not be true. Thankfully, tears soon blurred what my will alone could not.

"IT WAS TERRIBLE," he said.

"It was," I affirmed. It had been my intention to shield him from the truth, to dismiss the king's jest with a few words and a shrug. I could not. Triptolemus' grasp gave me a vessel for my shudders, and so I placed them there. He himself felt shaken too, as if he'd heard more about the pageant than I would have told him myself.

His sweat held a sharper edge than usual, and though I could smell the drift of garlic and meat from the kitchens, I had no stomach for a feast.

"I should have been there," he said.

"I'm glad you were not."

"We should not speak of it." He was not being kind. The king learned gossip from the roaches in the walls, it seemed, and if he wanted to add two of his favorite clowns to his next spectacle, no one would raise a word against it. Best, then, to speak of nothing and pretend that nothing was amiss.

"We will not." I gave Triptolemus a brief, but firm, embrace and then stepped back away from his arms. "How go the revels' preparation?"

His mouth bent in silent dismay. "Well enough," he lied. "By an hour past dinner, all will be ready for His Majesty's pleasure."

Such was our discourse: a forest of mirrors casting false reflections. Aware that any wrong word would bring the weight of our lord's wit and humour upon us, we chose our words like grapes among a half-ruined harvest. I nodded to him. "Surely the feast will provide welcome relief for such grand hungers."

"I hope," said Triptolemus, "that it will satisfy him." We both knew, of course, that it would not. Our lord's blood ran hot for amusement, and when it was up, no simple foods could appease it.

"I should sleep while I can," I told him, my head still spinning from the afternoon's wine.

"Will you be well alone?" he asked, his face searching my own.

It was my turn to lie. "I will."

My dreams ran wild with sharpened trees.

HUMOR HAS THE BREATH OF CRUELTY. Any jester knows this, and I more than most. By the time the servants tendered up their feast, the king's halls rang with noble laughter. Though I had no belly for food that night, I accepted the plate Triptolemus brought me. Starving jesters tender ill jests.

As I ate, I watched Triptolemus fly. His agile limbs cast him in an angel's role, too high and graceful to be bound by earthly weight. He danced in the ropes above our heads, shining with the glow of his exertions. Despite the swamp in my belly, I felt my heart fly with him.

Soar, my young blind Icarus,

Shame Heaven with your grace

Unbound by the dull chains of man

Gone to touch our Master's face...

And then I saw the courtier Bartholomew whispering in the king's ear, his face like countenance of a late-winter wolf.

The two men laughed. Our lord nodded.

Though Triptolemus still flew, I felt my stomach fall.

And when the angel descended, the devils caught him and brought him to the throne.

I hobbled over to where they stood, but Triptolemus warned me off with a glance. His expression closed tight, like men-at-arms in war formation. He nodded to our king, but I saw his shoulders shake.

Bartholomew nodded to one door, and Triptolemus bowed, then strode toward that portal. I looked to him. He closed his eyes and walked away.

"*Hop-Frog!*" The king's voice cracked through the chamber.

"My lord?" I knew better than to delay. Bowing, I felt my knees shudder. My thick skull blackened with the thoughts locked inside.

"To the ropes with you," he said. "We would see who flies best: the angel or the ape."

The courtiers laughed, of course. It was their nature to obey and their pleasure to observe.

Though I'm sure I fancied it, I would swear that Triptolemus' sweat lingered in the ropes, drifting over the smell of food, wine and candle lard.

In the arc of angels, I dreamed a demon's plans.

THERE ARE BARBARITIES to which no man nor woman should accept. And yet, we bear them with silent shrugs and empty eyes. In such a state Triptolemus returned, stumbling to his cot with unaccustomed frailty. I rose to greet him, but he shook his head.

Some novel iniquity had cut him in places my smile could not reach. "We will not speak of it," he said.

I nodded.

Our clowns' court was silent and cold that night.

"A MASQUERADE?" our lord asked.

"Indeed," I nodded. "Like those of the Venetian courts." With words, I painted frescos of delight that should have shamed Great Michelangelo had he beheld my art. "All the kingdom will speak of it," I said. "Word of your cleverness will spread from the cold pagan reaches to the sand-courts of the infidels!"

"*What* cleverness would they speak of, Hop-Frog," he said. There was no question in his voice. For all my art, our king was no fool.

But I, of course, am a *great* fool. And though it took all my art, so I fooled him in turn.

We laid plans for the masquerade, Triptolemus still rigid from his secret pain. He embraced me while we felt ourselves unwatched, but his arms felt stiff as paving stones. I tried to will some heat back into him, but whatever had chilled Tripolemus lingered there beyond my grasp.

It took time and no little effort, but soon all things were arranged. The night our of king's masquerade arrived, dressed out in devilish finery.

The costumes I'd prepared arrived as well.

"Apes?" Our king seemed dubious. His advisors eyed the fur-suits with unnerved curiosity. I had taken pains to ensure that the costumes would radiate a grotesque potency. Great teeth gleamed white in the shaggy masks, and jewels glittered against night-black fur. I had coated that fur with sweet-smelling musk, oils ripe with seductive masculinity. Best of all were the claws – scimitar talons carved from bone. Such props appeal to predatory men. True apes, of course, have no such claws… but each artist must have his liberties.

I had taken mine. And in Tripolemus' distance, I had taken to drinking, too.

My head whirled and my tongue danced. Flatteries spilled from my lips like wine. "It will terrify them all," I said. "Imagine the ladies fainting with horror. Imagine the brave men trembling in the face of your ferocity! *All* will fear you – and then applaud when you remove the masks and reveal the handsome men beneath the image of fierce apes."

"It would be," the king remarked, "a most *poetic* jest." His face tightened to a grin. "And should any man flee the court, we'll know him for his cowardice. A fine jest, my Hop-Frog… and perhaps a useful one as well." Behind his eyes, I saw trees dancing with the bodies of men.

When all were attired, I produced the chains. The king's eyes narrowed behind his mask. Though I had made certain that the men would be refreshed with strong spirits as they dressed, my king's wits had managed to peek through the clouds. "*Chains*, my servant? Do you forget yourself?"

"Not at all, my king." My wits glistened with the spirits' taste. "It is an essential element of the masquerade. Who would believe that mere *apes* could be loose within the palace? You are to be *demon*-apes, my lords, straining against the very chains of Heaven. Look here," I added, opening the door. "I have even brought an angel to hold you all."

Triptolemus stood waiting, his face stern as Heaven's messenger. A pale wrap girded tight across his loins. His muscles gleamed with oil and candlelight.

It was no great task to get them into the chains after that.

IT'S SMALL WONDER that folk crave masquerades. Our passions chase us from God's sight, warding us from Eden by flaming swords we carry in our grasp. To admit to our hearts' desires is to fall from grace like the poor acrobats we are. And so, we bar the gates to our inner natures, dressing them in costumes that hide honesty behind façade. In masquerades, of course, one's true face is revealed beneath a stylish confection. We may excuse its presence with cobbled finery, but we all know (though few will admit as much) that only in such deceptions may we be free.

And do we not have excellent teachers in such masques: The Lord, our cruelest jester, and His clergy on this earth? The God of sacramental tortures, the men who bless the engines of our pain – they speak of gentleness, yet show none of it themselves. The silky kitten is tormentor to the mouse, and the laws that speak of justice give free rein to the cruel. We hide our truths from the face of the Lord, and yet it is that Lord who makes us what we are. Such ironies bind our earthly lives, and so I found rich irony in binding our lord with chains.

In the grand hall, vast candelabras shed smoky light across the ballroom. Bright-clad apparitions spun and glided on polished stone. Musicians kept a heavenly reverie, their art echoing through stone chambers to each corner of the hall. Outside, darkness swelled with the rustle of bat-wings and the skitter of vermin beyond the candlelight. Hungry servants, huddled against the cold, shivered in their rags or slapped cards and flesh and pitiful wagers in vain efforts to keep warm. Horses snorted gusts of foul-breathed mist. Dogs gnawed on bones cast there once the best part of the meat had been consumed by the revelers inside. Like a body on the verge of rot, the palace swarmed inside with pale-skinned maggots of ravenous degree. Not far off, the scraps of our king's jests still hung suspended on sharpened posts, their crow-tattered corpses rich with grubs. The masquerade continued apace, trading truth for falsehood with ever-present glee.

Our king and his man-crows clanked their chains. Through hidden corridors, Tripolemus and I led them towards the hall. "Wait here, my lords," I whispered as I handed the full rein off to my companion. "I will shout alarms to the masquerade, priming them for your infernal appearance."

"And what then?" asked Bartholomew, his glance skipping between myself, our king, and the angel holding his chains.

"I have prepared a shot of brimstone to herald your arrival – a fierce but harmless fire-burst. When you hear it, and the screams begin, crash through those doors and howl like the fiends of Hell."

By this time, the king and his retinue were (as goes the saying) drunk as lords. I had made certain that wine was close at hand, well-sweetened with concoctions to muddle one's wits. Truth be told, my king and his advisors stumbled like veritable *Hop-Frogs* in their chains, their normal grace hobbled by dizzied limbs.

The king's guards, too, had been plied with wine. We all laughed with liquid cheer. Only Tripolemus did not laugh. His face held implacable angelic calm. My chest hurt when I looked at him.

Still, my office was to play the fool, and so I did, jigging like a frog on the end of a rough boy's noose.

"We are prepared?" I asked the company, but it was Tripolemus I looked to. He nodded. We had never, he and I, held much need for words between us.

In shadow, I loped up the stairs to a balcony where the brimstone cannon waited. I aimed it near the ceiling, then lit the fuse.

The hall shook with the thunder of its blaze.

Into the smoke-filled hall, I cried: "*My lords and ladies! Flee! The devil has burst the gates of Hell and set his minions loose! Save yourselves! Pray to God! The demons are free! Fly, my friends – FLY!*"

I took some small satisfaction in the ensuing pandemonium.

On cue, the king and his advisors charged into the room, their claws gleaming wicked in the candlelight. Bared fangs flashed in their fur-clad heads. Poor Tripolemus clung tightly to their chains, a gorgeous coachman with a furious team. The brimstone singed my throat and nose as I howled theatricalities to the room below. "*See them, my lords and ladies! See the angel wrestling with their chains! Fear the hot breath of their corruption, gentle souls!*" I made it clear that this spectacle was part of the masquerade. Soon, terror turned to hilarity.

The guests and men-at-arms joined the play. Ladies swooned with exaggerated flair. Men-at-arms brandished their weapons with obvious caution, wary of any true threat to the king.

The demon-apes raged about the room, tearing dresses and scattering furniture. Servants fled their approach, their faces pale with genuine fear.

The king and his advisors were clearly having the time of their lives.

Leaping from the balcony, I caught one chandelier and swung out in an arc. My hand clutched the torch with which I'd lit the brimstone. "*My lord and ladies,*" I cried, "*let us have an end to this! Let the devils stand revealed!*"

Our wise king caught my cue. He stopped and roared with infernal majesty. Reaching up, he shook free his demonic ape-mask, pulled it off, and roared again.

The crowd roared in approving response.

I glanced down to Tripolemus. He glanced back to me.

And tossed the chain in my direction.

It was, by my design, long enough to reach the hook I had hung from the chandelier.

Never harm an acrobatic fool.

I swung the hook to catch the chain, caught it, and pulled. The arcing chandelier snapped the chain tight around the men below. With a heave that near-tore my arms from their sockets, I pulled the chain to anchor it on the chandelier.

The king and his men were yanked high in the air.

We swung back and forth as I drew the cursing men toward me. Years of bitter exercise gave me the strength of an angry god.

"*Good people,*" I shouted, my lungs tight with exertion and brimstone smoke, "*Who is this I here behold?*"

"*It's the KING!*" some woman shouted.

184

"*Indeed?*" I yelled. "*Let me get a closer look!*"

And I shoved the torch in his face.

The musk-oiled fur flared. My noble lord screamed.

Indeed, I *had* prepared this jest – had crafted the costumes with an eye towards vanity *and* ignition. Within instants, the king, Bartholomew and the other courtiers shrieked in their prisons of burning fur.

Atop the chandelier, I cried:

The lord is my jester, I shall not want.

He maketh me to cry near still waters.

He lieth down with innocents and turns them to bawds.

I am Hop-Frog, and this is MY LAST JEST!

With that, I leapt to the balcony and ran for my life.

It has been said that Triptolemus and I fled the kingdom together that night; this much was true. Some tales even cast him as a woman… and this much was *not*. In a merciful world, I could say that we lived a blissful life from then on outward – and to some degree, we *did*. Through cleverness and luck, we secured a home near the edges of those lands, far from the wars and searches that combed the countryside. A wiser king soon rose to claim the throne, and the hunt for us ended with nothing to show but legends of my infamy.

And yet my angel had flown. His haunted eyes looked out toward some horizon that neither of us dared to speak of. Though his arms wound close about me at night, they held an ever-bitter chill. He trembled from the lash of some dire whip inside. No jests, no tears, no endearments could soothe him.

Tripolemus lived like a walking corpse. Not long afterward, he stopped walking and simply died.

If this was a kinder tale, I would have passed on with him then, going to whatever Hells or Heavens await creatures such as us. Yet the vitality that guided my hand that night has kept me strong through all these years. The seasons have fled. My life has not. Of all the souls alive that night, I may be the last one drawing breath today.

My vibrant strength has faded, though. What little grace I had is gone. Yet the heart beating in my chest pounds like a blacksmith's favorite hammer on the anvil of each night and dawn. I crave release, but cling to life.

It's justice, I suppose. To recall sweetness in such sour age. To smell the brimstone even when I sleep, its scent lightened by the sweat of love.

I thought myself clever… and so I was. Clever enough to see the humor of our Lord.

And even in my solitude, I have to laugh.

We are as frogs before our God

Tumbling through our graceless fall

Mortal men might play at jests

But time's the cruelest jest of all.

186

CLOWN BALLOONS

The floor at my feet is littered with clown-balloon corpses. Bright rubber screams into nightmare shapes. My ears ring. My wrists throb. This is my damnation, to twist and strangle rubber 'til my brain runs dry.

It isn't working, though. I'm running out of balloons.

I MAY HAVE BEEN EIGHT when the clown first appeared, a looming bright Satan against a sea of children. Flies buzzed lazy in the summer heat but if the clown felt dizzy in his painted prison, it didn't show. He laughed instead, and did magic tricks, his face swollen and flat behind red-slashed masking. Marcie Meyers, the Birthday Girl, flounced about all pink and pretty, but it seemed like the clown was intent on me.

My world tilted. I recall that much. Sickness bloomed in my belly, greasy-sweet from too much cake. The birthday-hat elastic bit into my chin and throat. I wanted the bathroom. I wanted to go home. I nearly wet my pants when the clown leapt suddenly from the bushes, scattering children in a screeching herd.

189

Laughing harder, he beckoned us back… and trusting, we returned to him. The Birthday Parents beamed and reassured us as the clown went back to work. The other children giggled and clustered beside him. I held back, though, sniffling. His laugh held tiny screams just for me.

I stood apart. Is that why we watched me?

I didn't need to see his eyes to know that he watched me. The feeling was clear enough. His eyes burned my skin like sunburn, prickled like peroxide on a scrape. When I dared a glance, our eyes met and locked. He seemed to giggle, then, but that may have been my imagination.

Then he fetched his balloons and it all grew worse.

I didn't want to be there. To be watching. To be caught. I didn't want to see him pull things from nowhere, to see sun glare on bright baggy clothes. To feel flaming eyes set on black-rimmed white, eyes that scurried over me like roaches. I tried to brush that gaze away.

"*Timmy!*" cried Birthday Mom. "Don't touch yourself there! It isn't nice!"

"Can I go inside?" I begged, or something like it. "I gotta…"

"I see," she said as she led me by the hand. But she didn't. Not really. The clown did, though. I caught him smiling at me as we went inside.

I heard balloons scream as we came back from the bathroom. I wanted to stay inside but she wouldn't let me. She said it was time to have fun, time to laugh, time to play. Marcie had wanted all her friends to be there, and I didn't want to miss the *clown*, did I?

How little we recall kid fears.

He caught my eye as I came out through the door. He'd been waiting for my return. At the middle of the yard, he tortured two balloons in his white-gloved hand, much to the children's delight. I winced as tiny screams broke me into goosebumps. My friends didn't notice, but I did. Dancing Marcie held a balloon-beast in her eager hands. Bruce and Katrina did, too. The clown gave his weeping balloons a final, vicious twist, then handed the result toward me.

It was hideous.

The clown was a master of his art. His creations were bent and broken things, agonizingly alive. The balloon-beasts quivered and mewled. Wet eyes pleaded for release. The one in Marcie's hands looked worst of all. I wanted to puke.

So I did.

It took forever 'til Mom showed up to take me home. I burned as the other kids laughed. Even the clown seemed amused. I wished he'd stop looking at me! On the ground at his feet, balloon-things writhed. The clown smirked as he squashed one beneath his oversized shoe. It squealed before it burst. Bright blood spattered the white of his pants. Why didn't anyone see this but me?

And still, he brought freakish things to life, handing them out like treats. Like sacrifice. He seemed to sneer beneath his paint as he wrenched pathetic beasts from garish rubber. That grin promised similar treatment to me.

Later.

I still felt him watch me as Mom came to take me home. Marcie never forgave me for puking blue birthday cake at her party.

191

The clown came to see me that night in my dreams. Red, wet, sticky dreams smelling of greasepaint.

Bruce Taylor called me "Party Puker." Katrina Watkins called me "Timmy Toilet-Face." Marcie called me things I never expected from a girl, and Gary Bright did a lunchtime impression of me that got him sent to Mr. Jordan's office. I was out-cast all that month, and it would be a long time before anyone invited me to a birthday party again.

I still can't eat cake, even now.

It wasn't over, though. There was more.

I was in my backyard, pitching dirt clods at my G.I. Joes a week later or so when I heard the squeak of rubber behind me.

"I *know* you want a balloon, Timmy."

Nobody saw the clown with me, then. Nobody saw his hands on me. His eyes. His blazing white suit. I didn't scream or cry or run away. I could see the sweat sheen on greasepaint as he held me close. The whisker-tips beneath it. His hot clown suit smelled unwashed against the pine-needle scene of my back yard.

I recall a finch feeding worms to her children that day.

In high school, I could never come through. I graduated virginal, not quite a man. I'd go out on dates, sure, but when things got close the smell of greasepaint turned me small and useless for the night. Word spread between the girls by my junior year. I didn't date again 'til college. My girlfriends, though, couldn't hear the squeak of rubber in my room back home. I didn't share that part of me at all.

The clown, I'd soon learned, had passed his gift of creation on to me that back-yard afternoon. Now *I* could make animals, too. I hid balloons underneath my bed, and when I returned from dates with Jane or Alexa or Sherri or Mo I'd dig out the bag and blow up and twist balloons until the skin pulled back beneath my nails and my head swam dizzily. Then I'd put the suffering things out of their misery with a pin, muffling their bursting bodies with my pillow before I slept.

I didn't want to do clown things.

Once, in college, feeling brave I dropped some acid. Big mistake. The room quickly filled with balloons and the laughter of clowns. Colored light crawled across the walls like blood. My feet brushed the bones of long-dead children as the clown stood, laughing, at the center of the room and blew bubbles shaped like heads. Balloon-creatures writhed, broken, at his feet. All around me, stoned girls watched my eyes and giggled when I met their gaze. My friends weren't really my friends, it seemed. I started at the floor to avoid their eyes. Besides, there were bones on the floor to be careful about, too.

I just wanted my balloons.

"I know you *really* want to be a clown, Timmy," said the bubble-blowing trickster. I don't think he was right, but back then I wasn't sure.

"Hey, Tim," said a soft voice. Alison Richards, from my chem class. She took my hand in her own warm one. "Let's get you some air," she offered. "It's kinda close in here." I didn't disagree.

Outside, we walked hand-in-hand as dying stars fell to the wet cement. Branches shook with nighttime wind. Our clothes clung tight in drizzling rain. We brushed damp hair from one another's faces as we kissed beneath a streetlight.

The next time I recall seeing Alison, she covered her face and ran away from me. When I saw the clown again shortly afterward, he looked pleased. Although I never learned what else happened that night, I also never touched acid again.

I MADE MANY BALLOON-THINGS on my wedding night. My new wife Helen never saw them. I went outside and popped them in an alley while she slept. If the clown was there then, I didn't see him.

I see him a lot now, though. At the edges of my sight, he waves at me. I buy plenty of balloons, and then fashion horrors to make him go away. Sometimes, I miss pieces of them when I'm cleaning up. Helen finds them and wonders where the rubber scraps come from. I haven't dreamed up a good enough lie.

"I know you really want to be a *clown*, Timmy," he insists. No matter how far away he stands, I smell rancid greasepaint, sweat, and birthday cake.

My fingers ache, stained and stinking of cheap balloon rubber. Helen keeps to her side of the bed now, watching me with chilly eyes. Maybe I should have told her about greasepaint and pine needles. If I had, she might not look at me that way.

I *should* tell her, but I can't anymore. It's too late. Things have changed. The clown leers from every shadowed corner, now. He might tell the police where to find Alison. I don't know where she is myself, and I don't want to know.

Maybe I should tell Helen that I'm running out of balloons.

So, I sit in my den, surrounded by gasping shapes wrung from rubber, nightmares looking at me with glistening eyes. It's late out, too late to buy balloons. The clown's shadow falls across my shoulder. He brings the taste of sweet sugar cake and the tang of pine needles, and he's chuckling.

Only two balloons left. Two balloons between me and my young son's bedroom door.

Please help me, God.

I really don't want to do clown things.

THE LEGACY BOX

Men don't cry. The boxes cry for them.

It's a mystery we women weren't meant to understand. The small wood boxes that men carry in their packs or pockets hold their tears. When a man feels the pain of an opened wound or the burn of humiliation or the wrench a heart suffers as it's pulled from its orbit by a loved one and cast into the flames of bitterness, he opens up his box and lets the tears fill up inside.

My father had two boxes: a pocket-sized black case carved from what looked like burnt bone, and a sturdy one the height of one male hand and the length of two hands pressed together side-by-side. The sturdy one sat on the top of his dresser, polished to a warm shine and carved with precious sigils and whorls. My father used to wax it every Sunday, taking the box down to his workbench and closing the door. He thought I couldn't see him then, but by the time I'd reached my seventh year, I had mastered the art of slipping behind him soundlessly and easing the door open on hinges I oiled for just that purpose in the night, standing tip-toe on a stool, reaching with the oil tin to drip little bits of liquid silence to the hinge. On Sundays, then, I'd slip down to the workshop door and slide it open just a crack. Just enough to let me see.

Father would sit in the glow of a single lamp, polishing both boxes with a soft checkered cloth. The scent of wax polish drifted to my nose as I'd watch. He'd sit in the dim light, tending carefully to that most male of mysteries. His face would catch the shadows from the lamp, sliding into an elderly mask unlike that face he usually wore. If he saw me watching, it never showed. In time, he'd stop polishing, examine each box with warm precision, and put away his polish and cloth. I'd know then to ease the door closed again, slipping the knob back into place with a faint snap that always caused my heart to skip. Then I'd dash back upstairs on silent feet, ducking through the back door to seem as though I'd been playing outside all along. My father would come to find me soon afterward, hoisting me on his shoulders like a warm, lean giant. His face – so old just slightly earlier – looked radiant in the sun, as if it could never age.

The boxes are a legacy, sometimes handed down from fathers or uncles to boys as they hit puberty, sometimes carved specially and given to them as gifts. Each one is made by hand. I've heard that some men make their own boxes, planeing and sanding and gluing the joints through some inherent male alchemy of wood. All the boxes are made of wood, too – no stone, no glass, no metal. I suspect that wood holds the property of tears, the ghosts of felled trees lending a primal bridge of sadness there.

On bad days, when my mother and father quarreled, I'd see him slip the box from his pocket when he thought no one could see. He would flip the lid open and stare into the box. His eyes held the shine of pending tears, but then that shine faded, and his eyes grew hard again. He'd snap the box closed and shove it in his pocket like something shameful. Once or twice, he caught me looking at him. Father never yelled at me at such times, but his grim expression shouted me to tears.

Usually, when I'd cry, my father would pick me up and cradle me with warmth. If I'd seen him looking at his box, however, he'd stuff his hands into his pockets and stride away as if he'd been caught sinning. We never discussed the boxes' purpose. He never offered and I never asked.

As I grew, I noticed that each man above boyhood had a box. My first sweetheart had one. My first lover had one. My husband has one, too. Every male relative I've had has possessed a box, and though I've rarely seen them open these containers in my presence, the hard outline in a pocket or the shining presence near a bed proclaims the box's ubiquity. They're as common as shirtsleeves… and as silently accepted. Each man has one. No man speaks of it.

We all have our mysteries.

When my mother caught sick that final time, my father's large box sat open near her bed. I'd see it sometimes, slick with moisture, its inner sides stained with decades of pain. Sitting at her bedside, he seemed to lose all care of my discovery. I was almost a woman by then, not the little girl who'd spied on him those Sunday mornings long ago. And so, perhaps out of respect for my age and the mysteries that came with it, he'd left the box lid open by her bed. Again, I never asked, and he never offered. We accepted the box as furniture whose purpose went unquestioned. When she died, he stood beside the bed, still as oakwood, his eyes set staring off at horizons past the wall, his face aging like the shadows of his workshop mask. The open box spilled over. My father's eyes stayed dry.

As my son grows quickly toward the day when he won't need me anymore, I cherish each tear that stains his dirty face. I hold him close and cradle him with warmth. Somewhere in our home, there's a box waiting for him as well. And on that day when his father hands it over and speaks words only men would understand, I'll keep my silence and pretend, as always, that I never saw tears there at all.

DRINKING THE MOON

For Sandi, who holds my heart

She was thirsty, they said, to drink the moon. She sighed like a forsaken queen and left her features bare. The young men painted their faces crimson, and powdered their chests with emerald dust. Still, she had eyes for none of them. Instead, each night the girl climbed the hill beyond their home, hushed whispers in her wake.

Her mother, it was said, had been an errant harvest wind that caressed a farmer boy to sleep. He had slumbered 'til the next full moon, when storms rattled the tall trees and brought some low and shuddering. As that storm-moon yielded to the sovereignty of day, the young man awakened in the healer's lodge, a bawling infant on his chest. He had raised her with tender strength until the night another storm came and carried him away. Since then, Wind's Daughter had subsisted on the kindness of her people, growing lean and beautiful as thunder.

Still, she thirsted, and not jhala-wine nor poppy syrup nor clear water fresh from the sky could slake that thirst.

Old Tor, whose laughter caused the ground to quake, mulled whip-grass into heady brews. She smiled as she drank them down, but shook her head with sorrow. Smiling Orishala, whose arms clattered with bright bangles marking favor in men's eyes, steamed wet earth from the dancing grounds, then mixed it with tears and washes of spring rain. The girl drank 'til her belly swelled above her skirts, but still the thirst remained. Each night, though, above her, the moon called out, sweet with glowing promise. *In me alone*, it seemed to call, *shall your thirst be fulfilled.*

And so, she sought to drink the moon.

On dark nights, when the sky-witch hid her face and the crops muttered restless in their beds, the girl tossed and turned on sweet-smelling grass and warm furs within the virgins' lodge. The other women watched her warily, their eyes dark with awe. No lullaby nor brew could bring her peace. Old Tor wove soft chains to bind her to her bed, but they broke apart on contact with her skin. Orishala, who knew about unruly sleep, sang ballads of warm water and old stone. Still, the girl rolled and sighed each night until moonlight shone again.

When moonlight bathed the landscape and made the lodge-roofs shine, the thirsty girl would slip past the brave eunuchs outside the virgins' door. Her cool touch upon their backs soothed them into sleep each night, and even the most steadfast among them could not resist that touch. Free to wander, she climbed the highest hill each night, picking through the wild darkness on feet light and sure as gold. Guided by the glow above, Wind's Daughter rose past tigers, wolves, and serpents to reach the peak unharmed. There, upon the stark crown of that highest hill, she'd throw back her head and stretch up her arms and try to drink the moon.

But there are voids in heaven and emptiness on earth. Though her devotions held her still and silent through each night, the moon-glow could not soothe her thirst.

Each morning, as mists fled before the dawn, the girl returned to the lodge, heart-dulled and dusty-throated. Her eyes still shimmered with cold luminescence, but her touch was cool as autumn rain. Old Tor, then, would hold her as she wept; Orishala would brew her bale-herb tea and talk of lovers until the sun rose high. In time, Wind's Daughter would sleep, waking just before the skies blazed orange with the fading day. Returned – as was proper – to the virgins' lodge, she'd escape once more and try to drink that moon. It was enough to make wise men chew their beards, and maidens burn their braids and eat the ashes.

One morning, as she lowered aching arms and coughed to clear her dusty throat, Wind's Daughter wept, enraged. Her skin still rippled with the moon's cool touch, but her throat felt tinder-parched. In a flash of rage, she stamped her heel into the peak's bald head. A sudden arc of water burst across dry ground like rain. Within ten heartbeats, a spring ran down the hillside, chuckling to itself with riddles only water knows. Wind's Daughter bent to taste that stream, but it scourged her bitter throat. Fists clenched, she wandered down the hill toward home.

That dusk, as harsh winds swept the trees, the thirsty girl slipped once more through the doorway of the virgins' lodge. Once again, she ventured up the hillside, eyes luminous with unshed tears. And once again, she reached the peak, spread her arms, and threw her head back thirstily. Wind's Daughter opened her mouth wide, and crooned a wordless song so rich that fireflies rose from the woods below and danced around her, shining. The cool winds chilled her skin like stone and tossed her wild hair. Eyes closed, she reached out and up, as if to touch that moon.

At her feet, the water whispered. Its voice flowed across the silence of her calm. Finally, she opened her eyes, looked down, and saw the stream. And in its face, she saw the moon as well.

Bending down, she cupped her hands. Between them, moonlight swelled. Eyes open, she brought those waters to her lips. Wind's Daughter drank with eagerness, and down her throat slid the moon.

They say the sky-witch dimmed her light. Old Tor whispered that the wind-mother had come home. Orishala smiled and drew her lovers close. Amidst their furs and blankets, the people settled deeper into dreams. Children stilled to restful slumber. Old aches and pains faded; nightmares fled.

At the hilltop, Wind's Daughter drank the moon.

In morning, she descended, eyes shining, finally fulfilled. Those who saw her then said she left footprints of light. Mist embraced her as she walked.

And then, smiling, she faded and was gone.

GRAMMA WOLF'S GARDEN

Not all wolves eat little pigs or children. Some eat flowers, magic or secrets. You never hear about those wolves, though. They keep to themselves at the far edges of the forest. The moon, for them, is communion enough. A girl's sighs of woe or pleasure can sustain them for weeks on end. Still, it's not wise to trespass there. All wolves have teeth, you know, and a predator of secrets may be the most dangerous kind.

In the perpetual shade of a balenor tree, there's a cottage overgrown with ivy. Though it gives the grave impression of unspeakable age, its windowpanes remain unshattered and its door glows with fresh paint after each new moon. Around that cottage sprawls a garden of such rich proportions that in spring it swells to engulf the house. Its blooms blaze bright as summer lovers, save for those which bloom at night; these trap the graceful shiver of the moon and shine it back in muted hues. No flagstones mark the thick front yard. No axe sticks proudly from its chopping block. Welcome to Gramma Wolf's Garden, where Grandma never died.

Long ago, a woman made her home deep in the forest. She labored hard to build it safe and strong. Her old name has been lost to time, so calling her Gram will suffice.

Back then, they say, Gram was vibrant and beautiful; the bloom of each moon's blood still crept between her legs, and she'd grind herbs into autumn-scented powders and then drink them with her tea on the nights when she'd take a strange lover to bed. The widow of a woodsman and the daughter of an herb-wife and a stonemason, Gram had hands strong as winter winds and a heart warm as a crackling hearth. Silver strands peppered the fall of her hair, while eyes the brown of fresh-turned earth caught the laughter of a child and the gloom of a poet with equal measure and grace. She spoke little, but the few words she said fell to the ground and sprouted flowers. Kindly children who picked them sang in their sleep, while spiteful ones tossed whining through dreams of wild hells.

When Gram had been a child, her mother taught her to seed small gardens with sweet whispers; her youthful tantrums wove briars between the flagstones and wrapped rose-vines dense with thorns and black petals among the rafters of their home. As that child grew, Gram's mother taught her to speak flattering bouquets and murmur healing herbs into moonlit soil. She sang crops to fullness and gardens to bloom. Gram's reputation blossomed like a rainy-season wood, and when a fever took her mother down, Gram – scarcely more than a girl by then – became the cherished herb-wife in her place.

Not long afterward, Gram met a woodsman with tangled hair and shining eyes. His skin held a sapling's rough suppleness. Sunlight glistened on his bare shoulders. He smiled often and needed few words to gauge Gram's mind or speak his own. Though he'd built his cottage far beyond the village paths, Gram slipped often through the shadowed woods to see him after dark. In the bloom of young love, she'd whisper white havermusk beneath the window of her beloved. Their cries of ecstasy made twigs bud

210

on the contours of his furniture, and filled forest clearings with dazzling red forget-me-nots. On the day they married, every flower for a thousand miles opened in full bloom. The birth of their first and only child cracked trees with the power of her screams. Her husband brought Gram handfuls of long-stemmed honeywine as she nursed their child, and her milk pulsed with the throb of wild life.

Sadly, life is often cruel. Just as Gram's mother and father had died before their season, her husband broke his leg at the bottom of a ravine and perished in a tangle of thorns. A kind-eyed passing wolf heard his cries, crept down into the ravine, and nuzzled the dying man to sleep. As he slipped beneath a soft and endless slumber, the woodsman whispered a promise to his beloved. No man living knows his final words, but the wolf caught them between lupine jaws, licked the woodsman's brow, touched one paw to his forehead as his spirit passed beyond the pain, and then clambered up the edge of the ravine.

When darkness wrapped the cottage the woodsman had built, Gram set out to find her mate. Strapping their child to her back, she had just stepped out on the forester's path when the wolf emerged from the mist. Behind him, a grim pack gathered on the path. Kind eyes shining with sorrow, the wolf bowed his head low to the ground. Gram raised her walking staff high, as if to bash out his brains, but stopped when he would not defend himself or flee. The wolf met her gaze, opened his jaws, and let the woodsman's whispers out. They scattered on the ground like acorns, blossoming into his final words to her. Eyes blurred with unshed tears, she beckoned the wolves into her yard, fed them dinner, and murmured her thanks. Jarrowbane flowers, pale blue and glowing like the moon, grew at the wolf's feet, and from that moment forward Gram, the wolf and his pack remained close as roses and thorns.

211

People whispered. People swore. Men came from the village to drive the wolves away. Gram had none of it. She muttered viperweed at the gossipers, and shouted briars at the hunters' legs. In time, the grumbling townsfolk shunned Gram's cabin. Though brave market-children still tangled at her skirts, and people still came to purchase remedies, rumors of Gram's wolfpack chased familiarity from her life like ducks before the sticks of angry boys.

Gram used solitude to weave lush gardens around her home. Her wolves ate flowers, not lambs, and they basked warm in the sunlit yard. Strong-nerved customers won themselves an honor guard of lupine company. No one was ever robbed or injured along the path to Gram's cottage. The gardens brimmed with herbs and flowers beyond naming. Some folks claimed that Gram's wolves paced the village at night, stealing secrets and bringing them home to bloom. Indulgence curdled into curiosity, into gossip, into fear. As her son grew toward manhood, Gram's name sent sweet sullen whispers around the wells and cottage tables of her town.

Those whispers stung Gram's son. A bold-featured boy whose face recalled his father's ghost, he lacked their family's gift for nature. He was a shaper, a moulder, a grinder, a hammerer. Forsaking his mother's garden and his father's axe, the young man took up the smithing trade. His ears echoed with the pounding of the forge. His hands tingled with the blows of steel on steel. His words huffed and clanged with blunt impatience, and the cottage gardens soon groaned behind stone walls and iron fences. The wolves snapped at him and he snapped back. What few words passed between Gram and her son held a ragged edge as he reached manhood and took a wife.

Gram's son claimed the weaver's pretty daughter as his mate; Gram, though, had little patience for the bitter-tongued girl. The wife, in return, had no great love for Gram, and though the three shared the cottage Gram's husband had built, its walls soon paled from the venom of their words. Fence posts bristled with glistening hooks. Stone walls crawled with restless ivy or abruptly collapsed, crushing frail shoots and crackling bushes beneath their weight. Distressed, the wolves fled the garden and feasted on caged lambs and shrieking cattle. By the time the first grandchild swelled the weaver's daughter's belly, Gram had bundled necessities in a heavy leather pack, gathered up her wolves, and headed off down a path as thin as treachery through the spring-dappled woods.

Now, these were not the slim and sickly woods at the borders of man's world. These were the edges of the Old Wood, where the first seeds of Creation took root and grew. Gram hustled her bundle and wolfpack through ravines, bore them over rivers, wrestled them up stark cliffs from which you could see ten thousand kingdoms at a glance. In her wake, Gram left toadstools ripe with curses, and glens bold with flower-songs. When she spoke to herself or to her wolves, the syllables blossomed into crimson stagweeds and spectre-pale widowcrook; when she'd meet a fellow traveler, her words tumbled to the ground and grew into succulent fruit. She sang at the birds, dusted the dirt with pollen, and muttered at nothing in particular, leaving briars where she'd stood. The deeper she went, the more her words flowered. What had been a strange talent in the village where she'd lived now became a lush inheritance. Gram loved the Old Woods, and they loved her in return.

The wolfpack flowed through those woods at her sides, at her lead, at her heels. The merciful wolf paced beside Gram, often drifting ahead but never out of sight. Each evening, they surrounded her, carrying back torn rabbits and ravaged deer carcasses as she kindled fires and sang up herbs. She tended them, they tended her, and though all but the bravest living things dashed off when Gram's pack neared, the season cloaked them in mist, bathed them with cool rains, and anointed them with filtered sun.

Four days and three nights out from Gram's old cottage, one clearing finally felt like home. Perched on the edge of a deep pond fed by nearby waterfalls, the moist soil hosted festivals of bright-hued magnificence. Lush spans of bright blue candlemere bobbed their heads in the faint breeze. A rash of violet roses climbed the balenor trees at the clearing's edge. Mist filtered the early morning light, ghost-breath-like and luminous as love. Gram set down her pack, took out her tools, and began to shape the wild to her will. Slowly, day by day, she plied the skills and talents of her family, raising a fine, if tiny, cottage and surrounding it with song-birthed gardens.

Each night at dusk, the kind-eyed wolf came to visit her, bringing gifts of fresh meat and company. Each full moon, Grandma reached naked to the sky, a crone dancing to deep wolfsong. The wolf brought packmates to her clearing and they helped her pray all night. Each morning of those exultations, new flowers bloomed outside the cottage. In no time, they filled the clearing, drawing, in turn, birds and beasts of all descriptions.

But wild places breed wild things… and the wild shaped her, too.

As time passed, Gram grew gaunt and feral-lean. Twigs and thistles wove themselves in her hair. Dirt blackened her fingernails and soles. Woven pelts soon replaced her threadbare clothes. Gram smelled of musk and sweet-turned earth, the herbs she gathered, and the beasts she ate. Gram's eyes glowed wolf-shine in the early morning mist. Yet her cottage remained clean, its contours shaped with skilled precision. She swept the stone floors clear of dust, and carved statues out of wood and stone. Filigrees of unknown languages danced across the walls and etched themselves in the earth. Were they warnings? Tales? Enchantments? Only Gram could say.

At times, the ancient presence of the Wood bore down on her with all the pressure years could bear. She awoke some mornings weeping for her son, stirred by dreams of bellies swollen with fresh life. As the seasons turned, Gram envisioned grandchildren sired and birthed in the cottage built by her husband's hands. Her own hands gnarled like old kindling, but her voice stayed strong and her step held the lightness of the girl she'd been. Her wolfpack never seemed to age; like stones, they held time to their breast and watched man's seasons fade.

Once or twice per season, Gram trekked back through the forests toward town, flanked by runner-wolves and her kindly-eyed companion. As she walked, time turned back upon itself, as it so often does in the Old Woods; one trip might last a single day, another passed in an afternoon, and still other trips seemed to last a week or more. Although Gram followed the path she'd blazed, it never ran the same way twice. So long as Gram kept to that path, she'd always reach her destination. Once, in curiosity, she wandered off to form a new path, and then got lost for weeks. It's said that she eventually found the edge of the world, where raw cliffs plunge into nothingness, and might have been lured off the side by the voices of the dead had the kind-eyed wolf not found Gram and led her home again.

Gram never strayed from her path after that.

But solitary woods breed monotony for human minds… and so, she'd wander from time to time back into town, sun-browned skin ripened like old apples, and silver hair spilling from her hood.

215

Children ran to cluster in her shadow, plucking flowers of endearments as she bent to rustle their tiny heads. She would trade precious herbs with the merchants in their stalls, fetching salt and tools and cloth to take back home.

Once or twice in these visits, Gram thought she'd seen her son and his family; if so, however, the years had gnarled them both. Where he'd once been slim and strong, the man she saw now trundled with unhappy weight. The viper-faced woman at his side stood thin as parchment, dense with sure unspoken threats. The children crouched at their sides, drowsy monks shorn of the vitality that proper children know. Each time, like a pack of sullen monkeys, the family slid into the market crowds before Gram could call out to them. In the thin cover of the marketplace, they seemed elusive as scared deer. Gram frowned at this but refused to chase them. Whispers slipped from her pursed lips, though, and grew thorny flowers where they fell.

Some folk in the village remembered Gram well; others drew back from her presence and held their children close. She was a rumor, a demon, a flicker of nameless dread. Where certain folk smiled, others cringed. Mama Thistle, they called her… or Gramma Wolf.

Gram did not come to the village alone. Though he stayed well out of sight at the borders of the town, the kind-eyed wolf and his pack watched for her return. When she would emerge from the market, heavy with tears and trade-goods, the wolf licked her hand and nuzzled her face and sang wild songs for her. In time, they'd leave the town behind, Gram's step lightening with each league until she walked with sure and feral steps. Each journey into town became a trip through time – a visit back to youth that left her old until she left the town behind and became young again.

Years passed. Trees grew. Children became young adults while their parents soon turned old. Whispers crept out of the woods, settling in hungry ears. Gram, the whispers said, was wealthy, was a witch, was hiding gold beneath her garden's soil. She was younger now, claimed the tales, than her own son was. Back in town, Gram's son and his wife creaked with bitter age. Their own children, thick as mossy stumps, became mirrors of their impermanence.

And so, the son and his wife decided, they would visit Gram in the woods, and coax from her that secret of eternal youth.

Knives and axes struck bright sparks from the whetting stone that night.

The next morning, Gram's son, and his three sons, and a daughter who was more boy than girl all set off to find the path that led to Gram's clearing. They whispered to one another of plans and treacheries. Dull words fell from them like stones, shot through with glimmers of fool's gold and iron red. They hefted sacks and axes, with sharp knives clenched along their belts. Back home, the wife and three more daughters brewed grim bread and razor tea. Their garden rustled thick with worms and dead things left for soil. A stout chair with iron bands awaited Gram's return.

In the woods, the wind caught snatches of the plan and brought them to the kind-eyed wolf. He ground them between his teeth like bones and then spat them into the dirt.

The ground shook, and the brooks shivered, and the trees rose up their roots to trip the ironsmith and his children. Boots tangled and men swore. Branches wove in tight together, plunging the forest into early darkness. Overhead, the birds cried warnings.

And the pack prepared.

The kind-eyed wolf called his kin. From all across the land, they came: red wolves and black wolves and wolves as gray as slate. They slipped through the woods on ghostly paws.

Gram felt the land shiver, and she howled with despair.

There are winds born on the tongues of mothers, rumbles beneath their bones where new lives begin. The hearthfires of eternity beck and crackle in the wombs of every birthing woman, and their embers never truly still. For Gram, those winds and bones and fires coiled into wordless tears that spilled from her in coruscating streams. Sorrow cracked through her like a whip-strike in still air, leaving Gram bent and shivering in its wake.

Sensing the approaching wolves, the smith and his children struck flint into fire and raised torches toward the meddling trees. Their mouths tumbled curses. Calloused palms and fingers tightened around worn-smooth axe-handles. Their eyes flickered, watching the trees. And yet they walked further into the forest, intent on the treasures of Gramma Wolf.

She saw them through the trees, watched them move along the path, spied on them through leagues of distance through the power of the Old Woods. If she'd willed it, her son and his children would be lost, wandering through the Old Woods until the skin slid from their bones.

Gram considered this.

Watched it in her mind's eye.

Saw days and weeks glide along their starving limbs until, one by one, they fed the worms, never once approaching her home.

And her tears became flowers of ripe and pulsing blue.

"Let them come," she told the Woods. "Let him come to see my home."

Gathering her tear-flowers up, Gram took an earth-formed vase and called out to the kind-eyed wolf. With firm cries, she howled him home. Her voice pricked the ears of the gathering wolves. Ashamed, they slipped into the shade and left the smith alone.

Emboldened, the smith and his children spoke of wealth and immortality. They joked about the gold of Gramma Wolf. They laughed as the sun cut through the trees again, but their laughter held the edge of broken slate.

The kind-eyed wolf ran home to her, and he caught the family's secrets in his jaws. Those secrets turned to flowers as he ran. He dropped them at her doorway and called out to her. Gram let him in, gathered up those blood-bruise blossoms, and placed his flowers in the vase alongside her own. Watered, the flowers began to speak: about her son's treachery, his wife's ambitions, their children's selfishness, the plans they had for her in the house her husband built. She learned what the townsfolk said of her, heard the whispers of her wealth.

"Let them have it," she finally said. "Let them have it all."

Gram dashed the vase to the floor. The flowers scattered and went silent. Reaching for the wolf, Grandma melted into him. Wolf and woman became one, and Gramma Wolf ran off into the forest.

The family arrived just in time to see Gramma Wolf disappear beneath the trees. Finding nothing but a smashed vase, dying flowers and a lifeless cottage, they invented a tale of

Gramma-eating wolves when they returned home two days later, their sacks heavy with food and flowers and pillaged goods.

Lies breed lies, but Truth grows in fertile ground.

The girl who looked like a boy heard the whispers first. The blue flowers told her that she had been another man's child. She quarreled with her mother, who cut out the girl's tongue and pushed her down a well.

The youngest grandson heard the bruise-red flowers speak. They told him to cut open his eldest brother's throat. He did, and a diamond fell out. The boy grabbed the diamond and fled into the night.

The food they'd stolen turned to rust in their bellies. Their pots and pans crumbled into dirt. Bright leaves sprouted from their fingertips. The forge threw itself at the smith, shattering his legs and feet. Each night brought new whispers. Each day brought fresh calamities. The garden's night-blooming jarrowbanes, once deep blue, soon glowed with bright red spots. Curses flew and axes flashed. Only one of the smith's sons escaped alive, and he remained mute until his dying day.

Soon the townsfolk came and burned the old house to the ground.

Ash-white flowers grew in its dust.

Deep in the woods, Gramma Wolf still lives. Her two spirits transcend one flesh. To this day, she keeps a cottage near her waterfall, dancing in its garden each night. Since the old house burned, she has nothing to fear. Each spring, some folks say, she looks younger than she had the year before.

Townsfolk still visit her. They bring her goods from the marketplace. No one speaks of treasure anymore, and if they plot or gossip, they do so quietly. The wolves are listening, and the wind, and the flowers and the trees. Gramma Wolf no longer comes to town. The Old Woods speak her name.

If you follow the path past the ash-white grove, you may find the way to Gramma's house. Be careful where you step, and be kind to everything you meet. The forest watches, and it never forgets.

Near a waterfall, you may find her, dancing or brewing or tending her garden with the wolves. Her hair shines gray but her skin holds the freshness of youth. Even so, her eyes could match the stars for age. When she speaks, which is rare, her words sound smooth as polished wood. There's no iron in her home, nothing forged. Each tool and vessel has been shaped from earth or wood or skin or stone. Her hearth and kitchen hold the rich scent of trust.

Gramma Wolf brews heady mead, thick with the promise of ever-bursting spring. The vivid blooms of her garden are said to be among the finest found in any realm.

Just be truthful around them. You never know what they might say.

THE GREEN TUNNEL

For Shadow, Hyper, and Pooka

Together we stand rooted on the edge, staring off with perfect clarity toward infinite horizons.

You can't download this. You can't watch it on YouTube or hear it on Spotify. The magic of technology can't share or capture this. The only way to experience it is to get sweaty and leave your comfort zone, strapping your life on your back and taking on the Green Tunnel in the flesh.

Hikers call it "the Green Tunnel" because that's how it feels inside: a vast corridor of trees and dirt and vegetation, snaking along the Appalachian Mountains, tucked between towns like some pocket dimension of incomprehensible age. You won't see it from your car window on the Interstate, though trail-heads flicker on the edges of rural roads. In settlements along the way, gamey specters drift in and out of the Tunnel's course – matty-haired and earth-redolent, hauling weather-beaten packs buckled to their bodies with arcane arrays of straps. Hyper and I joined that vagabond horde a few years back; now, on the cusp of afternoon, we rise from misty wilderness and stare out speechless at the rolling scene.

Humps of earth and greenery slope up from cloud-wrapped eternity. Light-jewels of distant towns sparkle on the landscape. A pearly sheen glows across the contours of the sky, ringing rainbows in silent symphonies below. "Wow," breathes Hyper, shrugging stiffness from her shoulders. Silence. And then again, "Wow."

If I seem hyperbolic here, it's because no simple words do justice to the sheer magnificence of humping your way up a mountainscape in time to catch the last bits of afternoon clinging to a late-April sky. Hyper and I have been on the Trail for three weeks now, shedding what little fat we'd acquired and replacing it with lean tanned muscle. I've never been truly *out* of shape in my life, but twice-a-week gym routines won't give you *this* kind of build. As for Hyper, she's got the glow and eagerness of the track star she was in high school. Scraping the edge of our fourth decades, we could each run rings around kids half our age. Still, by the time we hit this clearing, not far from the mountain's peak, we're both ready to drop our packs and call it a day.

Not yet, though...

"I wish," she says, "that we could share this view with everyone on earth."

I nod. "Maybe if they could see it," I add, "folks would spend less time in front of TVs and computer screens, and more time doing shit that *matters*."

It's an old gripe of ours – one we've shared since we met up in REI almost ten years ago. It's one reason we've been friends. A big reason we'd split up this past year from the folks who'd tried to tie us down. Hyper and I both share a draw toward the woods, and we're impatient with people who think life comes over the counter in a box.

The night she'd called to tell me she was leaving Greg, Hyper's voice had held a spark I hadn't heard from her in years. My own voice might have held the same quality a few months later when I told her that Veronica and I had given up trying to make things work. When she showed up in her Amazing Flying Pumpkin Truck – a huge old Ford painted a grotesque shade of orange – to help me pack up my things, Hyper's grin had flashed like Arctic sunshine. "Ready to join the dating pool again?" she'd asked.

"Not really." I wasn't. Dating sucked.

"Oh, good," she'd replied. "Then we can just fuck."

"Huh?"

"Jerry," she told me, stepping close, "we both blew a really good thing by getting married to people who weren't right for us. I don't know what that means for us long-term, but right now..." She grabbed my shirt. "I want to do things to you that I've been thinking about for *years*."

And we did.

And oh, God – she was right. We really *did* have a good thing going on between us.

Hyper's the kind of friend you knock back beers with after shitty days at work. The kind who'll challenge you to a good-natured arm-wrestling contest – and the loser buys the next round. The sort of charismatic powerhouse who either drives guys wild or drives 'em away. She and I had seen each other through more failed relationships than God. When we finally hopped the Just Friends barricade, we both realized what we'd been missing all those years.

And so – once we'd both hashed out our respective divorces, set aside vacation time, and recognized that neither of us was "just fucking" when said fucking involved each other – Hyper and I dusted off our gear, replaced a few items that had gone creaky with disuse, and did something we'd been talking about for almost as long as we'd been friends: We hit the Appalachian Trail with plans to through-hike it from Georgia to Maine.

Three weeks into a five-month trip, we're having the time of our lives.

Hiking and camping can be an acid test to love and friendship. Paired with the wrong people (as both of us had been before), outdoor trips can become nightmares of resentment and complaint. Paired with the right people, though, a long hike becomes communion – a sharing of selves and memories that deepen more the further you get from what most folks call "real life." The aching muscles and primal smells and meager food and green monotony carve away the working-week façade. Even with top-shelf gear, you recall what it's like to be an animal.

Most people can't handle that. We can.

We'd gone rogue from the white-blazed Trail sometime early yesterday. Following deer-trails and renegade campsites, we'd decided to literally go off the beaten path. Crisscrossing the edges of the usual course, we'd bushwhacked our way to dead ends, rotting cabins, hunting blinds, and old moonshine stills gone rusty with age. Each night, we'd lay down camp, curl up in zipped-together sleeping bags, and roll in one another's musk. Four days out from our last decent bath, we smell like raw earth, raw sex, and all other good things in life.

"Wow," she sighs again, gazing out across the empty space. The cliff in front of us curves down and out, a steep slope riding into the fog and trees below. A faint purple spot darkens the haze near a ledge of the cliff, just before another sheer drop to the forest at its foot.

The cliff reminds me faintly of Devil's Tower, a tourist spot in North Carolina. According to local legend, Native American boys used to climb the cliff as a manhood rite. If they turned back, they weren't yet considered ready to become men; if they slipped, they didn't *survive* long enough to be men. I have no idea whether or not the story's true. But as we gaze off down the slope, I see mind's-eye phantoms of Cherokee ghosts struggling for a peak they'll never attain.

Hyper snuggles close to me, and I keep such thoughts to myself.

"Still glad we did this," she asks.

"Gladder than I've been about almost anything in my life."

"Me too," she agrees. "But I'm hungry. Let's make camp and have some chow."

As we pick out a spot and break out our gear, Hyper and I follow silent rhythms. Our first few tries at making camp – like the first few times you share sex with a new partner – soon gave way to a comfortable flow. Hardly needing words, we now select a good site (smooth, no bug-nests, relatively flat but not in a low spot that might flood) and then fall into the habitual tasks. I clear away sticks and stones. Hyper rigs a spot to hang our food. We pop the tent together and rearrange a ring of stones that had clearly once been a fire pit.

As I unpack the cooking gear, she walks up behind me, runs her fingers through my tangled hair, then ducks off to score some firewood. I hear her boots crack off through the underbrush.

"Hey, Scruffy," she calls softly, using my Trail name, a few minutes later. "Check *this* out."

By that point, the daylight's beginning to shade into nightfall. The thick tree-cover screens out most of the remaining sun, so when I rise to follow her voice I snag the small red flashlight I carry in my pack.

A faint deer-trail slopes up away from our campsite, winding upward toward the mountain peak. The official Trail runs close by, but our spot's tucked off to one side – close enough for safety, far enough for privacy.

Now, normally the Appalachian Trail hugs the tops of each mountain, sliding across the peaks like some back-snapped serpent. That's not true, though, everywhere. In some places the blazed Trail slides away from the peak itself, hugging the summit but leaving the top alone. On this mountain, a dense crop of old-growth trees crowns the peak. Thick thorny underbrush congregates around those trees, dressed with flashes of bright purple flowers. A soft plushy scent, like fresh ground beef yet not exactly meaty, drifts nearby.

"Hey, Hyper – where'd you go?" My voice feels muffled in the cool humid air. I don't shout (that just feels *rude* in the wilderness) but my voice should carry more than it seems to do.

"Here. Over here." Her voice sounds muffled too. It's weird, the ways in which woods and atmosphere can play hell with acoustics. Stepping carefully around the briars, I follow the sound of the woman I love.

Yeah, it feels odd to say that: *the woman I love.* After V-Ron and I had split up, I figured I'd burnt out every shred of poetry in my soul. Much as I hate to admit it to myself… and, to be blunt, haven't yet admitted it to *her*… I fell in love with Hyper years ago. Back when Veronica and I were waltzing through hot ashes, I'd been kicking myself on a regular basis for choosing her over Hyper. What the *fuck*, I'd asked myself through many restless nights, had I been *thinking?* Until she'd made the first move, though, I'd locked Hyper up in a vault labeled "Friendship." Months later, it's still kind of awkward opening that door, even from the inside.

The Green Tunnel rustles with a rising wind. There's more than a hint of rain in its bite. "Hey, Hyper," I repeat, "it's starting to feel stormy. We'd better grab some wood and finish setting up."

"Yeah," she agrees, somehow suddenly next to me, her arms cradling a wealth of kindling. "Still, though – check *this* out."

She points toward a gathering of stones: smooth, configured, wound up in purple-flowered briars. The trees on either side give them room, as if – and I don't know *why* this occurs to me – frightened of what those stones might say, and yet fascinated by their possibility of speech.

They don't seem random, these stones. They look *purposeful*, as if huddled for some awful judgment.

"If I didn't know better – and I'm not sure I *do*," she whispers, "I'd swear someone *built* stuff up here."

"We're on top of a mountain in the middle of nowhere," I reply. Still, I think she might be right.

"People build weird shit on mountains all the time." Hyper's voice remains soft, her words half-lost in the deepening wind.

By now, the clack of branches sounds like dancing bones overhead. Again, I don't know why that image occurs to me. The Trail, to me, is usually a place of peace. This spot, though, creeps me out.

Hyper's freckled face slips into that grin of hers I adore. The breeze picks at the frazzled remnants of her braid, making it tic like a snake-tail running down her back. Her rich trail-scent blooms with mischief. "I think" she says, there's graffiti on those stones."

Flicking on the flashlight beam, I slide it across one grim stone face. She's right. There's lettering. Nothing I can read, but it combines spraypaint with age-weathered etchings. Old and new, shaming the stone.

"God," I mutter. "Some people are such *dicks*."

Hyper shakes her head. "Yep. Losers. I wonder what it was."

"Probably some old Native American stuff. Or a Civil War fortification." You see that kind of shit all over the Appalachians: mountain-man monuments, hunting lodges fallen to ruins. Civil War bunkers and pre-White Incursion sites, jumbled up with more recent additions by artistic hikers, hermits, and just plain weirdos. Most of it's pretty far off the Trail; every now and then, though, you'll find something closer to the beaten path. Since we're slightly off that path to start with, it's not really that unlikely.

See now, I know what you're thinking: *Get the fuck out of there.* Yeah, I've seen the movies. Don't camp near spooky stones.

Thing is, by that point, we don't have much choice. With night coming on and the wind picking up, we'd have to break down our campsite, re-pack our gear, and head off down the Trail in the dark… very probably in the rain as well. *Not* an option if we can help it. You want a horror movie? Try busting up a campsite and blundering around on a dark mountaintop as a storm blows in. Who needs Freddy Kruger when Mother Nature can kill you just as dead?

So yeah – while I admit that the place kinda creeps me out, I keep my mouth shut and nod back to the campsite. "We can check it out in the morning," I tell Hyper. "We should set up our stuff before the rain comes in."

"Good idea." She nods, stepping carefully but noisily through the brush. "Let's see if we can get some fire going before that storm rolls in."

That *meat-not-meat* scent rides on the breeze as I reach for some of the wood in her arms. Hyper grins again, handing some of her horde off to me.

"Hey Scruffy," she says softly. "Thanks."

"For what? For the wood?"

"For the You. Thanks for that."

"I'm just me."

"I like you."

"I like you, too."

I kiss Hyper's forehead and we take the wood back to the pit.

Thankfully, the rain holds off until after we've built a fire, had dinner, hung the food up away from our tent, and snuggled a bit by the fire. Heavy woodsmoke drowns the scent of those purple flowers up the hill. Which, I realize when it hits me, I'm good with.

"How ya doin', Scruff?" she asks me as I stretch out the kinks in my back. Sloshing a bit of filtered water around in our tiny cooking pot, Hyper cleans the dinner gear. Rolled sleeves flash the eagle-feather tats on her forearms. I've traced each design countless times with my fingertips. Hell, I was *with* her when she got the second one – the design she got after she'd dumped Greg. I haven't been inked myself just yet… but I'm thinking about it.

"I'm good," I tell her, "Hyper." Her birth-name's Hilary, but no one – on or off the Trail – ever calls her that. She picked up her name in high school, where she'd run circles around jock-boys who thought they were God's gift to girls. Even now, she shakes the sloshing pot around with fierce energy. Three weeks in the wilderness hasn't calmed her down. I'm not sure much *can*. "As usual," I continue, "you wore me out."

Hyper barks her trademark laugh. Something probably runs off in the woods at the sound. "You poor thing," she replies, "I hope you're not *too* worn out."

I lean over her and prove that I'm not. She tastes like smoke and sweat and rehydrated chicken with rice. I savor that sensation.

Two things about the mountains:

First off, when it gets dark, it gets *DARK*. Dark in *ways-city-folks-don't-understand*-level Dark. Unless you've got a decent moon that night, the only other light is star-shine… and if you're in the woods, the tree-cover blocks that light. Darkness on that level permeates your world. It surrounds you like a physical thing. You breathe it – just one more scent in a realm washed through with scents. Unless you're out in the open, it gets dark long before the sun goes down. In the Green Tunnel, you move through twilight as a matter of course. Full sunlight becomes the exception, not the rule. And as for the electric haze that fills any modern settlement, it's gone. Stand on top of a mountain as the sun goes down, watching the gleam of distant towns and cities, and you'll realize just how small we really are.

Secondly, it's *cold*. In spring, it can still fall below freezing at night. And while the days might grow sticky-hot near high noon, the thin air, raw earth and tree cover keep things moist on the East Coast and dry further out west. Without the heat-trapping properties of paved civilization, Mother Nature's curves stay cool by day and get downright cold after dark.

By the time wet drops of rain start to catch in our hair, the wind's picked up and the trees sway, drunken, in its pull. Braches clack their primal tongues as we gather up our gear, douse the fire, and stir the ashes black. Stripping off our boots and socks, we climb inside the tent, bring them in, and pull the zipper closed. Hollow patters on the roof and walls let us know that the storm has arrived.

Shivering with chill, we peel off our layers and slide against each other's skins. Pebbled flesh warms beneath our hands. Our lips brush against each other, then open, then go wide. Our own tongues catch the rhythm of the trees outside, tangle like vines, and seek each other's heat.

The sky cracks open with shattering light.

The answering thunderclap shakes the whole mountain.

"Holy *crap*," she whispers. I agree.

A wind-borne slash of rain bows the tent's fabric. I'd swear I hear the plastic poles creak.

Too damn close, something big cracks, breaks, and falls. Brittle things smash beneath its weight.

"Somebody," Hyper says, voice hushed, "is trying to remind us who's boss."

"She's made her point."

She didn't stop there.

Here's another one of those things you forget when you're in a nice safe house: Mother Nature's *BIG*. Bigger than us. Bigger than our gadgets and technology. When Mama ain't happy, ain't *nobody* happy. And while I can't know her mind when the storm hits our mountain, my guess is she's in a mood tonight.

Our tent ripples and snaps, its nylon sides billowing from the force of the wind. The poles bow with alarming strain. Rain pounds the mountaintop, stirring up a heady wild smell. Mud and ashes mulch into gray burnt smells blending, in my nose, with a wet-nylon bite.

"Wow," I mutter. "Glad we're not out *there*."

Flickers and blasts rock the sky in dazzling fractures of darkness and bright. Trees scream with enduring agony. Everything that can run has gone to ground, huddling – like us – in a state of terse amazement.

Skin to skin, Hyper and I wrap ourselves together. The sleeping bag suddenly feels too small to contain us. We shuck the bag, and cling, and burn. Muddy nails and unbrushed teeth dig past flesh and draw each other's blood.

Inside and outside, it's a storm we'll never forget.

Somehow, the tent holds.

In time, as they do, all storms pass.

"Didn't use the condoms, did we?"

"Uh…" I think about it. "Nope."

"Y'know," says Hyper, "I'm okay with that."

Despite the cold that snaps through me at her words, I think I might be, too.

Neither one of has used the L-word yet. Not seriously, with regards to Us… whatever Us is.

I suspect we've grown too wary to talk about it. Words like love get brittle when they've been burned. So, in the dark, we roll together and slip back into the sleeping bags, ripe with the smell of Nature's kiss.

I keep kidding myself that the poetry I used to write had run off and died when V-Ron and I called it quits. I'd felt it cowering in dark corners of my head for years, like some kid beaten past the point of tears. With Hyper, though, that poor kid's been sticking his head up more and more often. He's not quite ready to sing just yet but at least he's remembered how to speak to me.

As for Hyper, she doesn't say much along those lines to begin with. Feelings are something she *has*, not something she talks about. At times, when I back away from asking, I try to read her face and body language. Sometimes that's like reading Newsweek, and sometimes it's like reading Braille.

The dark has taken over now. Raindrops rustle down the tent, translucent vagabonds on a downward trail. *Wow – this woman's really turned me inside-out.* I hope she can't read the scares blooming in my head when I realize that.

As the realization settles in and we snuggle deeper into ourselves, I kiss her greasy hair and realize it's okay.

This time out, it'll all be okay.

I'm hungry.

A growl-gutted craving for something bare...

Naked walls paneled in dark smooth woods, a Brady Bunch lair gone bad. Silver implements sparkle across a white-clothed table, bright-spotted with red flowers of romance.

Cables drawn in sharp fixations bloom and open. Rose mouths crying for the sun. Pucker tight and then slide free. A course, of course. The road to blank fulfillment, wrapped in grease.

Light too spare to see by. Shadow-blank with lamentation. Reliquary blossoms quiver in the air.

Bright-synapse fires near the verge. Sliver-moon and meat perfume. Soft clenching between my jaws. Salt-slip of pink-white flavor red.

"He was hungry, so he ate himself."

I'm up.

Man, sometimes I hate dreams.

Listen to the rain hiss against the tight tent walls. Feel the curve of Hyper's back against my side.

In time, I fall back asleep, meat-perfume curling on the edges of my mind.

A warm breath in my ear. A whisper. "Hey."

A touch along my shoulder. A soft slide of fingertips.

A kiss on the back of my neck. Am I dreaming?

"Hey, Scruff. Get up."

Solid dark. Not even a hint of light. The sleeping bag rustles as I stir. Cold skates across bare skin, raising ripples in its wake.

"Huh?" An insight – the true gift of a witty mind. "Something outside the tent?" I add. All I hear is her breath and the rustle of our bags.

Chilly fingers slide down to wrap around… "*Damn*, Hyper! Your hands are *cold*."

"All the better to wake you up with." Her voice glides warm and close to my ear. "C'mon, sleepyhead – get up."

"Not with *those* cold hands."

"I don't mean *that*," she replies. "At least, not yet. Let's go outside and dance."

Is this another dream? I'm not certain. Either way, she takes my hand and we crouch naked in the tiny tent. The zipper's growl seems especially loud in the all-but-silent night. Is it Hyper's fingers, or mine, that guide it open? Again, I'm not sure. Our skin prickles with the chilly rush of night. Knees popping, Hyper rise from the tent's doorway. She steps out, and so do I.

Outside our tent, the air trembles with pearlescent gloom. A faint shine illuminates the night. Chilly breeze stirs our hair, raising sheets of goosebumps across our flesh. I sense, more than see, Hyper's crazy grin. The cold mud, course with sticks and stones, slides against our feet. Wet sounds mark our progress as we leave our tent behind.

Something high above us shimmers, hazy constellations of uncanny luminescence. Looking up, I feel myself fall into the void. My feet stay rooted to the mud, but it seems as though some perverse gravity draws me upward without moving me at all. Vertigo spins through my guts, and I have to look down and away.

Hyper raises her hands to the sky, her nude skin glowing in the half-light. Eyes closed, she arcs her head back. Her ragged braid dangles to her waist, flicking restless as she starts to move. Her hips rock back and forth in slow-motion imitation of our dance beneath the storm.

I feel myself begin to move as well – not conscious but with pure instinct.

The night begins to sing.

It vibrates up through the ground, through my feet. A vast chorus, deep as valleys, deep as mines sunk underneath our world. Root-blind and shivering, it twines itself around my bones, a sound too low or high for mortal ears to hear. Hyper's head swivels in her neck, mouth open, a faint rumble swelling in her throat. Her hands reach for the hungry stars, crawling softly in time with the music.

Meat-perfume blossoms in the hazy air, sliding down my throat as I, too, begin to sway.

Our throats make no human sounds at all. But we *do* join the chorus as we dance.

As if standing outside myself, I see us bend and shimmer in the haze. Sweat blooms on once-chilly skins. Our heads hang back at incredible angles, our arms coiling like sunlight-shattered worms. The sounds bubbling from our throats seem to glisten in the air like slime, sounds given viscous and repugnant form. It's a dream again – it *must* be. We dance impossible things.

Sticky sounds draw me off from the eerie spectacle. I leave Hyper and myself behind and slide noiseless to the edge of the cliff. Out past the edge, the sky still boils with pregnant clouds, their bellies torn by lightning wounds. Vertigo pulls me up and down at once, drawing my sensations in torturous directions. Back in school, I'd seen a picture in some old history book of a man being pulled apart by horses. Standing now at the edge of that cliff, I feel the way he must have felt.

A wordless scream boils up from nothingness inside.

Up the sides of the cliff, something shiny rolls across the sheer surface of the drop. Glistening balls of translucent slime, leaving slug-trail rivers in their wake. Each one larger than our tent, they roll *upward* on the steep stone. Away from gravity. Towards us. Shimmering ghost-boys made of tears.

Turning with immense effort from the cliff, I see Hyper and myself dancing near the tent.

At least I *think* that tangle of limbs and mouths is us.

But there are too many limbs and too many mouths, and it seems to be eating itself.

And we have no faces, just bristling braids twined together like snakes.

And the stars draw me up into silent cold nothingness.

The red void sings to me.

"JERRY?"

Hyper's voice. Distant. Echoing. Alarmed. "*Jerry?*"

Fucking dreams…

Um…

Oh.

That's not good.

My legs aren't supposed to bend like that.

My arms are supposed to work. But they don't.

Purple flowers and meat-perfume.

Sharp rocks and my own shattered limbs.

When I wake up, this is gonna hurt like hell.

"Jerry? Holy fuck, where *are* you?" Hyper's voice holds *another* spark I've never heard from her before: brittle bright panic.

Somehow, that chills me deeper than what I see.

Soft luminescent haze gleams in morning twilight. Shimmering motes catch the early rising sun. Tangled purple flowers grow from sharp red stones.

The stones on the ledge where I landed when I fell.

I'd like to think that's plant-juice spattered on the stones. Somehow, though, I don't think it is.

I really want to wake up.

Except I *don't*. Not really.

Hyper's voice floats on a haze of empty space, high above me, too far beyond to see.

I *do* see something else, though.

It's not good.

Plants shouldn't grow out of your chest.

Vines shouldn't burrow into your arms and legs.

Purples flowers shouldn't inhale when you try to breathe.

Meat-smell perfume and the scent of unwashed man.

And blood – yeah, *lots* of blood.

Try to call out.

Instead, I sing.

Without words, without breath.

Sounds vibrate through my bones, grimly wrestling with the first dull seeds of pain.

"JERRY! C'mon, motherfucker, where ARE you?" Hyper's voice edges over into rage shot through with fear rushing swiftly towards terror. "Don't make me look…" She doesn't finish the sentence, but a vaguely Hyper-shaped darkness appears on the cliff's edge high overhead.

I can hear her voice but the words are too faint to understand.

Then, pleading: *"Please,* Scruffy – tell me that's not *you* down there."

Around then, the pain digs in, a galaxy of spiders biting on my bones.

The song in my mouth grows sharp and mournful.

My mind drifts between my body and the air.

The pain should overwhelm my thoughts.

I wish it *would.*

But my mind hovers with perfect detached clarity, *aware* but not *submerged* in my horrific circumstances.

"Hang on, Scruffy. I'm gonna climb down there and get you out."

Don't, I try to say. But nothing works. Nothing but that damned demented song rising from my throat.

The Hyper-shape disappears above me. The purple plants rustle on my limbs. I try to close my eyes… but, damn it all, I still *see,* as if I'm a prisoner stuck watching some shitty horror flick where I can't take my eyes from the screen.

I'm naked, of course. My skin glows bright with vivid red paint. It's *too* red, though, *too* vivid to be real. This is a dream. Another fucking dream. Oh, good.

I'm ready to wake up now.

Really.

"No fucking cell reception here." Hyper's voice again, moving through the mist. And again, I try to warn her off. There's nothing here she can do. But then she's on the edge and moving down, barefoot, dressed in a sweatshirt and cargo pants, her hands and feet grasping for holds on the steep cliffside. "Hang on, Scruffy," she repeats. "I'm coming down."

Quicksilver anguish swells in my throat.

Trails. Glistening silver trails. As if left by giant slugs rising up the face of the cliff.

Hyper hits one of them.

Fumbles.

Slips.

Hangs in the air.

For an endless instant.

Falls.

She cracks open like a piñata filled with blood.

Her limbs shatter in impossible designs.

We both try to scream. Neither can.

But the purple flowers sing their meat-perfume aria as vines dig into her skin.

We lock eyes in awful clarity.

Then, together, helpless, we also join their song.

Rooted, endless, to a ledge lined with broken bones and flowers, our bodies quiver with lost voices and green thoughts.

And above us both, the haze darkens, and the rain begins again.

Sometimes

At night

I miss you

Spans

So deep and wide

Not even stars

Can jump across

I FEEL LUCKY

She was my girlfriend once, y'know. Before the brawls and black leather, she called herself Linda and lived with me for about two years. No, that wasn't really her name and I knew it even then. People got reasons for their secrets, though, and I respected that much. She never gave me reason to ask 'til after she left, and by then… well, you know the rest as well as anyone.

I'm still not sure why she took the path she chose, but I recall the girl she was back then. Haunted but sweet, so much so that it made my heart hurt sometimes just to look at her. Linda was always a big girl – not fat, never, but tall and strong-shouldered. She had a softness to her that you'd never guess to see her now. That sharp look you see on the news… no, that wasn't my girl. I guess there was a ghost of that running 'round in her long before we met, and I guess it kinda won in the end. For a while, though, she had a tender side. Sometimes I think about going after her and seeing how much of it – if any – is still alive in there.

Oh, hey, that reminds me – hang onto this for me, will you? Thanks.

We met in Charlie's, back before the Scotts took over. It was a high fine blues joint back then, all wood and beer-sticky tables.

I was there with Matt and Chris and Marty, checking out the Wednesday open-mic night. Place was packed, on account of Julie Penn and Cheryl Mack. The fans were going but the place was thick with sweat and smoke. I was propped up against the bar and Linda was standing nearby, and both of us kept shifting aside to let people pass by. She had her shoes off. "You're gonna get stepped on," I said. I think I was smiling.

"Oh, yeah – like *that'd* be something new." She grinned when she said it, but there were broken-glass edges in that smile. Her voice was clipped, her eyes wary. Challenging. I think that's why I kept talking. I never did like skittish girls.

We wound up sparring all night, like Hepburn and Tracy in a blues bar. She was smart. I wasn't bad, either. She bought me drinks, refused to let me return the favor. Even then, her actions said *don't own me*. She was good at being owed but never good with debt.

Speaking of drinks, you up for another round?

We kissed in the parking lot that night. It was weird. We looked at each other for a long time when I stopped by my car. She refused to let me walk her to hers. The streetlights caught her eyes, made 'em shine. We stopped breathing, I think. I leaned in a little. She never closed her eyes, so I did it for both of us.

Next thing I know, she's got me shoved up against my car. Hard. Strong. Her fingers are in my hair. There's Jack Daniels in my mouth. Hungry lips on mine. Teeth. *Damn!* I'm not sure if or when I started breathing, but we'd been there a while by that time. Suddenly, she jerked back away from me. Shook her head. "Oh, yeah," she said to herself. Shook it again. Nodded. "Oh yeah, oh yeah, oh yeah." She picked up her shoes, then. Smiled kinda shyly.

"Give me a call, huh?" I think I nodded. She walked off fast, like she was trying to get away.

She moved in three months later. The getaway came two years after that.

Yeah, she was always strong. Not like some of 'em, you know, flipping-over-cars strong. But she was a lot stronger than me, even back then. I gotta admit, and don't take this the wrong way, but I liked that. Some girls, you've gotta be careful you don't break 'em. With Linda, she was the one being careful. That first few times we made love – and yeah, it *was* love we were makin' then – she broke stuff. Three ribs. My nose. My dresser. Heh. Remember when I had that cast on my wrist? It wasn't stairs that did that. I've still got scars down my back from… well, that was a long time ago. Good thing I had good medical insurance – heh! And fast. Damn, she was quick. I had to slow down for the both of us. I don't know, sometimes, what she saw in me then. I mean, she could have worn down a football team. But she seemed satisfied with me.

Yeah, it *is* a new jacket. Nice, huh? I should have bought me one of these years ago.

Linda loved country music. Can you imagine? She had a thing for Lyle Lovette – thought he was cute. And she could sing every Trisha Yearwood song. Linda used to say that Mary Chapin's "I Feel Lucky" was her personal theme song. I think she was joking. She'd put on Rosanne Cash and cry. In bed sometimes she'd sing "City of New Orleans" when she thought I was asleep. One day, I found her listening to "Blood and Fire" with wild eyes and a throat too full to speak. Seeing those eyes, all tears and unscreamed things, I wanted to hold her, yet run far away at the same time. She sensed that hesitation and slammed the door so hard the wall cracked. Not long afterward, she left.

Maybe if I'd reached out, she'd still be here with me.

I don't know what made her that way. She had nightmares all the time, but never talked about 'em with me. I'd just hold her then, tight as I could. Run my fingers through her hair. Talk soft, like to a spooked horse. Stare into the dark and wish I could just take it all away from her. There wasn't any of that "It's just your imagination" shit between us, not even at four a.m. I wouldn't have insulted her that way. Whatever happened, it was real and it was bad and it still had bits buried deep inside of her. I think she's still trying to rip 'em out, even now.

I think that's why she does what she does.

Reporters know *nothing*. She's no sadist. She doesn't like to hurt people... 'cept maybe certain people. Every time she'd hurt me, she'd cry and say *I'msorryI'msorryI'msorry* over and over and over again. Linda had soft fingertips and gentle lips and... aw, hell, I don't wanna go there. But they're stupid and they're wrong. And I need another drink.

Heh.

We watched a lotta TV, she and I. Picture that: me and Riplash, curled up on a maroon love seat with a big mixing bowl full of popcorn, watching *Seinfeld* reruns Funny, huh? Butter breath, husks in our teeth. She wasn't Riplash then, just Linda. Big and beautiful with bed-head. Heh.

I wonder if she still remembers.

You can tell when someone's not there anymore. I mean, you can feel 'em when they're close by, even if you can't see 'em, and you know when they're not. You can feel an empty room, too, when it's really *empty*. Does that make sense? Me, I've become an expert on empty these last few years. I keep filling up the space and it just keeps feeling empty. I keep waiting for the sound of feet heavy on a hardwood floor. The creak of wood that means you're not alone. And yeah, I wake up sometimes with someone next to me, all warm and breathe-y. But they just feel like reruns. Songs I've heard too many times and that never meant that much to me the first time out. When they're gone, there's just dead air.

You're a good friend, dude. That's why I trust you with this.

Keep the key for me. I paid the rent for the next three months. After that, if I'm not back, you can have whatever you want from in there. Sell the rest, give it away, whatever. If I'm not back by September I won't be coming back. The bike's paid off, and I already took what I needed. Yeah, I should probably sober up first, I guess, but if I don't leave now, I'm not gonna. And I can't stand another morning waking up to dead air.

Heh.

I don't expect she'll be around here much longer. Linda doesn't stay where she's not wanted. I wonder if she'll recognize when she *is*. Or if she's too far gone to care. So, I wanna get on the road before she gets too far away. Right now, I have a good idea where she is. Tomorrow morning it'll be too late.

Gotta go, dude.

It's late.

But I feel lucky.

CHASER

"We've got to talk."

Gerald's words held an ominous chill. Rachel glanced up at him as they walked. His eyes seemed cold and distant as the San Francisco mist. *Here it comes,* she thought. She'd seen it coming but felt no better for the knowledge.

He quietly refused to meet her gaze; instead, he looked off into the fog. The sheen on his face reflected the orange glow of streetlights. Up above, a slice of moon glowed fuzzy in the sky. Finally, he spoke: "I think that it may… we might… maybe we shouldn't see each other like this anymore."

A blow prepared for hurts just the same. Rachel swallowed. For a long time, she said nothing, just felt the damp sand shift beneath her feet.

They walked in silence for a time before she answered. "Just like that?" The words grated in her throat like glass. Gerald nodded. He had no answer. Rachel hadn't expected him to. "Well, this certainly comes out of nowhere," she said, but she was lying. She thought she knew exactly where it had come from.

"Stand by the fire!" His eyes shine in the bonfire glow, flat and lambent as an animal's. His shirt hangs open, sleeves rolled up. Each curl of body hair catches that light and casts it back at her, gold slivers on dark skin. Their packmates, restless, pace and pose. Rachel meets his eyes, drops her gaze and shuffles forward in the sand, legs thick as iron bars.

Around her, wolves and people prowl, sand flecks glittering in their fur and skin. Some, curious, crouch forward as she steps toward the flames; others look away, grooming themselves or nuzzling one another in mock boredom. Feral malcontents, just another San Franciscan tribe… though wilder, perhaps, than most. Bandannas and dreads, young faces perched on age-worn leathers. Raw as saplings with old-man eyes. Holy sinners on the edge of the sea.

Her mentor, Beth, stares hard at Tanglewood, lean Alpha of their pack. Beth's eyes glare but her lips stay closed. She knows her place and will not speak.

Fury ripples through Rachel's skin. Again she raises her eyes to his. Won't look away. Salt air swirls with woodsmoke and prickly musk. Not far off, waves slide in, whispering. Rachel's voice catches in her throat. "This is bullshit…"

"Quiet." Soft but with the snap of command.

The rich scent of him darkens with anger. It hums in her nostrils, seeps to her bones. Each strand of familiar hair shines across his skin but now he stands distant, refusing to touch. Her toes brush sea-smoothed stones, their surface warmed by the fire they surround. Her fingers flex, their knuckles cracking in the stillness.

No one moves.

"Songchaser," he says at last, "choose."

Rachel swallows but won't look down. Beth had named her "song-chaser" as a friendly poke at Rachel's awful singing voice. The heart-name held a sense of Pack. Each one among them had a name like that. Beth went by Runnerwolf, Chuck by Tailspin, Aliea by Singefur because she sat too close to their fires. The others' day-names remained hidden from her, one more step of separation between their human world and this netherspace they shared. This shelter of impossible grace.

"Choose what?" She hates the weakness in her voice.

"Whether you're with us," he says softly, "or alone."

"So," she asked Gerald, "how long have you been thinking about this?"

"A few weeks." Gerald, oblivious, walked beside her, searching the night mist for answers.

"How long?"

"Over a month," he admitted.

Rachel glanced up sharply. The pack had ditched her three weeks earlier. "Any particular reason?"

He shook his head. "Lots of reasons. I can't put them into words."

"How about trying?" She looked at her feet, sticky with sand, as they walked. Doubt, fear, fury swirled up the back of her throat and burned. Eyes closed, she bit her lower lip. "I need answers."

They walked for a while, no one speaking but the waves.

"I haven't felt too good about us lately," he admitted. "It's a lot of little things."

"So you said." Feral things surged beneath her skin. "Care to be more specific?"

Garlic fear-sweat buzzed between them, drowning out the sea.

"Look," he said, stopping, "we're pretty young, okay?" This was true; Rachel was just shy of twenty, Gerald slightly older. "Let's be real," he continued, "things never last at this age." At her silence, his voice rose tight to a whine. "I still want to try college after all, and I don't want to go to U.C. Berkeley. I just wanna go somewhere else."

"And leave me here." Was she whining too?

"You never needed me to take care of you or anything," he shot back. "You'll find someone else."

"So will you." Rachel started walking again. She felt scabs pulled off deep inside, and the cuts still felt raw underneath. The blood from her lip tasted good. "Bastard," she muttered. Gerald didn't answer, and they walked again in silence for a while.

"Well," she demanded at length, "don't you have anything else to say?"

He shook his head and extended his hand. She refused to take it. "Rachel," he implored her, "don't be this way…"

"What way?" Her words tasted bitter. "Was there some other way I was supposed to take being dumped?"

"I'm not…" he started, then trailed off. "I guess not. No."

"I saw it coming, you know" she snapped, staring at the sand. Pinpricks sizzled on her skin. "I did. I just want a reason. I want an explanation. After almost two years, I think I deserve one." She raised her eyes to his. Gerald flinched. "*Why* are you doing this?" The question held a plea for some normal, rational, human reason. She said it knowing that Gerald had no answer, but yet wanting one regardless.

His helpless shrug said more than words could say.

SHE'D MET GERALD a few weeks after first waking up naked eight miles from home, with blood in her mouth and wolf-musk clinging to her skin. Before Beth and Tanglewood had appeared in her life, he'd been there at Cindy's party, spotting this cute wreck of a girl curled up in the corner alone. There'd been shitty wine and sloppy kisses and her eyes had been swollen from crying. Gerald touched her shoulder and asked, "Hey, there – you okay?" Rachel had always been a bad liar before, but she'd refined it to an art form since that night.

He'd been a sweet guy then, cute and awkward, too polite for his own good. It was always easy to keep her temper around him, and he accepted everything she told him with quiet deference. Her packmates, even in their human guise, made him nervous but Gerald never complained to her. He'd drifted past them, ignored their stares, won them over with calm acceptance. Rachel built a house of deceit to shield him from her life, and had kept him as a barrier against the wolf. Gerald was soft in a good way, a comfortable anchor, and she felt freer with him than she did with the pack. Their walks on the beach became a ritual, a cleansing of her spirit.

He'd stood at the gateway to her humanity, grounding the woman that the wolf could not command.

Now his voice felt ocean-cold and his eyes were hard as glass.

He stopped and turned away, looking out into the endless dark. Waves rumbled and hissed just out of sight. Mist danced across the slivered moon. "I'm not sure where we're going, Rachel," he said after a while. "We've been together for a long time, but I don't see where we're going."

"That's a lot of crap." Her tone was quiet and sharp. She restrained sudden urge to shove him in the water and scream out the fury just beneath her words. Deep below her skin, Rachel felt other, darker urges. Something inside her twisted and uncoiled. Sensing it, he stepped back. She pursued him, caught by fury and instinct.

Sea air blossomed with hunting scents.

Rachel snarled. He backed up further. "Don't give me that shit, Gerald." The words grated in her throat. "I know you too well." She met his fearful eyes, her own stare predatory-flat. "Be straight with me," she purred. "Is there someone else or are you just bored?"

Her words stung. "*Fuck* you! This isn't easy for me–"

"Well it's a real treat for *me.*"

"You don't–"

"No, I *don't!*"

"*Listen!*"

Their eyes locked.

A thick pulse, beating.

A moment, a surge where she thought perhaps he might rise to what she needed.

Then:

"You're asking," he said softly, "for something I don't have."

Waves, not words, filled the silence.

Gerald glanced down to the sand. "There's nobody else, Rachel," he finally added. "No. I just… Feelings don't always make sense. We can't…" He slumped. "I have to go. I'm sorry."

You will be, said the wolf.

"*I get this hierarchy thing and all,*" *she says.* "*It's really just not me.*"

His mouth twitches. "*You don't know what's 'just you' yet. That's the problem.*"

"*It doesn't have to be.*" *She spreads her hands, placating.* "*Look… Jesus, we're* people, *right? Not animals–*"

"*Wrong!*" *Tanglewood snaps.* "People *are* animals. Especially us. Especially* you. *That's the part you don't want to understand.*" *He smells now like an animal – an angry one.* "*You're still too young to wrap—*"

"*Y'know, I'm truly* sick *of hearing that.*"

Even the sea holds its breath.

Rachel doesn't catch the hint. "You keep telling me how young and stupid I must be and that's just fuc–"

She can't see him move until her feet clear the sand.

Lean muscles hold her easily at arm's length. Rank musk boils between them. Strong fingers choke the words in her throat.

He pulls her close enough to smell the wolf on his breath. Flat red shimmers in the back of his eyes. His snarl sets her hair on end.

She swallows hard, drops her gaze to the sand and closes her eyes.

He drops her at the fire's edge. Steps away.

Behind them, the others stir. Beth rumbles at the back of her throat. Singefur yelps and draws back. Shapes move in the dark mist, shifting in the sand like phantoms.

His nails rake slow across her scalp, gentle but still sharp. She shudders in the fire-warmed sand. Her hair follows his stroke, caught in his nails, falling strand by strand.

The last one drops. He draws his hand away.

"Without rules, without structure" he says, softer, "we're creatures of confusion. Without them, we don't know when to bite and when to hide. Our limitations keep us safe. Until you realize that, Songchaser, you're a hazard to us and to yourself."

"Give her more time." Beth's voice rustles just above the waves.

"She's had time," Tanglewood replies. "See how much good it's done."

"She's a kid–"

"We can't afford 'kids.'" His words catch the sea's cold finality.

"Meaning what?" Rachel's voice feels dead against the sand. Opening her eyes, she looks toward Beth.

"Meaning we won't kill you," Tanglewood replies. "Not yet, anyway." Beth's strained expression shows this decision was a near thing. "Still," he continues, "you can't stay. Not like you are. Not with us."

She rolls over to face the Alpha Wolf, careful now to avoid his eyes. "I thought you said I had a choice."

He stiffens. "You did. You just blew it."

She shuts her eyes, bitter. "Fine. So who am I with now?"

Again, his mouth twitches. "Both sides of yourself."

The wolf inside her reared its head. Rachel felt its heat behind her eyes. It bared its teeth and she fought to drive it down again.

Gerald took her silence for speechlessness and reached for her.

"Don't!"

He flinched. Rachel's vision sharpened. Her heart jumped. The mist around him seemed brighter, seen now through predatory eyes. The taste of Change, like a mouthful of summer grass, rose sudden in her mouth. A voice inside her screamed *Not now!*

A strong gust blew in from the sea, biting through her damp jeans and leather jacket, raising goosebumps on her skin.

She shivered, but the thrill went deeper than a random breeze. She snarled.

Gerald met her eyes.

She pinned him in place without raising a hand.

With fur and spit, seawater and blood and red silk cords, they bind her. She struggles underneath their grip, held down to cold sand while Beth whispers in her ear.

There's wet fur between her fingers, fear-musk in her lungs, panic crying in the back of her throat and rage clawing through her gut. His words blur, meld together and sink beneath the waves.

They cut shapes into the sand. Arrange the stones in black circles around her. Paint her face with bloody lines, one splitting it straight down the middle.

Above them, the misty moon hangs like a judge.

"Wolf and woman are not one within you." The chant rings heavy in their human throats. "Two hearts war 'til one heart wins." The wolves croon counterparts as Rachel sobs. "No breath share you among us," the chant continues. "Run too free, run alone."

The Alpha plants his foot in the middle of her chest, his rangy weight pushing her into the sand. "Turn your head."

"No."

"Turn your fucking head or lose it!"

"Rachel..." Beth warns. "Please..."

Tears blind the girl. Finally, she bares her throat.

Tanglewood nods, face hard, eyes luminous. He stoops to gently brush a bit of sand from her cheek, then presses his hand beneath her chin.

A faint growl. Beth lowers her head, eyes staring straight at Tanglewood. A wash of something —sadness? regret? – passes over his face. Again, his mouth twitches in one corner. He looks down at Rachel and softly closes his eyes.

With implacable slowness, he squeezes his fingers across her throat. The others croon a single tone. "Songchaser," he speaks with ritual precision, "we send you out. Until you walk with a single stride, until you feel the call of the pack, until you calm the storm in your heart, we cast you out to walk alone."

The packmates, save Tanglewood and Beth, turn their backs on her. Tanglewood hesitates, shakes his head and, shoulders rigid, shuts her out. Beth lowers her gaze to the sand, closes her eyes, and joins them.

Rachel looks up at their flame-washed forms, seeing only the rough sympathy of wolves.

She'd wandered the park for hours after the rite, daring strangers to hassle her. No one had. When she reached home, her rage built to a fever pitch. Clenched rigid by sheer will, she paced the hardwood floor, muttering to herself until the dam broke inside and she snatched the first thing that came to hand – an incense burner shaped like a Chinese Fu dog – and hurled it against the mirror. The bright smash sent her into a frenzy of destruction, ripping furniture, trashing knickknacks, baying in rabid fury.

The wolf had her in its jaws. Its rage shredded everything in sight.

Her fury spent, she sagged, weeping, to the floor. Her clothes hung in tatters. Mirrored glass bit into her knees. Blood welled up with tears. She cried until she couldn't breathe, then reached at last for the phone.

When Gerald came, he asked no questions. Only held her 'til she finished shaking. He whispered words that meant nothing, stroked her hair, cradled her in too-thin arms. When Rachel finally calmed down, he helped clean up the mess, his brown eyes clouded with concern.

"Rachel?" Gerald's eyes were wide, his voice uncertain. The wolf in her wanted to rip those eyes from his head. It would be so easy, here, alone, to share her pain with him. Words, bloodlust, torrents of fire and much, much worse seethed too close for safety.

"Go home, Gerald," she muttered, breaking eye contact and turning away.

Was he to blame? Would this have happened without the pack's exile? Did the problems between them run deeper than deed or ritual, below the surface of things they'd never said? Should she blame Gerald? Tanglewood? The pack? Herself? *Think about it, really*, she mused, and settled on herself. *If you're honest*, that voice continued, *you know damn well who to blame*. Her belly boiled with recrimination stew, seething and shifting like greasy red soup. It bubbled up the back of her throat and peppered across her tongue.

Honesty? That's fucking rich. Where should she begin? *I'm a werewolf? I'm alone? I hate myself for loving you and I hate you for letting me do it? Yeah, sure – let's go* THERE *now.* That'll *work…* Honesty was a leg-hold trap, one she'd chewed limbs off to avoid. Rachel had built a wall of lies – to her pack, her lover, herself. Didn't they *both* do that, though? Didn't *everyone*? Even Tanglewood, with his precious integrity, lied his ass off when it suited him. So what lies had *Gerald* maintained? What truths had he kept to himself? He knew so little about her, really; how little did she know about him in return? What went on in his head when Gerald stopped talking? Two years gone, and far too many lies.

She thrashed around cages in her skull. Her gums ached as they drew back tight. Locked teeth sharpened behind her lips. Any words were the wrong words. Rachel shook the thoughts away. She hurt too badly to think this through. Better puzzle through it later, when the wounds weren't quite so raw. *Get away now. Heal.* Maybe a party. Maybe a drink. Maybe a run past the end of the world.

"Hey, wait," Gerald called as Rachel walked away. "We can talk about this!" Now he was beside her, reaching for her arm.

She pulled away. "There's nothing to talk about. You've said enough. Just go."

"Hey, look – I'm sorry."

"So am I, Gerald. Leave me alone." Hurt lodged in her chest like glass. "For your own good, go home."

"Is this it?"

"That was your decision." The wolf gnawed at her self-control. Pain and loneliness, rage, confusion, sadness washed through her like ocean waves.

Had she loved him, ever? Did she *now*? Too many questions, too many doubts. "Please just go."

SHE'D SENSED THE DIFFERENCE in Gerald after that. The half-hidden glances when he thought she wasn't looking. The stale drift that smelled like fear. No questions, though. Ever. He hadn't asked her what was wrong. He simply withdrew, like the pack but without their anger. Roughly three weeks after that crazy night, he'd cast her out as well. Was this the pack's doing, or Gerald's, or her own?

"I'LL TAKE YOU HOME." He reached for her again.

"Go!" She lashed out, spun. He cowered from the wolf in her eyes.

Change bristled just beneath her skin.

Rachel stepped forward. Her prey stumbled backward, sprawling in the sand. The fear in his eyes dimmed as she blocked the light, throwing her shadow across the sand. She smelled his sudden sticky fear. Her fingers curled into hooks, claws itching to extend. Her teeth throbbed. Sharpened into fangs. Shards of humanity kept her claws from his throat. Flickers of will kept the wolf inside.

"Get out of here."

Gerald scrambled to his feet, eyes rabbit-wide. Rachel trembled, wanting to hug him, wanting to kill him, and turned away instead.

Striding waist-deep into the freezing surf, she forced the wolf back down. Cold waves slapped her. Crashed against her legs. Drenched her belly. Soaked her chest. Sent her shivering.

Rachel waited there, hugging her sides until the fury stilled. When she turned around, he was gone.

She howled until her throat went raw. The sound got lost in the roaring surf.

THEY STRAIN: wolf and woman, struggling. Red cords burn across their skins, biting deep enough to bleed. Rich scents coil as they breathe, reaching in and drawing out again.

The wolf thrashes in her grip. She dodges its teeth and wrestles it down. Locking eyes, they snarl. The sound becomes one with the ocean's roar.

It pulls her, draws her, taunts her, dares her.

Furious, she dives…

Thrashing, spinning, no air, no light. Cold weight, dragging. Darkness. Sand.

Shedding bonds. Shedding leather. Bursting up through cold sharp stars.

Up above, a chill moon glaring. Slivered. Rimmed with fog.

*Furious, she sputters. Gasps. Starts to swim. Not toward the beach —
away. Toward deep water solitude. To drown? To fight? To escape?*

To tear the moon to pieces from its sky.

*Sounds boil, wordless fury. Stagger from lungs washed cold with
salt. Choke from tight throat howled raw. Burn in boundless frenzy
mind.*

I will kill the moon, she cries.

*Wolf and woman strive as one. Two hearts share a single pulse. Two
throats share a single breath.*

Storms burst against them, and they fall...

GASPING, Rachel broke the surface. Cold waves shook her like
a soggy rag. *What the hell am I doing?* Far off, faint stars of orange
flickered. Bonfires. The beach. Behind her. She'd been heading out
to sea.

Clarity broke colder than the waves.

No fucking WAY, she thought. *Not happening.*

Arms heavy, she chased her way toward shore.

SHE ROSE spitting from the surf, drenched and shaky and salty
and alone. *God, Tanglewood,* she thought, *you* suck*!*

Disgusted, Rachel shook herself. *Lost my jacket. Marvelous.* Still in all… she looked back toward the hungry dark.

Her legs dropped out from under her.

And for a time, she lay numb on the sand.

HOURS LATER, Rachel stood alone on the beach, cleansed by the Pacific wind. Her eyes stung but she refused the luxury of tears. The sliver moon now hid itself, wrapped in mist like a blanketing womb. There was pristine beauty in the night, and both wolf and woman welcomed it together.

Rachel's breath misted near her face. Waves washed across her feet. Breeze soothed the jagged spots inside. Her sadness lingered, but the bitterness waned. *It's about time*, she thought, *for rebirth.*

The wolf and the woman, they'd said, *are not one.* That curse no longer seemed true. After the last few hours, perhaps they'd reached some understanding. They would clean up future messes themselves.

In the raw distance along the beach, bonfires warmed the flickering mist. From one came the sound of drums, laugher and off-key songs mingled with the wash of waves. Rachel paused, recalling similar nights with Gerald, with Beth and Ray, Shelly and the mousy blonde with a name no one could pronounce. Wet evenings in cool fog with beers and fires and old friends. With the pack, even Tanglewood, and sea breeze light against her skin. Gone now, only memories. She shivered. It was a good night for sorrow… but sorrow was a waste of time. Her life was smashed to slivers, now. Best to bury the pieces and move on.

Down the beach a ways, firelight glittered on a rash of broken glass. Cans and bottles jutted from a blackened mound of sand. Rachel swore as she approached the mess. The campfire embers guttered. Smoke rose into fog. The tracks of the bastards who'd left this mess led up to the pavement and away. By the look of their fire, they were long gone. Pity.

She let out a thick disgusted sigh. "I fucking *hate* when people do that." Folding carefully to her knees, Rachel knelt beside the fire and sifted through the sand. Some asshole had built a beer-can Stonehenge, the metal wet and gritty to the touch. A soggy paper bag held fast-food wrappers and two more cans. The cheap scents grated on her nerves.

Cursing, she threw the first few slivers in the bag. The flat *clinks* matched her mood. She stopped. Thought. Looked back out toward the waves.

Damp fur brushed against her hand.

She glanced down. Nothing there. *Of course not.* Still…

The next few pieces fell softly in the bag.

Sweeping fingers through the sand, Rachel searched for broken glass. Her efforts carved designs, wedged damp grains underneath her nails. As she worked, she thought of Gerald, cleaning up her broken mirror. *I guess I'm not the only one who got stuck with someone else's mess,* she mused. *I guess it's time to clean up my own.*

The larger pieces were easy to find. The hard part involved the slivers, stubborn shards half-hidden in the sand. *No matter how carefully you pick them away,* she thought, *there are always some waiting below the surface. You could sift sand all night and never catch them all…*

But leaving a few tiny shards behind beat large fragments lying around. Given time, the sea would wear the slivers down until shards and sand became one. *'Til then, I guess, you just take your chances and hope no one steps on the glass.*

Her legs had cramped by the time she finished. She stretched and grunted, then carefully raised the bag. The glass inside rustled as she cast a last slow scan across the sand. "You can never," she repeated aloud, "get them all." Rachel brushed damp hair from her eyes with a gritty hand. It was better than nothing and would have to do.

Off a ways, the songs continued. *Wow,* she thought, *they* really *suck. Maybe they could use some company…*

Rachel grinned as something settled warm beneath her skin, put its face on its paws and went to sleep.

Dumping the bag in a nearby trashcan, she headed back down the beach to chase a song.

WILLOW AND WIND

For Kristen Leigh Elmore
and SJ Tucker

Once, as they say, upon a time, there was a tree – a willow standing in a forest on the fringe of the world, far from the woods known by man. And although this willow bent himself near a clean and soothing stream, he felt alone.

Then one day, an errant east wind rippled through the willow's branches. In their rustling and ticking, they wove enchanting songs, and the wind lingered long past the time when a breeze should have passed on. They grew to love one another, the willow and the wind, and beside the stream on the fringe of the world they made precious music together.

But winds are fickle things, and soon the restless breeze blew far and away. Once again, the willow stood alone. Then one day, a young woman stepped up to the tree – a girl in the woods where no human foot had fallen. And she sat in the willow tree's shade, singing familiar songs. She took up fallen sticks and clacked them together. The tree rustled his branches and she whistled her tunes and then she turned back into the breeze and played among his limbs.

As the sun set, they made love, and by the light of a waning moon the woman-wind taught her beloved to dream himself into the form of a man.

Filled with bright enigmas and tales of precious lands, they took one another's hands and ventured into the woods. Following the whims of the wind, they crossed strange paths and wove new passages through places without names. In time, they stepped beyond the forest's edge and entered the world of men. The willow trembled and the wind wavered, but soon the lovers found their place in this dense and thorny realm.

For a time, the willow-man and lady breeze prospered in the mortal lands. They played and sang and loved ten thousand human pleasures. The wind shimmered with rare beauty, dawn-haired with sunset eyes. The wind stood tall – lanky, rangy, handsome in a hangdog way. His fingers struck wonders from wood and steel; her voice drew pictures on the contours of each heart. When they played and sang together, people flocked like hungry birds to hear.

But soon the wind grew restless and the tree felt rootless, and when men offered them gold and glorious chains, he refused.

They quarreled then, the willow and the wind. They tossed and they stormed and they broke treasures without price. Their fury scoured walls bare and scattered dreams like autumn leaves. Fathomless with sadness, the willow reached into his chest and broke off a branch from deep inside his heart. He left it on her pillow as she slept. "With this," he whispered, "you will always have our songs. But as long as you wander the world of men, you may have their gold and praise and chains, but you will never again have me." And he left her then, stalking off into man's world to find his way back home.

But man's world grows thick on you, like moss or ivy. All paths seem to become one, leading you back to the place you stood before. The willow soon found he could not find his way back to the edges of their wood. The more he sought them, the fainter they became. Home-songs drew him onward, but each back-alley and dead end chased his path a little further off. Now, it's said, he sits by the edge of a stream, struggling to sing or weep or dream his way back home again. Some folks say he's trying still. And the wind blows empty through the world of man, seeking a familiar touch and the rapture of their song.

THE ICE FIDDLER

For Denise Jones

Every season has its song. Surely, you know what I mean? Spring with her shy promises, summer with lusty barefoot glory. Autumn burns with tawny heat, her melancholy shading in toward winter. And winter? Don't you think she's got one, too? I'd say she does. I've heard it, right here, in fact. Listen up – I've a tale to tell.

This happened a few years back, when ice had turned the world to glass. An exquisite coat of winter wrapped the city in its sleeve. Every tree and house and lamppost wore a glistening silver sheen. There were closings and blackouts and chills and even deaths. Still, there are no words for the beauty of that time. Each morning caught the ice like diamonds; each night re-froze it to that glassy state. When the wind blew – which was often – the ice tinkled like mystery chimes. It was a magical time, that storm, and it carried magic with it.

As you might imagine, tempers flared. Words grew brittle as the ice itself. On TV, warnings crawled like refugees across the bottoms of our screens. *Disaster*, they said, and *tragedy*.

The talking heads stayed deaf to the chiming ice. They spoke instead of money, holidays, and ruin.

Oh, yes – the holidays. The air was filled with canned carols and plastic cheer. The stores flocked with people spending that greatest of illusions, wealth. Wealth they did not have, spending for things they did not need, often for people they did not love. It's our ritual, I'm afraid – the brace of commerce beneath the guise of faith. Like the ice, it lends a sheen to its surroundings. And like the ice, in time it melts away.

Outside, that fresh ice chimed and sang. That, I think, was the first I heard of the song of Winter. In a way, it's soothing, like a chilly mother's hand. *How must it feel*, I sometimes wondered, *to be Winter?* That loneliest of seasons when the world goes to sleep? Spring has her acolytes, and Autumn, and Summer. But winter is our slow time, our cold time, a time to snuggle underneath the covers and hide.

We were snuggling that night right here at Pook's Hill. The power was down but the tavern was open. Libra'd posted a sign to that effect at the gate, cleared the path to the door and illuminated with candles. Inside, a handful of us sat – die-hards, mostly, with a scattering of strangers. It was Bardic Night then, but business was slow. Frozen roads and frozen cars had kept most folks away.

There may have been twelve of us, total. We clustered near the fire for warmth. I was there, of course. Libra, naturally, though not Tomika. Sweet, feral Ashley with her rainbow hair; John and Leena Ravenscroft, bundled in black wool and leathers. Sir Ragnar was his usual Viking self, but even *he* seemed chilled. Kaylina brought her silver-bell voice, while Megan and Scott sat quietly. The other folks, I didn't recognize.

Yet.

It all seemed quite old-fashioned that night. With no power, we felt *truly* medieval. Libra'd hauled out every candle she had, but it was the fireplace, not their flames, that kept the place alight. At that fire, Kaylina sang madrigals; the rest of us hunched over hot cups of spiced cider and wine. In the fireplace, logs crackled and spit. Woodsmoke breathed its perfume. We were more cheerful than we *might* have been but not as happy as we *could* have been. Winter weighed heavy on us all.

She flowed in that night like breath on a windowpane: a young woman with a fur-wrapped violin. When she entered, I saw flames dance in the hearth. Fresh cold cut through my coat, and I shivered. "Close the *door*," someone muttered, but I'd never heard it open, myself. As I turned, the newcomer regarded the room, then drifted to the far corner past the door.

"Hail and welcome," Libra called, but her voice seemed weary. She was working the room alone. "Come in close by the fire," she said, "we'll make room." The visitor smiled but cocked her head in gracious refusal. "You *sure*?" Libra countered, disbelief in her voice. When I really *looked* at the stranger, I saw why.

Although she wore furs, our stranger was too lightly clad. Her night-blue dress rode to mid-calf; her legs and feet remained bare. A white cape fell from her shoulders to the floor – fox fur, from the look of it, and quite real. She was pretty in a cold way, all sharp angles and deep-set eyes. Her hair, ice-white, spilled free across her shoulders. Where light touched it, it shimmered like rime. "Aren't you... *cold*?" asked Libra. The woman shook her head, still smiling. Libra sized her up for a moment, then shrugged. You get all types here in Pook's Hill. It doesn't pay to ask questions of most.

"Want a drink?" Libra said. The newcomer shook her head. Behind me, Kaylina kept singing, though her tone shook a bit.

"If she changes her mind," added Sir Ragnar, "I'm buying." Still, the woman did not reply.

After a moment, Libra nodded and returned to the fire. "If you decide you want something," she said, "let me know. If not, you can still stay. I'm not turning anyone out tonight."

I tried to catch the woman's eye. Beneath her smile, though, something cold made me look away.

I turned back to Kaylina and her song. She finished to scattered applause. I sipped hot cider while Kaylina sat down next to the Ravenscrofts. A stranger took her place at the hearth. This one was a man about forty, clean-shaven and a bit stocky, too. His thick wool coat spelled working-class. He'd been sitting with a friend – a third stranger, and a man as well, dressed in jeans, work boots, and a corduroy coat. They both looked a little flushed and I don't think it was just from the cold.

"Those were beautiful," said the man in the wool coat. "And I'd like to toast that young lady who sang." I recognized his voice as the one complaining about the open door. He had that tight look folks get when they're about to do something stupid. It's a look I know well, from the mirror.

We applauded him politely and raised our mugs to Kaylina. The man's cider steamed, still fresh, as he pulled up the stool. He started to sit, stopped, thought better of it, and stood back up.

"Another toast, too," he cried, glancing to his friend and then saluting us with his mug: "To Christmas, and to Christ our Lord!"

Behind me, I heard Libra sigh. "Not *this* again."

Pook's Hill hosts a pretty Pagan crowd. That's expected when the hostess is a witch. Every so often, someone gets it in mind to save our souls. They mean well but their efforts are wasted. Folks here believe what they will. I don't know why they bother, really – it's not like we storm their churches to sing "Merry May Folk" on Easter Sunday – but there it is. It happens once or twice each Christmas season, especially since that "war on Christmas" stuff began. Someone makes a scene and Libra gets stuck with the mess.

The man's companion raised his own mug. "To *Christ*mas," he said, stressing the "christ" with an edge. Beside me, Ashley growled deep in her throat. I put one hand on her shoulder. Megan and Scott, Christians themselves, shook their heads and glanced at one another. No one else acknowledged the toast.

"Look…" Libra began, raising her hands in a firm but peaceful gesture. "We appreciate the season…"

"*GOD REST YE MERRY GENTLEMEN…*" the stranger sang. He had good voice, actually – rich as hot spiced chocolate. He went a'caroling, I'm sure, each Christmas. If not, he certainly *should* have. "*LET NOTHING YOU DISMAYYY…*"

"Remember Christ our Savior," his companion sang, "was born on Christmas *Dayyy!*" The two of them had done this before, if not for an audience like us.

Ashley growled again. I shook my head. "*Don't,*" I whispered.

"*TO SAVE US ALL FROM SATAN'S POWER,*" they continued in baritone harmony, "*WHEN WE HAD GONE ASTRAYYY…*"

"With tidings," muttered John Ravenscroft, "of fuck you all, boys."

Libra clapped her hands once. Hard. The crack echoed through the room. Everyone silenced.

"That's enough," she said, very quietly. Outside, I'd swear I heard ice snap.

The man sat down. "It's Christmas," he protested.

"Yes it is," Libra agreed, still quiet.

"Elsewhere," John added. "Not here."

Libra glanced icicles at him. "No," she said. "It's Christmas here, too." Libra looked to Megan and Scott, then smiled. "We honor *all* traditions and holidays here." Her gaze moved to the two new men. "As they honor ours as well."

To see her then was to see Goddess speaking. Libra's not tall, but she sometimes *seems* to be. That night, the fireglow made her shine. Her shadow on the far wall swelled. Her voice deepened. She became, at that moment, the true Mistress of Pook's Hill.

Behind her, the pale woman watched but said nothing.

Libra breathed deep. The hearthflames flickered. I suspect we all took long breaths in unison. She closed her eyes, smiled, and opened them again. "Another song, perhaps, in the spirit of our holidays?"

The singer nodded. His stance softened. He smiled. "Okay," he smiled. "That's fair." I saw Megan sigh in relief. She has a temper, that one, but she's not fond of losing it.

Something ugly passed us by.

"How about 'Rudolf the Red-Nosed Reindeer?'" he asked. Applause. A few cheers. My hands stung from the cold as I

284

clapped. It seemed to have deepened in the room. My breath, I noticed, came out in a puff. It hadn't been doing that before.

"RUDOLF THE RED-NOSED REINDEER..." the man in the wool coat sang. His voice rang rich as ever. A few of us joined in – Sir Ragnar, Kaylina, Catherine, Scott. His friend, though, was not amused.

"No." He cried. *"No."* He stood. "This is *Christmas*, and we should be able to sing Christmas songs!"

"Oh, for..." Scott protested. "That *is* a Christmas song!"

The man shook his head. "I mean *real* Christmas songs. *Old* ones! *Real* ones!"

"Come on, Justin," the singer protested. "Don't start that here."

"Why not?"

"Just *don't.*"

Kaylina spoke up. "*I* sang a Christmas song. A real one."

"A real *old* one," Sir Ragnar agreed. I heard anger in his words.

"I *like* Christmas songs," said Ashley, near-whispering.

"Me, too," I agreed. The puff of my breath, this time, seemed thicker.

"Jus*tin*..." said the singer, "let it go."

"*No!*" Justin snapped. "I won't, and I shouldn't *have* to!"

Libra glared. "Actually," he said, "this is *my* establishment and my home. If you can't deal with the rules here, leave."

"I'll *help* him leave," John added.

"Me too," said Ragnar.

Something ugly returned.

The candles went out.

Silence…

A note keened out from the back of the room, low and thick as a dawning bruise. Another followed, and the fireplace dimmed. We stopped, as one, and turned. The young stranger stood on the table with her violin, furs thrown back across the chair. She wheeled the bow across the strings, and as they cried out I saw that both bow and strings shimmered like new frost. Firelight glistened on that violin, which was clear ice, not wood at all. Notes whirled like snowflakes, cold and lovely, and as we watched the air itself began to shine and fall.

It started snowing in the room.

The door blew open and the wind came in. It danced with frosty promises. The fiddler's hair danced too, like ice fire licking across her bare shoulders. The dress rippled in midnight-blue cascades. Her skin gleamed with a soft skim of rime. Her eyes were closed, her face serine. She caressed her bow across the strings, and the sound from them was ecstasy.

My shivers had little to do with the cold.

I felt stripped, naked, exposed to the wind. Through layers of clothes, my skin seemed to burn. Her notes held the crackle of icicle cries. I heard Winter's song, and I wept.

The ice fiddler sang of hacklebush and cinders, of burnt logs and dead cats frozen to the road. She sang of Christmas lights and ambulance lights, of coughs, hot chocolate, and soggy footprints in the slush. She sang of ghost leaves under snow, and buds that had yet to be born. She sang of rest and struggle and hearts burst while shoveling the walk. I heard trees snap and crystals grow in the notes from her violin. I felt carolers and lost dogs and 3:00 a.m. curses when the car winds up in a ditch. There was fellowship in that song, and grief and hate. I heard lawsuits and snowsuits and birthday suits, all. Sad birds that would never return. Bright lights in a neighborhood sky. I held hot chocolate and slushballs and torn Christmas wrapping. I held *nothing*, then, and that made me weep.

She sang it all without speaking a word. And I wept for Winter's lament.

I wasn't alone. But I *felt* alone.

And then I felt heat rise behind me.

Libra stood by the fireplace. The flames had flared again. This time, she stood before the light, and the silhouette she threw seemed implacable. Beside her, Ragnar held the spear from above the mantelpiece. The man in the wool coat stood by them both too, grasping the stool like an awkward club. "I *said*," Libra spoke with an air of command, "that this is my *home*. There's plenty of ice outside. You don't have to freeze my *tavern*, too."

The woman arched up on her toes. Icicles dripped from the tabletop. Eyes closed, she spun out a cascade of notes: red berries, pine trees, a skitter of snow...

"She *said*," declared Ragnar, "to *stop*."

"What *is* that?" said Justin. He looked like a cat in deep snow.

"I think," Catherine murmured, "that she's Winter."

"How do you stop her?"

"You don't."

To accentuate that point, the fiddler spun a flurry of sound, a gallery of magical glass. Her song burned us marrow-deep, cascaded with longing. It spoke of white fields and dirty-gray slush. Of frozen ponds and frozen bones. In my mind's eye, I watched glaciers rise and fall. Saw icicles shatter on cold stone. Through my own frozen tears, I watched the young woman weep. Ice trails swept down from her eyes to her chin. As she sawed at the fiddle, she opened those eyes. They glittered like a sub-arctic sea.

The fire roared louder. The light seemed to surge. Between Libra and the ice fiddler, I stood – half-burnt, half-frozen. Snowflakes whirled through the room. My bones started to ache.

With a glare, the fiddler shot a sharp note from her strings. And in the hearth, the fire blew out.

A voice in the darkness. A single word: "Oh."

Winter can be a world sheathed in ice.

For a moment, we all hung suspended and silent.

Then Kaylina began to sing.

Her voice rose high and bright, a spear of winter sun. It matched the pitch of the fiddler's song, slid into harmony like a scabbard and blade. She sang wordless, a torrent of sound. And in a moment, a man's voice joined in. The man in the wool coat had begun singing, too.

The fiddler called to them, cried to them, led them like a wolf with her cubs. She sheared dagger-like notes from her instrument; they replied with ullian cries. She dipped deep into half-tones, screeched high like a shattering pond. They followed, spiraling, sweeping, tumbling. He poured the bass foundation; she wrapped it in silver bows. The fiddler danced like a huntress, and her hounds were musical chords.

I began to drift, to weave, to fade. The music became my whole world. I fell into myself without moving a step…

…and a flame burst to life by my side.

Libra stood with a wreath in her hand – a branch-woven wreath made of rowan. Beside her, Sir Ragnar held a freshly-lit a candle. He shook out the match and took up the spear, glancing up to Ashley. All of them wore frozen tears. As Ashley reached for the candle in Ragnar's hand, Libra raised the wreath high. There were flecks of snow in her dyed-blue hair. "*Winter*," she declared in invocationary tones, "why is it tonight that you're *here?*"

"I think," whispered Ashley, "she just wants to be… *heard*." And you know, I believe she was right.

Think of it: There you are, an incarnate spirit of the loneliest season. You create a work of vast beauty – perhaps to celebrate this "holiday" thing, perhaps just because it's your *pleasure* and you *can*. But instead of appreciation and acclaim, your masterpiece gets scraped and salted instead. So, you snap the wires, crack the trees, wrap the landscape up in ice and then go looking for someplace that reminds you of bygone days.

Maybe you sense the magic of this place; perhaps you hear songs sung from *real throats* instead of machines. Past the primal glow of firelight, you see incandescent souls. Fiddle in hand, you go in to play.

And stupid *people* greet you inside.

Wouldn't *you* be upset? It wouldn't be the first time we'd let Nature down.

Now, this is all just speculation. Our fiddler never spoke. But as Kaylina and the man in the wool coat blended their songs with her own, the cold wind stilled. Frost still danced in the air, but the chill gave way to shivers, then to warmth. I felt that same wordless song slide up my own throat, reach into their harmonies and wrap around their notes. I saw Ragnar open his mouth to sing, and Ashley, and the Ravenscrofts. Libra held the wreath at arm's length as everyone joined in.

There's power in songs shared by winter's light.

It was when the last voice, Justin's, joined the chorus that the rowan began to bloom.

Green shoots budded in the tangled boughs. Tiny berries swelled from yellow to red. Within seconds, the bare woven wood sprouted fresh foliage. By the candle's light, we watched it grow. A dapple of frost sparkled across the wreath, but its colors burned with spring-like élan.

Libra's eyes widened. Her face glowed. Her fingers clutched the rowan bark with white-knuckled awe. Sir Ragnar boomed a profundo refrain, his red beard gleaming with frost. Justin glanced warily from face to face to wreath and back, but the miracle seemed to enchant him as well. Candlelit faces sang to the wreath, and the fiddler carried our tune.

We sang of fast sleds and skinned knees, dead cars and dying gardens. We called elk to the run, and we slumbered with bears. We became squirrels and crows, old deer and cold hunters. Our song rippled with moonlight, cracked with thaws. And through it all, not a word – *not one word* – was said. We sang with a voice *beyond* words.

I'm not sure, but I think winter smiled.

A high keen on the violin. A falling note, deep as a crevice. The fiddler drew her bow once more across the strings, and I swear I heard thunder echoing across the ice.

The candle blew out.

Vast silence.

When Kaylina struck a match to light it, the fiddler was gone.

Where do you *go* after that? What can you *say*? What could you *do*? We all stood a while, silent, no one daring to speak the first word. Eventually, though, we began shivering, and moved back again toward the hearth. Sir Ragnar got the fire burning in no time, while Libra regarded the wreath at arm's length. It still blazed with bright berries and shimmering leaves, and after a long, long pause, she hung it over the mantle with a single silver nail.

In the silence, the wool-coat man and Justin paid their bill. Libra nodded in mute acknowledgment but seemed glad to see them go. I wondered then, as I watched them leave, how *they* would explain tonight's revels. Perhaps their Lord will sort it out for them in the end.

I wandered up to the door, opened it, and stepped out myself. Starlight shone on a world made of glass. Above us, an implacable sky burned blue-black with distant snowflakes. The city's light warmed the edges of that sky, but I could tell then, just for that moment, how that sky must have seemed in the days before electrical light. A vast clarity called to me. *Remember*, it said with silence. A scattering of stars arced up and away, expansive in their infinity above me, and for a moment I could almost feel myself falling into them from a great and terrible height.

And then across the street, the lights came back on. And I fell back instead to who I *was*, not into who I *might have been* beneath that cold sky. I'd like to claim that I heard her then, her ice fiddle calling the tune. But Winter is a changeling child. And in her wake, there was nothing to say.

JOHNNY SERIOUS

Not long ago, there was a boy with a hole in his heart. All the joy ran out that hole, and all the sadness of the world seeped in. After his father died in the war, this boy dressed only in somber colors. He kept his sleeves long even when it was hot outside, and he never wore short pants except in gym class. He grew his hair long to hide his face, and he rarely talked at all. The other kids called him Johnny Serious. They didn't bother waiting 'til his back was turned to do it.

Johnny Serious had secrets. He listened only to musicians who had died. Sometimes he cut and burned himself to see if he could still feel pain. And he had a friend named Thorn whom nobody could see. Nobody. Not even Johnny. Sometimes this made Johnny wonder if he also had a hole in his *head*… but because his other secrets weren't very sane, Johnny didn't care if his friendship with Thorn seemed strange as well. In Johnny's world, Thorn may have been the only thing that, to him, made any sense at all.

Long ago, Thorn had been a shadow with a voice. When Johnny was little, Thorn used to play hide-and-seek with him. Sometimes, Thorn would make toys move and seem to speak. Or he'd leave trails in the woods for Johnny to follow.

As Johnny grew older, the games turned to talk. In time, the shadow disappeared. Now Thorn was just a voice. He would talk about girls and other boys and seasons and sports. Johnny listened and learned from his invisible friend. And he told Thorn things he never said to anyone else. When Dad died, Johnny cried to Thorn, but said little to Mom about the hole that had opened in his heart and let the world's pain spill in.

Sometimes, Johnny Serious glimpsed Thorn in the bathroom mirror or saw his shadow outside a window. By the time he'd wonder about it, though, the image would be gone. Johnny found dried leaves on the carpet or saw bare footprints in places everyone wore shoes. Sometimes when he'd tried to cut himself, Johnny found that his pins and blades and lighters had been hidden away. This really pissed Johnny off. If Johnny wanted to cut, he figured, then Thorn could just go fuck himself.

Johnny Serious was always cold. He moved into the basement so that he could draw curtains against the sun. Only one window led to the world outside his room. The curtains on that window rarely opened, and Johnny liked it that way.

Johnny was skinny. He hated his body. He hated being weak. He covered his body as much as possible and got Mom to write notes to get him out of gym. He preferred the autumn to the spring and the winter to the summer. As the leaves died, Johnny felt himself draw up into himself and fall. When winter came, he'd draw back the curtains on his lonely window and look out into the snow.

The white fields of winter woods draped the world in chilly shrouds. To Johnny Serious, it looked as though the world had dressed for its own funeral. He'd spend nights staring into moon-glowed fields pricked here and there by dark bare trees. The branches poked and raked against the sky. Instead of redness, that sky bled snow.

In the streets outside, shovels and plows tore furrows in the white. They pulled the snow away, baring bones of black concrete. People walked on those bones, and drove their cars, and moved as though nothing was wrong in their world. But Johnny felt the earth ache beneath their feet. His own bones shivered at the sight. So, he walled himself inside his room, with his darkness and dead rock stars and the endless call of white.

The fields and woods glowed beneath a winter moon. Night after night, Johnny sat, restless, on his bed or stood chilly near the window, his breath fogging the glass to mist. As the world slept, he stared out to the winter as if the snow could answer questions he hadn't thought to ask.

And then one night, he finally saw Thorn.

It *had* to be Thorn. Who else would be standing outside Johnny's window, naked in the snow? Who else would have antlers growing out of his head, or frost melting in the curls of his broad and furry chest? Who else would look like Johnny – a Johnny who'd grown confident and strong, with lean muscles and a sensuous smile? As Johnny gaped in wonder and desire and more than a little bit of fear, Thorn gestured to him and spoke.

Come and run with me, said the familiar voice. The words sounded close, as if the glass and winter wind did not exist. *Stop watching the world from a distance. Come feel it on your skin.*

And Johnny, who stood at the crossroads between boy and man, stripped off his clothing, opened the window, and ran out into the snow.

They played hide-and-seek for hours in the night. Thorn left trails to follow in the snow. When Johnny caught him, they wrestled in the woods like wild boys grown lean and fearless with desire. When they kissed, it was Johnny's first time kissing *anyone*, and that kiss tasted like heaven.

Thorn laid Johnny on his back and ran rough fingers down his hairless chest. *Like the trees,* Thorn said without speaking, *you will slumber. Like them, you will awake. Your rest is dark and deep with cares, but it is not the* ending *you would seek. Life and death are wolves chasing their tails. In sunlight and storm, they run together.* Thorn kissed Johnny, his tongue rich with pine sap and promises. *The beat of their hearts is the pulse of our world. Listen for it, and it will guide you home.*

In the white nothing of the snowy fields, Thorn made love to Johnny Serious. Ice melted beneath their skins. They touched, and they tasted, and they felt very much alive. When dawn pinked the fleeting clouds, Thorn traced the cuts on Johnny's arms. *You are mine,* he whispered.

I am yours, Johnny replied.

Let there be an end to sorrow then, said Thorn. *And an opening to life.*

They stood alone in the white dawn, cold gone from the heat of their embrace.

The next day, Johnny put his pins and blades and lighters away for good. He went out and bought new clothes – still dark, but sleek with fashionable purpose. He got his hair cut differently, and soon the other kids stopped laughing and began to stare. What had been sullen glowed with confidence. When he smiled, people smiled back.

There were rumors, of course. That he had a girlfriend. That he had a boyfriend. That Johnny ran through snow in his underwear, shouting like a madman at the skies. Some kids laughed. Most did not. Johnny's eyes looked through winter towards the spring. What he saw there glowed like bonfires on the hills.

When spring arrived, Johnny put on cutoffs and walked barefoot in the grass. He chased shadows through the woods. He laughed and grinned a hunter's smile. He still listened to dead musicians and rarely spoke, but no longer wondered if he could feel.

Life holds pacts sealed with tree-sap and tears. Wolves chase their own tails in the dark. Blades cut and dreams kiss and snow and rain fall from the same sky. There are strangers in the mirror and saviors in the woods and boys whose hearts well up with secrets in the night.

Those secrets have thorns. But they hold kisses too.

NO EXIT ANGEL

D on't let that "art" talk fool ya, kid. Music is *work*.

When I have a gig, that's my *job*. There are no sick days on the road. I might feel like shit, hate my crew, have a headache from last night's bender – it doesn't matter. It's time to go to work. I don't do that, I don't get paid; do it too often and I might *lose* my job for good.

You ever play No Exit, down in Baton Rouge? It's hot as a sauna on the low side of hell, and the bartenders water their drinks too much. This well-named sweatbox is dug about as deep as you can dig a hole in Louisiana without taking a swim in the local swamp. What the original builders were thinking, I don't know. I guess it might've been some pirate hangout or some such shit. Certainly had that vibe. Anyhow, we've played that club more times than I wanna recall. The worst, though, was around 2016. It was August, and whatever passed for the air conditioner was on strike that month. I'd just busted up for good with the boy-toy whose name I won't speak out loud anymore, and my gut felt like I'd gone six rounds with the high-school bullies who used to hold my arms and punch me 'til I threw up. I still had bits of last night's puke burning up my nose. My hangover could have killed God with a glance. Did I pull an Axl? No fuckin' way. No Exit's owner, Allen, had a no-cancel policy. Somehow, he'd packed that place like a Japanese commuter train that night, and if we'd backed out, we would have nuked both a payday and a bridge.

So yeah – no shit, there I was, head pounding like a jackhammer before we'd even begun. I'm nursing a beer whose vintage wouldn't have passed muster in a low-end frathouse. Right then, I'm convincing myself that a 40-hour punch-clock gig with paid vacation wouldn't be such a bad ride. The smell out front could have come from Satan's swampass when this adorable kid pokes his head into the sweltering graffiti-ridden pit that passed for a greenroom. He looks *maybe* drinking age if you squint real hard, but my girly-bits do a Hallelujah chorus just the same.

Okay, so this kid's a lean angel whose sculpted shoulders make a lovely hanger for his ragged white Sid Vicious T-shirt. Kid clearly wasn't even *alive* when Sid kicked it, but the audacity makes him even more adorable. His razor-shredded Levi's looked like they belonged on a chick, but the way they hugged him in all the right places proved he was very much a dude. This scraggly mop of curly black mess sat on top his head and hung into his eyes, teasing a pair of shock-blue peepers that stopped my breath halfway out my mouth. He's a kidling for certain, but y'know… I'm thinking right then that a nice little choirboy might take the edge off.

"Yo," he says, "two-minute warning."

"Kuh…" I stammered, my breath still trying to process the memo. "Kay. Um, thanks."

Kid smiles then, and… aw *fuck*. I had to close my eyes or wind up struck by God into a boozy pile of salt. Closing my eyes made my headache flare. I probably squinched my face like some Judas Priest shotgun-rider.

"Hey, yo – you okay?"

I gritted out something that probably sounded like "Not really" translated into *Please-Make-Me-Die*-ese.

"C'mere," he says, stepping into my bubble of carefully maintained me-space. Kid holds out both hands. Not thinking much past the shock of oh-shucks high-school hormones, I lower my head into his hands. He smells nice, a buzz of musk underneath the bartender stickiness.

Kid kisses my head, and *BAM!* No headache. Fuck-me *gone.*

"There," he says. "That oughtta help. Now get your ass out there and rawk those fuckers dead."

And I *did.* And *we* did. And while I'd like to say I shagged that kid until my eyes exploded after the show, I never saw him again.

So, yeah – music is *work.* Don't let anyone shit you. If you can do *anything* else, do it.

But fuck… if you need it like a crack whore needs that next blast of heaven, then *do* it. Karate-do *yes* or karate-do *no,* just fucking say *Yes.* And maybe, just maybe, you'll find some backroom guardian angel out there, too. Just knowing he's out there for me makes this shit a little easier to take.

LIGHTNING DUST

She would never forget the day they met. On a desert morning, she'd crouched down near her tent, watching lightning play across the peaks of distant mountains. *Will that storm reach me*, she wondered, feeling small, *and what will I do if it does?*

"It won't," a man's voice said behind her. "It's going the other way." She looked up, shocked. He hadn't been there before. No one had. Sensing her alarm, he took off his cowboy hat. His face held the rugged grace of stone. Sun caressed it, unafraid. He seemed at home here. "Sorry to startle you," he said. "Sometimes I forget myself."

He sat down then. They talked for hours. He seemed to know and love the land. Her bravery impressed him – the way she walked alone. He told her of another trail, one that led away from the stormy peaks. They wandered, and he showed her clear water and sweet sage. Their boots grew bright with desert dust. Their shadows made love to the earth.

That night, their bodies made love as well. His arms and chest held her like warm stone. And in the morning, he was gone. No footprints, no goodbye.

Only a pile of small red rocks where none had been before. A cairn topped by three perfect desert roses, growing strong like they'd been seeded in the spring.

DREAM ALONG THE EDGE

For Cat, Ashli, Siren,
and Mermaid Melissa

I hit the beach running like I always do, lungs burnt by the chilly Northern California dawn. My sleepy limbs stretched as my back unfolded from its grouchy snarl. Sandy pavement woke my bare and retail-achy feet. Mornings there were colder than they'd been back in San Diego; by *that* particular morning, though, I'd gotten used to it.

On the day that things changed forever, I took my usual pre-dawn run, the backpack cinched tight so as not to throw off my stride. After a warm-up wander through the foggy streets of Half Moon Bay, I'd jogged the long way down Poplar Street, out across the Coastal Trail and away from the usual public spots. Down there, the streets give way to rocks, cliffs, farmland, the golf course, and lots of sand. Streetlamps and shoreline houses faded to foggy specks, then simply disappeared. Leaving the Trail behind, I dashed through pearly mist, the blue salt brine seething through my nose and throat. The run warmed me and I'd paced myself, opening my lungs for my morning dive. Most people use less than a quarter of their lung power when they breathe. I'm not most people, though.

That small a life would strangle me. There are fires inside me that never go out. So, I dare, and I challenge, and I dream.

Until six months ago, I'd had a prime job working as a mermaid in Siren's Cove, a San Diego tourist trap with grand aspirations. The pay wasn't great, but it beat flipping burgers or playing Girl Friday to some oily jerk with an MBA. I adored making people smile from the other side of a glass wall – hovering weightless in watery bliss, close enough to see them grin yet remote enough to remain untouched. Not the sort of thing you can do all your life; compared, however, to sitting in a classroom piling up student loan debt, it wasn't really a bad start.

These days, though, no one has money to spend watching mermaids play. The place went under, so to speak, and we all wound up high and dry. I scrounged a few gigs here and there. My skill-set's pretty specialized, though, and there isn't much call for it anymore. I'd done some pretty-girl-swimming-behind-the-glass stuff at various casinos and bars, but the attention felt more voyeuristic than flattering. Two tries at Cirque du Soleil in Vegas had come to nothing, and the waiting list for a shot at a job with Aquarium on the Bay was a mile long. So there I was, crashed out on a friendly acquaintance's couch and working at a Barnes & Noble a few miles away. Worse places to be, I guess, but not what I'd had in mind.

The beach, as usual, was deserted at that hour – just the way I like it: damp twilight sky, bracing surf and the chilly crush of sand beneath my soles. Every so often, I'd spot some kindred spirit or adventuresome tourist. Most times, though, I was alone. That early in the morning, the sun's too far to the east to light the beach. The gray haze presents a perfect netherworld for someone who wants to get lost.

Out about a quarter mile off the beach, buoys bobbed across the coast. Faint lights winked on and off like lightning bugs back east. I guess they were meant to keep ships from coming in too close to shore. Barely visible in the morning mist, they gave me something to aim for in the sea. Looking around, I slowed, stopped, stripped off my clothes, and shoved them into zip-lock bags in my pack.

Swimsuits, to me, are like shoes: uncomfortable social necessities to be ditched whenever possible. One of the reasons I like those early-morning swims is because out there in the fog, no one knows if you're nekkid and few folks would care if you were. Cold water is my wake-up call. Freezing to most people feels just right to me.

During my final high-school days, my then-boyfriend Todd would come up from college during Christmas break. We'd snuggle close beside his car, my warm feet bared to the ice and snow. "Don't you want to go inside?" he'd ask. I'd shake my head *no* and kiss him deep again. It was one of many things about me Todd never understood. Sharp contrasts between heat and cold help me feel alive.

Knee-deep in chilly surf, I readied myself to dive. Deep breaths, fast breaths, frictioning my hands together in a blur. I had a restless horny itch in those places Mama told you not to touch. Warmth flared outward from my palms and lungs, flushing my skin with dazzling heat. As I closed my eyes on that cool gray morning, I reached past limits, reached past fears. I reached out to my mermaid self and drew her to me like a last long breath.

And then, like a mermaid, I dove.

The Pacific's no tame ocean. This far north, it's dark, rough, and treacherous. Up here on the Peninsula, most folks wrap themselves in drysuits before diving in or surfing. I'm not most people, though. God willing, I never will be.

Reaching the buoy was easy enough for me. Once my body settled into the current's rhythm and the sea's blue bite, I turned inward and let instincts do their thing. *Kick-sweep-pull-kick-sweep-pull. Duck up, breathe, duck down again.* Head straight, breath held, moving through the dark. Salt in my nose. Sea in my eardrums. Shut my brain off. Set my body free.

The elemental slide of ocean against skin washed me hungry, clean, and raw. It stirred me, stroked me, surged deep enough to hurt inside. Something rich and dark as ocean depths welled up below my ribs. Three years and god-knows-how-many miles gone, and still I couldn't shake the pain.

Todd. Damn him anyway.

The details are as boring as they are stereotypical. Still, if some idiot cues up "Jesus of Suburbia," I have to leave the room. Todd got under my skin in ways I couldn't shake loose from. Like the dark Pacific tide, he drew me in and pulled me down and lit cold fires between my legs. I damn near drowned myself in him, and so as I swam, I dared the sea to do the same.

...Head up. Breathe quick. Head down. Dive again...

Close up, the buoy's light was blinding, a flashing glare against the mist. Halogen-bright, it seared my salt-blurred eyes. My fingers scraped against barnacled steel, *feeling* it more than *seeing* it. The ocean kicked me back toward shore, so I reached out to hold on. Grabbed a rust-rough strut and clung for dear life.

Gasping, I drew in one last huge breath, kicked down, and found the buoy's anchor chain.

I hung on underwater to the chain, feeling pressure build inside. Behind my ears. Behind my ribs. Between my legs, pulsing like a marathon heart. The rational bookstore cashier mind rebelled, but the mermaid wanted to go home.

The void called me. I responded.

With a pair of large caribiner clasps, I snapped my backpack to the buoy chain. I wasn't stupid enough to leave my clothes on shore. I'd done that once too often years ago, and some asshole had stolen everything. After that, when I'd strip down, I'd bring my clothes with me, moor them somewhere, and come get them when I was done. That way, those nude excursions remained my little secret. No one knew what I was doing except me.

Pack secured, I ascended, got my bearings, took in a last deep breath, and then kicked off down into the dark.

The swirling green around me lit up each few moments with the epileptic strobe of the buoy's light. I marked my descent by the heat beats between flashes and the dimming of their glow. Bubbles trailed up behind my kicking feet as implacable weight pressed in.

I could get lost. I could get dead. I could rise again from the waves like Aphrodite and go back to my job the same afternoon. Pitting myself against that vastness, I feel sacred. Alive and magical. I was never meant to spend my life on land. Water's always been my home.

I dared myself to reach the bottom. To swim so far down I might never rise again. I challenged myself to pass my limits – to grow great or die in the attempt.

And that's when I saw them.

Shapes flickering in the pulsing green.

A pod of dolphins, running deep. Blurry smears against the black. At first, I couldn't tell what they were. I wasn't in my element.

But *they* were. And they saw me there.

By the time I'd spotted them, they were heading toward me, their squeaky-door clicks ringing in my ears. I'd worked with dolphins back in Siren's Cove, so I realized what they were. Bottlenose dolphins. Holy shit. They don't usually swim this far north… but then again, neither do skinny-dipping girls. We were both out of our preferred habitat, so it seemed natural that we'd meet the way we did.

These weren't caged pets or New Age paragons. These were wild beasts with the strength of oceans cased in flesh. As I hovered in the pulsating depths, they slid through the water to my side. Rubbed up against me. Slipped with quicksilver suppleness against my skin. Nuzzled me and sang bright mysteries.

My fingertips chased up and down their skins, smooth tracings of magnificent flesh. My hair flowed in green-lit streamers past my eyes. I think I made sounds but I'm not sure… something primal humming in my throat. It felt holy in that weightless neverworld. Like dreams. Like worship. Like sex better than any sex I'd known before.

I felt the throb between my legs deepen. Bloom with luminous intensity. My belly kicked and fluttered, desperate for air, even more desperate for release.

My fingertips crackled with storms beneath my skin. My ears buzzed, pounding with pressures inside and out. One bottlenose slid his snout against my breast. I swallowed down a rabid scream. Lost in that instant of fierce insanity, I wanted to fuck the sea itself.

I was dying to come… and if I came, I would die.

I spread my legs to full surrender. I frog-kicked in the strobing dark, each inch of me ravenously pure. Smooth skins nuzzled up against me, driving me mindless at their touch. A blue bolt sizzled up my spine, shaking me like thunder in its wake.

Baseball-sized beneath my ribs, my lungs exploded in a bubbling cry. Ripping up my throat, all the breath I'd locked inside burst out.

I remember grabbing one dolphin's dorsal fin, but not a damn thing after that.

IF HEAVEN WAS A MAN, then Heaven's hands were on my tits.

Well, *between* them, actually, pressing down in sharp hard bursts. It hurt, not in a good way. I slapped at him with feeble, shaking hands.

Ow – you can stop now, I wanted to say, but my throat felt full of sharp wet cotton. A headache kicked me in both temples at once. I tried to pull away from Heaven's hands.

"Lie *down*," he barked through the fog in my head. "Stop moving around so much – you damn near died!" His voice had an odd accent, not one I recognized. Musical, sort of… almost Latino, but not quite that.

I coughed up something dark and hideous, a fluid terror from my throat. I felt, more than saw, him shaking his head.

"What were you *thinking* out there, girl? Were you *trying* to kill yourself?"

That self-righteous tone stung me… especially since he was right. "I was *fine*," I choked out with thick phlegm indignation. "I used to be a mermaid."

The flat silence I heard as I coughed up the last of my lungs made it clear he was not impressed.

We lay gritty with salt and sand, a few feet from the water's edge. Behind us, the tide seethed in and out, as if to bring us home again. I was naked, of course. So was he. His half-mast cock lolled with animal indifference. Strong fingers wiped a screen of pearl-gray hair from across his face. Despite that color, he looked young… about my age, more or less. And oh my yes, did he look *fit*.

I like swimmers. Always have. My first three crushes and first four boyfriends were all guys on our swim team back at home. That lean slide of well-honed muscle makes me flutter in my girly-bits. Chlorine's kinda like catnip where I'm concerned, so when I finally turned around to look at Heaven, I felt a budding wisecrack crawl up and run away.

The dawn haze shimmered across a smooth-cut swimmer's chest – not that bulky steroid-bunny bloat but the sleek curve of muscles shaped by liquid strength. Bold shoulders carried that impression of deep-sea confidence. Those fingers held the gentle certainty of a tide, and despite that pearl-gray slide of hair, his face glowed young and smooth beneath his soggy mane. No beard, no stubble, just silky skin.

He could have done ads for boxers, gyms, and razor blades. I got the impression, though, he'd never used any one of them at all.

I worked in a bookstore and I used to be a mermaid. I knew better than to doubt the thoughts blooming in my mind.

I knew better than to *speak* them, too. So instead I just stared like a moron and tried to think of something not-ridiculous to say.

Big black eyes looked back at me from that smooth-planed face – eyes huge and dark enough to drown in. They were *human* eyes of course, but barely, rich with the implacable pull of the sea.

For god-know-how-long, we sat silent, the cold breeze sticky on our skins.

"You're lucky," he eventually said. "I think some diving reflex kicked in back there. You should have died out past the buoys. It took us a while to bring you to shore."

Us. He'd said. *Us*.

The only people on the beach were him and me.

"I should have died?" I countered, shoving up against the sand. My chest felt like a basketful of rocks. "If I 'should' have died, then maybe you should have left me there."

"We you *trying* to die?"

"Of course not," I said. "Just trying to feel alive."

"That's a funny way of showing it. You people always forget your limitations." There it was again: an odd note – *You people*. He didn't *look* Latino, so it wasn't a race thing. Not Indigenous. Just *different*.

I had to wonder, though, just *how* different we really were.

"How do you mean," I asked, "*you* people?"

He sensed a trap. "Just a saying."

"*Whose* saying?"

"Mine."

He quickly stood up and brushed the sand off his ass. (*Nice ass, too, just for the record.*) That lazy-hung cock shook itself at me as he moved. No sense of modesty at all. Given his looks, he didn't need to be. Still, I've known plenty of gym-rats who wouldn't be caught dead with their goodies hanging loose unless some hot chick was about to play a skin-flute solo. This guy felt primal. Elemental. Uncaged by clothes or modesty or shame.

Things added up fast inside my head.

The strange accent, his musicality, those black eyes and the color of his hair…

No. Fucking. Way.

But he *was*.

He glared at my appreciation. "Stupid tourists," he snarled. "Trying to be one with nature."

"I'm not a tourist," I shot back. "I live here."

"You could have *died* here."

My bravado faltered. "I know."

He turned around and headed for the waves.

"Hey…" I reached out to stop him.

My fingers brushed his calf. Underneath the smooth skin, his muscles clenched. He looked down, almost angry. Heaven glared at me, and I pulled back to glance down at the sand. "Sorry," I whispered. My words got lost in the waves.

"I don't know why I bothered," he growled.

"Bothered *what*?" I said, glaring back up at him. "Not letting me drown?"

His stance softened. "I'm sorry," he echoed, looking away across the waves. The sky cast a pale pink glow on our skins. "I'm sorry too. I didn't mean to be…" The sentence hung unfinished in the air.

I coughed again, more from chest-pain than from awkwardness.

His mouth hung open, as if wondering what else to say.

A dolphin leaped up a few yards off-shore, scattering wet diamonds to the dawn. He cried out – I knew by instinct that dolphin was a "he" – for a high-pitched moment, then splashed back in the sea again.

"They're waiting for you," I told Heaven, my throat raw with salty phlegm. "Go ahead. Thanks. I'll be okay."

He crouched down to look me in the eyes up close. A briny musk hovered on his breath. Come to think of it, I could taste it in *my* mouth, too. I wondered what had happened while I'd been blacked out. He reached out, hesitant for the first time in the way he moved.

His fingers brushed against my face. I leaned slightly into them. His eyes seemed to swell as they looked into my own. I closed my own eyes and held my breath again.

I can hold my breath a long, long time.

Heaven's fingertips slid across my chin. My cheek. My throat. And then withdrew. The skin hummed where he'd touched my face. "I'm Rachel," I breathed at last.

"I'm…" He paused.

"Heaven." I replied, then laughed shakily. "You're Heaven. Just go with it."

He smiled – not that player's grin some guys get when they know they've scored, but a natural one. Like a dolphin's smile. Like the sun in the sky as it's heading toward dawn.

"Okay," he answered. "I'm Heaven, Rachel."

"See you soon again?"

His gaze ticked away. "I'm not sure."

"Go on, then." I pushed lightly against his chest, a casual tone forced across my words. "I'm good. Your friends are waiting." Then I touched his face, brought his glance back to my own. "Thank you," I said, weighing my voice with sincere gratitude. "I really appreciate what you did. What you are. That you were there for me. Thank you."

I leaned back in the sand, then, and let him go.

He moved through the tide with fluid certainty. Glanced back at me once more, then launched himself into the waves. I watched the sea burst open and take him in, welcoming Heaven home. Two dolphins leaped into the air, then three, then none at all.

I watched until the mist burned away, but I never saw him surface again.

320

It wasn't till the first car door slammed that I remembered I was naked on the beach.

By the time I'd fetched my backpack from the buoy chain, I knew I'd be late for work again.

"Dude," hissed Ashli, "where's your *shoes?*"

I winced. "I was running late."

"So you *forgot your shoes?*"

"I used to be a mermaid," I said, shrugging. "This 'wearing shoes to work' thing's new to me."

"Well, go get some over at the mall, real quick," Ashli replied, half-shoving me out the door. "I'll run interference until you get back. But *hurry.*"

My best friend at the new job, Ashli's a tattooed Tank Girl of grit and attitude. While the rest of the staff gave the San Francisco Shoulder to my East Coast earnestness, Ashli sorta picked me to be her pet project rescue hound. The first day I started working there, our assistant manager Margie decided I wasn't welcome anymore. Ashli helped me out when she could get away with it… but three weeks in, I was on thin ice with a blowtorch and we both knew it.

I snagged a cheap pair of sandals, shoved them in my pack, and headed back toward work. Heaven glided underneath my thoughts, peeking back at me with quizzical eyes. My bank account a bit further towards the red zone, I stepped into the sandals, headed through the door, and spotted my nemesis laying into the new shelver. Judging by her expression, this wasn't one of Margie's good days. Lucky me.

"Holy shit," Ashli muttered, trying to look busy. "You just missed getting flash-fried."

"I see that," I replied, hustling up the escalator toward the office with Ashli close behind. "What's her damage this time?"

"Who knows? Not getting laid enough, probably."

"Then she's got company."

Ashli drooped a mock-pity face. "Aw. Is the mermaid still high and dry?"

"Yep." We swept in through the break-room door, hoping no managers would see me hit the time clock late. Yeah, I'd show up late regardless, but I'd have happily avoided explaining why.

"Even in the Temple of Luuuv?"

"God." I squeezed my eyes shut. "Don't ever call it that again."

My crash-host Chalice has this thing: She used to want to be a mermaid; now she wants to be some kind of sacred prostitute. I guess she's good at it. When her last boyfriend died, he left her his house in Half Moon Bay, plus tons of cash to keep it with. She spent a fortune turning her place into this temple of holy sex or something. It's not my style, but she's more or less a sweetheart… and I've got to admit, she's got the nicest living room I've ever crashed in.

"I'll bet Yoni-Bunny could set you up with a dozen of her finest sex-slaves." Ashli's fondness for my housemate ran about as warm as the morning surf. My constant bitching to her about Chalice did not help matters much.

"Chalice's cool," I replied, half-guilty, watching my timecard go *ka-chunk* in the machine. "Don't trash on her."

"It's all good," Ashli said. Then Ms. Nemesis stepped in, and it wasn't anymore.

"Surf's up this morning, Miss Cooper?" Her voice oozed lightly from a *gotcha* face. The worst thing about Margie's sadism is that she manages to act so goddamned *nice* about it.

"I don't surf, Margie," I replied. "How's life?"

"Not as good as it must be for you to have been late again."

Dammit.

See, now I *hate* that kind of shit. Bad enough Margie has to go all dictator on everyone, but then she has to play dress-up first before she slides the knife in.

"Sorry." I grimaced, trying to act innocent. "I had a headache and I overslept." The headache part was true. Lack of oxygen tends to do bad things inside your skull.

"You sleep pretty late and dream pretty vividly," she observed, then added: "You still smell like salt, and there's sand under your fingernails."

Dammit twice.

"If you're late again," she said in that same light tone as she breezed into her office, "you'll have lots more time to spend at the beach."

Damn, I missed Siren's Cove. There, at least, I actually *liked* going into work.

Actually, I *did* enjoy working at the bookstore. I've been a compulsive reader since Day One. My mom used to joke that I needed waterproof books so I could read when I went swimming, too. I wish I could say that she meant it affectionately. Sadly, Mom and Margie had all too much in common. That took a lot of the fun out of my job.

The headache haunted me all through work. Every time I bent down, it reminded me how close I'd come to not being there at all. Another sensation nagged me, too: a warm swollen pressure somewhat lower than my head. All through my shift, I felt caught between the throb between my temples and the throb between my legs. I couldn't ignore this simple truth: Aside from the "almost dying" part, I'd had a blast. And I couldn't wait to do it again.

That afternoon and evening, I contrived to spend more time than usual between the Fantasy/Sci-Fi section and the Romance section. After close, I shelved armloads of paperbacks, glancing at the clinch covers and feeling like a cliché. That night, I checked out a book from the New Age section: a hefty white encyclopedia of magical creatures. My hands shook a little as I signed my name in the employee borrow-log. I hoped Margie wouldn't notice but was probably fooling myself.

"*THERE* YOU ARE." Chalice's happy chirp greeted me as I stepped inside and scuffed off those cheap, uncomfortable sandals. The living room lights glowed dim through incense clouds. Outside, the windows cast warm illumination through remnants of evening mist. Clearly, Chalice was entertaining in the temple… which meant I wasn't getting much sleep that night.

"Rachel?" Oh crap. Luke. Chalice's on-again-off-again "sacred soulmate" or whatever he was supposed to be that week. The scent of nag champa swirled in the entranceway as I shucked my backpack and retreated toward the kitchen. "Hi, Chalice," I called, avoiding their love-nest. Maybe I could curl up on her massage table in the other room again until after Luke left.

I heard the hardwood floor creak as I opened the refrigerator and reached for some orange juice. When I looked up, Chalice was belting her robe closed. Luke, as usual, hadn't bothered with one. He stood there with forced casuality, his proud cock gleaming in a mess of bronze fur. "God, Luke," I muttered, looking away. "Don't they wear clothes on the planet you come from?"

"Clothes are a lie," he intoned, "meant to cut us off from our animal natures." Sometimes I loathed the Bay Area. Walking clichés seem to breed from thin air in San Francisco, spontaneously manifesting from raw pomposity.

"After the day I've had," I told them, "I could deal with less nature and more lies."

"Oh, honey." Chalice moved in to hug me. I let her. The contact felt good. She may be a fruitbat but her heart's genuine. She used to work the gift shop at Siren's Cove, aching to become a mermaid but unable to pass the physicals. "Luke," she said without looking back at him, "I invite you to go get your kimono and honor Rachel's boundaries."

"Of course," he said, withdrawing from the kitchen and taking his shiny cock with him.

"Bad day at work?" she asked as I gulped my juice.

I nodded. "Any day's a bad day when Margie's on the schedule."

"You can still work with me in the temple."

"Thanks, Chalice, but not right now. I'll consider it, though. Thanks." Sure, I'd consider it... when hell froze over. Gifting pretentious jerkwads with my magic yoni or whatever holds no appeal for me. I'm glad – honestly glad – that Chalice finds fulfillment in that role. She does a lot of good, I guess. It's just not my path at all.

Luke's pervasive aura of rarified creep threw Heaven into deeper contrast. I'd been thinking of him all day, of course, and the things I'd read about dolphins during the long bus ride home just made me more intrigued. Sacred to Apollo, Eros, Neptune, and even Jesus? Shapechangers in Polynesian and Native American myth? Soul-guides and mermaid-companions? How could I have spent so much time with dolphins and not realized before how magical they were?

By that point, I'd given up on asking *how* Heaven was what he was. When you see the faces of people who *know* you're manifesting the impossible but love you for it anyway, you start appreciating magic's pull. Myth's been with us a lot longer than science has... and as anyone who works in a bookstore can tell you, myth commands more real belief. Religion's just magic with a God complex, and if folks can believe in a Jewish zombie from the sky, I can believe in dolphin-guys from the sea.

Chalice padded after me as I fixed myself a sandwich. "We won't be much longer," she said as Luke reappeared, draped in a black silk kimono with silver dragons chasing one another's tails. He put his hands on her shoulders and she settled against him, eyes closed with genuine bliss. He looked down at her with what seemed like real affection. For a second, I could almost stop hating him. Then his dark eyes flickered back up at me with the slick predation of a panther crouched above a corpse and spotting his next meal.

I took my juice and sandwich down the hall and closed the massage-room door behind me.

I'd like to say I dreamed of dolphins but honestly, I can't remember a thing.

"HEY, BEACH-HIPPIE," Ashli said. "Someone take a dump on your aura or what?"

"*Huh?*" I grunted like a lobotomized cavegirl. I was on shelving duty that hour, a chore that's hell on higher-brain functions.

"You've been sloshing around in a pool of mope since I saw you punch in this morning. What's up?"

"My roommate's creepy boyfriend sleazed all over me last night, and I wound up sleeping on the massage table again."

She wrinkled her pierced nose. "That explains the mystic hippie-stink I smell all the way from over here."

It wasn't an honest answer, but the truth wasn't something I was about to share. A night on the massage table feels good only when someone's got their hands on you. That dawn, I'd done my morning run, slipped out of my clothes and gone back in the sea. I swam out naked to the buoys again... but nada.

No dolphins. No Heaven. And not nearly enough sleep. In place of invigoration, my swim had left me exhausted and sore. It's dumb to feel rejected by a magic sea-mammal. Somehow, though, that just made me hurt worse.

"I don't know how she puts up with him," I replied instead. "I'm in the kitchen just trying to eat some food, and she's all snuggled up with him while he leers over her head at me. It's gross."

"Maybe you should go all Corn King on his Rod of Power."

"Now *you're* being gross. And a total geek."

"That's what it says on the label," she shot back. Ashli's ink includes a half-dozen comic-book characters, some occult symbols, and a cartoon on one arm that looks like Bill the Cat on speed. She'll probably hate herself when she's 60, but I'm not sure Ashli plans to live that long.

"That mystic hippie-stink you smell," I said, "comes from those fucking clove cigarettes you smoke incessantly."

"You *are* in a mood. What's up?"

I shrugged. "Girl stuff. Guy stuff. Total cliché."

"Clichés only suck when they're not true."

"Wrong," I countered. "They suck *worse* when they're actually true. Case in point: Chalice's boyfriend."

She grimaced. "*Dude.* I just had *lunch.* So, who's the boy?"

"Some guy I met yesterday. On the beach."

"You total *slut*," she cried, delighted. "No wonder you were late."

"Not so much, no." I tried not to sound dejected. Failed miserably. "I was hoping to catch up with him again this morning, but no luck."

"What's his name?"

"Um… Heaven…"

"*God*, I hate the Bay Area." She leaned close. "Seriously, dude: *Heaven?*"

"He didn't call himself that. I did."

Ashli stopped the remark rising in her throat. Looked past me. Closed her eyes.

"*Ray*-chel," sang a familiar voice behind me. "Would you please come into my office to fill out some forms?"

They were, of course, termination forms.

Well, Margie was right. Now I'd have more time to spend at the beach.

I'd HIT THE MALL. No one hiring. Grabbed a paper. Nothing I could do. I'd checked back at the Aquarium. Same old story: hiring freeze.

I spent all day riding buses that stank of desperation. By the time I got home, I felt like death. The house was dark, so I grabbed myself a sandwich, fell onto the couch, and dreamed of stocking shelves with empty air.

The next day, I slept in. Didn't do my morning run. Instead, I found myself staring at the pile of crap I'd piled in the corner. Not a *lot* of crap, to be honest – just some clothes, toiletries, my laptop, phone and charger, a heavy jacket, some books, my sleeping bag and hiking pack, the smaller backpack, two pairs of sandals, a pair of beat-up boots, two swimsuits, and random junk. I didn't take up much space in Chalice's house. Maybe soon I'd take up even less.

Since arriving at Chalice's, I'd been living out of that hiking pack. It had history. For my 19th birthday, I'd gone backpacking in the Shenandoah Mountains with Todd. He'd bought me that green-and-purple inner-frame Highlander, a North Face sleeping bag, a pair of boots and other goodies. It was supposed to be our Happily-Ever-After prelude: the mermaid and her Suburbian Jesus. We thought we'd bond with the wilderness and all that crap. Instead, we wound up fighting the whole trip, cutting it short, and disappearing from each other's lives at the end of summer break. He transferred to Radford, I dropped out of UVA, and we haven't spoken since. Last Christmas, I looked him up on Facebook. He ignored my Friend request and blocked my page. I should've ditched the hiking pack by now, but it's too damn useful to waste on bad memories.

When I'd left San Diego, I stashed most of my stuff in my friend Alice's basement, shoved what I could carry in my hiking pack, and lived out of it ever since. It wasn't bad at first; kind of adventuresome, really. Luke and the couch, however, were getting on my nerves. Luke had been cool when I'd first moved in, but these last few weeks his eyes drifted my way far more often than I liked. I'd broached the subject with Chalice a few times; "He's just intense," she told me. "His animal aura makes some people uncomfortable." I know animals and I know Luke, and the closest he gets to "animal" is the sounds he makes in bed. Those sounds had gotten louder lately… as if he was showing off for me. Until I had a better option, though – something not quite on the table yet – I was stuck with Luke for now.

Aside from a bunch of books and a few new changes of clothes, I hadn't added much to my load. It occurred to me that afternoon that I could give the books to Chalice, pack or give away the rest, and simply leave. It was tempting. But I wanted to consider my options first.

I spent all afternoon in the temple living room, putting what little yoga I recalled to work. Ghosts of incense tickled my nose. After three months there, all my stuff smelled that way. It was kinda pleasant, actually – comforting in an exotic way. The various god-statues and that large crystal penis were a bit much, but they were nothing I couldn't deal with. The colorful pillows and comfortable rug were delightful enough, and I enjoyed the candles more than harsh electric light. If you took away Chalice's sleazy dude, the temple was a pretty decent place to crash. As I tried to meditate that day, though, Luke's musky scent dogged my peace of mind.

And underneath that scent, a hint of brine and the sharp taste of a guy from the sea.

I stretched, breathed, tried to step outside myself and let the cold knot in my belly fade away. No luck. A lump of ice-cancer fear wound its way through my guts and I couldn't shake it loose. All the money I *didn't* have cramped my karma and tangled up my limbs.

It's a paradox: the more you have to lose, the less freedom you have to get lost but the more you have to get lost *with*. Unless I wanted to start turning tricks, my travel-cash was pretty limited.

I had no desire to mooch off Chalice, and even less to earn "tributes" servicing her creepy friends. In this economy, it could take weeks, even months, to find another job. I didn't have that kind of time or money to lose. Every option I saw looked like one more box to trap me in.

So finally, around dusk, I jogged down Kelly Avenue, past the sun-washed houses toward the beach. Maybe I'd find Heaven again. Perhaps some magic-dolphin mojo could make my world right.

My bare feet scuffed the sandy asphalt as I ran, each shock of impact humming in my groin. That warm feeling swelled again between my legs. Underneath the shorts and sweatshirt I wore, my swimsuit chafed in interesting places. Fleet impressions of Todd and Heaven traced sparkling paths across my skin, faint memories of fingertips more exquisite than any skin could match.

Chilly breeze blew in from the ocean, rustling my ponytail and bangs. The cooling afternoon air promised mist and dampness after dark. Bright colors danced along the waves and turned the sky to a stained-glass masterpiece. Margie's tiny kingdom seemed pitiful compared to this glorious pagan cathedral. She *had* done me a favor, really. Why, then, did I feel so scared?

The rawness, I realized, terrified me. That wide-open vulnerable space where anything could happen scared me on an elemental level. Yet I craved. Needed it. Want to draw it into me and fuck it ragged. Like that sea beyond the buoy-line, I needed to feel adventuresome and wild.

And Heaven was most definitely an adventure.

He wasn't human. That was obvious. The parts were right, but his heart seemed alien to the land I knew.

I didn't need him to *save* me – by all Chalice's Gods, *fuck* no! But I needed, right then, to feel a kindred spirit's touch.

What if I reached out and he wasn't there? If, like Todd, he wanted the cute swim-team chick but not the complicated critter underneath her skin? What if I said or did or presumed the wrong thing and drove him away again? And worst of all, what if I never had the chance to find out because he was already gone?

And then there was the whole animal thing. What *was* Heaven, anyway? Human, beast, something in-between? Did he even *he* know what he was? I didn't want to be one of those gross hags that gets caught up in the whole furry-fantasy thing and goes over the edge into a bestial abyss. I've heard of them – researchers and zookeepers and New-Age nutjobs who project their fantasies onto unconsenting animals. The thought of being one of those people hit me like a cold shock to the skin. My feet stopped running while I waited for my mind to catch up.

What a beautiful evening it was.

That brilliant sky-cathedral arced overhead like a gateway to eternity, sun sparkling across the waves, igniting them with Nature's impossible passion for itself. Cascades of colors too rich for words to capture painted that sky and everything beneath it blazing. Some teenagers passed a Frisbee back and forth, their skins orange in the dusklight. A girl about my age did yoga in the sand. A pair of gray-haired dudes meandered like lovers, ankle-deep in surf. Far off, the buoys pitched and rolled, warning off the ships that slid through distant currents. Evening fog drifted in patches on the edges of the scene. That moment, though, burned me with its perfect clarity.

Screw the job. This was life outside the box. With or without dolphins, I was looking Heaven in the face.

I scanned the horizon, but if my dolphin-buddies were around, they were keeping low. Slinging off my backpack, I headed over Yoga Girl's vicinity. "Hey," she breathed as I approached. Her smile could have lit up Brooklyn.

"Nameste," I said, grinning back from a respectful distance. I've done the classes, I know the protocols.

"Nameste," she replied, sloping out of tree pose and nodding a bow at me. Whoever woke up next to that smile was a lucky person for sure.

"Mind if I spread my stuff out near your mat?" I asked her.

"Go for it," she answered. "Planning to stretch out?"

"Planning to swim," I said, unrolling my beach towel from inside the pack.

"Really?" She laughed as I stripped down to the suit. "That water's *cold*."

"It's okay," I told her, grinning. "I'm a mermaid. I'll adjust."

Given the daylight and the number of people nearby, there was no question of going naked this time. *Which*, I thought as the chilly waves hit me, *brings up an interesting question. What does HE do if he wants to walk around on land?* If and when I saw Heaven next, I'd have to ask him. Or bring him some pants. Or both.

The thought of seeing him again made me flush despite the cold. The thought of seeing him without *pants* again made my girl-parts do the Happy Dance.

I swam until the sun went down. Yoga Girl waved to me as she rolled up her mat and headed back toward the parking lot. Waving back, I felt a little sad. She seemed neat. Maybe I'd see her again.

On the edge of sight, I thought I spotted a dolphin's dorsal fin break the water. You can tell them from the sharks if you know what to look for. Even so, a chill hit me that had nothing to do with the Pacific cold. Great Whites hunt along these coasts. If I had another undersea encounter, I'd better pray for dolphins, not a shark.

Gulping a breath, I kicked down deep and scanned as far as my eyes could reach. Without the accustomed clarity of aquariums, pools or the Atlantic coast, that wasn't nearly far enough. The salt stung in that familiar way, but the dark water revealed nothing. I saw fish and flotsam, nothing more.

I thought I noticed that pricking-scalp sensation of being watched, but couldn't be sure. Finally, after the fog rolled in and the sun had long since vanished, I headed home alone.

I DEFINITELY NOTICED being watched when I returned to Chalice's house. Tracing the crawl across my skin, I noticed Luke eyeing me from her front window. Lit candles threw him into silhouette but he was being pretty obvious. Chalice's car wasn't parked up front. I knew she'd given him the key, but he was in the living room now. *My* spot. Near where I slept. What the fuck was he doing there?

I eased some mace out of my backpack's side pocket as I reached for my keys.

Scraping sand off my feet on the hemp-woven doormat, I unlocked the door and turned on the light just inside. I knew already that he was there but my nerves jumped anyway. Luke hadn't even bothered to stay in the living room acting innocent. When the light flared on, he was standing within arm's-reach of the door.

"Nameste, Rachel."

I didn't bother being courteous. "Where's Chalice, Luke?"

"At the *puja* down in Oakland. At Francesca's place." His eyes didn't blink. The shiver I felt had nothing to do with my wet hair.

"And you're here *why?*"

He leaned against the wall with forced relaxation. "I was feeling a little out-of-sorts. Chalice suggested I lay down until she got back."

I stayed outside, just beyond his reach. Glared at him. "You were sleeping in the temple, then?"

"Um, yeah."

"Where I sleep."

"Is that a problem?"

"Definitely." I kept my voice flat to avoid showing fear. Luke was big enough to be a problem if he chose to be. Unlike Heaven, he *did* lift weights. Probably used steroids, too. Definitely did yoga almost every day. I've been swimming most of my life, but he could bench-press me easily.

"Why does that bother you?"

"For starters," I said, balancing my weight in case I had to move fast, "I didn't invite you to share my space."

"It's sacred space. Chalice made it for all of us." He didn't move.

"Chalice made it *safe* space," I corrected.

"Don't I feel safe to you?"

"Don't make me answer that."

He closed his eyes. "I'm sorry if you got the wrong impression."

"That's not why you should apologize." My heart beat out a Morse code message of astounding length and complexity. My voice, though, stayed as level as I could make it at the time.

"I'm not used to communicating with normative-culture terms. Or dealing with such hostility."

I didn't take the bait. Silence is often the most effective weapon.

"Look," he said, opening his eyes with a *forgive-me* pitch in his voice. His stance softened. He spread his hands in surrender. "I know I come off too strong sometimes, and I apologize. I'm a really intense person, and I know that, and I'm sorry if that crossed boundaries."

For a moment, it almost worked. So few guys actually *apologize* that I almost spoke the reflexive "That's okay" response.

Then I stopped. It was *not* okay.

My scorched-earth voice began rising in my throat.

No. Uh-uh. I could *not* afford to lose this space. Ashli shared a one-bedroom apartment with her partner Forrest and five cats. She wasn't an option and I didn't have any better choices.

For now, somehow, I had to make nice.

"I want to acknowledge you," I said in the Bay-Area hippie-speak I was learning whether I wanted to or not, "for admitting to your limitations. And I invite you to consider the effects it might have on a woman's boundaries when she finds you staring at her from where she sleeps at night."

"You're right," he said, a contrite bad boy accepting punishment. "I wasn't being cognizant of the energy I was projecting in your space."

God, I needed to leave San Francisco.

"I… acknowledge and appreciate your… um, cognizance of my situation. I invite you not to do that again."

He stepped back inside the house, toward Chalice's room and away from the temple. His hands stayed wide and he tilted his head down. "Thank you, Rachel," he said. "I appreciate you speaking your truth."

"Thank you," I said, stepping into the foyer, still hiding the mace among the keys in my hand, "for acknowledging me. Let's not need to have this conversation again."

"Agreed," he said as he turned on Chalice's bedroom light and shut the door.

My host and I needed to have a talk soon. I wasn't sure I liked the possible results.

CHALICE CAME HOME around midnight, shiny with excited sweat. If I'd been so inclined, I could have said her aura was glittering. Luke had stayed in her room for the most part, venturing out to grab something from the fridge but leaving me alone. I, meanwhile, had been reading the borrowed magic-creatures book. Sometime soon, I'd thought, I really needed to raid Chalice's metaphysical library. She probably had *something* in there about dolphin-fucking, though I'm not sure I wanted to know for sure.

Oh, Heaven, I reflected as I read. *What the hell am I going to do with you if I find you again?*

According to the book, dolphins shape-shifted into human form to – and I quote – "dally with young women from the tribe." Heaven, though, didn't seem like the player type. His nakedness felt natural, not seductive. I hadn't stripped to get his attention and he hadn't stripped to get mine. His total *lack* of self-consciousness, in fact, made him all the more appealing. Thinking of those muscles rolling underneath his skin, I'd found myself caressing my pillow with awkward intimacy as the front door opened and Chalice arrived.

"*Hey*, Rachel," she called as she slipped off her shoes and tossed her messenger bag on a nearby seat. "How's your day?"

"Well," I answered, rising from the couch, "Christmas came early for Margie this year."

"You got fired?"

"Kinda, yeah."

"Oh, sweetie…" As I stepped into the foyer, she hugged me tight. I let the contact wash over me, not realizing until that moment how much I'd needed it. I hugged her back, and so when Luke opened her bedroom door, he found us embracing and decided to join in.

Yay.

After a few minutes of catching up, they both assured me I didn't have to worry about a place to stay… not yet, anyhow. "Do what you can," Chalice said. "As long as I can have this space when I need it, you're still welcome here."

"You're *totally* welcome here," Luke added. Chalice didn't contradict him. I didn't either. That discussion would go nowhere good.

They retreated to her room to play Kama Sutra Bingo while I squirmed on the couch trying not to feel jealous. After the third screaming orgasm, though, I needed to take a walk.

By that time, the fog had rolled in thick. Each streetlamp held a greenish-yellow haze. Along the road, houses glowed like Christmas ornaments, half-artificial in the twilight. Most windows were dark except for the blue flickers of occasional TVs. Two or three cars passed me as I walked. Aside from that, though, I had the night to myself.

Underneath my sweatshirt, my nipples sang arias to a genital chorus. My cutoffs scraped soft skin with every step. Storms of lightning seemed to dance across my flesh. I'd ditched the swimsuit when I got home. Where I was heading, I wouldn't need one anyway. The thrill of possible discovery drove my horniness insane. If I didn't find Heaven, I might just Jill myself comatose without him.

I heard the waves before I saw them. Even from the sand's edge, the surf remained invisible. Far off down the beach, bonfires fuzzed an afterglow. Not *totally* alone, then. I'd have to be careful. As I reached the tide, I stopped, shrugged my backpack off, slid out of my sweatshirt, and stepped out of the cutoffs. Darting glances to all sides, I wrapped the clothes in zip-lock bags, rolled them all into my pack, tugged it on and waded into the coldly hissing waves.

The icy blast shocked me awake. My skin rippled. My nipples clenched. I waded in, kicked off, and dove beneath the freezing black.

Cold or otherwise, it's no wonder Aphrodite preferred the sea.

Since long before I knew what sex is, water's been my aphrodisiac. Is it any wonder I became a mermaid? It was their magic I related to, but I'd be lying if I said sex wasn't part of the appeal. Todd, weirdly enough, wasn't a water-baby by choice. I think, at first, that's why I liked him.

After a run of arrogant swimmer-boys, I'd enjoyed the soft touch of Suburban Jesus and his mountain bike. As I kicked into deeper seas, I felt his ghost skim against me and then disappear.

Ghost? Or something more magical?

Or, worse… perhaps more *dangerous*?

I knew what dolphin-skin felt like. I knew what fish-scales felt like. I even knew what shark-hide felt like.

This felt a bit too much like shark.

Shark-hide features sharp ridges. Rub them wrong and they'll tear your own skin open. Thankfully, the brush against my side didn't hurt.

It wasn't the skin I was worried about.

Panic slammed through me, clutching hard across my chest. The lump of my held breath froze halfway down my throat. My eyes strained but the dark was absolute. *Don't thrash*, I commanded myself. *Don't freak out or you're dead.*

A stray current waved against my side. *Something* big was in my space. I stopped kicking and clenched my fists, floating in blind stillness underneath the waves.

Nothing.

I floated motionless until currents and the need for air forced me up.

Surfacing, I spun in the tide, drawing small breaths of foggy air. Any second, I expected to feel teeth snap a leg or two off at the knee.

Nothing.

And damn it all, the roaring hornies felt worse than before.

Eventually, I swam out further, filled my lings with air, and dove down as far as I could reach. If something was gonna eat me here, I planned to go out in style.

The dive took me deeper than I'd expected to go – judging by the pressure, thirty feet or more. When my hands scraped the rocky bottom, I glided along through the black by feel, parting sea-plants and tiny lifeforms as I passed. Terror faded into joy. This was the way I loved to live. I'd taken dive certification classes years ago, but the tanks and mask always felt *wrong*. Scuba diving was just another box to get stuck in. I'd adapted to the fake tail and air-hoses at my job. *This*, though, was what I wanted most: just me, a breath of air, and the sea.

Again, I felt something swim nearby. Something big. Then two. My heart punched hard behind my ribs. My skin waited for the slash of teeth.

A familiar door-squeak rang against my water-dulled eardrums.

Dolphins.

Heaven?

My sub-skin lightning flickered with delighted lust.

More cries sounded from the other side. Two dolphins, then, at least.

The shapes paced me until I had to kick up toward air. As I rose, they followed me. They broke the surface just before I did – two of them.

Two?

Where were the others… and who was missing?

I sputtered out a greeting, but they seemed to be alarmed. The one closest to me jumped and jittered and cried. Once I'd caught my breath, I realized they were trying to lead me somewhere. Parallel to shore. Out beyond the buoy-line. The hazy lights, chain-moored, bobbed with the tide. As I blinked my eyes clear of the salty blur, I realize that something big was thrashing near a buoy further down the line.

The dolphins squealed impatiently at me.

"There?" I asked them, pointing to the disturbance. "Over *there?*"

It's amazing how much dolphins nod like us when they say *yes.*

"Then take me there," I said, took a deep breath, grabbed their dorsal fins, and hung on for dear life.

The Roman naturalist Pliny declared the dolphin to be the fastest animal alive. While that's not actually true, you'd never know that if you caught a ride on the back of two dolphins blasting flat-out across the sea. A breathtaking shower of mist and spray later, I found myself at the verge of a vast clotted mess, twitching with frantic life.

Shit.

A ghost net: tangles of abandoned fishing nets, swept along by ocean currents, that snare and murder anything caught inside. Wild with terrified sea-life, the net rippled in the dark waves. Faint moon-haze and spectral flashes from the buoys lit a nightmare of struggling forms tossing on the waves. My escorts called out piercing cries as I released their dorsal fins and kicked hard to avoid being tangled there myself.

The webby mass surged and buckled in the tide. My flesh prickled at the thought of the fins, spines, coral and teeth gnashing in their plastic prison. Currents dragged me toward the ghost nets. The mess brushed against my feet and legs and hands. My mind warred between kicking back toward shore and staying here to help. What could I do, though? It's not like I had…

I still had my backpack on. And in the left pocket, the box-cutter I'd been bringing to work with me.

Ducking back under, I swept one pack-strap over my shoulder, started digging for my box-cutter, and realized – in a flash of buoy-light – that I wasn't the only person there.

Heaven!

Wrangling with his bare hands, he tried to free a shrieking dolphin from the net. My escorts joined him, chirping furiously. They didn't have fingers… but *he* did. He kicked naked in the frothing darkness, his lean legs pumping, his long cock bobbing free.

Oh, God, he was gorgeous… every muscle tensed in warfare with the net. His hair billowed wild in the current, bubbles bursting from his nose and lips as he clawed at pale, impossible strands. The snared dolphin nuzzled and cried, biting at the net with carnivore teeth. The pulsating buoy cast uncanny lights and shadows on them all. If I'd slipped into a Herculean myth, the scene could not hold more erotic thunder.

This wasn't myth, though. That magnificent horror could strangle every one of us. The others had teeth. I had a knife. A small one, granted, but sharp as hell.

Clamping a muzzle on my hungry girl-parts, I swallowed hard to hold that breath. Dug my hands through that backpack pocket. Heaven seemed not to notice me, determined as he was to free the dolphin from the net. Kicking back to the surface, I exhaled hard, brought out the box-cutter, slid the strap back over my shoulder, and took the biggest breath my lungs could hold.

My skin sizzled as I kicked back down to Heaven's side.

The glowing tangle seemed to have snared the buoy and its chain. Heaven tore at the strands, stretching them with incredible strength. Strength alone wouldn't break those webs, though. Sharpness would. Gently, I patted him on one shoulder. He turned, furious, his black eyes fierce in that angelic face.

His fury crumpled with surprise. In less-fatal circumstances, I might have laughed.

Scowling again, he waved me away.

I smiled at him and brandished the box-cutter, hoping he'd know what it was for.

He did.

I reached into the swirling mass, grabbed a handful of slimy plastic strands, and began sawing at them with the blade. A few frustrating heatbeats later, the strands parted and waved free. I pointed near the dolphin's head and made a stretching gesture with both hands. Heaven understood, nodded, and grabbed two handfuls of the net.

As I leaned in, his tense arms swept against my breasts. The throb between my thrusting legs pulsed so hard I feared I might black out again.

My heart jackhammered against my ribs as my belly clutched and bucked for air. These double-handful strands were tougher, thick with salt debris and clutched tight between Heaven's fists. My ears pounded and squealed with pressure. I hacked at the netting with everything I had, kicking hard just to stay in place.

Inside the net, the trapped dolphin and other creatures thrashed, twisting the chords and shaking their entrapment. Bubbles, raw skin and flowing hair strobed pale in the cold abyss. I heard myself moan in frustrated agony, fighting my body, the net, the sea. Pain ripped through every inch of me, blending with arousal in a silent scream of lust.

Heaven wrestled like Laocoön in the coils of the sea-snake. Rigid muscles bunched beneath his skin. His teeth snapped and gritted behind drawn-back lips, champing at the sea with elemental rage.

As the blade tore through the ghost net's strands, my lungs rebelled. A bolt of anguish tore from my belly to my mouth, pushing out a throat-ripping cry. Bubbles exploded as I sucked…

…air.

Heaven had clamped his mouth over mine, filling my lungs with a stale but potent rush of breath.

I fumbled the box-cutter.

Caught it by the blade.

Salt burned my cut fingers. I kept hold of the knife.

For some vast interval, we hung there in the pulsating depths. Heaven pulled me close, and every molecule within me sang.

For a time, there was no net, no danger, no other living thing. For a hovering eternity, we hung suspended between worlds.

Then the swirling net surged in on us, and we had to fight for our lives.

I don't know how long we fought the damned thing. No idea how long I held my breath. Cuts and abrasions clouded the water with blood – from the fish, from the dolphins, from our pale naked skins. My muscles burned with passionate exertion. My eyes went blind with salty chaos. Finally, the trapped dolphin pulled free. A gout of other fish followed close behind.

I can't tell you how long we were there, only that there was *no rational fucking way* that even *I* could have held my breath that long. As we pulled back at last and kicked wearily toward the surface, I knew that "science" was bullshit and magic was real.

For obvious reasons, he broke the surface first, then reached down to help me up those final desperate feet. My limbs felt like concrete but my mind spun cartwheels in the dark. Watching those bubbles rise and burst into light above us, I stretched for the sky with exhilarated bliss. I'd *found* him. And *helped* him. And saved *dolphins*. And *defied human limits beneath the sea.* The box I'd feared was shattered. *Anything* now was possible. As Heaven's powerful fingers wrapped around my wrist, I wanted to scream with pure joy.

I broke the surface hauling in gasps of misty air. Heaven held me while I caught my breath. Nearby, the other dolphins chirped and splashed, a safe distance away from the drifting nets. I swear I heard the trapped one pour out his *No shit – there I was!* account as the others celebrated his escape.

And then there was us. Me and Heaven. Oh my God.

Now we actually had to talk or something.

Holding lightly on to one another, we kicked away from the drifting mass still boiling with tangled or escaping creatures. My head buzzed with euphoria; my body burned with weariness and lust.

Heaven brushed his fingertips across my face. "Are you all right?" he asked, his gentle voice not quite lost in the sound of waves.

"I'm…" I had to think. "I'm fine," I concluded, nodding. "I'm… really *good*, actually."

"What *are* you?" he asked, oblivious to that question's paradox.

Still choking a bit, I laughed. "Told you – I'm a mermaid."

He didn't even sound winded. "You," he said, taking me in with those dark eyes, "are gloriously insane. Maybe dangerous. Certainly brave."

I didn't know how to respond to that.

"*Thank* you," he declared with rich sincerity. "I don't know what else to say to you, but… well, thank you."

The dolphins brushed against us. The *other* dolphins, reminded myself. Heaven might look human but he was one of them.

The one we'd freed still vibrated with half-restrained panic. Swimming over to him, Heaven ran his hands along the dolphin's sides. Nuzzled his face. Touched his heart and held his other hand against the dolphin's chest until the dolphin's terror eased. The other podmates joined in, nuzzling and whistling comfort. I wanted to help but didn't know how.

Finally, the scared dolphin calmed. Nuzzled Heaven's face. Swam over to me and poked his… no, I realized, *her*… snout against my hand. I stroked her, feeling skin shed across her nose as my hand passed over the dolphin's face.

Heaven smiled. "She thanks you as well."

I smiled back, but the water suddenly seemed colder. I shivered without meaning to.

"To return your question," I asked, hesitant. "What are *you*?"

He smiled a human approximation of that bottlenose grin. A wave of weakness that had nothing to do with exertion washed through me. I could get used to that grin close by, forever. "That," he said with a wary tinge in his voice, "is a very complicated story…"

He explained things as we swam toward shore. "I am," he said, "what I *am*. I don't think there are words for it. None that I know, anyway."

"But…" I gasped out between breaths, "you *can* speak English."

"Not as well as I'd like… but I'm learning, yes."

"Were… you born… on land?"

"No. I'm a dolphin by birth. The rest… happened later."

I still felt drained from our battle with the net, yet flush with energy from the primal nearness of him. The other dolphins helped me, offering their dorsal fins and pulling me along as Heaven laughed.

"What are their names?" I asked him as we neared shore. "Do they *have* names?"

"Of course," he said. "Though you couldn't pronounce our *real* names with a human mouth."

I barked a raw-throated laugh. "I *knew* it! People keep debating the intelligence of dolphins… whether or not they…" I squeezed my eyes shut in embarrassment… "I mean, *you*, have intellect comparable to human beings. Obviously, you do."

This discussion brought back the queasy acknowledgement that Heaven and I came from different species. What the hell was

I thinking, wanting to fuck him... maybe even wanting to...? Uh, uh – *not* going there.

My body had other ideas.

Distant bonfires still sputtered among the mist, their flames and the figures around them fuzzed by Bay Area fog. I was shivering by now, though I couldn't tell if that shaking came from exhaustion, cold, lust or nervousness. Probably all of them at once. I finally felt the sand beneath my feet and stumbled from that liquid sense of flight back to the world of gravity and weak-kneed legs.

"It's a different kind of intellect," he said, gliding beside me till the draw of shallow tide forced him to stand upright. The dolphins (*other* dolphins...) squeaked and chattered as we shambled toward the beach. I wish I'd known what they were saying.

Without the sea to hold me up, I tripped and fell face-first in the surf. Sputtering, I felt Heaven's hands wrap around my arms and pull me up. It had been ages since a man had held me with such intimate ease. A shadow of Todd swept through my mind. My eyes itched with more, perhaps, than just salt water.

"Can you stand?" he asked. "You just... *did* a lot."

A short dark laugh blew its way out from my chest. "Yeah..." I said in a complicated tone. "I... yeah, I kinda did." Still, I let him bear my weight. It felt good having someone else do that for a change.

I'm stronger than most girls. Swimming all your life will do that. Some guys seem intimidated by that strength. Heaven held it effortlessly. He leaned into me, shifting slightly to keep us both upright in the tide. I closed my eyes and pressed against him. The lust deepened to more complex sensations.

I *missed* this. Missed the level of contact we shared in that moment. More intimate than sex – naked but not interlocked. You don't need condoms for that kind of closeness. It won't get you preggers, go limp or fall off-beat. That kind of closeness often *leads* to sex, if only because that's what we expect from it. It doesn't *need* sex, though. Intercourse just joins the loins the way the spirits feel connected. You can fuck all year and never reach it, or share that feeling with nothing more than shaking hands. It's connection on a depth no stupid human words describe. Standing there in the night tide with Heaven, our warmth ran deeper than the cold of our skins.

I felt his cock bloom hard against my back.

His fingers slid down and dipped into…

"What the *fuck*, Heaven?"

Caught off-guard by confusion, lust, and flat-out being *pissed*, I smacked his hands away. "What are you *doing*?"

He released me, stepped back, his own face confused… and his cock… oh my God…

Folks say dolphins have prehensile penises. That's not quite true. They are, however, flexible, muscular, and – by human standards – gigantic. Those traits carried over into his human shape. Heaven, if he'd wanted to, could have had a *very* good future in porn.

I'll be honest. It scared me. Todd was a very comfortable size, and this… well, it didn't look comfortable. Yeah, it freaked me out a bit. I'd be lying, though, if I said I wasn't dying to try it out and see what happened.

My conscious mind had other ideas. "Back *off*, for God's sake," I snapped. "You're an *animal* or something!"

In the grand pageant of *Things Rachel Wishes She'd Never Said*, this statement flew to the top of the list.

Heaven looked as though I'd slapped him. His face boiled through a spectrum of shock, hurt, anger, and cold rage. "I thought... you had..."

"Oh, shit." I spread my hands with apologetic speed.

"Go home," he snarled. "*Tourist.*"

"I'm sorry... I didn't mean–"

"You were clear enough."

"Jeeze, just *give* me a minute here..."

"I could tell you wanted sex."

My gut felt like an empty elevator shaft. "I *do* want... I *did* want... I... *still* want... I'm just..."

Behind him, the other dolphins whistled and squeaked.

"You're *confused*," he shot back in sub-zero tones. "After all, I'm just an *animal*."

Heaven stepped back, his cock deflating. Stammering, I tried to pull us back together. "*Please*," I begged him. "I'm *sorry*. I'm sorry I said that. It's just... it's been... everything's..." I reached out but he pulled back.

"Oh, I understand." His face showed unfathomable hurt. "I *do*, I think. But I also know," he added, turning away toward his mates, "what happens when a confused person fucks an '*animal*.'"

The bitterness behind that word could have frozen the sea.

I had nothing to say to that. As the waves slapped against me, I tried to grab him. But he slipped away, and dove.

The dolphins followed him where I could never go.

My BRAIN played connect-the-dots during that long, cold walk back to Chalice's place. Seagate Paradise, a second-rate seaquarium outside Los Angeles. A bit less than two years ago, one of the dolphin-trainers and her boyfriend had been caught by security cameras messing around with a few of the dolphins. A guard had posted the videos to YouTube, and hell was a playpen compared to the shitstorm that broke loose. The trainer had been fired, arrested, and sued. Cops went looking for her boyfriend but the guy had simply disappeared… along with all eight dolphins there. Animal-rights groups claimed the management had killed the dolphins to cover up the scandal. The place was sunk, so to speak, by the scandal.

I figured I'd discovered the truth.

Heaven clearly wasn't an ordinary dolphin. His podmates obviously *were*. If they're been able to shape-change the way he could, our fight with the ghost net would have gone down differently. Lingering memories of the rumors I'd heard played around my brain. I'd never seen the videos myself, but some of my fellow mermaids *had*. They described a young-looking dude with light gray hair and an enormous cock. Charlaine wouldn't shut up about how big it was. The missing boyfriend became the talk of Siren's Cove. We all kinda hoped he'd show up there someday.

Apparently, I'd found him.

And then botched *everything*.

I have a long list of times when I wish I'd kept my trap shut. For all the lost jobs, arguments, and drop-dead dramafests I'd sparked with my big fat mouth, *this* one took the cake and ate it for breakfast, lunch, and dinner. Sure, he was weird, but Heaven had every right to get pissed. I didn't know what he was, but he'd deserved better from me than *that*.

Luke was sitting on the porch when I arrived.

Chalice wasn't with him.

The porch light cast thick shadows over him. Luke sat spread out across the top step, his bare feet propped against one edge of the outside entranceway, his back leaning against the other. Reading – or at least *pretending* to read – he looked up in false surprise as I stopped on the driveway and cocked a glance at him.

"Did the director finally go home?" I asked sweetly.

"What?" The remark, as I'd intended, threw him off-stride.

"The director of the porn flick you and Chalice were shooting in the bedroom." My mouth was running away from me again. "With that much theatricality, I figured someone must be filming porn."

He glared. I winced inside. My frustration was looking for a target and this creepy bastard was in my line of fire.

"I'm sorry," I said. "I'm in a bad mood. Didn't mean to take it out on you."

Luke gave me a generous smile. "It's okay," he said. "We were being inconsideratly passionate."

He pulled his long legs aside to give me space on the doorstep beside him. I didn't take it. "It's Chalice's house," I said. "She can do what she wants in it."

"The rest of us are just passing through," he added. I shrugged and nodded with an offhand air. God, I was tired… more tired than I wanted to admit. A headache gnawed like some alien thing inside my skull. Gravity dragged my bones without mercy. My legs trembled. My feet throbbed. My soaking backpack dangled at my side, clutched in shaking fingers, too wet and heavy to strap across my half-dry clothes. As my adrenaline ebbed, the chilly air bit chewed at me. I wanted nothing more than to curl up under a pile of covers. And Luke was blocking the way.

"You look cold," he said. "Come on over."

"That's okay, thanks."

"I was reading. Couldn't sleep."

"I noticed."

"I get like that," he offered. "Insomia. No matter how busy a day I've had, it wakes me up in the middle of the night and I have to read or go for a walk until I'm tired again."

I'd noticed. For some odd reason lately, his insomnia seemed to lead him past my crash-couch a lot.

"I see I'm in good company." He nodded in my direction. "Midnight swim?"

"Kinda like that, yeah."

"Someone I know?"

I closed my eyes. *So* not a conversation I wanted to have.

"No one you know. Just me."

"It's dangerous out there," he said. "Especially for–"

"If you say, 'a pretty girl like you,' I am pounding you to paste and burying you in the garden."

"I hadn't meant it that way."

"Just let me inside, Luke. Please."

He shook his head in mock concern. "Why are you so filled with negativity, Rachel? Is that why you lost your job today?"

Dammit, Chalice.

Opening my eyes, I met his own. "No, actually. It's not. I'm sorry if I'm snapping at you now, but it's been a long day and a longer night and I really just need to get some sleep."

"Fair enough." He got up and moved to one side, offering the doorway to me.

"Thank you, Luke." I stepped past him and went inside. "Sleep well."

The book in his hand read *The Way of the Superior Man*. I guess everyone's gotta start somewhere.

IT HAD TO START WITH ME. I realized that as I shifted, restless, on Chalice's couch. Despite my weariness, I couldn't sleep. Eventually, I heard Luke come inside and pad past the temple. His footsteps paused by the entrance to look in on me. I pretended to be asleep. Eventually, I heard Chalice's bedroom door open and shut. Maybe, I thought, I should give Luke the benefit of the doubt. If nothing else, I should stop baiting him. If Chalice wound up having to choose between us… well, one of us was on her couch and the other was in her bed. It didn't take Einstein to figure out that equation.

The shower I'd taken hadn't helped me sleep. If anything, it woke me up again. I'd tried to ease my horniness but the release I needed wouldn't come. I kept envisioning Luke right outside the door… or worried myself about the hot water I was wasting on selfish self-pleasures. Most of all, I beat myself up and down mental avenues, each word I'd said that night flogging me with iron-studded whips.

Finally, I gave up. "Fuck it," I whispered aloud, gathering up a towel, my cutoffs, a fresh sweatshirt, a pen and pad of paper, and – as an afterthought – a stretchy pair of sweatpants with little skulls on them. Wrapping up the sweatpants, pad and towel, I tossed them in my still-wet pack and headed toward the beach again.

I guess I wanted to leave a note for Heaven. An apology or something like that. I wanted to recapture our common ground. As I wandered through misty streets and pondered black swirling gulfs of farmland, my thoughts tumbled over one another like fog. Moodiness and misery and leg-shaking horniness tangled up between them. Inside and outside, I felt unmoored, drifting in things I didn't quite understand. At that hour, what little light there was came mostly from streetlamps and a vague shine in the sky.

The darkness shimmered with transitions as I picked up my pace and began to run.

Once I started jogging and breathing, vitality flowed back through me again. My feet slapped against the pavement as I ran. That familiar half-light haze enchanted me. As I neared the beach, the sound of ocean welcomed me again.

By then, the bonfires had gone out. I probably had the beach to myself. Stepping catlike through the sand, I peered into the night.

Nothing living… but something gleaming in the sand where I'd come ashore hours earlier.

Pale patterns, catching ghosts of stars and streetlamps.

Cautious, I stepped closer.

Smooth stones, piled in a cairn.

Beside them, letters.

Words.

Spelled out in sea-shells and still-wet ocean stones across the sand:

I was an idiot

I'm sorry

Let's talk

Animal

So, Heaven knew how to spell. And how to apologize. And how to impress a woman with more than quick hands and the size of his cock.

He'd taken something that had hurt his feelings, and he'd turned it into an affectionate joke. He knew how to sign a message only I would understand. In nine words, he'd changed everything bad I thought of him. Score one for Heaven, and color me impressed.

The pulse between my legs beat hot and strong as I stripped off my clothes, packed them, and waded into the cold waves.

Again, I swam out to the buoy where we'd met.

Again, I clipped my backpack to the chain.

Again, I surfaced and took as deep a breath as I could manage.

And again, I dove as deep as I could go.

There in the black, water pressed skin-tight against my muscles. Crushed my lungs beneath my chest. Pushed against my eardrums 'til I equalized the pressure in my head. A faint trail of bubbles slid between my lips as I focused on the heat inside. In that deadly paradise, each sensation stoked my inner fire. Hovering in the current, I reached down to stroke my chest and run my fingers through the folds below.

Years earlier, I'd realized that I held my breath best when I'd found something to occupy myself.

Growling softly in my throat, I occupied myself until I heard familiar clicks and whistles in my ears.

Dolphin echolocation sounds.

And a greeting.

I realized in that moment that I'd staked my life on getting his attention. The sudden pounding in my lungs matched the furious throb between my legs. My belly clenching, I followed a burst of bubbles from my lips up toward the surface. Dolphin-cries echoed in my ears.

Too deep.

I wouldn't make it...

And then a slide of water announced a dolphin's approach. I felt him close beside me in the dark. As I reached out, fins brushed against my fingers.

I grabbed on tight and emptied my lungs as I rode him back to the surface again.

Sputtering, I swam over to the buoy so I could catch my breath. My escort swam beside me, circling the buoy 'til he made sure I was okay.

"That *is* you, Heaven, isn't it?" I gasped in between breaths. He nodded, chirped, and skated backwards on the waves.

This was going to be a very strange relationship.

"I saw your note," I told him. "Thank you. And yes – please, let's talk. I'm sorry too, and I promise not to be an idiot myself again."

He nuzzled my hand with his bottlenose snout. I had to laugh. "Can we do this on or near the beach? I'm kinda spent tonight, and I'm not sure how much longer I can swim."

Again, he nodded and squeaked agreement.

"Lemmie dive back down and get my backpack," I said. "It'll be dawn soon and we might need some clothes."

He clicked at me in apparent protest.

Rubbing his face, I shook my head and laughed again. "I'd rather we stayed naked too, but the neighbors might object. And yes…" I finished, "I brought something for you, too."

After I'd fetched the pack, Heaven offered me his dorsal fin and towed me in to shore. When I released his fin in shallow water, he dove down as a dolphin and surfaced several yards away as a man. That was going to take some getting used to.

As we waded toward shore, I reached out to touch his shoulder. It felt smooth and warm beneath my palm. "I'm sorry," I said, meeting his eyes and holding contact. "What I said earlier tonight… it was unfair and untrue. I didn't mean it. I'm as much an animal as you are… as much as your podmates are. I was just…" Oh, God – I swear I wanted him in me right there, that minute. Still, I kept my voice calm. "I didn't have words for what I felt, and I should've just shut right the fuck up then."

He reached back – to touch my shoulder, not my crotch, this time. "I…" Heaven gathered his thoughts. "I don't think there *are* words for what I am. You were right that I'm not…" He paused, and when he spoke the word, it held vast complexity: "*human.*"

I blew out a heavy sigh. "Humanity," I said, "is highly overrated."

We both laughed. Then stopped. Then regarded each other. Our breathing deepened.

"Just please kiss me," I whispered, "before I say something stupid again."

He did.

Oh, God.

There aren't words.

If I swam in a single breath to the bottom of the sea, it could not match the abyssal depth of that one kiss.

There were more.

Each one drawing me, drawing *us*, further down. Further in. Further beneath the waves. Beyond restraint.

Behind closed eyes, I caressed his chest. Swept fingertips across smooth muscles. Dipped them into the crevice between his pects. Slid them over his thundering heart. Flattened my palm against his ribcage as his own hands slid down my salt-sticky skin, pressed me against him, circled my ass-cheeks and drew me close. My breasts pressed blissfully against his own, their soft warmth crushed tight to lean musculature. My hand, trapped between us, seemed to blend into his skin. Slide through it. Sink into the warmth where his heart beat for me.

...Warm sea of blood where hearts tremble and merge

We're sinking into one another with no need or time to breathe...

A wave splashed up and knocked us over.

As we slid forward, Heaven rolled to catch the impact of our fall. We landed in the water, me half on top of him. Sputtering through mouthfuls of sand and seawater, we laughed. Somewhere behind us, the other dolphins laughed as well.

"Did they do that?" I asked Heaven.

He shook his head. "We're not *that* strong. It's just the waves."

"Mama Ocean…" I nodded. "Unpredictable."

He nodded too. "She is."

"You know what I want right now?" I asked, kissing the tip of his nose. "More than anything else?"

"What's that?"

"To get away from this gritty sand and go fuck each other breathless in Mama Ocean's lap."

"I thought you were tired."

"I thought so too." I nipped his throat and got a mouthful of seawater. I coughed it up and laughed again. "Guess I was wrong."

Heaven picked me up, then. Just stood up and lifted me out of the waves like I weighed nothing. I snuggled close against his chest. Squeezed my eyes shut. Breathed deep and felt his heartbeat in my ear.

"You're sure, Rachel?" His words vibrated deep in his chest.

I nodded. "I think so, yeah." Opening my eyes, I looked up. "So: have any fascinating STD stories you want to tell me first?"

He smiled. "Not that I'm aware of, no." His eyes got a distant look. "I've… had sex… with only one other… um, female like you."

"Another terra-centered biped."

He chuckled. "Yes."

"I like that you know what that means."

Heaven's voice went faraway-soft. "She… was… a scientist."

"Seagate Paradise. The dolphin trainer."

He looked surprised.

"I know now," I told him. "It's okay."

His voice grew tight. "It was… a long time ago."

"We can talk about it later if you want. I don't mind." I paused, searching his expression. "Did you love her?"

He went quiet. Unreadable. Then nodded. "Yes. I think I did."

"Good," I replied, my own voice soft. "I think I needed to know that. I think I really *wanted* to know that you did."

We didn't say anything after that – just stood in the tide and let the water and the closeness and the inner heat wash over us.

We synchronized our breaths. Our heartbeats. The rhythms underneath our skins. I felt the slide of muscles as they strained against gravity. The wet backpack squashed between us. The waves washing against the two of us. My lungs swelled. His cock did, too. The pulse between us grew and surged, two full-bodied heartbeats pumping as one.

Above us, dawn began to light the haze.

Heaven whispered: "Ready?"

"More ready," I replied quietly, "than I've ever felt before."

Heaven softly set me down on my feet. I straightened up. Stretched. Took several deep breaths. Looked him over in the dawn-light.

I was the luckiest woman on earth.

Heaven took my hand. I nodded. We waded out until the waves splashed cold against my breasts. Then we dove together beneath the waves.

Kicking out into deeper water, we slid against each other like dolphins at play. His warm skin held the moist texture of dolphin hide with the supple warmth of human flesh. I dragged my nails across his sides. He grabbed me, shook me, let me go so I could come back and dart in at him again. We caught salt-water mouthfuls as we bit each other's skins. We tangled up each other's limbs. Hunger flared between my legs, a pulsing ache to be filled beyond capacity.

We clutched each other, weightless, tossed in tides external and within. He clamped my nipple in his teeth. The pain blossomed into rainbow sparks. I felt electric, as if my touch could illuminate the depths. Sweet sounds buzzed in my throat, my poor imitation of a dolphin's cries. As the hazy sun rose above the waves, I could see Heaven close to me, his pale skin green with deep refracted light.

Heaven dove then, and I hung on as we ran deep.

He was fresh and pure and natural, and I ached for him like starved lungs ache for air.

Finally, it kicked in: the need to breathe again. I pulled free and tried to orient myself. Dizziness nailed me right between the eyes. I lost myself. *Rapture of the deep*, divers call it: when you can't tell where you are and really don't care. Delirious pain spun whirlpools through my chest. I coughed up the last of my nitrogenated air.

Then he grabbed my hair. Pulled me close. Kissed me 'til my eyes went blank.

My lungs filled with briny oxygen. Seaweed-green but pure enough to breathe.

We clutched one another in the dark. Hunted and captured and frolicked and spread.

Oh, *God...*

We don't have words for how it felt. There isn't language for such sensations. If I tore a thousand adjectives from *Roget's Thesaurus* and burnt them with white phosphorus it couldn't equal one-tenth of a bright sliver of how Heaven felt in me.

It was bliss. It was pain. It was fire inside. It arced through me like neon-blue typhoons. He bucked in me. I bucked back. We pounded ourselves raw against the tide.

I bit his shoulder to keep from drowning. The blood bloomed salt-copper in my mouth. I dug my teeth in 'til my jaws cramped.

I don't know who came first, but we both exploded in the dark.

No human being could have survived that blast. I should have drowned. I should have died.

Instead, I settled into Heaven, blowing pearls of spent breath toward the surface in our wake.

EVENTUALLY WE SURFACED. Ten seconds later, ten minutes, ten hours – I couldn't tell. By the time our heads broke through the waves, the mist had brightened into morning light. I could see the beach through a fading screen of fog. Headlights cut like needles through the distant parking lot.

"Oh," I said when we'd finally caught our breaths. "Looks like it's morning over there."

We laughed. It held a shaky sound. What *now*?

My backpack dragged and chafed my shoulders. I'd been tempted to ditch it, but the last thing I wanted to explain to Luke… or to some cop… was why I'd walked home naked from the beach. As we bobbed in the current, the other dolphins nuzzled us. I'd stroked and petted them but still felt like a stranger. Maybe more than I had before.

Dull aches settled in – physical and otherwise. The tossing of the waves seemed exhausting now. Heaven ran his fingers through my hair but felt distracted, as if the same cloudy melancholy had settled over him as well. We held each other skin-to-skin. Our hearts, though, followed different beats. A cold stone gathered in my belly. Could he get me pregnant? Did he have some weird disease? Worst of all, was he now thinking of that woman at Seagate Paradise – missing her, regretting me? What if one of these dolphins was his mate? They didn't *seem* angry, but I couldn't know.

This was why I hadn't had sex since shortly after Todd and I broke up. The fears. The regrets. The *I-never-knew-that*'s bunched behind someone else's eyes. Those missed connections in the dark. This *felt* different… but I couldn't trust it. Didn't it *always* feel right until you finally hit the truth?

"What's wrong?" Heaven asked me in a searching voice.

"Nothing," I lied.

He snorted with soft amusement. "People lie to themselves. To animals. To each other. All the time. I can't speak for the people, myself. But the animals can always tell."

"Yeah," I breathed. "I guess you can."

"Is that what's bothering you now?"

"A bit. Kinda. Maybe. Yeah."

"That I can tell? Or that I'm an animal?"

I sighed. My chest hurt. "Please just let that go. It was stupid. I shouldn't have said it."

Heaven's fingers took my chin. Guided my face up softly to regard his own. Waves lapped our chins and chests, reflecting dim sunlight back at us. "I dreamed one night that I was a man. I woke up in the tank as me. I've been trying to figure out since then… since *before* then, really… who I am and where I fit in. I think we have that in common, you and me. Diving in strange seas, halfway between what we see around us and what we are inside."

He kissed my cold lips tenderly. "You are," he added, "more *like* me than anyone else I've ever met before."

I couldn't help it. "Even the trainer at Seagate Paradise?"

He nodded. "Even Rose. That's her name. Rose Dean. Doctor Rose." He looked deep into me. "And yes… even *her*. I loved her. *Still* love her. But she's not you."

"Who *am* I to you?" I asked.

He smiled again. "A puzzle. A dream. A kindred spirit." He kissed me again. "The mermaid you always knew you were."

God, he was good. I think I felt myself smile. "Okay," I allowed. "Maybe I am."

We floated for a while. The other dolphins splashed and dove, escorting us but keeping a safe distance while we talked.

"What about them?" I eventually asked.

"My siblings? We grew up together, may have even been born together, I don't know. Rose never said. I'm not sure she knew herself where we came from or how we were related."

"She probably did."

"If so, she never told me."

"Where are the others?"

He said nothing.

"The sea's a big place," I finally said. "And dangerous."

He nodded.

Eight dolphins disappeared. Five were here, plus Heaven, now.

I touched his face. "I'm sorry."

"It happens," he replied. His expression didn't match the offhand words. "Things die in the sea."

"Speaking of…" I said, wrapping tight around him. "I'm cold. And didn't sleep all night."

"You need to get back home."

"It's not home. But yes. I need to sleep"

By now, fuzzy figures were moving on the beach. A few people starting off their day. There weren't many of them, but I didn't have the energy for explanations. We swam up to the beach far enough away from them for plausible deniability. Once we'd waded from the waves, I shucked the backpack, unrolled my clothes, and toweled myself off.

"Here," I said, handing him the baggie with my skull-faced sweatpants. "These might fit you."

He cocked a grin at me. "Am I escorting you home?"

I thought about it. Seriously.

"Not yet," I finally decided. "No. I need some time to process stuff. Besides, my roommate's boyfriend is a dick. He'd probably try to New-Age guru you or something, and…" I steadied myself on Heaven's shoulder while I slipped the cutoffs on… "as fun as that might be to watch, I don't have energy for that kind of drama right now."

"Then keep them safe for me," he said, handing back the pants. "Come back tonight if you can."

"I will," I replied. "If I can." By now, a pair of female joggers approached. I felt the prickle of watching eyes. "You'd better get back in the water," I told him. "Before you're fending off cops… or worse yet…" I grinned. "Admirers."

We kissed twice more, draining what little strength I had let in my legs. My girl-parts sang a sore yet happy song. Heaven's cock swelled. I patted its head. "Down boy," I warned, "before you get us all in trouble."

"*More* trouble?" Heaven said, amused.

"Yes," I said, kissing him one last time. "*More* trouble. Now *git*."

He slid into the ocean as the joggers arrived. "Good morning," I said, pleasant… but it wasn't me they were looking at.

Out in the water, Heaven's podmates capered and squeaked, welcoming him back with the aquatic equivalent of *DUDE! You scored!*

Chuckling to myself, I waved, then began the short, achy walk back home.

"HEY, BEACH-HIPPIE." Ashli's voice burst through my cellphone speaker. "Why aren't you here today?"

"I got *fired*, remember?" My groggy voice sounded harsher than I'd intended. Every inch of me hurt. By the time my face had finally hit the couch, Chalice was on her way to work and Luke had already left. Hours later, the *True Blood* theme rattled from my phone. *I want to do bad things to you*, indeed.

"So what?" she shot back. "It's *payday*, bitch. Come get your check."

"I do direct deposit."

"Come in anyway."

Chip set firmly on my shoulder, I did.

Admittedly, the place looked less ominous when I didn't have to work there anymore. I've always been a book lover, and that fun wouldn't stop when the paychecks did. Besides, I'd just been paid so I had a little something to spare. I brought the magical beast book with me when I went, planning to buy it outright this time. Maybe, I thought, my employee discount might even still apply.

"So," said Ashli as we sat down for cheap Caesar salads in the taproom next to B&N, "did you hear about Margie yet?"

"No. She get promoted or something?"

"She got *shitcanned. SHIT. CAN. DUH.* Buh-*bye*-evil-bitch-*bye*." Ashli's face glowed with radiant vindication.

We clinked our glasses to toast the Evil One's demise.

"So…" Ashli continued when we'd finished a round of gloating, "maybe you can get your job back now."

"Huh." I thought about it as my tongue tried to dislodge a piece of romaine. "Does it make sense to say I'm not sure I *want* it back anymore?"

"Aw, *c'mon*." She scowled. "Don't you miss my pretty face?"

I laughed. "I don't need to work there to see you, Ash."

"It's *lonely* over there without you, Rache," she complained. "Everybody else is a *douche*."

"I'll think about it. Maybe," I promised. For a moment, my thoughts drifted.

"Who is he?" she said.

"Huh?"

"The stud who's written all over your *face*, bitch."

I probably flushed. "It's that obvious?"

"Like a big neon sign screaming *Just Been Fucked*."

"Okay," I surrendered, wincing with a smile.

I left out the dolphin stuff and told her the rest.

"So... *DOLPHINS*, HUH?" she said.

"What?"

"The dolphins," Chalice said when I got home that evening. "The ones Luke saw you swimming with this morning."

God. Damn. It.

I shot a look at Luke. He acted casual, hands clasped behind his head as he propped his feet up on an empty chair. Luke smiled with rank innocence. "You guys were beautiful, Rachel. I thought about saying hi but didn't want to interrupt."

Bombs went off in my chest. Behind my eyes. That passive-aggressive little fuck. I *knew* I'd felt eyes watching me on the beach... and if I hadn't seen Luke there, then he hadn't *wanted* to be seen.

"Gee, Luke" I said, my voice as even as I could manage. "I hadn't noticed you out there. What were *you* up to at that hour?"

Chalice has lousy taste in guys; she's not stupid, though. "Yeah, I was wondering where you were, myself, Luke. I got up to hit the bathroom and you weren't there. What's up with that?"

"I had insomnia again," he said with just the merest edge of pity in his voice. "I know that Rachel goes for early-morning runs when she can't sleep, and that sounded like a really good idea." With a nod, he indicated a sand-crusted yoga mat bag near the front door. "So, I grabbed my mat and went out to go do some forms on the beach." He smiled at me without a trace of irony. "It's beautiful out there, Rache, and…"

"Ray-*chel*," I corrected him.

"No hostility in my temple, please." Chalice warned.

I'm not stupid either, so I kept quiet as Luke continued.

"Rachel," he amended with a conciliatory nod. "And yeah – it's *totally* beautiful out there. The fog's like this gorgeous borderland… kind of a world between worlds, which is what some legends say mist *is*, anyway." He painted pictures of his words with his hands: "I had set up my mat and was going into my first downward dog when I saw shapes out in the water. As I watched them, I realized they were dolphins – and Rachel was out there swimming with them. Diving down, riding them, nuzzling each other…" His face got a beatific faraway look. "It was *beautiful*, Chalice. I wish you could have seen it."

I glanced over at her. She'd bought every word on the layaway plan.

Slippery as a greased ninja, that boy.

"So, how'd you find them?" Chalice asked. "Or did they find you?"

I stumbled out an off-my-head response that mixed the truth of our midnight-swim meetings with the omission of a certain gray-haired paramour. Watching their faces, I tried to gauge just how much Luke had seen. His expression remained as enigmatic as a bronze Buddha: placid with a hint of knowledge, but letting you puzzle out the rest for yourself. I left out the sex of course, winding things up with my spied-upon exit from the tide this morning.

Then Chalice dropped the bombshell: "Can we swim with them too?"

I was gonna *kill* Luke.

I shook my head. "They're wild animals, Chalice. Not pets, not even trained aquarium dolphins. I don't think they're accustomed to human beings."

"But they swim with *you*," she countered.

"I've been training for *years*, Chalice."

Her expression slid from request to resistance. "I remember." Icicles slid off her words.

Crap.

Too late, I recalled Chalice's face back at Siren's Cove. The hangdog look of envy she often wore. She had tried three times to pass the dive exams, but always got stuck behind the gift-shop counter. She'd worked hard, I suspect, to stay pleasant toward the water crew. Still, her friendliness held a bitter edge.

"Then you remember," I said, careful with my tone, "how hard we trained. How hard it was to pass the physicals."

"Yeah." The word curdled on her tongue. "But Hardass isn't *here*, Rachel. *You* are."

"Hardass" Jordan was our dive coach at Siren's Cove. If you didn't impress her, you didn't make the grade. Depending on who you asked, that nickname came from her sculpted butt, her attitude, or both. I figure it was both. She'd been the one to flunk Chalice in the tests – the one who'd kept her watching shows while the rest of us performed. Hardass had been *right* to keep Chalice out of the tanks. Pointing that out, though, wouldn't win this dispute.

Luke tried not to get caught smirking. I noticed anyway.

"Chalice," I said, "it's dangerous. Really. You could *die*. I almost have."

"Life without risk," Chalice declared, "is a lot like death."

"I agree with you, Chalice. I *do*." And I did. We were kindred spirits in that regard. I reached out for her shoulder; she held back. "Out there, though," I continued, "it's different. Even *I* have a hard time in deep open water, and I've got years – I mean *years* – of swimming and diving experience."

"I know. You're a *mermaid*."

Ouch.

"Maybe," I replied. "Maybe not. But I'm *not* a lifeguard." I shifted my gaze to glare to Luke. "I'm on my own out there. My business is my business. If *I* get hurt swimming with dolphins, it's *my* problem. If I take someone else out there, though, I'm responsible. For you. For *them*. For everything."

"We wouldn't *sue* you," Chalice countered.

"I could get *arrested*. I could go to *jail*." I lowered my voice. "Worse still, I could get the *dolphins* hurt… which would be bad for *them*." I stepped back slightly, addressing Luke and Chalice both. "This isn't just risky for you or for me, guys, it's risky for *them*. For the dolphins maybe most of all."

Chalice nodded, unhappy but convinced.

"I've swam with dolphins in Hawaii," Luke said, overstressing the second-syllable accent: *Ha-VAH-eee*. "At Lori's estate in Maui. I can take care of *us*. And I know what I'm doing with *them*."

I sensed a lie but couldn't confirm it.

"Besides," he went on, "there's that gray-haired dude you were with this morning. He can help keep an eye on things, too."

Bastard.

"I mean," Luke concluded, glancing between Chalice's face and mine, "if the two of *you* can swim with them, it should be okay to share that experience. I'm sure the dolphins wouldn't mind. They might even…" he said, addressing the last words to Chalice, "welcome us being there among them."

I was pretty sure they wouldn't.

But the matter was settled.

And I *really* needed to find a new place to live.

For a mad moment, I considered it.

Running away with the dolphins. With Heaven. Just disappearing that night into the sea.

Sitting alone in the temple later, eyeing my scatter of stuff and feeling like Judas on the half-shell, I considered just plain *leaving*. Stripping off my clothes at the beach and never coming back again.

But that would be stupid.

For starters, Heaven and I hardly knew each other. Would *you* move in with someone you'd just met? Okay, the sex was hot… but the Pacific wasn't. Sure, I might be able to hold my breath a long time, but *then* what? Catch and eat raw fish all my life? Swim until

I got exhausted and drowned? Get busted by the Coast Guard for indecent exposure while my dolphin boyfriend swam away? *Not practical, Rachel. Not real.* Magic was fun in faerie tales, but real life doesn't end with Happily Ever Afters.

I thumbed through the book on magical beasts that I'd purchased that afternoon. It already fell open to the Dolphins entry, and I scanned the words, restless, as I pondered my next move.

I'd finally agreed to Chalice's demands. That conversation set clocks ticking in my head. We'd finished the discussion on shaky ground, and while Chalice never said as much, I knew my welcome mat had been more or less withdrawn.

San Francisco had proved to be a tangle of self-important New Age twits. Luke wasn't even the worst of the ones I'd met so far. I'd have no problem finding a place to crash if I really needed one; I wasn't sure, though, that I'd be willing to pay the price. My options, at that point, looked pretty damn small. No *real* friend I had had space for me to land, and of the people I knew in town, Ashli was now the only one I trusted.

My thoughts chased one another's tails as I laid down and tried to sleep.

"No," said Heaven.

"That was my answer too," I told him on the beach, long after midnight. "They didn't want to hear it."

"They can't *force* you," he said. We were curled up in the sand, his arms warm around me. I'd arrived edgy; he'd asked why. Instead of blowing up, as I'd been worried he might do, he simply held me on the beach. His refusal had been quiet. Calm. And firm.

"No," I agreed, "but she can kick me out. She pretty much said as much last night."

"That doesn't seem like much of a loss," he rumbled, his soft words vibrating from his chest to my ears. Heaven's fingers slipped, salt-sticky, through my hair. We hadn't made love but the closeness remained.

Heaven's skin felt good against my own. The breeze raised goosebumps on my arms. We were naked again, as usual, but sitting on the land. In the distance, his brothers and sisters chased each other through the waves, now and then leaping into the air. Their cries and splashes echoed through the mist.

By now, I could tell them apart from one another. The one we'd freed from the net had mottled skin and three small scars running along her snout. She was a prankster even by dolphin standards, so I called her that and she seemed to like it. The smallest of the boys was a real charmer, so I gave him that name: Charm. The largest sibling had big fins and could out-race the others; for obvious reasons, I named her Race. The darkest of them was also the most beautiful – sleek with perfect lines and a face that would make sculptors reach for marble and tools. He seemed so majestic I just had to name him Apollo. These weren't the names Heaven called them, of course; when I used those names, though, they answered. That seemed to please Heaven. It certainly pleased *me*.

I hadn't wanted to risk this fragile bond. Still, I didn't want secrets between us, either. I'd had enough of that crap a long time ago. Secrets never last. And when they pop out, usually at the worst possible times, they leave bigger messes than the truth would have made. So, I'd rolled aside the boulder in my throat and leveled with Heaven about Luke and Chalice. To my vast relief, he hadn't freaked.

I was getting to kinda like this guy.

"That's true," I replied. "I'm sort of low on options, though."

"Friends? Family?"

I made a face. "My best friend lives across the country, with a new baby and a full-time job. Her husband doesn't like me, and the feeling's mutual. Most of my other friends scattered when Siren's Cove broke up. And you couldn't *pay* me enough to live with Mom again. Jobs are scarce, money's tight, and may every god help you if you don't have a permanent address. I've been doing what I can, but decent choices are running out."

He puffed a half-laugh through his nose. "You're a mermaid," he said, looking down into my eyes. "Land doesn't seem like home to you."

"Yeah." I looked away. "It never really has."

"It never really *has* to be," he said. "Not now."

Though not underwater, I stopped breathing.

Searched the darkness of his eyes.

I held my breath while clashing feelings whirled against themselves.

"Are you inviting me," I whispered, "to move in with you?"

We both started laughing – two nervous chuckles that built into an edgy disbelieving tide. Every time one of us stopped laughing, the other would start again. We cried with salt hilarity.

"Yes," he said finally, "I suspect I am."

I expressed my reservations. He shook his head, smiling. "Did you think," he asked me, "that'd I'd been living in the ocean these last few years, alone with my family, like Tarzan of the Waves?"

"Um…" I scrunched my face. "I kinda did." Reaching out to comb his dripping hair, I added. "Does it make sense that I'm relieved you know who Tarzan is?"

"I'm no Lord Greystoke," he said. "I'm not rich, and there's a lot of about people I don't know. Still, I've got friends at the Aquarium – *human* ones – and places to stay when I get bored with the sea."

I scrunched my face in disbelief. "You get *bored?*"

He laughed loud enough to echo off the waves. "Yes," he said, "I get bored. Why do you think I became what I am?"

"Did you consciously *decide* to do it?"

He looked contemplative. "I'm not sure," he finally said. "I hadn't *planned* to do it, but I suppose on some level that I did."

"How?"

"I don't know." He ran his fingers down my cheek, raising little blue chills along my back. "I was born…" He nodded toward the sea. "Like my brothers and sisters. To this day, I don't know really understand why I'm different. I used to watch the people watching me, wondering what their lives must be like. Sometimes it seemed

382

as though I could slide behind their eyes and watch me watching them. A part of me could wander off with them, seeing the park from a human perspective." His own eyes got a faraway look. "I started dreaming I was a man. And then one night I woke up in the tank…" He looked down at himself. "Like *this*."

"That must have been scary," I said, holding my palm to his heart like I'd seen him do with Prankster.

He chuckled. Took my hand. Kissed it. Looked at me. "I've had," he said, "much worse experiences."

Close-up, I could see the scars I'd missed before. Old cuts, bite-marks. Healing gashes from our ghost-net fight. I laid my face against his salty chest and listened to the strong pulse beneath his ribs.

Heaven's face got that faraway look again. "There's a lot about me you might not like, Rachel. A lot of ways I'm more like *them* than like *you*. I'm not sure what I can offer you, and I'm not sure what you can offer me." He turned to look down at me again. "But I dreamed of being a man for a reason. I escaped my cage and freed the rest of us. I want to help you leave yours, too."

"What about Dr. Rose?" I said, cursing myself inside from bringing her up again. Still, I had to know.

"She's not in jail anymore." His face slid into something that looked like sadness.

I still wasn't sure how to read Heaven's odd inflections or the expressions he showed to me. In ways, he was an ocean inside.

But then again, aren't we all?

"Do you still see her?"

He shook his head. "Not these days. Not in a while. No. I sometimes wish I did. But she carries her cage in her head, and no matter what tricks I performed…" His voice took an acidic turn. "I could never get through to her. It was there before she met me. It's there now that I'm gone. Rose has her journey. I've got mine."

"And me?" I said. "Where am *I* headed?"

Heaven kissed my nose. "I just *love* you," he said with casually ambiguous affection. "If you needed *me* to answer that for you, we wouldn't be here now."

"True enough," I answered.

For a while, we snuggled in silence.

We heard his siblings through the misty darkness, playing in the sea. I swear on some levels that I was starting to understand their words.

"Did you ask *them*," I said, nodding my chin toward the sound.

"About what?"

"About me?"

"Of course."

"And they didn't mind?"

He chuckled. "They're the ones who suggested it."

"Did they?"

"They did. I just wasn't sure, until now, that I'd ask."

"I get that."

He nodded. "They like you, you know."

384

"That's mutual. I think. It's hard to understand them now."

"You'll learn," Heaven added. "If you want to. You have time to do that if you take that step. To learn all that, and more besides"

If I took that step...

Passages, I realized. *Thresholds. Worlds.* Dolphins guide souls between life and death in legends. According to my book, they're *psychopomps*: god-like entities that lead people through transformations. Their name comes from the Greek word for *womb*. The place of gestation. The place of birth.

But they're animals, too. Capricious. Sometimes killers. Implacable like the sea. The ancient Greeks thought that dolphins were descended from pirates who'd tried to rape the god Dionysus. He turned the men into dolphins, and all dolphins still share their ferocious sense of fun. People underestimate our sea-going cousins, and those misconceptions sometimes kill. Flipper's smile can be a nasty trickster's grin. And you'd never know until you took that step, reached out and held your breath, just what might happen when you did.

Doctor Rose Dean had loved Heaven. That love destroyed her life. What might his love do to mine?

"Did you mean it?" I asked him.

"Mean what?"

"That you love me."

He ran his fingers through my hair. "To be honest, I don't know yet."

Heaven kissed me, then, and I felt us sink beneath each other's skins. When we drew back, he eased my eyes open with his fingertips. "I don't know," he repeated, looking into me, "but I want to find out."

"Y'know," I said, kissing him again. "That was actually the right answer."

"Show me," I told him.

"What?"

"Show me," I said, "who you *are*. *What* you are." We were back in the sea, treading water past the buoy line. Their lights scattered on the dancing tide. The waves had kicked up stronger. I ached to go below.

"You've seen me," he replied. Heaven's voice held a faint note of hesitation.

"I want," I said, "to see you change."

For a moment, I thought he'd swim away. Even in the flickering light, I saw some ugly ghost pass across his face. Then he nodded. Drew in a deep breath.

I did the same.

We dove.

Trails of bubbles sparkled in our wake as we pulled down to colder depths. The other dolphins followed us. Race offered her fin to me as Prankster flashed past Heaven and called to him. Heaven kicked faster, stroked harder, bolted down at a speed no human swimmer could match.

In pulsating shadows, I saw him shift.

Prankster and Heaven sped back toward us. Heaven glided in Prankster's wake, letting the dolphin's speed become his own. As I watched, his human skin seemed to slide away in a bubbling haze, leaving the sleek-muscled form of his dolphin self.

And oh God, was he beautiful.

Heaven's skin held the pearl-gray tone of his hair. His eyes maintained their dark curiosity. My own salt-clouded eyes caught the quirk of his grin as he angled off and headed toward Race and me.

I let go of Race and caught Heaven's fin.

In a blast of speed, we flew toward the surface again.

We burst up, exultant, from the tossing waves. Heaven leaped into the air. For several seconds, he seemed to hang in the hazy air. Then he crashed back to the waves again, his splash filling my mouth and nose with sea. My heart followed that magnificent leap.

As I spit out the water, he slid up to me. I ran my hands across his hide. Caught my breath. Kissed his skin. Held him against my humming flesh as we cut through the water toward deep seas.

"Take me down," I whispered. "As deep as you can."

Heaven barked a protest.

"I'll be fine," I assured him. Somehow, I knew that I would. "If we're gonna do this thing, I have to *know*. I can't just be your girl-toy floating on the surface, Heaven. Lemmie grab a big breath first. And then take me down as far as you can go."

This was it. A dream along the edge.

As a little girl, I used to wish I could swim to the bottom of the sea. Growing up, I realized that was impossible. Even at the slightest depths, the weight of water becomes impossible to bear. I never stopped dreaming, though. Taking the deepest breath I could, I held on tight and reached for that dream.

The light, the surface, everything I knew of my world slipped away. In the burst of Heaven's speed, we fell into all-consuming dark.

The freeze crushed against my bones, pounded my eardrums flat, made my heart throb dull inside its cage. My lungs soon burned as I emptied them of all but the smallest trace of oxygen. Heaven's fin cut deep into my grasp. I clenched my hands to his slippery hide. His muscles pumped power to my own. The icy rush cut across my skin like razors as an elemental void drew us down.

Inside I burned. Inside I hungered. Inside I dreamed and loved and cried with joy.

The pulse between my legs was an animal thing, beating stronger than my heart. All pretense and politeness had been stripped away. I *wanted* like a beast wants, with the hunger of a siren with her prey. I understood the lure of dark depths and the secrets locked beneath the waves. I saw nothing, felt everything, and craved even more.

Time slid away. Nothing mattered but sensation and the hungry dark. Echoes rang in my aching ears – dolphin cries cutting through the night. We swept along through an endless crush where *forward* was the only direction possible.

Finally, as the last of my air soured and my throat cramped with the need to breathe, I felt us rise toward the surface again.

We broke through in near-darkness, so far beyond the buoys that I could barely see their light.

I was in agony. I was in ecstasy. I felt so blessed between the edges of pain and rapture that all I could do once I got my breath was laugh until my throat felt raw.

After making sure I was okay, Heaven left me with Race and Apollo as he dove down and shifted forms. Surfacing as his gray-maned self, he swam over and held me tight. "Are you all right, Rachel?" he asked, his voice tight with concern.

"I am…" I gasped. "So far *beyond* the shores of just 'all right' that I never want to feel just 'all right' again." I took his puzzled face between my hands and kissed him ravenously. "That means," I told him when we'd finished, "that I'm having the time of my life."

His face spread in that happy-dolphin grin. "So, what," he asked, "do you want to do now?"

"I want," I told him, "to go back down there and fuck you until I can't walk for a year."

I still managed to walk when we'd finally made it back to shore near dawn, but I was far from disappointed.

I TOOK MY STUFF to Ashli's two days later. "Can you hang onto this for me?" I asked, shoving my sandals into the hiking pack.

"*Dude!* Of *course*," she insisted with her usual emphatic tone.

"Thanks." I breathed much easier now.

"So, when you coming back?"

"I don't know." I shrugged one shoulder. "Maybe tomorrow. Maybe never."

That last word hung in the air for a second.

We took the moment in. Held it quietly.

"I got *promoted!*" Ashli yelled out of nowhere. "Can you *believe* that shit?"

"Congratulations, Ash." I hugged her. Hard.

"If you need a job…" she said into my hair.

"I'll remember. Thanks," I said into hers.

"*So*, beach-hippie," she asked, "You're *really* running away with this dude? For *reals?*" Her face scowled a few inches from my own.

"Maybe," I confessed. "I don't know. But I'll hate myself if I don't find out."

"Go *crazy*, then, bitch," she whispered. "Without some crazy, you might as well be dead."

"Do EXACTLY," Heaven told them, "as I say."

"It's cool," Luke replied. "I know dolphins. They love me. I swam with them in Ha-*vah*-eee." He *so* deserved whatever Heaven had in mind.

It felt weird seeing Heaven wear clothes. It felt weird wearing clothes around him, too. I'd scored him a set of tight black trunks (*with dolphin designs – I couldn't resist*) during the week we'd spent together since that night. I'd lived mostly on the beach that week, building my endurance and acclimating myself to the great outdoors. It was easier than it should have been; my inner fire kept me warm. Like icy winters and crushing depths, hypothermia didn't bother me. Oddly, I seemed immune to it, as if gifted with a magical inheritance of my own.

For food, we'd scrounged up goodies or shared meals throughout San Francisco and Half Moon Bay, spending the rest of my bank balance and the money Heaven earned doing odd jobs for his friends. One of those friends, Grace, owned an estate on the water's edge of Tiburon Bay. She seemed happy to feed us, offer crash-space, and put us to work around the house. I liked Grace but wasn't certain how far to trust her. Grace's eyes watched Heaven – or, as she called him, "Ariel" – while we worked, her gaze sliding along his naked muscles. She maintained, as she put it, "a clothing-optional home," and preferred it when folks opted not to. For some reason I never heard about, she and Chalice didn't like each other. That didn't exactly break my heart.

Chalice and I, meanwhile, had grown more distant. We pretended pleasantries that neither of us meant. More than anything, I felt sorry for her. As for Luke, I didn't bother. He was Chalice's problem now, not mine.

I had expected Luke to wear a Speedo to the beach, but he chose somewhat tasteful jams instead. Black, with a blue-and-white flame pattern. Honestly, he looked good in them. In another life, in another world, I might once have found Luke attractive. Now, though, he nagged me like a rotten tooth.

And the dentist was most definitely *in*.

There's a way guys stand when one's trying to be dominant. Shoulders back, chest out, chin either propped up or dropped low for a fight. Luke stood that way now, his thumbs hooked in the waistband of his jams. Heaven didn't bother posturing. Instead, he shrugged at Luke's insistence. "Well, you're obviously experienced," he told Luke, "so do what you will."

"*Do what thou wilt,*" Luke misquoted, "*is the whole of the law.*"

We stood together on the sand, near sunset, as the sky burned vivid colors mirrored back across the waves. I wore my swimsuit with a diving knife I'd purchased earlier that week. A change of clothes and some towels lay stashed in my backpack at our feet. Breeze blew in from the sea with chilly promises of night. Out near the horizon, Heaven's family splashed and leaped, making themselves obvious to the people on the beach. A few kids pointed. Their parents smiled. For that while, the world looked innocent.

As usual, folks wandered or waded through the sand. Yoga Girl was there; her name was Kim, and we'd since gotten to be friends.

"*Nameste,*" she called out, waving. Kim was one of the few folks I'd met around the Bay who didn't make me grimace when she said that phrase.

"Nameste," I called back, ignoring Luke's sudden glance toward Kim. As I'd seen that past week, she had better taste in men than Chalice did.

As for Chalice, she wavered between excitement and trepidation, her lime-green bikini half-covered by a small floatation vest. Luke, of course, was too cool to wear one himself. His gym-fed muscles flexed their glory to the sea. He stretched theatrically for Kim's benefit, then padded down to the incoming tide. Chalice trailed behind him. We followed the two of them.

"You're not planning to *hurt* them, are you?" I whispered to Heaven.

"That," he said flashing his trickster's grin, "depends on them."

Thigh-deep in the waves, Luke performed an invocation – some New-Age nonsense about "the children of the sea." From someone else, it might have seemed reverent. I wanted a stray wave to knock him on his pretentious ass. Chalice stepped beside him, closed her eyes, and tried to ride the spirit of the moment. I sensed her anxiousness and moved to take her hand.

"You okay?" I asked.

She jerked her hand away. Fear flowed into a familiar grudge. "I'm fine," she said with false confidence, "*mermaid.*"

Luke had apparently peeled some old scabs back while I was gone. I tried not to show how hurt I felt.

"Ready?" Heaven asked. They nodded.

We swam out.

There's a vast difference between the ocean and a pool – a restless weight that never stills. Within seconds, Luke and Chalice were panting hard. "Want to go back?" Heaven offered. Luke sputtered. Chalice hesitated, then shook her head.

"Remember," I told them, "your safety's *your* responsibility, not ours."

We felt the ground fall away. Felt the cold distance of the ocean grow. Waves and currents pulled our bodies in capricious waves. *Is this what I'm choosing*, I asked myself. *Is this what I want my life to be?* A struggle on the verge of endless depths, skirting the surface of some unfathomable void? Each stroke, each kick, took me closer from stability.

But then I looked at Heaven and watched the sunlight burn across his skin. His clean strokes cut tiny droplets from the sea. He caught me watching. Grinned his precious dolphin grin. For that instant, I would've given up the touch of land beneath my feet forever. He dove, then, and I followed him down.

We spiraled deep to where darkness plays with light. Sent our bubble-breaths searching for the sky again. We slid against each other, skins chafing at the strain of clothes. Far down below, we kissed while fishes ran their endless errands through the sea.

His family – *my* family! – joined us then, and we all headed back above.

The dolphins got there first.

As cute as they appear to us, dolphins are really fucking *strong*. Well over five hundred pounds of ocean-honed torpedo. Bottlenoses kill sharks, seals, porpoises, and sometimes men. Luke and Chalice were about to get seriously schooled.

Prankster, true to her name, opened the game, brushing Chalice's foot with her dorsal fin. Chalice's shriek echoed through the water down to us. Race began to swim fast circles underneath the waves, drawing strong currents in her wake. As Luke and Chalice struggled in the pull, Apollo darted in and bumped Luke with his nose. It looked playful but I knew it hurt. Charm flashed through the waves above, out of reach, too fast to clearly see.

Not one of the dolphins had shown themselves. For all Luke and Chalice knew, they had sharks, not dolphins, at their feet. Heaven's siblings darted in and out around the swimmers – nipping them, bumping them, taunting them with elusive speed and predatory silence.

So much for Luke's "children of the sea."

When I surfaced, Chalice coughed up a small scream. Clearly terrified, she stared at me with huge blue eyes.

Charm breached, then – leaping high beside them and then splashing down in a blinding crash.

Luke and Chalice disappeared beneath the wave.

I reached out underwater toward the flash of Chalice's life-vest. This time she didn't pull away. I grabbed her hand and hauled her to the surface. Below us, Luke kicked as Apollo pulled off his blue-black jams. Cold water, I noticed, had its usual effect on Luke.

"Okay, come on now," I told Chalice as we surfaced. "Breathe."

She sputtered.

"You okay?"

She nodded.

"I'll go get your boyfriend."

I frog-kicked down in time to see Luke give up on trying to catch Apollo. Dolphin laughter clicked and echoed in our ears. I swam toward Luke. He waved me back. Heaven rose nearby, leaving Luke to struggle up alone.

Race broke off her circling, sped toward the surface, and breached just as Luke inhaled. Again, the surge washed over us all. I saw it coming. Luke and Chalice did not. Bobbing back up, they coughed with throat-racking urgency.

"Let's go in now," I suggested.

Chalice nodded.

"No fucking way," Luke spat with forced bravado. "That was *great!*"

Charm and Race danced across the surface, cackling at Luke's words.

Curious shouts rang up from the beach. People must have noticed the distress. A few surfers bellied out on their boards, paddling in our direction. "Okay, folks," I told the others. "Playtime's over. C'mon – let's go back."

"I can't go back," Luke protested. "That dolphin's got my jams."

"You're lucky," Heaven snorted, "that's all he took off you."

"Hey, *fuck* you, Tarzan!"

Heaven glared.

"That's *it*," I snapped. "We're done here."

"Fuck you, too. I don't need chaperones."

"Luke." Chalice shut her eyes in frustration. "Stop being a macho ass."

By now, the surfers and a few swimmers were headed our direction. I spotted Kim grabbing a towel and running into the surf. Brave girl. That made me like her even more.

Heaven's family darted through the waves, setting up a serious chop. "I used to do this in Ha-*vah*-eee," Luke said. It was obviously untrue. "I know what I'm doing," he insisted. His gasping voice said otherwise.

"*Luke*," I shouted with all the lungpower I could raise. "You are embarrassing your girlfriend and endangering the rest of us. Knock off your bullshit or we're leaving you here."

"So, *go*." He gurgled as the dolphins laughed.

"Chalice?"

"Fuck 'im. Let's go."

Race breached high right next to Luke, then crashed down sideways, sending up a wave that could have swamped battleships. Luke went down again. This wasn't cool. If that moron drowned himself, the Coast Guard might clamp down on the dolphins. Luke's dumb ass could wreck everything.

"Can you get them to chill?" I asked Heaven as Luke sputtered to the surface again.

He shrugged. "I can try. We *are* our own creatures, after all."

I hoped Chalice didn't catch the subtext there.

Now Luke was roaring half-garbled insults at the dolphins. Heaven dove down, probably to change. I hustled Chalice toward the surfers. Back behind us, Apollo surfaced with Luke's jams in his mouth. He skated across the waves on his tail, cackling at Luke's rage.

Prankster and Charm broke through ahead of us, then raced in our direction.

Chalice, panicked, pulled away from me. "It's okay," I assured her, hoping I was right. The waves tossed heavily, reminding us all just how small we really were. Then Prankster slid up alongside me, squeakily offering me her fin.

"Prankster," I asked, "can you take her in?"

My dolphin-sibling bobbed up in the waves, nodding.

By now, Apollo and Race were playing catch with Luke's bathing suit. They reminded me a bit too much of bullies with the new kid's lunch. True, *Luke* was the real bully here. Still it bothered me. I sighed. Enough was enough.

"This is Prankster," I told Chalice. "Prankster, this is Chalice." I slid my hand along her scarred snout. She nuzzled me as Chalice's eyes went wide. "You're *both* my *friends*," I said with emphasis. "Prankster, could you please take Chalice home?"

Again, she nodded.

"It's okay," I told her. "She knows you now."

I saw a maze of questions behind her eyes. She didn't voice them. Her wary hands reached for Prankster's fin. "Hold on," I told her.

She did. Together, they raced toward shore.

Now for Luke…

Heaven, in his dolphin-self, was trying to talk Race and Apollo into playing nice. Luke, caught between them, struggled to stay afloat. I took Charm's fin and headed toward them. I tried to call out to Luke but swallowed a spray of sea instead.

Race ducked in to give Luke a final nudge. Luke, furious, reached out to grab Race's dorsal fin. He barked out a vindicated *"HA!"*

And then disappeared in a shower of surf.

Idiot.

Grabbing a dolphin is like hanging onto a speedboat's ski-line without the skis. As winded as he was, Luke could drown before Race even realized he was there.

"Charm, my friend," I said, gulping down a breath, "let's fetch that jackass."

Heaven bolted after Race. Apollo darted after Heaven. Charm and I flew after all of them. We bolted through the waves, more or less across the surface. I kept waiting for Luke to let go, but he was too scared, too arrogant, too stupid, or all three.

Whatever he *did* do, it pissed Race off. With a sudden arc, Race leaped high and then dove, dragging Luke down with her.

"Crap," I snarled. Patting Charm's side, I caught a fresh breath and whispered *"Down."*

Ahead of us, Heaven's body flexed like sunlight through the waves. Though I couldn't see details, I could *feel* him through the distance. Some strange empathy revealed each rippled contour of his skin. As Charm and I sped behind them, Luke finally let go of Race's fin. Heaven caught Luke's thrashing body by one arm.

Shook him lightly to establish dominance. Then hauled Luke back to the surface again.

I hugged Charm, then let go and kicked upward toward the sun. I realized, as I swam, that feats which would have winded me a week before seemed easy to me now. My lungs hardly hurt at all, and it seemed as though a dolphin's strength – or a mermaid's – had become my own.

That final race drained Luke's attitude. Naked and shivering, he held tight to Heaven's side. "Are we done now?" I asked once I'd regained my breath.

He nodded.

"Sweetheart," I said, stroking Heaven's gorgeous face, "let's go home."

"I COULD FEEL YOU out there today," Heaven said. "Inside my skin. Like part of me."

We stretched out naked on the sand. I wore the knife-belt and nothing more. Dusk had long since faded out, and the fog turned streetlamps and bonfires to bright haze along the beach.

"I felt it too," I admitted, nuzzling at his neck. "What does that mean?"

He cocked one shoulder. "I don't know."

"Never happened before?"

He waved one hand toward the sound of our family. "Only with them. No one else."

"Not Rose?"

"Not even Rose."

I pondered that for a while.

"You realize," he told me, "that you've done impossible things this week."

"I *do*, yeah," I said, nodding. "And I want to do more. *Lots* more. With you."

Our breaths rose and fell in unison. Our hearts beat in a single pace. I realized then that *I'd* never felt anything like that, either. No other lover, not even Todd, had ever felt so close to me.

Was this what we look for all our lives? What we beat our heads and hearts bloody trying to achieve? Was it this connection, this sense of being *met* and carried in separate yet united selves, the essence of love we crave?

"*Do* you?" he asked, his voice almost lost beneath my own thoughts.

I turned to face him.

My body knew the answer.

"With everything I have," I declared, "Yeah – I *do*."

We stood up, then. Brushed the sand from our skins.

He reached out, firm. I took his hand, strong.

Strength to strength. Breath to breath. Skin to skin.

Nearby, the tide shushed itself against the sand – the rolling endless threshold between land and sea. My last change of clothes was stashed in my backpack, hidden deep in a brace of rocks and driftwood. Somewhere out beyond this beach, Heaven had a life he wanted to share with me. I looked forward to discovering it – and to see how far I could dive when land no longer felt like home.

I waded with Heaven into the sea.

The sea reached up and took us in.

I had dreamed of being a mermaid.

He had dreamed of being a man.

With one last breath, I whispered, "So now let's see what *else* we can dream…"

AUTHOR NOTES:
TALES BEHIND TALES

As a member of the audience, I've always loved learning the "stories behind the stories" of the media I enjoy: author notes, liner notes, directors' commentaries, bios, that sort of thing. And because my work is intensely personal, drawn near-inevitably from my life, I want to offer the following "tale behind tales" for the stories in this collection. If you enjoy this sort of thing too, feel free to keep reading. If not, thanks for your time and I hope you liked this book.

Cheers either way, y'all. Take care and be well!

TASTING THROUGH
THE ROOTS

My PRIMARY childhood home was surrounded by woods. Built in the late 1960s and early '70s, the development had been constructed *within* the land, not *upon* the land. As a kid, I used to spend uncountable hours in those woods – climbing trees, swinging from vines, digging in creeks, and shaping stories around my surroundings. Later, as a teen and young adult, I'd run off to those woods at all hours, sometimes in nothing but a pair of cutoffs and my own sense of primal abandon. In later years, I'd bring girlfriends to the woods, and we'd make out in the dirt or along the banks of forest creeks. I felt a keen *belonging* in such places; when I connected with my Pagan beliefs, those roots could literally be found in the woods where I grew up.

Originally written for my *Deliria* sourcebook *Everyday Heroes: Adventures for the Rest of Us*, "Tasting Through the Roots" was directly inspired by my then-partner and still-friend Ann Lenore Taylor, who I was living with when I wrote that book. The narrator's sentiments reflect some things Ann herself said, and you can also find her influence in the stories "Ravenous" and "The Green Tunnel." The first time Ann took me to meet her parents, she introduced me to the oak tree she had grown up climbing in and retreating into. Ann insists that she can feel trees speak to her, and I believe her. One of my many nicknames for Ann is "Magnolia Faerie," and although the observation about ants and birds and the memory of trees is my own insight (one I had years before I met Ann), the narrator's voice is totally the Magnolia Faerie talking.

SWALLOWED

There's nothing "fantasy" about this story, save the fantasy of becoming a legend in your own mind. And yet, beyond the obvious play on godhood and that faerie-tale punchline, "Swallowed" is about identity, determination, and the chance to manufacture myths if you've got the guts (and the stomach) to push past those moments when life tries to bring you down.

Identity, as I've realized over time, is a primary theme within my writing. Although my gaming work emphasizes inspiration and empowerment, my fiction deals largely with identity and a tension between two disparate yet associated senses of self that usually (though not always) resolve into a balance. That idea is probably most obvious in stories like "Swallowed," "Ravenous," "Chaser," and "Johnny Serious," but it carries through even in separate and contrasting characters (Elynne Dragonchild, Lord and Father, the lovers of "Willow and Wind," Riplash and the narrator of "I Feel Lucky," and so forth), where such characters bounce off one another's contrasts while caught in the inexorable ties between them. For Ravenwolf Grigori, that tension comes through in the rock 'n' roll persona he crafts for himself, and the insecure guy underneath. Speaking as a person who always disliked his given name, adopted new name, writes occasionally under a third name, and never really felt much like a "guy" to begin with, that's a tension I understand. I've got a secure sense of myself now (as much as anyone can have one, I guess), but it took me a lifetime to get here and the stories in this book reflect that journey.

I based the Psychlotron on the outside stage of Atlanta's late, lamented club The Masquerade, perhaps my favorite venue from the White Wolf days. I saw the Ramones play one of their last gigs on a humid Georgia evening there, and that sweat-soaked celebration provided a real-world basis for this tale. The Henry Rollins spoken-word piece I refer to in "Swallowed" is called "Nothing Can Go Wrong," and it deals with Hank knocking himself unconscious in the opening seconds of a major gig. That moment became my story's key inspiration, and I hear "Swallowed" in my head (and perform it out loud during live readings) as coming through in Henry Rollins' voice.

Ravenwolf's bandmates, Brian and Chipper, originated in "Ravenous," and have since joined the ranks of my favorite creations. I made versions of them both in *Rock Band*, and I have several stories featuring the two friends which are currently in the works as I write these words. You're quite likely to see them again…

THE KING OF SLEEP

As SHORT as this story is, it's among my all-time favorites. Like Marlene, I envisioned the King of Sleep's tale in a short burst of inspiration. I have no idea where it came from, and I don't question it. Although the King himself resembles a spirit named Ojala the Benevolent (who I'd created for *The Sorcerers Crusade Companion* back in 1998), both that figure and his story came straight from my imagination. Thank you, King of Sleep!

ELYNNE DRAGONCHILD

A MILESTONE STORY for me, this tale took shape when I was working at "Virginia's Largest Shoe Store" – a job I loathed every second of the five years I spent there. Initially inspired by paintings from Rowena Morrell and Boris Vallejo, "Elynne" took shape across a collection of index cards I kept in my back pocket and wrote on when I had a chance. Liking what I saw, I transcribed my notes at home and then completed the story in a long day's push.

Polishing it up, I sent Elynne's saga to Marion Zimmer Bradley – an editor who'd said she didn't want to receive any more dragon stories unless they showed her something she'd never seen before. In her forward to the tale's appearance in *Sword & Sorceress IX*, Marion wrote that "Phil seems to have thought the subject through, and brings us a different dragon story…" This tale became both my first attempted submission to a major publisher, and my first mass-market sale. That victory encouraged me to keep writing; thirty years after the story appeared, that's still my full-time career.

As I noted in the Author Notes of my 2013 collection *Wyldsight: Tales of Primal Fantasy*, the figure of a wild, elemental, rebellious, and often female character is a hallmark of my work. I used to look for her in other people, but eventually realized that person is an innate element of my self:

Whenever I've needed to clear my head, I've headed off to the woods or a beach. Thankfully, such places have always been close to where I've lived. In later years, I learned long-distance hiking from my friends Heidi and Kelly; those treks invested me with a sense of the World Beyond the Cities, where you could dance in a thunderstorm or wander through mists without seeing another human being for days.

Age and injuries have limited my ability to do those sorts of things these days, but the wilderness will always be a part of me, my faith, and the stories I tell.

The Wild Girl has been a part of me for almost as long as the woods themselves. I've seen her run barefoot between the trees, sometimes in the flesh, often only in my mind's eye. I've been involved with some of her earthly manifestations too, but her true connection to me is internal. On a lot of levels, she is me – my Anima, or female aspect, tied eternally to primal Nature. These stories are hers, are mine, are beyond us both.

"Elynne Dragonchild" marked that figure's first appearance in my professional work. It wouldn't be her last. In the years since Elynne's debut, I've delved deeper into Jungian and post-Jungian archetypes and shadow-theory, embracing Whitman's sentiment that "I contain multitudes," and recognizing my artistic creations as reflections and manifestations of my identity. Where I once saw a mysterious and alluring wild Muse, I now recognize myself.

An amusing sidenote: Not long after I'd sold the story, I had sent a copy of it to my cousin John, a professional artist and lifetime fantasy fan. "It's kinda purple in places," John responded, "but you might be able to find a publisher for it somewhere." I laughed and said, "It's already been sold." "Well," he replied, "there you go then." He was right.

Even closer to home, my wife Sandi has said that she'd first encountered the story as a reader of the *Sword & Sorceress* series, back when the book originally appeared in the early '90s. "Huh," she recalls thinking, "A *guy* wrote this? I'll bet he'd be interesting to get to know." She got the chance a decade-and-a-half later, and she didn't even realize that I'd written this particular story until I'd seen it on her bookshelf after we had moved in together. Like I said, this tale's a milestone.

LOOPHOLES

BETWEEN 2000 AND 2004, I went from being a married home-and-business owner with tens of thousands of dollars in savings, credit, and investments to being a divorced ex-homeowner and struggling business owner with no savings, credit *or* investments, plus almost $50,000 in debts. I got to know Jack Dunning all too well during those days, and so I created that Money Ogre to describe the constant pressure of anxiety I felt. Although bankruptcy helped me slip free of Jack's weight in 2005, by the Autumn of 2007 he was back. A client screwed me out of $4000 that year, leaving me stranded in Seattle with a rapidly depleting bank account, a dead car, and an apartment back home in North Carolina. One night, while "practically vibrating with stress" as Sandi puts it, I told my then-new then-girlfriend Sandra Damiana Buskirk (now Swan) about Jack Dunning and how much I hated him. "I don't hate him," she told me. "I think of him as an aspect of your Knight – the part of you that honors commitments." She suggested that I write a story about him. I did. "Loopholes" is the result, and the character Dami is the first of many tributes to Sandi in my work.

Aside from the climax, for which I consulted my lawyer friend Clary Pollack (who'd helped with my bankruptcy two years earlier), I wrote "Loopholes" in a day-long frenzy. The story draws heavily on my Siciliano family, with Sal being inspired by my long-dead Uncle Gino who was, as I understand it, "family" in more ways than one. The remark from our protagonist is my father's actual response when I'd asked him once if he'd ever taken advantage of various "offers" I knew he'd had. The element of being fucked over by a trusted friend comes from life, and although that incident didn't leave me quite as desperate as the fictional Gino, it *was* partially responsible for my financial situation in 2004.

Sadly, life robbed both of us of any satisfying resolution. Then again, that real-life guy didn't wind up facing Jack Dunning, so I guess he got off easy in some respects.

GRIMBLEGROTH

MY OLD FRIEND and former roommate Danielle Curry inspired this story, which I wrote while living with her in 2002-2003. Though Danielle would never be caught dead tossing trash along a hiking trail, she went hiking almost every weekend when the weather allowed. The bit where Jenna's roommate worries about her safety came from a real incident: Danielle didn't come home one night, and the weather had gotten bad. This was before either of us had a cellphone, so I couldn't call her, and she couldn't let me know – until she returned the following day – that she'd spent the night at a motel because of bad weather and a sudden drowsy spell which left her unwilling to risk driving home. Both Danielle and I loathe people who litter the wilderness, so Grimblegroth emerged from one of our gripe-sessions about people who didn't pack out their fucking trash; as I recall it, one of us said something about wanting wood-spirits to teach such people a lesson. You've seen the rest.

VALHALLA WITH A
TASTE OF LETHE

ONE OF MY FEW comedy stories, this one came out of nowhere and decided to write itself one day. The original version was straight stream-of-consciousness, but it took several revisions before the humor and dialog fell together properly. Though I wasn't consciously satirizing the divinity, I enjoy the inversion of Thor – normally the most Metal of Gods – being a washout as a rock star. A fan of both music and mythology, I amused myself by peppering the story with all the inside jokes I could fit into the text. If you understand them all, consider yourself an enlightened entity.

The original version of this story was accepted by NewWitch magazine; I revised it and sent in a better version before that tale saw print. This version is a considerable improvement on the earlier publication, giving more character to Thor, Pan, and the serpent while also smoothing out some jagged transitions and tangled exposition. The title is perhaps my favorite story-name thus far, a nod to Harlan Ellison (one of the cornerstones of my writing career) and his gift for poetic nomenclature.

RAVENOUS

MY MOST FREQUENTLY REPRINTED short story, "Ravenous" began as a "heavy-metal faeries" pitch for the first volume of the *Bad-Ass Faeries* series. I envisioned a fey Iron Maiden; instead, I got one of my rawest and most personal tales.

Like most of my fiction, "Ravenous" draws upon real-life experiences. Although the band and its musicians are totally fictional, the on-stage implosion of my band actually occurred… complete with a flying drum thrown at the singer's head. Thankfully, I wasn't around for that one myself, having been kicked out of the band several months earlier. But the bubbling animosities curling up between the notes you play together, and then striking like some sort of phantasmal giant snake… that part I remember all too well.

"Ravenous" also deals with one of my reoccurring themes: The clash of a divided self whose split between "civilized" fear and "primal" freedom becomes too much to endure. In Kelsey (whose name I'd inadvertently nicked from another story, "Special Guest," which I'd written almost fifteen years earlier), I brought out the hungriest, most alluring form of the Wild Girl aspect I mentioned earlier. Nikita, meanwhile, became the anxious impostor-syndrome poster child, bulldozing her fears through sheer attitude while they eat her up inside. Though I didn't intentionally satirize it, that clash also mirrored my conflict and breakup with Ann Taylor, the Magnolia Faerie. I had – in an effort to get my shit together after one of the craziest periods of my life – pushed a lot of my "magic" off to one side. Although Ann wasn't the one responsible for me doing that, I'd perceived, at the time, that she was at least partially causing me to do so. Back when I wrote this story, I *had* been feeling like I was cannibalizing myself for other people's sake… which in turn spurred the "Ravenous" theme of parasitic self-destruction.

Old Man Ivan is also a legacy of my time with Ann, whose family home has a huge oak tree in the back yard. The first time she took me home to meet her parents, she also introduced me to that tree; we climbed up into it and spent some time hanging out in the branches, where Ann told me that in her younger years she had curled up in that tree with a book whenever she felt like being left alone. The barefoot faerie-girl here, though part of me, is also inspired by Ann, who still has a penchant for wearing wings and going without shoes whenever she can get away with it. At her core, however, Kelsey is the sexy yet infuriating *anima* who lures, drives, seduces, and withdraws according to a secret agenda only my creative subconscious truly understands. As for the name-changing Nikita, I see her as an aspect of my more insecure self – the would-have-been rock star who wondered why I was still writing "that fantasy stuff" for a financially precarious career as I entered middle age. The slamming doors and identity shifts echo my own later teenage years, although I was always on better terms with my parents than poor Nikita is.

Some of the band names, incidentally, came from brainstorming sessions for real-life monikers. Attila's Waltz almost wound up being called Jesus on the Half-Shell and I kinda wish in retrospect that we *had* gone with that name. As for the lyrics and song title from "Centrifuge," that was an actual song by Lonesome Crow. The band's drummer Mike Stillwell wrote the lyrics, and he gave me permission to use them in this tale. Chipper's nickname came from my own nickname for Mike – "the Wood Shop" – because I once glanced back at him during a gig and noticed the shower of splinters flying from his drumsticks as he played. Mike's the only person I've ever heard of who cracked a brass cymbal by hitting it too hard. And yes – this is the same Brian and Chipper who appear in "Swallowed," although "Ravenous" predates that story in both publican and in-world chronology.

As mentioned earlier, I have more plans for this pair, as they're two of my favorite supporting characters.

"Ravenous" was originally accepted for publication in the first volume of *Bad-Ass Faeries*. Just before publication, though, one of the editors told me that as much as they loved the story, they had decided to drop it because its tone and content clashed with the rest of the collection. I totally understood that, sent it instead to Weird Tales, and had it immediately accepted. A year or two later, it was reprinted in *Weird Tales: The 21ˢᵗ Century, Volume 1*. Not long after that, it was reprinted again in *Ravens in the Library: Magic in the Bard's Name*, the benefit anthology that launched Quiet Thunder Productions and showed Sandi and me just how well we worked together as a team. I find it amusing that a story that was partially inspired by the breakdown of one partnership wound up being part of a project that cemented another. I've heard that Sandi did a kick-ass reading of the story's climax at the *Ravens in the Library* release party, although I was at work that day and wasn't able to see it for myself.

I guess it's also worth noting that "Ravenous" inspired my phrase *green-room writing*: the writing an author does "offstage" to fill in a scene that doesn't actually appear in the story but informs the things that *do* see print. In theatre tradition, the green room is the place where performers wait when they're not onstage – so named because the walls are often (though not always) painted a calming shade of green. In nightclubs, that room's typically painted black instead, with graffiti, band fliers, and other memorabilia pasted over every square inch of that often-tiny space.

My first stabs at "Ravenous" began in the green room, shortly before the show begins. The tensions between members manifest as the character bicker with one another. That scene introduced the people, their relationships, the reasons they were about to fly apart onstage.

And yet, it didn't work. It was exposition, not activity. I banged my head against that opening for hours until I realized *why* it didn't work.

The story begins when they step onstage. And so I cut the green-room scene entirely and kicked off with Nikita facing that "just-before-the-cages-open feeling in my chest" – a feeling I know well from my own experiences with an audience. That was all I needed. From that point to the arrival at Old Man Ivan, the story wrote itself in a few blurred hours. With a few minor tweaks of phrase, the story you read here is the story I wrote in that first pass.

And I could not have written it that way, that well, that *fully*, if I had not already known, by that point, who my characters were and what they were fighting about.

Thus, I turned "green-room writing" into a thing. Just as actors hash out the offstage details about their characters and motivations, sometimes even improvising scenes that don't actually appear before an audience, so I hash out notes and occasionally whole scenes that don't make it (and aren't intended to make it) into print. Those scenes give the characters substance and the story urgency. I often recommend that technique, especially to writers who feel stuck at a particular point, or who are grasping for hints about characters and the relationships between them.

KEYSTROKES

More of a vignette than a full-fledged story, this one also comes from *Powerchords* but first appeared several years earlier in my 2014 collection *Tritone: Tales of Musical Weirdness*. Unlike most of my stories, this one has no fantasy content at all, not even a nod to faerie tales. And yet, the original meaning of *weird* is *fate*, and it feels to me like there's an element of fate involved in both this story and its characters.

The real story here isn't the amazing adventures of two hot musician boys; it's the self-reflexive loathing and confusion we so often feel when faced with a seemingly impossible crush. The added weight of what Sandi calls "imposter syndrome" – the feeling that you don't belong in your crowd because you're not as good as they are at what you all do – brings a familiar heft to the tale as well. And spinning around and through those emotions like a weave of thread, the trickling piano line of Kraig's unseen fingers leads poor Brady to the door of his personal labyrinth. But the unseen inner minotaur tears him up inside, until Carla's Ariadne confronts him with the truth. It's Brady who speaks, Carla who listens, and Kraig who opens the door and invites Brady to either retreat with his demons or risk facing a new adventure.

That's the story, really. And it's just as long as it needs to be.

Employing the "write what you know" technique, I envisioned Kraig and Carla as my real-life friends in the story's dedication. Those people are not actually like those characters, but I see the characters in my head as looking and sounding like them. As for the practice hall, that's real… or at least it used to be.

I mentally staged the climax in the annex of the Virginia Commonwealth University music department as it was when I went there almost 40 years ago. I had several friends in the music school, and so I often hung out in the annex between classes. From what I understand, that area's no longer used as a practice space. But as the story says, I can still hear the pianos behind those doors, and recall the human dramas going on behind them too.

ECHO CHAMBER

INSPIRED BY A DREAM about a dorky guy fighting zombies in the halls of the original White Wolf Game Studio offices, I initially wrote "Echo Chamber" for an anthology called *Crimson Pact* back in 2009. The book's original editor accepted it, but after he stepped down his successor passed on it. The new editor included some astute criticism of that story, which he said wasn't especially funny, starred an annoying protagonist, and featured a rather gross interlude wherein that protagonist gets startled while taking a huge dump. I agreed with his critiques, and decided to revise the story; that revision, however, got sidelined by my work on *Powerchords*, *Open Your Heart to the Magic of Love*, the *Werewolf* and *Mage 20ᵗʰ Anniversary Editions*, and my subsequent seven-year tenure on the *M20* line.

When I returned to the story in 2020, I recognized a number of other glaring flaws, notably an inadvertent sexism that crept in through the main character's perspective, a failure to set up the zombie angle properly, and the massive changes in the RPG industry since the advents of Kickstarter, DriveThruRPG, and other self-publishing opportunities that didn't exist in the 1990s or the early 2000s. After pruning the sexism, cutting the bathroom scene, and making Dennis more likeable and less annoying, I decided to set "Echo Chamber" in that interregnum period of the early Obama years, between the economic slide which began in 2007 and the establishment of crowd-funding and virtual distribution as a primary venue for roleplaying media.

Although I removed some of the initial inside jokes (the bathroom scene, for instance, was a commentary on the restrooms of the early White Wolf offices and the tendency many of us had toward reading on the can), the story still includes shout-outs to my early days on the WWGS staff. Echo's office is my own, with the addition of a few dangerous grimoires on the shelf and practice swords on the walls instead of leaning in a corner. The "all-hands on deck" GenCon mobilization was an annual tradition for White Wolf staffers, and the bit about selling a banned book out of our rooms and backpacks is a reference to how we sold the original *Clanbook: Malkavian* after GenCon refused to let us sell that book at the booth in 1994. (We later did the same with *Clanbook: Tzimisce*, *Destiny's Price*, and other "forbidden books" throughout the 90s.) The character Echo is a fictionalized mashup of artist Echo Chernik, designer Jennifer Hartshorn, and White Wolf's original warehouse manager, Rebecca Schaffer. Chesh is a shout-out to my old friend Norita, whom I'd nicknamed Cheshire when we'd dated briefly in 2007, and Dennis is a mixture of the dorky guy from my dream, my own youthful insecurities, and the star-struck folks who sometimes visited our offices. The errant interns were based on a pair of real-life White Wolf interns who were escorted off the premises (amid threats of bodily harm) and banned from our presence after they'd made gross remarks about our sales director; thankfully, the real interns did *not* raise a zombie horde. The idea of grimoires on a game designer's shelves comes from a few books in my real-life collection (including a really nice leather-bound *Lesser Key of Solomon* that a *Mage* fan gave me some time ago), combined with "satanic panic" clichés wherein RPGs are linked to occult rituals.

We really *did* have a cemetery about two blocks from White Wolf's offices in Stone Mountain, GA; we often wandered around that graveyard when brainstorming about World of Darkness projects. The concept of a BDSM RPG came from a bullshitting session in which the real-life Echo and I enthused about the idea of doing such a game (with really high production values and art by Echo herself) as a Kickstarter project, before realizing that we'd both have to change our names in order to publish such a thing without burning professional bridges neither of us could afford to torch. That said, we've also discussed a project titled *Love, Sex & Magic*, and might well release such a book someday.

WAVES

Why must the Little Mermaid surrender to the loss of love? I envision her saying *"Fuck THAT noise!"* and using her superhuman powers to bring a world of hurt down on the kingdom and the man who spurned her. This tale began as a sponsor award for *Powerchords: Music, Magick & Urban Fantasy*, and although I thought about expanding the story, I eventually decided that it stands on its own as it is. Padding it out, I felt, would weaken the impact of the tale.

THE LORD'S GREATEST JEST

Dad used to read me Poe stories when I was a kid; later, I began reading them myself, thanks to Dad's complete collection of Poe's work. My gruesome take on Edgar's already-gruesome "Hop-Frog" was written for Steve Berman's excellent collection *Where Thy Dark Eye Glances: Queering Edgar Allen Poe*.

As readers have probably noticed by now, my own gender and sexual identities are best described as "complicated." I've been part of queer comunities, and identifying as some sort of "nonstandard" gender and/or orientation since my early-80s college years. Aside from "Keystrokes" and the pansexual Johnny Serious, though, I had not written specifically from a queer male point of view before, so I ran with Steve's invitation into some of the darkest realms of my career...

CLOWN BALLOONS

...ALTHOUGH *THIS* STORY may rate as my darkest self-owned work. Inspired by a nightmare I had after an afternoon spent blowing up balloons at my job with "Virginia's Largest Shoe Store," this tale essentially wrote itself within a few hours in the early 1990s. I initially submitted it to a horror anthology edited by the now-infamous Ed Kramer; he told me, "It's an excellent story but if I publish this, people will hang me from a tree." Years later, I realized why. A second editor purchased it for an anthology which never came out, and because my career veered further into fantasy and less into horror, I left "Clown Balloons" aside until my old friend Angel Leigh McCoy (who'd published "Chaser" a few years earlier) invited me to contribute to a horror collection she was editing. After polishing the prose and dialog a bit, I handed it in; Angel and the editors declared it among the most disturbing tales in that anthology. I tweaked it again for this collection, if only because the G-slur doesn't fly anymore in sensible company. Allison was inspired by a girlfriend I had in college, but thankfully I have never felt tempted "to do clown things" myself.

THE LEGACY BOX

ALSO INSPIRED BY A DREAM, "The Legacy Box" is a product of my transition between *Powerchords* and *Mage 20ᵗʰ Anniversary Edition*. By then, I favored a more surreal approach than I used in my earlier tales, and I'm especially happy with the way this one came out. Unlike most of the other stories in this collection, "The Legacy Box" isn't based in real-life inspirations – except, of course, for the strain that toxic masculine "traditions" put on people, relationships, and societies at large. I had this dream after writing several essays about the damage we often do to ourselves and each other in the name of masculinity, and "The Legacy Box" contains those observations.

DRINKING THE MOON

I'VE BEEN KNOWN to tell bedtime stories to my partners as they fade off to sleep. Generally, I forget those tales by morning. This one, though, stuck in my head, so I wrote it down the day after I'd told it to Sandi in bed. Shortly afterward, I sold it to *Cabinet des Fées*, where it became my first publication in that Journal of Fairy Tales. Like so many of my stories, it deals with someone outside the norm who finds her place in a greater world. I guess we're all sorta looking for that place. And sometimes, when we're lucky and dedicated enough, we even find it.

May you always find your joy in a world that's big enough for you.

GRAMMA WOLF'S GARDEN

This one began as a flash-fiction intro to a shop presented in my book *Goblin Markets: The Glitter Trade*. Although it came pretty much from nowhere, I enjoyed its inversion of the traditional Red Riding Hood dynamic and those images of whispering plants and the wolf-lover with flowers in his jaws. I'd submitted the original version to *Cabinet des Fées*, but the editors rightfully turned it down because it wasn't really a *story* quite yet. I expanded the fragment a year or so afterward, turning my cherished Wild Girl aspect into a grown woman who really *does* run with the wolves.

Keeping the faerie-tale approach intact, I worked in themes of family dysfunction, unconventional relationships, and domestic treachery. Beyond that, I integrated that sense of "bent time" you get when you walk away from all the usual landmarks of civilization. The wilderness operates on a different schedule than the industrial pace of our societies; in a vision I'd had along a California road years ago, Brother Crow referred to it as "crow time": the pace of Nature that couldn't care less about human concerns. Building the narrative around love, loss, "crow time," and elemental affinities, I turned "Gramma Wolf" from a vignette to a full-length story. When I read it aloud at HowlCon 2012, everyone wanted to know where they could purchase the story. I first published it *Wyldsight*, and my beloved heart-sister SJ "Sooj" Tucker read it for the audiobook version of the collection in your hands. If you haven't heard that reading yet, you should.

THE GREEN TUNNEL

IN SPRING 2006, I spent roughly three weeks hiking barefoot along the Appalachian Trail with my friend Pooka; several years earlier, I'd taken my first long-distance hike in Utah with my friend Hyper Heidi. "The Green Tunnel" draws from both experiences, and I wrote it for a Lovecraft-themed anthology called *Maelstrom*. Because Lovecraft so often wrote about reedy, neurotic, academic loners, I decided to write about a vigorously physical, happy couple. The presence of enigmatic ruins and "altars" in the American wilderness is absolutely factual, and the legend of young Cherokee dudes proving their manhood by scaling a precarious cliff, while probably untrue, comes from a precipice Ann Taylor showed me back in Asheville, NC. The deep woods are eerily sublime; experiencing a thunderstorm when you're camped on top of a mountain provides a quick lesson in just how fragile we are when faced with the implacable force of Nature.

SOMETIMES

THIS POEM essentially wrote itself in my head one night back in 2003. Within a few short months, I had broken off one relationship, ended another after a traumatic incident with my then-lover, suffered an intense depression and a flu, sold the house I'd bought with my second ex-wife, and then lost (to old age and kidney failure) my longtime companion, Salome – the cat who'd slept on or next to me for over 15 years. To say that I felt down was an understatement, and the words to this poem welled up in me as I lay in bed crying for everyone and everything I had lost. I wrote it down, and the ambiguous phrasing of that poem is intentional. I also intentionally left the title off this piece because I think it looks stronger on the page without one.

I FEEL LUCKY

AMONG ALL my short-fiction offspring, "I Feel Lucky" may be my favorite. It hurts, in large part because so much of it is rooted in several real-life relationships, especially my second marriage and divorce. The Mary Chapin Carpenter song was a favorite of Wendy's back when we were together, and I doubt I'll ever hear it without thinking of her. Although we'd split almost four years before I wrote this tale, two recent breakups had me feeling especially raw and nostalgic at the time Frank Fradella invited me to write for *Cyber-Age of Heroes*. The narrator's wounded optimism recalls my own dedication at that time to throwing myself off cliffs in the name of love. I'm healthier than that now, thank gods, and I didn't need to have a supervillain girlfriend accidentally break me first.

As he and I have talked about since then, Frank was way ahead of the pop-culture curve, publishing novels and anthologies about the human side of superheroes over a decade before that sort of thing became a literary genre. Personally, I wanted to show a metahuman not from the perspective of an awed bystander (*a la* the comic series *Astro City*, *Marvels*, and *Kingdom Come*) but from someone in a dysfunctional yet loving relationship with one. Linda /Riplash is a composite of several friends, now-former lovers, and my own dark side. The "Love and Fire" bit was me, though no one saw me crying at the time. The narrator, meanwhile, speaks with the soft accent I sometimes slide back into when I return to my old stomping grounds in the American South.

CHASER

INSPIRED BY THE IMPLOSION of my first marriage, crossed with an incident on a San Francisco beach in 1993, "Chaser" hits a familiar theme for me: the tension between a person's primal impulses and the more "civilized" behavior people so often expect from us. As a Pagan, I can't stand to see people treat our environment carelessly; as an avowed barefooter, I've got a special hatred for folks who smash glass all over the place.

During a visionquest on that San Francisco beach, I nearly stumbled into a discarded bonfire site in which some bunch of troglodytes had meticulously smashed *Every. Single. Bottle* they'd brought with them before leaving the whole shattered mess and the smoldering fire behind. Half in the spirit-world already (I was tripping on acid, and the beach was wreathed in thick summer fog), I spent what felt like hours choking down my rage as I sifted through the sand to pick out the shards of glass, metal cans, and paper waste. Thankfully, the assholes in question had left their beer-bags intact; I put the wreckage into the bags and eventually cleaned up the site. I have no idea how long I spent on that chore, but it took quite a while. Over the course of that clean-up, the task became a meditation. I'd had a lot of shit to work through that night, and so sorting that mess out seemed like a perfect metaphor for me at the time. Like Rachel, I came to some conclusions that night that changed my life from then on out.

An early version of "Chaser," titled "Shards," appeared in two collections during the 1990s. Because that tale was written as a work-for-hire piece based on White Wolf's *Werewolf: The Apocalypse* line, however, I don't own the rights to it. This has always been a special story for me, though, so I rewrote "Shards" around 2009, taking out the shared-world elements, adding bits of my life since then, shifting the voice and tone, and making various other changes too. The revised tale is stronger and more intimate than its original form was, but its most personal elements – the wrenching choice, the broken glass, the end of one life and the acceptance of another – remain as vivid for me now as they were when I first lived that part of the story almost thirty years ago.

Incidentally, it wasn't until the final consistency edit for this collection that I noticed that the protagonists of "Chaser" and *Dream Along the Edge* share the same name. Considering that I've occasionally done the same thing with other characters and stories, it's fair to say that I have a fondness for certain unusual names which does not become apparent until you collect thirty years' worth of my writing into one place and realize how often certain names pop up in my work. I thought about changing the repeated names, but eventually decided against it – partly because it would be a pain in the ass, and partly because those names fit those characters. Altering them long after they've attained this sort of life just feels wrong to me.

WILLOW AND WIND

BACK IN EARLY 2004, a bunch of us were touring to promote my then-new book *Deliria: Faerie Tales for a New Millennium*. For me, that project offered a fresh start after my White Wolf days, and I hit over a dozen conventions that year to bring it to the fans.

A few months earlier, I'd encountered my close friend Kristen Leigh Elmore online; at a small convention, we met in person and clicked like mad. It wasn't a romantic chemistry, but rather a bond of kindred spirits. She helped me run the first of many convention games that year – a story that I came up with the night before the con. "Willow and Wind" is based on my notes for that story: the tragic tale of Ariel – a restless wind-who-becomes-a-singer – and her lover Stickman, the tree-who-becomes-a-musician. Kristen and I, with two groups of players, ran wild with the story, taking it to emotional highs and lows that had folks literally in tears and cheering by the end.

A few months later, Kris and I – along with my then-business associates Kevin Divico and Burton Taylor – were planning to take the next portion of that story on the road to DragonCon at the end of our tour. Ariel would be doing a concert there; problem was, Kristen could not play guitar. We were tossing around options when a tricky pixie with a huge grin and an even bigger guitar showed up at our booth to ask where she might find a place to play. We were at the FaerieWorlds festival, the pixie was SJ "Sooj" Tucker, and we were all looking at one of those life-changing encounters.

As with Kris, our bond was essentially instantaneous. I looked around for a performance space for Sooj and her two friends, but we didn't find much worth working with. I had to return to our booth, so I asked Kris to find a spot for them. She did so.

About ten minutes later, she came back to the booth. "You *have* to hear this," Kris told me.

"In a minute," I replied.

"*NOW*," she said, grabbing my sleeve and hauling me over to where Sooj and Company were set up and playing. When they'd finished, Kristen told Sooj, "Sing him that song you just sang for me a minute ago." Sooj opened her mouth, and this *VOICE* boomed out – a swell of power and passion that left me speechless. We had found our Ariel. Sooj joined us a few weeks later in Atlanta, and we've been close friends ever since. Sooj even introduced me to Sandi (also at FaerieWorlds, three years later), so once again, a fantasy story laid the groundwork for real-life magic.

Seriously, this stuff is *POWERFUL*.

THE ICE FIDDLER

ORIGINATING as a commissioned story and birthday gift I wrote for web-cartoonist Denise Jones in 2005, "The Ice Fiddler" enjoys the cruel distinction of having been parodied (rather brilliantly) online by the friend of a woman I had recently broken up with. The story's setting comes from Denise's webcomic *Eversummer Eve*, although only Libra and her tavern actually originated in that strip. I also name-checked a few friends of mine: Scott and Megan Walters from the *Deliria* crew, plus my now-late partner Coyote Ashley Ward, whom I'd first met shortly before I wrote this tale.

The inspiration for the story itself came from a cross between that obnoxious "War on Christmas" crap and an ice storm that hit

Atlanta in 1999, doing exactly what it does in the story, minus the personification of Winter.

As for Winter herself, my impression of her came from Ruth Thompson's print *The Shaman*, which I had hanging on my wall back when I wrote "The Ice Fiddler." Regarding the narrator's reflections upon the season of winter, those thoughts came from a long, cold walk I took on Christmas Eve one night in the 1990s, looking up at the stars and wondering how Winter must feel to herself.

JOHNNY SERIOUS

ANOTHER STORY expanded from an early version written for *Deliria: Faerie Tales for a New Millennium*, "Johnny Serious" essentially presents Teenage Me meeting his freer, queerer, more confident future self. The first several chapters of my *Cult of Ecstasy Tradition Book*, starring scared Cassie and her future-self Aria, also feature an earlier and more extensive treatment of that theme.

Thankfully, I wasn't quite as despondent in high school as Johnny Serious is, if only because I didn't know about Gothic rock and self-harm at the time; to be fair, the Goth subculture hardly existed when I was in high school… but if I *had* known about it back then, I would have been eyebrows-deep in it. The bit about going outside, though, sometimes during snowstorms, in nothing more than cutoff shorts? Yep – I totally *did* do that for real. Back then, that sensual rebel part of me was a secret I hid from everybody else. Years later, though, during college, I became more like that in my everyday life.

NO EXIT ANGEL

Also from *Powerchords*, this tale began as a mental monolog about why, as a performer, you can't just call in sick if you've got a gig. Its direct inspiration came from the Storm Large song "Under You," which is seriously worth checking out next time you're online. The idea of an underground club in Louisiana is patently absurd, so of course I went with it. The image for that club came from a narrow basement dive featured in the documentary *Anvil: The Story of Anvil*, and I made the story up as went along… which I often do. No Exit was the name of one of my favorite Atlanta Goth clubs. As for the angel, I hope for the sake of musicians everywhere that he's out there someplace too. I like the idea of an angel who digs music and holds compassion for lost souls while still accepting them for who they are.

LIGHTNING DUST

A short vignette from *Everyday Heroes*, "Lightning Dust" draws upon my experiences crossing the American West in 2003 and 2004, specifically some brief stopovers in Arizona, New Mexico, and Eastern California. During one of them, I watched a train recede into the Big Sky sunset and realized that country-western music, Indigenous flute music, and the Old Testament God resonate at a whole other level of significance when you view them under that implacable sky. Credit for inspiration goes also to Terri Windling's *The Wood Wife*, which is one of the strangely few fantasy novels set in the myth-rich territory of the American West.

Going from the dry West to the Pacific Ocean seemed like a natural contrast for the final tale in this collection…

DREAM ALONG THE EDGE

Originally written for a paranormal erotica anthology for a now-defunct publisher, this novella draws from my short yet memorable time living in the San Francisco Bay Area. All of the locations are real, and several of the characters are unflattering but accurate mashups of people I knew when I lived there. Ashli was inspired by a real coworker of mine in those days, and her real-life counterpart and I remain friends to this day.

For this story, I consulted with several other friends who are professional mermaid performers, and though I've never gone skinny dipping out past the buoys at Half Moon Bay, I *did* do similarly stupid shit long after midnight on a lake in Minnesota in the early 1990s when I felt too horny and keyed-up to sleep. Jogging barefoot through the empty Half Moon streets around dawn, on the other hand, was a common activity for me when I lived in Burlingame. The scene where Rachel shows up at the bookstore barefoot was inspired by a real-life coworker (ironically, at my shoe-store job) who'd arrived at work unshod and needed to go buy shoes because she'd just spent a long weekend at the beach and was running late that morning; unlike Rachel, thankfully, that real-life person did not get fired.

Dream Along the Edge also marks the first time I've drawn from the persona /aspect of my pen-name Cedar Blake during the writing process. Although I'd published several pieces under that name before this tale was written, I consciously channeled that part of myself in order to write this story.

At the time, I had recently kicked a toxic friend and collaborator out of my life; consequently, my Muse-self went on strike and my ways with words went with her.

Shortly afterward, I received an invitation to write for the aforementioned anthology. After several weeks of trying and failing to write "as me," I decided to use the Method acting technique of assuming a different (if related) psychological identity. Though I didn't dress as Cedar or call myself by that name, I tapped into a different headspace to get past my writer's block. It worked. *Dream Along the Edge* was written in a bit over two weeks, and the block – once banished – stayed gone. I used the same trick a half-decade later, after the deaths of several loved ones stalled my work on the *Mage 20* book *Gods & Monsters*. Because "Cedar" wrote *Dream* and part of *G&M*, I gave her author's credit for both, accepting her as a conscious part of my admittedly complex identity.

Thanks to a hinky contract I refused to sign, I withdrew *Dream Along the Edge* from its intended publisher; a year or two later, when my friend Janine Southard invited me into a paranormal romance collection, I revised *Dream* with slightly less explicit content. Although I may publish the uncut version someday under Cedar's name, I prefer this version over the more explicit original draft. And as parting stories go, I couldn't resist making this novella our final tale… for now, anyway.

Dream also taps into my longtime fondness for romance novels – not the clinch-cover stuff, but rather the bantering modern-romance books so often derided as "chick lit." Personally, I find it relaxing to go on an unapologetically emotional roller coaster ride where the stakes are high but not catastrophic. Especially these days, vicarious drama with minimal tragedy provides a fun wild ride for me.

If those lovers in question can dream themselves to another level in the process – as my spouse Sandra Swan and I have done in real life – and find levels of magic they hadn't recognized before, then I call that a win for everyone.

434

I hope y'all can bring such dreams to life yourselves. We could use more magic in this world.

Cheers, everyone.

For now, anyway...

A SPECIAL PREVIEW

FROM SATYR BRUCATO'S

URBAN FANTASY NOVEL

RED
SHOES

WAS ALL THIS FOR REAL?

B lue was dancing like mad when she burst into flames.

It didn't happen suddenly. She'd been busting chaos-angel moves on stage when I'd noticed smoke rising from her hair. Blue's feet flashed and spun beneath her jingling skirt. Sweat shimmered on her tattoos. Her eyes rolled back till all I could see were the whites. Her pale skin began to glow.

"How's she *doing* that?" Ashley whispered.

"I have no idea," I whispered back.

Flames flickered from Blue's scalp, then swept across her skin. Her black vest caught fire in a sudden puff, the flames shining on the tiny mirrors woven into it.

"Holy *shit*," Ash hissed.

We launched ourselves at the stage.

For dancers, fire is *bad*. Modern bellydance gear tends to be full of artificial materials, which often melt on contact with flames. Lots of us – especially the ones who dance with fire – stick to cotton garb when dancing for just that reason.

Blue's gear had Lycra, Spandex, and lots of other things that don't like fire. And it was melting to her skin.

She didn't scream. Not once. Aside from the sound of the flames, she was totally silent.

Still dancing, too. Dancing like flames.

Booming over the sound of those flames, "Maiden Goes to Bollywood" set up a counterpoint to the horror show on stage. Ash grabbed two glasses of water off nearby tables and threw them both on Blue. The water hissed and spit across the fire.

I whipped my head around, frantic, looking for something to roll Blue up in to smother the blaze. Nothing. Ah, hell – I leaped onto the stage, sprinted to the bundle of clothes and stuff I had set off to the side behind the curtain, and grabbed the leather jacket my last ex-boyfriend, Karl, had given me for Christmas.

Blue whirled around the stage like a flaming dervish, still utterly silent. Ashley tried to tackle Blue and roll her on the floor, but the heat kept her leaning in and then pulling back out of sheer self-preservation.

The audience – realizing this wasn't part of the act – freaked out. Yelling, pushing, chairs and tables scattered, knocked over… a mosh pit at the bellydance party.

Blue's skin crackled. Her hair blazed. I yanked my jacket from the pile of crap backstage and dashed over to where Ashley and Blue were weaving back and forth like MMA fighters too scared to throw the first punch.

FWUMP! I threw my jacket over Blue's flaming back and slammed her down.

Our feet skidded on the water-splashed stage, and all three of us fell on top of each other – me on Blue, Ashley on me.

Blue never made a sound.

I heard thumps nearby as some vague shapes hopped up on the stage with us. Ash was screaming in my ear. Blue stayed quiet. Her skin kept burning around the jacket as I rolled us around trying to put the fire out.

I felt the heat from her body through the leather. If my jacket had been cheap-ass leatherette, it would've melted to my hands.

Someone pulled Ashley off me. Someone else had a fire extinguisher. He blasted us with the extinguisher. The whole thing seemed to be going on somewhere way outside my reality, which is a good thing because otherwise I'd have totally lost my shit.

My best friend Meghan says that in times of shock, your mind disassociates from your present circumstances. And so, as Ashley flailed around in the grip of some big dude I'd never seen before, and the guy with the fire extinguisher hosed us down, I felt myself looking at the whole scene through the length of a long mental tunnel. *Oh*, said that distant part of my brain, *I hope this doesn't mean I'm gonna pass out.*

I didn't.

All around me, I felt people moving: Inky and Caroline from our troupe, Arcana Darque. Chalice and some other dancers from different troupes. Tabi, the owner of the Hearthstone. Other folks I didn't recognize.

And right there, under my jacket, my friend Blue, who wasn't moving anymore.

441

It didn't look like Blue. It didn't look like *anyone*.

That's when I passed out, halfway through throwing up everything I'd eaten for the last week...

A young dancer descends
into her hometown's underworld.
The things she'll discover there will change her forever.

RED
SHOES

www.ingramcontent.com/pod-product-compliance
Lightning Source LLC
Chambersburg PA
CBHW021213260626
47172CB00002B/402